*Pride Publishing books by Jason Wrench*

**Single Books**
Twelve Days of Murder
Till Death Do Us Wed

**Up on the Farm**
Finding a Farmer
Bewitched by the Barista
Sanctuary for a Surgeon
Catching the Composer

**Love and Liquidation**
Boy Bands and Bullets

**Collections**
A Wolf in Billionaire's Clothing: Wolf Island

I0662164

# Love and Liquidation

# BOY BANDS AND BULLETS

# JASON WRENCH

Boy Bands and Bullets
ISBN # 978-1-80250-584-9
©Copyright Jason Wrench 2023
Cover Art by Kelly Martin ©Copyright December 2023
Interior text design by Claire Siemaszkiewicz
Pride Publishing

Published in 2023 by Pride Publishing, United Kingdom.

# BOY BANDS
# AND BULLETS

# Dedication

To the curious souls who dare to venture into the wild unknown of my imagination,
I dedicate this book to my puggles, the best friends a man could ever ask for. Daikin, who didn't even get to see his tenth birthday, and Teddy, who I recently lost after sixteen years, four months and eleven days. I also dedicate this novel to Max, who faithfully sits by my side whenever inspiration strikes, ensuring the inclusion of the finest gibberish known to humankind. He's only six and a half right now, but he is one of the kindest, most gentle souls I've ever known.
To my loving friends, who kindly refrained from questioning my sanity as I spoke of fictional worlds and characters as if they were real.
To that one barista who kept my caffeine supply steady and my dreams of becoming a bestselling author alive, I owe you more than a lifetime of lattes.
And to my family, who patiently endured my ceaseless ramblings about plot twists and story arcs, I promise I won't move back in — even if there's another global pandemic.
To you, dear reader, who decided to give this book a chance, may you find laughter, adventure and a few valuable life lessons hidden among these pages.
I originally devised this novel's idea in the late nineties. Sometimes, an idea needs to percolate — just like my coffee.
With a cheeky grin,
Jason

P.S. Thanks to all the boy bands who helped inspire me.

# Prologue

Dr. Phillipa Hennigan watched the sun set on the horizon. The last rays of light glittered over Lake Pontchartrain. She pulled the black sedan to the curb in front of an industrial building a block away from their target. From Mardi Gras to the Jazz Festival to any night on Bourbon Street, New Orleans was always one of the most happening towns in the United States. And as much as she wanted to grab a hurricane, kick back her heels and take a load off, she wasn't in town to enjoy the debauchery with drunken tourists. She had a job to do.

After throwing the car into park, she took in her surroundings. In the distance, a large group of people were boarding a vessel for an evening cruise. She'd read in a brochure that nightly excursions left from this part of the lake. The evening trips around Pontchartrain, or any of the rivers that fed into it, were combined with exquisite seafood and seemed to be a requirement for any knowledgeable vacationer. From the way some tourists down the block wobbled on solid land, she could tell the revelers on the dock had been drinking long before they arrived here. One tourist almost missed the gangway completely, but a shipmate grabbed her before she could fall into the waters below.

Dr. Hennigan glanced at the brick building they'd parked in front of. 'Pontchartrain Fishery Buyer and Processor' was stenciled in fading black letters across the side. She'd chosen to park here because the people who worked for the fish buyer were in bed or would be shortly. From the intelligence her team had gathered about this area, the workers would start unloading the previous night's hauls around four in the morning, so the building should be vacant this time of the evening.

She looked across the lake and could almost make out Bayou St. John. While many of the lake's boats were neatly tucked away in their rented spaces, she'd done enough research to know many crews were already setting traps and getting ready for a long night of fishing, either in the lake or the Gulf of Mexico. She turned her head and looked down the street toward a clump of houseboats that swayed in the night air. She wasn't interested in all the houseboats, just the second one.

Two other women sat inside the sedan with her. Her two colleagues wore khaki shorts, loose-fitting polo shirts and new tennis shoes. Her colleagues' wardrobes were recently purchased, but the only part of the outfits that gave that away was the bright white of the shoes. They looked like thousands of other tourists shopping or stalking the streets, hoping to glimpse their favorite soap opera star. Since the hit show *NOLA Nights* began shooting in the area, paparazzi and lookie-loos had been clamoring to get photos with and of the cast. Some international press members had been camped out for months in various hotels throughout the city.

Dr. Hennigan wore a more conservative gray pantsuit with six-inch stilettos. At five-feet-eleven-inches with short-cropped black hair with a tint of red in it, she looked like any power CEO. She reached into her bag and pulled out a rifle telescope, then examined the scene down the street. The boat with the drunken revelers was finally pulling away. As for the houseboat she was interested in, the boat's internal lights were lit.

"How many people are in there, Richardson?" she asked. Richardson picked up a pair of binoculars and scrutinized the houseboat.

When satisfied with her answer, Richardson said, "One."

"You had better be right," Dr. Hennigan said.

Dr. Hennigan checked to ensure her Browning Buck Mark with the Silencerco suppressor was ready. She liked how accurate the gun was and how quiet the silencer made it. She glanced around and noticed her two operatives doing the same with their standard-issue Glock nineteens with Octane nine suppressors. Their weapons were not as silent as hers but were quiet enough to get the job done that night. Next, she double-checked her backup gun in her jacket, a small handgun explicitly designed for The Foundation. It was a nine-millimeter short with thirteen point-thirty-eight hollow-point rounds inside, which she could easily hide under a light T-shirt. This weapon was not a standard police-issue weapon. It was created using a special plastic polymer, making it undetectable by the most stringent airport security. As for the bullets, they were ceramic and shattered on impact to maximize damage.

Dr. Hennigan's mother always told her, "*If you're going to level your gun and shoot, plan on putting the target down.*" For a second, she wondered what would happen if terrorists ever got this specific technology for themselves. She grinned, noting it would be impossible, especially since the designer was dead — the first victim of his own creation by her hands. Satisfied, she opened the driver's-side door and walked toward the houseboat. Without saying a word, the other two women slipped out of the sedan and matched her stride.

When Dr. Hennigan was almost to the boat, she turned and looked at the women. For the first time, she realized how ridiculous they looked. She would chastise them later, but for the moment, she had a job to do and wanted to get it done.

"We are going to do this exactly like we planned. Richardson, go to the rear and up the back ladder but stay on deck in the shadows. Take anyone down quietly and quickly if they come on deck while we're inside. Denzili, you're my backup. Follow my lead." The two women nodded.

The three made their way around to the side of the boat. Richardson went along the wooden surface between the boats to the rear. Dr. Hennigan stepped on the ladder and scaled it before jumping on board, landing in a silent crouch.

Denzili landed next to her, and Dr. Hennigan made a series of hand motions to Denzili.

"Back deck is clear," Richardson spoke into Hennigan's headset, a tiny earpiece that used bone conduction to amplify speech. "Stage one complete."

"Proceed to stage two," Dr. Hennigan replied.

There were two sets of stairs, one going up to the target's office and one down to the living space. Dr. Hennigan and Denzili crept down into the lower living quarters. Luckily, nothing creaked under her weight, which had been one of the major concerns of this operation. Thankfully, the boat was still new enough that it didn't make the wrenching noises of an older vessel. Strains of classical music reached them from the bottom of the stairs, along with the faint smell of grilled vegetables. Dr. Hennigan flattened her back against the wall and peered into the room at the bottom of the stairwell. *Bingo*, she thought. The target was in the living room, standing next to the opposite wall, looking at a row of CDs. Dr. Hennigan slipped inside the cabin, just out of sight of the occupant.

As part of their surveillance research, Dr. Hennigan and her colleagues had found out the company that ran *NOLA Nights* had long realized that providing the stars of their show with houseboats was more economical than attempting to put them up in hotels in the city. All the actors had their own boats scattered around the lake. This one was two stories high and contained a posh living environment, which included a living room, kitchen, exercise area, office, primary bedroom and bathroom.

Richardson and Denzili had scouted the layout earlier in the day when the target was on set filming and security was focused on the set, not the boats. According to internal emails Dr. Hennigan had read after they'd hacked the producers' accounts, the company felt the threat was not substantial enough to hire guards, making this mission easier.

Dr. Hennigan moved across the thick carpet toward the subject. The lush flooring muffled her approach. Denzili was still against the wall, eyeing the back of the boat and up the stairwell with her gun firmly in her grip, just in case.

Dr. Hennigan quickly looped her arm inside the subject's left arm. With a sweeping motion, she prevented the subject from moving and yelling. A stifled screech came from the woman's mouth beneath Dr. Hennigan's hand. She pressed the nozzle of her gun against the woman's temple.

"Where are the files?" The subject didn't respond. Dr. Hennigan pressed the nozzle a little harder and asked again, "Where are the files?" As she asked the second time, Dr. Hennigan lowered her hand from the subject's mouth so she could speak.

"What're you talking about?"

"Where're the files?"

"I don't know what you are talking about. I swear, I don't!"

"Hey, Cynthia, where do you keep your oregano?"

Dr. Hennigan turned fast enough to watch the owner of that voice walk into the living room from the kitchen before she pointed her gun and fired. Cynthia shrieked as a man slumped to the ground. A pool of blood spread its way over the plush carpet from the bullet hole in the man's forehead.

Cynthia's sobs were muffled from beneath Dr. Hennigan's gloved hand. "You can stop with the theatrics. I taught you everything you know."

The woman stiffened under Dr. Hennigan's grip, but the fake tear-works stopped immediately.

"Go ahead, kill me," she said. "You can't stop the files from being made public. I already saw to that."

Dr. Hennigan grabbed the actress by the chin and forehead and violently twisted. A clear cracking sound was heard as the subject's body went limp.

"Denzili," Dr. Hennigan said into her earpiece, "check her office."

Dr. Hennigan heard the operative head upstairs to the subject's office. While Denzili was upstairs, Dr. Hennigan walked around downstairs, trying to determine how this plan had gone so completely wrong. In the kitchen, she turned off the stove. The spaghetti was still hard on one end as it leaned out of the boiling water's side. She looked around and picked up a stack of mail. She glanced at the return labels. On the third piece of mail, the mistake in the operation hit her. The address wasn't for the subject. The mail was for a Mr. Daniel Hawthorne. Either the subject had a live-in boy toy, or her operatives upstairs had totally fucked up her operation.

# Chapter One

*Ethan*

Five...Four...Three...Two...Action! Ethan and the other members of his band, ZERO, watched a monitor from backstage as a clear view of the New Orleans skyline came into view. The camera closed in on Bourbon Street and started flying down the street before shooting back into the sky, swiveling and heading right toward Jackson Square. The familiar statue of Andrew Jackson on his horse with the St. Louis Cathedral in the background was quickly framed before the camera turned in one-hundred-and-eighty degrees, focusing on the downtown building where the *Real Time News* offices are located. The shot angled downward, and, in the distance, the infamous logo of the Real Time News Network could be seen by viewers as the logo raced toward them. Finally, an extreme close-up on the logo filled the screen, and the station announcer's voice was heard over the RTN theme music, "*You are watching* Real Time News, *the only station bringing you groundbreaking news twenty-four hours a day with no pre-taped programming. You can also keep in contact with the world online by watching RTN at www.rtn.media.*"

As soon as the announcer finished, the shot went right through the wall of the RTN building, giving the viewing audience an overhead shot of the RTN media studios. After a second pause, the camera swooped down. Images of reporters hunched over computers, editors viewing segment footage and anchors standing around having coffee or getting their makeup ready filled the screen as the camera arched down toward the main broadcasting desk.

The main desk came into view, displaying a cheerful-looking blonde sitting behind it. She was clearly the woman of the moment in the RTN offices. She wore a smart navy-blue business suit with a cream-colored silk blouse under her jacket. Her naturally long blonde hair was pulled up into a clip on the backside of her head. Although other women constantly tried to emulate Tika Downs, no one could perfect the look of a woman who looked like she jogged in and was now ready to walk down the catwalk in a Paris fashion show. Her makeup lacked the same finesse. Tika insisted on doing her own makeup for the camera. When she didn't look like an orange pumpkin on top of her snow-colored neck, her fire-engine red lips jumped off the screen at the viewing audience. Industry insiders joked that her lips were the most memorable part of her entire career.

Tika shuffled a small stack of papers before glancing at the camera and flashing her award-winning smile. Once the viewing audience saw this smile, no one wondered why she was 'America's Most Trusted Newsperson'.

"Good evening, America. This is Tika Downs, live from the *Real Time News* Network's Main Studio in New Orleans. This evening has several brilliant shows being brought to you from around the world via the RTN Network. A complete listing of all shows can be found on our website at www.rtn.media. Next hour, Jeremy Price's *Business Hour* will be brought to you live from within the Japanese Stock Exchange. But first, Tom Dulce has chart-topping ZERO sitting with him on his couch today."

"Places," a voice said into Ethan's headset, causing him to look up from the monitor. *It's go time.* He climbed onto the small platform and took his position on stage. Another monitor on the ground allowed the band to see the RNN telecast. He watched as the shot went over the back of Tika's head, showing more people busy at work in the newsroom. The camera zipped out of the studio and down the hall before taking a sharp left into another sound stage. This time, as it entered the sound stage, the live audience erupted into applause as the image narrowed in on an older newscaster. Tom Dulce's face looked like any sixty-year-old man with a little Botox injected here and there. The only part of Dulce's appearance that gave away his actual age was his eyes. Although Dulce was not the oldest person in the news industry, his eyes had that aged look that came from a lifetime of memories.

Dulce had started his career as a war correspondent at another network. Even Ethan had heard the rumors floating around the news industry that Dulce had seen more live combat action than most single-star generals. Although the Pentagon had never confirmed anything,

Ethan surmised that there was probably more truth in the rumor than not.

The camera zoomed in on Dulce, who sat behind an enormous mahogany desk set against a clear window overlooking a busy Camp Street. On the monitor, Ethan could see the barricade set up by the NOLA Police Department, where fans of all ages stood outside screaming. The fans held various poster board signs, hoping to glimpse Dulce or his guests. Although the glass was soundproof, Ethan saw the frantic jumping up and down and imagined the screaming in his head.

"Welcome to *In Touch with America*. I'm Tom Dulce." The studio audience erupted into another round of applause. "This afternoon, I am dedicating the entire hour to the number one music group in the nation. You know them as Zach, Ethan, Ric and Orr — better known as ZERO."

Ethan heard the distinct sound of four clicks of drumsticks as the studio camera faded off Dulce and onto a side platform erected on the sound stage. In the dark, Ethan got into his first position, keeping his eyes on the telemonitor to see what it looked like to the audience.

A white screen was suspended between the ceiling and the front of the stage. A bright light shone behind the platform, causing the white screen to glow. The lights dimmed, and the camera framed the dais as the introduction to ZERO's number one hit *Baby, I'm Back* boomed through the speakers with the backdrop of screaming fans inside the studio. The song started slowly. As the introduction picked up momentum, green lasers shot at the white screen, forming various shapes. The notes built into a crescendo, the lasers spelled out the 'Z' 'E' 'R' 'O' logo across the white screen. The sound from the frenzied audience grew. Ethan had worried the introduction was drawn out too much, but from how the audience reacted, the choice was the right one.

A voice cut into his headset, "Curtain drop in five, four, three, two…"

The screen quickly dropped to the ground as fire burst from each side of the stage, revealing the ZERO members, who stood in a straight line across the front. For the first time, Ethan saw the live studio audience.

Ethan and the other members of ZERO executed their prearranged choreography, skillfully crafted by their choreographer, Sally Higgins. Sally may have had a background in ballet, but no one would have guessed that when ZERO performed her high-energy, hard-hitting steps.

Before coming on *In Touch with America*, no one had seen ZERO perform the new song live. The band's single had shot up the charts before the full album had been released. Today marked the launch of the full album and the start of their North American tour. After the performance, the group planned an autograph party at the Hard Rock Café, a couple of blocks from the RTN studio. Dan Rawlins, the group's producer, had planned on getting as much press and hype as possible to skyrocket the album to number one and break records, which would help ZERO sell out their one-hundred-city tour.

As the song ended, the pace shifted back to the melodic introduction, hushing the crowd with anticipation. Ric, the group's tenor, finished the song with a solo unaccompanied. As Ric sang, Ethan and the rest of the band made the same forward and downward hand motion as they tilted their heads and the lights dimmed. The last note hung in the air before the audience erupted into applause. Ethan let out an inner sigh of relief. *That went better than I thought it would.* The audience didn't readily see the repeated line Orr made during his solo or how Zach had botched a piece of choreography. Ethan realized that one of the nice things about an audience not completely familiar with a song was that they weren't as critical because they didn't know the material yet.

Ethan walked over to Tom Dulce's interview area with the rest of the band. Dulce, in his usual stoic, professional newscaster manner, had remained seated during the applause. As the band approached, Dulce stood to greet each of the young men with a solid handshake as they sat down beside him.

"Wow, what can I say after a performance like —?"

"I love you, Ric!" a teenage girl on the fourth aisle yelled, cutting Tom off.

Ric smiled before saying, "Thanks. We love you too."

Ethan smiled to himself. They'd all been coached to respond to these outbursts with the universal "we" to make it clear that the entire band loved their fans.

Four years ago, when the band's first album, *Dog Days*, had first come out, no one in the US had known who they were. The group had been steadily touring Europe for a couple of years before the album's release. Most boy bands got tested overseas to see if they were worth spending money on making the group a US hit. If a boy band became wildly successful across the pond, they might make it in the US. Within weeks of the band's first release, their title cut, *Dog Days*, had skyrocketed to the top of all the music charts globally. What had seemed like overnight, the four best friends from New Orleans became the biggest pop sensation in over a decade. Their first album had gone triple-platinum and continued to break records with each new country it was released in.

Zach, Ethan, Ric and Orr had not been ready for the media storm that ensued because of their success. Zach's parents' divorce had been dragged through a tabloid, and Orr had been accused of abusing a wide range of substances. Overall, the group had moved forward and defied all the odds. Most of the group's success could be attributed to two talented music industry insiders—Ron Hightower, the group's manager, and Dan Rawlins, the producer. While both Ron and Dan had believed in the group's musical talent, both men were music insiders who knew how to deal with the press. Despite all the problems during that first year on tour, the group had stuck together and thrived.

Their second album, *As Expected*, had come two years after the first one. Ron and Dan had believed in what they called the 'triple threat.' Ron and Dan had wanted the group to release three albums in a little over four years. Hopefully, all three could be on the charts at once, making record history for a boy band and boosting sales. So far, the first two still hung on the charts, and this third album had what it took to make that vision a reality.

"Ethan, what sets this album apart from the two previous ones?" Dulce asked.

"Well, Tom, I'm thrilled you asked that question, because people expected this album would be another typical 'boy band' album, but it's not. In fact, it has a completely different vibe than anything being done in the US. Our Producer, Dan Rawlins, hired an innovative DJ from Germany to create the record's rhythmic sound. This stuff is rocking the charts in Europe, and we wanted to incorporate it here."

"You think you have something unique, do you?"

"We know it's unique, Tom, and we're the band who gets to usher in this total hip music style here in the US," Rick said.

Zach, Ethan and Orr all nodded in agreement.

"Orr, what is the nationality of your name?" Dulce said, switching gears, "In my research for today's interview, I found several explanations attempting to describe its origins."

Ethan knew Orr was annoyed by the rumors surrounding his name, but he kept the smile pasted on his face as he answered. "Tom, thank you for asking. I have run into those same rumors. I've been accused of being from Iceland— Hello, I'm Black! Do I look like I'm from Iceland?" The audience politely laughed at Orr's attempt at humor. "Actually, my birth name is Orville Johnson. Not exactly the name you want to be called in junior high in inner-city Pittsburgh, so I started going by Orr."

"How does a kid from inner-city Pittsburgh end up in New Orleans?" Dulce asked.

Ethan sat back against the couch as the group quickly spent the next few minutes reviewing their history. The four guys had met in a college at Tulane. Zach, Ethan and Ric had all come to college from privileged backgrounds.

Ethan had been the captain of his high school football team and initially entered college on a scholarship. At six-foot-one-inch with his perfect V-shaped build, Ethan had been a stellar athlete and could have gone pro until he suffered a severe back injury. Ethan's neurosurgeon had replaced a ruptured spinal disk, but the doctor told him another injury could permanently paralyze him.

Orr came to Tulane after having been scouted by several university football teams. During summer training, Orr and Ethan had become best friends. Orr's mom had been a single mother and had told him he needed to work hard and get through high school to go to college. Orr had realized early that his mother's dream wouldn't happen easily, because there was no way she could afford it. He had known the only way he was going into college was by becoming a straight 'A' student and football star.

When Ethan had been injured during the fall semester of his freshman year, Orr had taken it upon himself to get Ethan out of his depression and help him channel his energy in a new direction. Ethan had not been ready to stop moping around. After many failed attempts at re-integrating Ethan into college life, Orr had realized Ethan would be a tough case to break. Eventually, Orr had stopped trying to take Ethan out of the dorm room. Instead, he had brought the fun to Ethan. Although Orr's constant insistence that Ethan "*be productive*" had grated on Ethan's last nerve, he had eventually come around. During this moping recovery phase, Orr and Ethan had met a couple of cool guys on another floor, Ric and Zach. Before long, Zach, Ethan, Ric and Orr had been inseparable. The guys did everything together.

After their freshman year, they had gotten a house a few blocks from the main campus. Orr had worked all summer and raised enough money to quit football with the help of other financial aid and scholarships. Orr had never taken to football how most expected. To Orr, football had been the means to get himself into and through college. Once there, he realized he had more options than playing ball.

One night during the spring semester of their sophomore year, the guys had thrown back a few beers when they came up with a scheme to make themselves known on campus. They had formed a band and entered the university talent competition. The initial goal had been to find some 'boy band' song and destroy it in jest. The group had settled on *Excess* by X-chro, a British import that had ended up being a flash in the pan but had been making headlines and waves in the music industry at the time. What originally was to be a spoof of boy bands ended up winning them the top prize and a consultation with an industry producer, Dan Rawlins. Rawlins, as they found out, was the British producer who'd signed X-chro.

The competition organizers had forwarded the video to Rawlins at the end of the competition. When Rawlins had seen the four guys and their raw talent, he went to New Orleans and had a development meeting with the group. Zach, Ethan, Ric and Orr had been dumbfounded by the offer Rawlins made to develop the group's talent and shepherd them. Less than a month later, the four had signed contracts and taken leaves of absence from the university. The following year had been a whirlwind of vocal lessons, choreography training and meeting with songwriters. Before they knew what had happened, the group toured Europe while developing material for their first album. After two long years, the group's first album *Dog Days* was released to outstanding reviews and impressive sales. Zach, Ethan, Ric and Orr rocketed from obscurity to superstar fame in less than four years.

Here they were, as the group prepared to release their third album, talking to the famed *Real Time News* talk show host slash anchor, Tom Dulce.

"So, guys, you know your fans want me to ask you *the* question. Are you all currently in relationships, or are you all still single?" Dulce asked.

"Tom," Orr said. "I guess I should make it public… I got engaged two weeks ago to my high-school sweetheart, Constinia." Several exasperated "*ahhs*" and "*ohhs*" were heard from the studio audience but were quickly drowned out by polite applause.

Listening to Orr talk, Ethan let his mind drift as he remembered how Orr had told the guys right before he popped the question. Sadly, as was typical with celebrity life, the group had discussed how Orr should handle the post-engagement press. Since this was unfamiliar territory for the band, the group had told Orr to ask their manager for his opinion. Hightower had immediately involved Rawlins. And before the band knew it, a complete media campaign had been developed for the post-engagement announcement press tour. Today's 'impromptu' appearance at RTN was the beginning of the publicity tour. Rawlins saw the engagement announcement as a great opportunity for Orr to sing a ballad from the new album, which could be dedicated to his fiancée, Constinia.

The audience died down as Ric and Zach admitted they were both single and currently looking for people to fill the vacancy. Several "I'll be your wife" yells came from the audience.

"Well, it looks like everyone has answered the question except for you, Ethan. You wouldn't be trying to avoid answering, would you?"

"Not at all, Tom. I am not married, for those of you who want to know, nor do I currently have a girlfriend or fiancée. I find it hard to meet people when you're on the road as much as we are." Ric and Zach both quickly agreed. Ethan continued, "When you are touring or recording in the studio forty-three out of fifty-two weeks in the year, you don't get much personal time. I only see my family on big holidays or when I fly them out to a show. Without these three"—motioning to Zach, Ric and Orr—"I probably would have quit singing long ago. Don't get me wrong. I love what I'm doing. I love you, the fans, but it takes a lot of work and energy to do what we do."

"And the four of you do what you do amazingly well," Tom said, looking into the camera. A stage manager signaled that it was time for the newsbreak. Tom looked right into the camera and said, "It's time for *News Minute* here on the *Real Time News* Network. Tika Downs is in the news studio. Tika."

"And we are off the air for three minutes," the studio director informed the audience. It was as if the balloon had been let go in the room. Everyone sighed and relaxed in unison. Ethan absently watched as Tom and the rest of ZERO started talking among themselves. Tom assured the group that the interview was going well and asked them if they needed anything during the break. The guys said they were fine and enjoyed taking a breather. Ethan stood and stretched his legs, lifting his hands over his head just high enough that his shirt pulled up, exposing the top of his boxers and the tuft of light brown hair on his stomach that led down into his boxers. A couple of the girls in the front row almost fell out of their chairs. Ethan saw their expressions and laughed on the inside. *If they only knew.*

"Places, everyone. Sixty seconds to go." Ethan looked at the monitor to see Tika reading the list of news items succinctly. He was about to move back to his chair when he saw a graphic of a houseboat with the words "*New Orleans*" underneath. Ethan paid attention to what was being said for the first time during the break.

On the monitor, Ethan watched as Tika glanced down at her script and read, "*This just in. A tragedy struck earlier this evening. As you probably know, New Orleans is home to the popular daytime soap opera* NOLA Nights. *The police are not releasing any information. We have confirmed from studio sources that two of the show's stars who were rumored to be dating have been murdered. Cynthia Dunning and Daniel Hawthorne, both age twenty-seven, will be sorely missed by the acting community and their fans.*" Cynthia and Daniel's *NOLA Nights* publicity headshots flashed across the screen. Their birth and death years displayed below. "*Our hearts go out to the NOLA Nights family and their fans during this tragic time.*" Tika's somber face stood frozen on the screen for a second before she continued, "*Now, we rejoin Tom Dulce with* In Touch with America *and the band ZERO. I'm Tika Downs. This was* News Minute."

Ethan watched Tika with transfixed horror as she reported the deaths of Cynthia and Daniel. The world seemed to slow down for him. He saw the news bulletin end but could not feel or hear anything else. He felt like he had an out-of-body experience. He shuffled back to his seat in the studio, but he was on autopilot. In the distance, he heard, "*I'm Tika Downs. This was* News Minute," but he wasn't sure where it was coming from. It sounded like someone yelling when you're submerged in a swimming pool. His eyes rolled into the back of his head, and he collapsed. In his last second of consciousness, there were sounds of screaming as he slipped into nothing but black.

# Chapter Two

*Blayne*

Blayne Dickenson was doing his best to pay attention, but the gorgeous fall day just outside the window called to him.

"Mr. Dickenson, how would you organize forms of pop culture into a history class?"

"What?" Blayne asked before he could fully articulate a response.

He turned away from the window to stare at his multicultural education professor, Dr. Madeline Reich.

"I realize it is a gorgeous day, Mr. Dickenson, but we still have content that must be covered."

"I'm sorry, Dr. Reich. It's just—"

"Don't worry, Mr. Dickenson. There is no one here who does not share in your desire to be outside. But, as I was saying, *'How would you integrate forms of pop culture into a history class?'*"

"Minimally, if at all," Blayne quickly responded. "We spend so much time catering to our students' desires for thirty-second sound bites that we teach nothing anymore. If anything, we must avoid blurring the lines between education and entertainment."

"Wait a second," piped up Hillary Smith, another doctoral student. "If we don't use the tools of the masses to educate people, are we not doing some kind of disservice to our students? I mean, if watching a commercial, movie or television segment can help our students thoroughly grasp the content...then why not?"

"Why not? Because they're college students. It's not like we're teaching middle-school," Blayne responded. "Besides, like Allan Bloom said, the further we get away from the basics, the dumber our students become and the worse we are as educators." Out of the fifteen graduate students in the room, only five appeared to agree with Blayne, so he continued. "The fact is, in today's educational climate, we are constantly watering down the content. As a result, we produce graduates who cannot read and write. We are creating consumers of pop culture who can't tell the difference between facts and opinions and between actual news and fake news. Maybe if we spent more time teaching people how to think critically instead of what a Real Housewife did, our culture wouldn't be in the state it's in now. Find me a show that can do that?"

"What about *Sesame Street* or *Mr. Roger's Neighborhood*?" suggested Dr. Reich.

"Okay, I'll concede that there are a handful of shows on *public* television and a few on the History Channel that have educational value. Instead of figuring out how to use the lyrics from the latest pop song to teach our students, we should focus on how we can teach our students to be critical thinkers. I've never seen a pop-cultural artifact foster original or critical thought."

"What about that boy band ZERO's Earth Day show on RTN? You had a boy band, can't be more pop than that, explaining to kids and teenagers why we should actively support and save the environment. How is this not useful?" asked Hillary.

"Well, I'm surprised RTN would stoop so low as to have a boy band on. But then, RTN is not exactly in the news business these days," Blayne groused. "Second, did ZERO foster thought, or did they tell their mindless followers what they should think? As you can tell, I'm slightly biased against the human cloning enterprise, otherwise known as 'boy bands'. And besides, I'm sure they sold another million albums following their little special on RTN. So, did they really care about the environment or were they just making another dollar?"

"Well, I never know what I'm going to get when I wake the sleeping giant," Dr. Reich responded as she smirked in Blayne's direction. After a brief pause, she continued. "Since we're coming to a close for the evening, I want to continue this discussion next week. But I don't want our discussion to be opinion-based. I want each of you to research and write a five-page reaction paper to the research you find from educational theorists about using pop culture in the classroom. Find at least five peer-reviewed sources to support your argument, not obvious ones like Newman, Bloom or Palmer. Really, see what research is out there."

\* \* \* \*

Blayne stood in front of his locker in the university recreational facility, dripping with sweat after his workout. After the debate in Dr. Reich's class, Blayne had been ready to get his blood pumping. At twenty-seven, people often mistook him for being in his mid-thirties, which irritated him. At six-foot-four-inches and two-hundred pounds, with brown hair and blue eyes, Blayne always stood out in a group.

Although Blayne was clearly athletic, he had never liked organized sports. Honestly, he didn't like sports as a general concept. He wasn't much of a joiner. He did, however, like watching soccer players running around in their shorts. And he liked it even more when there was a game of shirts versus skins on the field. There was something about a well-toned guy without his shirt in nylon and polyester. Although this specific sexual fantasy had been fulfilled on more than one occasion — especially with his high school soccer team's captain — it still amazed him how the sight of a hot guy in soccer shorts could so easily turn him on.

Blayne mostly did his job, teaching basic English composition and worked on finishing up his course work so he could write his dissertation. As a graduate student, Blayne felt more like an indentured servant than a faculty member. He was consistently one of the more popular composition professors in his department. He had recently found out that he received an 'excellent teaching by a graduate student' award from the university's College of Arts and Science. Although he was honored by the recognition, he had wondered if it was indeed justified. Half the time, Blayne felt he was winging it in the classroom. He would rush into class semi-prepared — only having barely finished reading the material himself. He was constantly afraid someone would find out he didn't know what he was talking about half the time.

Blayne stared at himself in the mirror inside his locker. His hair was matted to his head with sweat. He smiled into the mirror, realizing how vain it must look to smile at oneself. He stripped down, then carefully hung his workout clothes in the locker to provide ample drying room. He grabbed his towel and shower supplies and closed his locker door. He caught sight of a guy with impressive back muscles in a towel bending over to pick something out of a bottom locker a couple of rows away. Even though the guy was bent over, Blayne could see his perfectly shaped ass. As Blayne played Peeping Tom for a second, the blood quickly rushed to his cock. Blayne forced his mind to think about something other than that perfectly sculpted ass.

"Hey, Mr. Dickenson! Good run?"

Blayne spun around to hear the voice. The 'incredible ass' was talking to him. "Oh, hey, Todd. I didn't even see you in here." *Fuck, I can't believe I got hard looking at a student's ass.* "Yeah, I had a good run. Needed to blow off some extra steam. Don't forget your outline is due tomorrow." Blayne learned early in his teaching career that students would approach him anytime and anywhere. It didn't matter if he was stark naked standing in front of his locker semi-erect—students always felt the need to say "hi" and talk.

"Don't worry, Mr. Dickenson. I won't forget my outline. The dumb thing's practically written."

"It's not a dumb thing, Todd. Outlines help you write better. Trust me… When you're in the real world and you have to write a business report, you're going to be very thankful I've drilled this into your head. But anyway, I've got to get showered and finish grading your midterms." With that, Blayne strode to the showers and was thankful Todd hadn't followed him in.

Blayne didn't mind when students said hi to him at the movies or talked to him in restaurants. But when he was hot, naked, sweaty and desperately needing a shower, this was not the time to speak to him. One day, he had a freshman introduce himself while he was relieving himself at the urinal.

The showers in the recreation center were in a square-tiled room. In the center of the room, a circular formation of showerheads made it possible for up to eight people to shower simultaneously. Blayne stood under the warm water and almost drifted off to sleep as the warmth of the water flowing over his body took him away for a second. He broke out of his trance when he heard a couple of voices on the other side of the showers.

"Hey, Blayne, fancy meeting you here."

He glanced over his shoulder at his new shower mates to find Arnold Giest-Mueler and his partner, Harry. Arnold and Harry were the current advisers of the university's Queer Coalition. Although the couple was almost fifteen years his senior, he enjoyed talking to them about the days before they could be open about their relationship. The couple had been together for almost twenty years, and although they had a notoriously open relationship, they seemed very much in love. Blayne'd had a brief tryst with Arnold when he'd first gotten to Pennington. Arnold was a general surgeon at the Pennington University Hospital whom he had met when his best friend Kira's appendix burst, resulting in emergency surgery. One thing had led to another, and Arnold and he had had sex in one of the on-call rooms while Kira recovered. They'd fucked a couple more times over the years.

The first time they'd fucked, Blayne had just arrived in Houston and didn't know anyone. He'd pulled out his cell phone and the Giest-Muelers were the first people he'd met. Blayne had been relatively inexperienced at the time, and the Giest-Muelers helped him learn to top like a pile driver and take dick like a porn star. Blayne hadn't been a virgin, but in retrospect, he wasn't exactly knowledgeable of how a lot sex could be. He was thankful to the older couple for opening him up in more ways than one, but they were now more friendly acquaintances than fuck-buddies or lovers.

Blayne lathered up and was rinsing off when he caught Harry eyeing his ass. Blayne rolled his eyes and finished rinsing. He couldn't blame the man for looking. Hell, Blayne had just done the same thing. He finished his shower and said goodbye to the couple before heading to his locker to dress and get out of there.

# Chapter Three

*Dr. Hennigan*

Dr. Hennigan sat in the back of her stretch limo listening to Wagner's *Liebestod* from *Tristan and Isolde* with her eyes closed. She'd always felt a sort of oneness with the German composer. She reached over to the bar and opened the small fridge, pulling out a can of juice. One of her requirements was that she had a stocked bar in the limo. She pulled the tab back, popped open the can and held it up to her nose. She breathed in the bitter orange scent, lowered the can to her lips and drank.

Dr. Hennigan was very much a creature of habit. She had juice every morning on the way to work, then a bottle of water on the way back in the afternoon. She expected to have a copy of the *New York Times*, *Washington Post*, *London Gazette*, Paris' *Mondo Times* and Tokyo's *Mainichi Daily News*. The newspapers lay beside her in a stack. They wouldn't get read, but she wanted them there in case something important had happened in the middle of the night. If The Foundation pulled off an operation, she would also have a copy of the local newspaper that covered the event. She knew information was power, and in her line of work, she was probably one of the most powerful women in the world.

She didn't need to open her eyes as the car slowed down and her driver's window lowered. There was no point. The privacy partition was raised between the back and the driver's seat. The partition was raised in case of unforeseen events that caused concern for Dr. Hennigan's safety. She knew the women who worked for her would ensure she was safe and secure.

While she couldn't hear what the guard at the gate said to her driver, she didn't really need to. She had been driven every morning for fifteen years to the Vuélo airport twenty miles northwest of El Paso, Texas. This morning was slightly different because she had a new orientation group waiting for her on the plane. She lifted her half-empty orange juice to her lips and finished the can as the car jerked toward the tarmac. The vehicle then stopped in a few seconds. She could hear the rumbling of the plane next to the car. Her driver exited and walked around the back of the car to the passenger's side to free the doctor. Dr. Hennigan opened her eyes, pulled out a pocket mirror and looked at herself one last time as the driver opened the door. Her hair was still very much in order, and her makeup was sensible yet elegant.

As she exited the limo, she ran her hands down her pantsuit, attempting to release any wrinkles created during the brief trip. Today Dr. Hennigan was wearing a black pinstripe pantsuit with a cream silk blouse that folded across her chest, causing a V-shape right at the top of the crack in her cleavage—very professional, very refined. She reached back into the limo, pulled out a leather attaché case and draped her designer black trench coat over her arm.

"Dara, I won't need you to pick me up this evening. I am staying at The Complex overnight to oversee the initial stages of the recruit orientation. I'll call tomorrow to let you know when I'll be back."

Dara was a woman in her mid-to-late twenties who wore a bulky, black suit that attempted to hide the woman's athletic physique. Her raven hair was pulled back into a single ponytail that stuck out from the back of her driver's cap and flowed down her back, blending in with her suit coat. When in her uniform, most people naturally assumed she was a man. "Yes, Doctor. I called and received confirmation. All twelve recruits are ready for takeoff once you are on board."

"Thank you, Dara. Are we still on schedule?"

"Yes, Doctor. It is currently five-fifteen a.m. Central Standard Time. You should be at The Complex by no later than five-forty-five, so you won't miss your window."

Satisfied everything was on schedule, Dr. Hennigan turned toward the waiting plane. It was a specially equipped V-Twenty-Two Osprey that could quickly and quietly maneuver members of The Foundation to and from The Complex, a hybrid plane and helicopter. With propellers and jet engines, the Osprey could maneuver in and out of locations much more easily than a typical helicopter or airplane. The Osprey has two large propellers on either side of the plane's main body that tilted from a perpendicular position for lift, like a traditional helicopter, then tilted horizontally for thrust, like a traditional propeller plane. In its resting position, the propellers lay over the length of the plane's body, making the Osprey easier to conceal than a traditional airplane or helicopter because there is no wing or propeller span. The Osprey was fifty-seven feet long and eighty-four feet wide in flight mode, but only sixty-three feet long and eighteen feet wide when the propellers were folded in. Since The Complex only had limited above-ground storage space, they could store six Ospreys without them being seen through satellite imaging. The main cabin could hold twenty-four people comfortably. Because this was a recruit orientation, only half that many were on board.

When Dr. Hennigan entered, she felt the movement above her as the propellers transitioned toward their takeoff position as the propellers started spinning. She surveyed the new recruits. All the recruits were women, as per the policies of The Foundation.

The Foundation's primary goal had always been women's equal inclusion and involvement in politics. While The Foundation was established in the United States, the organization had expanded in the past eighty years and now had branches in most major countries, including England, France, Germany, China, India, Saudi Arabia, Japan and many more. Although only a few people knew the complete infrastructure of The Foundation, everyone who worked for the organization knew it was extensive. And it was often speculated by lower-level operatives that nothing happened in international politics unless The Foundation had arranged for it to occur. Dr. Hennigan knew the rumors were not wholly true, but she felt no need to contradict the extent of her power in the eyes of others.

The chairwoman position in The Foundation was passed down in a matriarchal fashion. Her grandmother, Sara Hennigan, was the current chairwoman. When she died, Dr. Hennigan's mother, Deborah, would take over. Then it would be Dr.

Hennigan's duty to run the operation. Dr. Hennigan's real name was Philippa, but most people called her Dr. Hennigan simply because it was the easiest way to distinguish between the matriarchs.

Dr. Hennigan glanced over at the twelve women with black sacks over their heads, who were sitting evenly spaced out around the Osprey. Having read all the recruits' files, she knew that among the new recruits was a pathologist from the University of Denver Medical School, a high-powered Constitutional law scholar, a housewife, a couple of ex-CIA operatives, three former special operations marines, two politicians, a prison warden and an actress. Dr. Hennigan had twelve weeks to turn this motley crew into members of The Foundation. Blindfolded, with small duffel bags in their laps, the group looked very stoic, but she knew they were terrified.

She entered the cockpit, sat in the co-pilot's seat and nodded to the pilot.

"We're ready when you are," the pilot informed the doctor.

"Let's get going then."

With that, the pilot pushed forward on the lever between her legs and the Osprey ascended straight up. Dr. Hennigan heard a quick yelp from one recruit and stifled her laugh. *If you're scared by this, you won't make it to the end of the day.*

Unlike previous tiltrotor planes that went from ninety to sixty-degrees angles in one stroke, causing the transition from lift to thrust to be very jerky, the Osprey transitioned from ninety to forty-five to sixty-degrees, which allowed for a smoother transition from lift to thrust. In a matter of seconds, the plane arced, then leveled off as it switched into thrust mode, propelling the aircraft forward through the early morning sky.

"Dr. Hennigan, how do the new recruits look?"

"Honestly, there are a couple I don't think will make it past today. And if they make it past today, I doubt I'll keep them through the week. With that said, the pathologist and actress have real promise. It will be interesting to see how quickly I can find their breaking points."

The two sat in silence for the next few minutes. The New Mexico branch of the Rocky Mountains was quickly below the Osprey. In the early morning dawn, the mountains were pitch black. Not a single living soul lived in this remote and desolate part of the state. The Foundation's International headquarters was in a valley north of the Mesa Juamenes Mountain Ridge in southern New Mexico. The valley was approximately three-fourths of a mile and about three-hundred yards wide. From the sky, the landscape looked empty. What could not be seen from satellite photos was the runway, which was purposefully designed to mimic the terrain's appearance. The storage for the Ospreys was a carved-out hangar in the side of the Mesa Juamenes Ridge. Since the ridge was primarily made of rock and not dirt, the carving out of the hangar had not been too difficult.

"Alpha Niner Epsilon, this is The Complex. Your ten-minute entry window will occur in five, four, three, two, one."

The Osprey's propellers moved from thrust to descent, and the plane was on the ground in eight minutes. "Alpha Niner Epsilon, welcome to The Complex. Your window closes in one minute and fifty-four seconds. Please move to pad five in the hangar."

Since the advent of satellite technology, planes were required to maneuver skillfully in and out of The Complex in a fashion that couldn't be seen by satellites.

The satellites hovering over the valley got blocked for ten minutes every two hours. And since leaving during the daylight was unthinkable, people could only leave and return six times daily, starting at eight p.m. and ending at six-thirty a.m. Most of The Foundation members had residencies in two locations, The Complex and wherever they called 'home base'.

The pilot switched off the propellers. Dr. Hennigan could hear them locking into position on top of the plane. With forty-seven seconds to spare, the pilot had secured the Osprey on pad five. Dr. Hennigan opened the main door, and her lab partner, Ms. Wilson, entered the Osprey with a team of ten armed technicians.

"My name is Dr. Hennigan. I will process you during your orientation phase. As you were told when you were recruited, you are all women here. Modesty will not exist. Without taking off your blindfolds, stand up and take off your shirts, then brace yourselves against the plane's wall. As a medical precaution, you will receive a quick injection."

Each of the ten technicians, Ms. Wilson and Dr. Hennigan held one of the gun-like apparatuses — AZ-five-hundred-fifty — and placed the nozzle to the lower right of the spine below the liver where a fatty bed existed that could easily be penetrated with high enough pressure. The AZ-five-fifty delivered a small microchip into the recruit's body using a high-air-pressure cannon. The microchip served as the recruit's permanent ID tag and could monitor their vital signs. "On the count of three. One...two...three..." The sounds of the AZ-five-hundred-fifties against the skin were muffled by the quick yelps. Dr. Hennigan learned long ago the only effective way to administer the chip was to inject all recruits at once when no one knew it was coming.

"I'm sorry about the pain, but the new method of inserting the microchips is much easier than it used to be. You can now remove your blindfolds." The recruits slowly removed the hoods over their faces and, for the first time, saw one another and the woman whose voice they had been hearing. Dr. Hennigan continued, "The microchip inserted into your body is your personal identification in The Complex. When you come to a door, your body will be scanned. If you have access to that door, it will automatically open. If you do not have access to a door, you will be informed you do not have. Do not try to remove the microchip. As soon as the chip is exposed to air, it releases a toxin into your system. If this happens, you will die rather painfully within five minutes. As a member of The Foundation, if you ever need surgery, you will be taken to one of The Foundation's surgeons, who can temporarily turn off the chip if necessary. Follow me, and welcome to The Foundation."

The recruits followed Dr. Hennigan closely in a single file line out of the Osprey. Dr. Hennigan had trained over thirty classes, so she did not need to look behind her to see the looks of awe that was registered on their faces. At the back of the hangar, a staircase led down to a brightly lit room. Armed guards stood on either side.

"Watch how I do this, because this will be your only instructional session on how to operate doors." Dr. Hennigan stood in front of the door, and a narrow green beam emanated from a round ball above it. The beam quickly scanned Dr. Hennigan from head to toe.

"Welcome, Dr. Hennigan, Senior Administrator, Security Clearance Zeta. Please hand the guns attached to your shoulder, ankle and lower back to the security guard for inspection. Please remove the pen from your right front coat pocket. No other weapons detected," a robotic voice said from over a hidden speaker.

Dr. Hennigan pulled out the gun on her lower back, unhooked her shoulder holster with the gun still in it, then rolled up her pants to reveal a small gun strapped onto her right ankle. In a matter of seconds, she gave the three firearms and the pen to the guards. The wall to the door's left contained small lock boxes. A small box pushed away from the bank. The whirring sound of the gears was heard before a slight click. One guard reached over, removed the lockbox from the wall, placed the items inside and relocked the box. The guard then gave the box to Dr. Hennigan, who put the box back into an open slot in the wall and entered a key code to prevent anyone else from retrieving her items.

"You are only allowed to bring clothing and footwear into The Complex. Any other paraphernalia will be scanned and confiscated before you may enter." Dr. Hennigan stepped in front of the door, and the scan reinitiated. The beam quickly re-scanned Dr. Hennigan from head to toe.

"Welcome, Dr. Hennigan, Senior Administrator, Security Clearance Zeta. You may enter."

The doors slid open, and Dr. Hennigan stepped inside before they shut behind her.

# Chapter Four

*Ethan*

The doctor slowly released the air from the blood pressure cuff attached to Ethan, getting an accurate reading.

"Everything seems good. Your blood pressure is one-twenty-three over eighty, which is about as normal as it gets. Your pulse rate is fine."

Ethan glanced over and noticed Dan Rawlins, the band's producer, who paced back and forth in the room's corner. *If Dan keeps that up, he will wear a hole in the carpet,* Ethan thought before focusing again on the doctor.

"And you've never had a fainting spell before?" the doctor asked.

"Nope," Ethan responded from the edge of his hotel bed. "This was a first for me."

"Curious," the doctor pondered. "Well, I see no reason for postponing your trip to Seattle. I would do the usual—ensure you eat properly and get plenty of fluids. If I were a betting man, I would guess you were dehydrated. The intensity of the studio lights caused the fainting spell. But again, this is a guess at this point. Make sure you take care of yourself, okay?"

"Doctor, I'll make sure Mr. Bond takes care of himself," Rawlins said. "Anything we should watch out for, though?"

"If it happens again, we'll want to do a more complete workup. But, as far as I can tell, he's in excellent shape. Once the lab runs the bloodwork, I'll have a better idea if there is anything to be concerned about—"

"Yes, but are we good to continue with the tour?" Rawlins asked.

"Like I said," the doctor started, "I see no reason he can't continue with the tour as planned." The doctor then turned back and looked at Ethan. "If you experience any symptoms, call me immediately." The doctor reached into his jacket pocket, pulled out a business card and handed it to Ethan. "My cell phone number is on here, so don't hesitate to call me any time of the day or night. That's what concierge medicine is for. You need me. I'm here for you. Got it?"

"Yes, Doctor," Ethan said.

"Great," Rawlins added. "Thanks for coming over, Doctor. Please, let us know when you get those test results back."

Rawlins ushered the doctor from his bedroom. He flopped back on the bed, feeling a slight bounce as he stared up at the ceiling. He knew precisely why he'd passed out. Still, he wasn't exactly sure how he would tell his producer, manager or the band.

"What happened to you, Danny?" Ethan said to himself as he wiped a tear away from his eyes. He'd been trying to keep his emotions in check all evening after the RNN debacle. He replayed the segment before the ZERO interview with Tom Dulce. *Murdered? Who would want to murder Danny?*

Ethan had met Daniel Hawthorne, the dreamboat star of the daytime soap opera *NOLA Nights* at a party the year before. Danny, as his friends called him, knew Ethan's best friend, Stephanie, from college. When Stephanie received an invitation to attend the previous season's premiere, she'd convinced Ethan to be her date.

When Stephanie introduced Ethan to Danny, they immediately hit it off — not only because they were both celebrities but because they each knew the other was secretly gay. Ahh, the joys of gaydar. They started seeing each other on the downlow. Thankfully, it wasn't uncommon for celebrities to hang out, so they had become friends. They were often seen hitting up nightclubs in town. They'd even had a couple of double dates with various starlets. Of course, they always had ended up back at either Ethan's loft or Danny's houseboat at the end of the night — together.

For Ethan, it wasn't exactly love. It was a friend with benefits — a convenience situation. Both Danny and Ethan were hot, so there had been sexual attraction and chemistry. But beyond hanging out and hooking up, neither had been looking for a relationship. They'd spent the night together two nights before. Danny and Ethan had gone out partying and ended up back on Danny's houseboat for a bit of fun before Ethan had headed back to his own townhouse in the Garden District.

There was a soft rapping at the hotel door. "Come in," Ethan responded, snapping him out of his trip down memory lane.

"Hey, buddy," Zach said as he entered the room. "How are you feeling?"

"Better," Ethan said, propping himself up.

"What did the doc say?" Zach asked.

"He guesses it was dehydration caused by the studio lights."

"And what do you have to say?" Zach asked, a quizzical look on his face.

He drew in a deep breath and let out a quick sigh. "As good a guess as any at this point. They drew some blood and will have the results tomorrow. If there's anything serious, he'll let me know."

Ethan heard some noise beyond the door frame. "Guys, you might as well all come in. I can hear you eavesdropping."

Orr and Ric poked their heads quickly around the corner.

"We weren't eavesdropping," Orr protested.

Ethan raised an eyebrow, "Thou doth protest too much."

"Okay," Ric started. "So, we may have been eavesdropping, but it's because we wanted to make sure you're okay."

"I'm fine. The doctor said I'm fine," Ethan reassured them.

"That's good to hear," Orr said.

"Totally," Ric agreed.

"Anyway," Zach started, "glad to hear you're all right. We're about to order room service. Can we get you anything?"

"Let me look." Ethan scooted around the bed to the bedside table, opened the drawer and pulled out the hotel room service menu. He glanced through the menu before saying, "Order me the lobster mac-n-cheese with a Diet Coke."

"Will do," Zach said. "Have you called Stephanie yet?"

"Dear God, no. I hadn't even thought about calling her. I'm sure she's panicked."

"Yea," Zach said, scrunching up his face a bit. "She's called me five times asking how you're doing and why you aren't picking up your phone."

"I'll do that now. Thanks for the heads-up."

"We'll let you know when room service gets here," Zach said as he shut the door.

\* \* \* \*

*Blayne*

Blayne had grown up in a small town in West Texas called Plainview. The name clearly exemplified reality. One could see for miles in any direction, and all they saw was flat dirt. There was not a hill or even a giant anthill in any direction from the town. Plainview was also a good representation of the way the city saw the world outside. The folks in Plainview were decent and kind, but they didn't understand they lived in a world with all different kinds of people who were not like them. As Blayne was growing up, he would escape to the metropolis of Lubbock, TX, a metropolitan community—in numbers at least—about forty-five-miles south of Plainview. In Lubbock, Blayne could experience culture—at least culture that didn't exist in Plainview or most of West Texas. Heck, Lubbock even had two gay clubs and a lesbian bar. Blayne had gone to Texas Tech University for his undergraduate work, but quickly discovered that what he saw as a culturally rich city wasn't. Although Lubbock had more culture than any other part of West Texas, the city was still a very conservative enclave. As soon as Blayne had finished his undergraduate degree in psychology and his Master's in multicultural educational studies at Texas Tech, he knew he needed to find a more liberal institution for his doctorate.

One of Blayne's favorite professors at Texas Tech had attended Pennington University and encouraged Blayne to apply to the program there. Blayne had taken the chance, applied and found himself at Pennington, a small but well-respected liberal arts university in a Houston suburb. The Pendlebrook subdivision, where the university was built, was primarily composed of university-affiliated personnel. Culturally, Pendlebrook truly opened Blayne's perspective on everything possible. If the university didn't have it, then Houston would.

For Blayne, coming out had been a non-issue. He had realized in junior high school he was not interested in females sexually. He had initially thought there was something psychologically wrong with him. Unbeknownst to his parents, he had seen a psychologist. Unbeknownst to Blayne, the psychologist had been gay. The psychologist helped Blayne understand that being gay was neither a sin nor a mistake nature made. Even after they had ended their counseling relationship, Blayne kept in touch with his psychologist to let him know how things were going. By the time Blayne's senior year in high school had rolled around, Blayne was pretty much out to everyone. And since Blayne was gorgeous, intelligent and athletic, most people were shocked when he came out in a school newspaper column. Although he hadn't been entirely prepared for the amount of support he received, the few negative experiences still upset him. Blayne hadn't understood why people had gotten mad at him for being honest and upfront about who he was. To Blayne, the idea of lying about his sexual orientation had been as idiotic as lying about one's religion or political affiliation.

Since high school, Blayne had always lived as an openly gay man. He didn't run around Pennington University screaming about his gayness from the top of his lungs. He simply lived it. He didn't gender-switch pronouns when giving examples in class. He didn't turn the picture of him and his ex-boyfriend around when students came into the office. And he didn't lie when asked. Blayne lived his life openly and honestly.

Blayne's ex-boyfriend had been killed in an automobile accident two years before he'd come to Pennington. Jeremy had been driving home from Christmas vacation and was killed in a head-on collision with a semi. Jeremy had swerved into the oncoming lane, and the emergency people on the scene said he'd died instantly. Although the investigators didn't know how the accident happened, Blayne did. Jeremy had regularly stopped paying attention to the road as he fiddled with his phone, picking the next album or podcast to listen to while driving. Blayne could easily see in his head what had probably happened. Jeremy had messed with his phone and swerved at the wrong time into oncoming traffic — such a senseless death.

Blayne hadn't gotten over Jeremy because Jeremy had been Blayne's soul mate. Both Jeremy and Blayne had figured they would live together for the rest of their lives. Neither had expected the rest of Jeremy's life would only be a couple of years. After Jeremy's death, Blayne had stopped caring emotionally for guys. He had friends he trusted and guys he fucked, and the two groups never crossed paths. Cognitively, Blayne realized this differentiation of relationships was unhealthy. Still, it helped him get through his heartache for a few years. When Blayne wanted to talk to someone, he spoke to his friends. When he had wanted to fuck, he found a hook-up.

Back in his apartment, Blayne hurried himself into the kitchen to make dinner. After arguing with a fellow student, running, getting horny, looking at a student's ass and getting ogled by older gay guys, he was totally famished. Blayne broiled a chicken breast and baked a potato. He wrapped the potato in foil and half-listened to the news on *Real Time News* in the background.

"Welcome back to *Real Time News*. I'm Tika Downs. With the primaries right around the corner, the world of politics is quickly reaching its boiling point. But before we discuss the current political hotbed our President has entered, let's go live to Lake Pontchartrain, where Stephen McNeil is investigating the tragic murders of *NOLA Nights* stars Cynthia Dunning and Daniel Hawthorne."

*Daniel Hawthorne? Why does that name sound so familiar? Must have read it on the cover of a magazine at some point.*

"Thank you, Tika. The horrific site of Daniel Hawthorn's houseboat this evening startled police officers. This investigative reporter obtained exclusive footage from inside the carnage. Warning, this segment is not for our younger viewers."

Blayne turned to look at the television when he heard the reporter's announcement about the live footage. *When did news agencies become so depraved?* The image on the screen was clearly taken by someone's cell phone. The person with the camera was going down a short flight of stairs. The image panned left at the bottom of the stairs, and Blayne could see a female lying on the floor. Blayne was glad the film wasn't great quality because he really didn't want to see the reality of murder. The camera panned right. A pair of legs stuck out of a doorway. The cameraman walked toward the body. The screen filled with the image of a handsome guy, probably in his mid-twenties, with a bullet hole in his forehead. As the face was in view, someone pulled a white sheet over the victim's head. *How do they get away with showing this crap on TV?*

"Stephen, those images are truly devastating. It looks like this is some kind of assassination. Have the police said anything yet?" Tika asked.

"Tika, ten minutes ago, an unnamed source from inside the New Orleans Police Department—NOPD—gave me crucial information about the case. In their investigation, the victims were not dating like was originally suspected. Instead, various articles in the house leave the NOPD to think Daniel Hawthorn was probably a homosexual," Stephen said with a slight grin on his face.

"Stephen, what kinds of *articles* were found in the houseboat? Can you give us any further details?"

"From what my exclusive sources tell me, some sexual paraphernalia and unsigned love letters were found in the houseboat. My sources say the police are currently following four potential lines of investigation. First, Hawthorne was gay and was killed by some kind of jealous lover, and Dunning was killed because she was in the wrong place at the wrong time. Second, Hawthorne and Dunning were having an affair and were killed by his ex-lover. Third, this was a ménage à trois gone very wrong. And, fourth, this is some kind of premeditated hate crime."

"Stephen, the police sure look like they have their work cut out for them on this case."

*Click.* Blayne hated it when the media got on some kind of gay kick. It never ceased to amaze Blayne how murder became even more scandalous when it involved a gay man. Heck, it was even better if it was a gay man who had killed another gay man. To Blayne, a crime was simply a crime. It didn't matter if the crime was perpetrated as an act of bias-related hate. It was a crime. In theory, Blayne thought the idea of hate crime laws was ridiculous. To classify certain crimes as being more severe because of one's thought process seemed like thought police. A murderer was still a murderer. It doesn't matter if he was gay, straight, Black, Hispanic, White, Asian— They were a murderer. Although this perspective was philosophically sound, Blayne also realized lady justice had only one eye peeking in today's world. When teenagers could kidnap, beat a gay kid and carve the word 'fag' into his chest and only get suspended from high school for a couple of days, injustice obviously existed. So, on hate crimes laws, Blayne realized they had to exist because the courts and public often could not be trusted to dole out justice.

Blayne finished doing his dishes and decided he had enough television for the day, so he checked his email and dating apps before calling it a night. Blayne had the newest computer model released earlier that semester by Harvester Electronics. For thirty years, Blayne's father had worked at Harvester designing software. The Harvester X-Forty-Eight contained the latest Internet protocols and protection software on the market. It was allegedly the only system that could break into an X-Forty-Eight was the FBI's carnivore system, which kept tabs on profiles and secure information on the Internet. He also set up the system to mirror his smartphone apps on his desktop to make life a bit more seamless.

Blayne sat down in his high-back-office chair and leaned back as he clicked his mouse and opened his personal email account. He had an email from his mother reminding him he needed to let her know about his plans for Christmas. He wrote back to her.

*Mom,*
*It's September. I have plenty of time to decide.*
*Love,*
*Blayne*

He then read an email from his best friend, Kira. Kira was a lawyer, and she'd been in Boston working on a case for her firm. Thankfully, she would be back in Pennington the next day, which made Blayne excited because he was lonely without her.

After checking his personal email, he switched to his school email account. He quickly responded to several student questions about their outlines that were due the next day. Most of the questions could be answered if the students would read the damn syllabus, but he refrained from typing this.

With his work-life taken care of, he opened a dating app he'd been using for a while called *EndZone*, whose slogan was "Because I'm Worth Dating!" Blayne wasn't looking to date anyone, but he'd met a few nice guys he'd corresponded with off and on. He immediately saw a message from a guy he'd been corresponding with for about six months named Roy or *0Time4Fun*. Blayne liked Roy almost immediately because they were both career driven. Roy had never quite told Blayne what his day job was, but he could tell it kept him constantly busy and on the move.

*Hey B.*

*Had to write to you real fast. I've had the crappiest day of my life. I wish I could go into details, but frankly, I don't even have them yet. Someone very close to me died today, and I had to find out publicly. I wish I was there with you. I feel trapped in my job right now. No one has a clue what's going on with me. Heck, no one I work with knows I'm gay. I feel like I'm at the end of my rope, and I'm about to get hung. I know this is probably way too much to dump on you right now, B, but I don't have anyone else to talk to.*

*Roy*

Blayne took a deep breath after finishing Roy's email, only now realizing he had stopped breathing while reading. After six months, Blayne knew Roy was gay, he had been dating someone and he was a total closet case. Beyond that, Blayne didn't know where Roy lived, he didn't know Roy's boyfriend's name and he didn't know what Roy actually did in life.

Blayne had messaged Roy initially because he'd mentioned musical theater in his profile. Blayne was a total theater geek. People often asked him if he wanted to be on stage, but Blayne knew his talents in life were not acting, singing or dancing. So, even though Roy didn't even have a face pic online, Blayne had messaged him and the two had become fast friends. When Blayne had asked about the lack of a face pic, Roy said his job was public, and he didn't feel comfortable with his face out there on the Internet.

Despite this lack of personal information, Blayne felt he knew Roy. He didn't realize the superficial information, but he knew Roy's soul on a deeper level than he knew anyone. There was something about Roy's defenselessness that worried Blayne. He knew Roy wouldn't kill himself—they'd already had that discussion. But Blayne was surprised by the urgent tone of the message. Blayne typed back.

> *Roy,*
> *I don't know what's going on, but you concern me. Are you okay? Please let me know if there is anything I can do for you. You're in my thoughts and prayers.*
> *Always your friend,*
> *Blayne*

\* \* \* \*

*Ethan*

Ethan picked up his phone, which had been charging. He immediately noticed the half-dozen missed calls and messages from Stephanie.

Stephanie Anne Mitchell was Ethan's best friend since elementary school. They were practically inseparable growing up but ended up going in different directions in college. Thankfully, with the abundance of social media and smartphones, Ethan and Stephanie kept up their friendship over the years.

Ethan hit the call button and waited for Stephanie to pick up the phone.

"Where have you been? Are you okay?" Stephanie asked. "I went by your place, and your doorman said you had packed up and left yesterday. What's going on?"

"I'm fine."

"Then why haven't you answered my phone calls?"

"After passing out, they brought me back to the hotel."

"Why are you in a hotel? Why aren't you at the townhouse?"

"Because of the release of the new album today, which I royally fucked up, I might add."

"It's not your fault you passed out on national television. I'm sure no one blames you."

"I'm sure they handled the Hard Rock Café appearance somehow. Hightower and Rawlins are good at covering those things."

"You still haven't explained the hotel situation," Stephanie reminded him.

"Oh, yeah. With the release, press junket and our upcoming trip to start the tour in Seattle, Hightower and Rawlins decided to house us in a hotel for a few days."

"Your world is so weird to me," Stephanie said.

"It's weird to me, too," Ethan admitted as he lay back down on the hotel room bed and stared up at the ceiling.

"So, what did the doctor say?"

"He figures it was dehydration combined with the intensity of the studio lights."

"What really happened?"

"Did you hear about Danny?"

"Yes, I did," her voice suddenly became very somber.

"Well, I was in the RNN studio getting ready for another part of the interview when the piece about his murder showed on the monitor."

"Oh, dear God!"

"Yep," Ethan said, trying to keep the emotion out of his voice. "I remember seeing the segment, the world spinning, then waking up as the band and everyone huddled around me."

"What a horrible way to find out," Stephanie said. "Not that there is a good way."

"What about you?" Ethan asked. "How are you holding up?"

"I'm still trying to process. I was so worried about you that I didn't even have time to think about it. I'm sure it will hit me at some point today, but it hasn't yet."

"Have you heard from his family?"

"I talked to his sister. She's still in shock. They haven't even made funeral arrangements. Besides, the police aren't sure when they'll release the body to the family."

"Well, if you need me, I'm here for you," Ethan consoled.

"Likewise. Make sure you answer your phone from now on."

"Scouts' honor. I will answer."

"You better."

"Anyway, the boys ordered dinner, so I should pull myself together. I plan on eating then trying to sleep. I'm exhausted."

"You and me both, dear. You and me both. Well, if you need me, call. Okay?"

"Will do. Love ya."

"Love ya, too," Stephanie said before the line went dead.

Ethan sat back up, his head swimming with a million-and-one thoughts. *What happened? Why Danny?*

Ethan pulled his phone into his lap and stared blankly at the screen. He wanted to reach out and talk to someone who didn't know him, didn't know he was in a boy band, didn't know he dated Danny, didn't know anything about him.

About a year before, Ethan had downloaded the gay dating app *EndZone* and randomly talked to some people. He'd hit it off with a guy named Blayne in Houston. The two had become 'friends', even though Blayne knew nothing about the real Ethan. Ethan had lied to Blayne early in their conversations, telling Blayne his name was Roy and that he worked in Internet marketing out of New York City. When they met on *EndZone*, Ethan had been in New York rehearsing for a tour, so it made sense to tell Blayne he was in NYC. They only connected on *EndZone* because Blayne had been in NYC doing tourist crap.

Over the last year, they had become 'friends'. Blayne had been a great sounding board for all kinds of problems Ethan had faced that year. Admittedly, all Ethan's issues had been disguised to hide his identity.

Ethan opened *EndZone* and quickly scrolled through his messages before finding the latest from Blayne. He typed.

*Hey B.*
*Had to write to you real fast. I've had the crappiest day of my life…*

# Chapter Five

*Agent Murphy*

FBI Agent Sarah Murphy walked through the crime scene. She was thankful the water on the lake was calm that day, because she got seasick easily. Walking around a houseboat was not her idea of a fun evening.

The New Orleans Police Department had requested the FBI's help on this investigation since it looked like a mob-style hit on a couple of celebrities. Sure, the New Orleans Police Department—NOPD—could probably handle the investigation, but they wanted the extra eyes and resources that involving the FBI could bring.

"What are you seeing?" Sarah asked FBI Agent Daniel Harper, her partner.

"Well, it looks like both were shot by one person, who surprised them."

"Why do you say that?" Sara questioned.

"Well, my best guess is the shooter entered from here," Agent Harper said as he walked through the crime scene from the door. "He grabbed Dunning, used her as a shield, shot Hawthorne, then shot Dunning to leave no witnesses."

"Makes sense to me, but..." she started, "you're assuming Hawthorne was the target. What if *she* was the primary target?" Murphy said, motioning to Cynthia Dunning's covered body on the floor. "Even though this wasn't her houseboat, someone could have tracked her here."

"Your theory works, too," Harper said, knitting his brows. "Why would anyone want to off two soap stars?"

"That is the question, isn't it?" Murphy finished up a few notes before she headed off the boat. She was glad to return to the dock as soon as possible.

"Agent Murphy?" a voice called from a distance.

Murphy looked for the voice and saw a woman standing behind the police tape. She took stock of the woman and her expensive suit. *Clearly, she's not a local*, Murphy thought to herself. Murphy walked over to the woman and reached out to shake the woman's hand.

"Agent Murphy," the woman started, shaking Murphy's hand. "I'm Denise Alvarado. I'm the senior executive for the production company that produces *New Orleans Nights*, Limitless Films."

"It's nice to meet you, Ms. Alvarado," Murphy said after noticing the woman wasn't wearing a wedding ring. "How can I help you?"

"So, it's true?" Alvarado asked with a smile on her face.

"Is what true?"

Ms. Alvarado shook her head from side to side to make sure no one was easily eavesdropping to ask, "Are Cynthia and Daniel dead?"

"I take it you heard the news?" Agent Murphy asked.

"Yes," the woman responded, narrowing her eyes at the agent. "No one called to tell us anything, which is why my boss sent me to find out what was going on."

Agent Murphy took a half-step back to take in the middle-aged woman. Her suit was tailored, and her heels were expensive. Her outfit was not made for the wooden planks of the pier where she stood. Murphy pulled out her notebook and jotted down Alvarado's name. "Can I get your title and phone number? In case I need to reach out to you later."

Alvarado picked out a business card and handed it over to Murphy. Murphy jotted it down in her notebook before sliding the card into the breast pocket on her jacket. She didn't care about this woman's information, but she wanted to make it clear Ms. Alvarado wasn't in charge.

"Thanks," Murphy said. "So, when was the last time anyone from your company spoke to either of the victims?"

"Victims?"

"Yes," Murphy responded, looking at Ms. Alvarado quickly. "You know they were murdered, right?"

The woman's face blanched. Murphy watched, figuring out the woman was sent here with zero information.

"They were murdered?" Alvarado said as her smile faded. "I thought there was some kind of accident. I was told to come over here and find out what happened. Oh hell, this is going to stop production for at least a week. Fuck!" Alvarado pulled out her phone, found a contact and pushed the send button.

Murphy stood there, a bit transfixed, as Alvarado called someone and relayed what Murphy told her. When Alvarado told the caller on the other end that the murder investigation would probably delay production, a string of expletives was heard through the phone. The voice was so loud, Alvarado pulled the phone away from her ears.

"What's going on?" Harper asked as he walked up behind Murphy.

"Woman from" — Murphy pulled out the business card and reread it — "Limitless Films. They own the TV show our victims were on. Apparently, someone isn't too happy this little murder of ours will delay their filming."

"God, I hate Hollywood types. It's always about them. Fuck the corpse. What about me? What about *my* needs?"

"Tell me about it," Murphy agreed.

Alvarado turned back around with an apologetic look on her face. "I'm sorry. As you can tell, the show's director is heartbroken over the news," Alvarado said through clenched teeth.

"Ms. Alvarado, this is FBI Agent Benjamin Harper." Ben didn't reach out his hand. He nodded in the woman's direction. Murphy continued, "When was the last time anyone at *NOLA Nights* saw the victims?"

"I'll be candid," Alvarado started. "I don't know. We wrapped production around six p.m. last night, which was pretty early for us. We shoot a lot of night scenes. After all, we are called *NOLA Nights*, so getting out before two or three a.m. is very early for us."

"We'll probably be around the set in the next couple of days to see if anyone on set knows anything. Who should we arrange that with?"

"Call my cell. I'll make sure you have access to anyone or anything. Obviously, this is an enormous shock to the entire *NOLA Nights* family and everyone who works at Limitless Films."

Agent Murphy was amazed at how quickly Alvarado went from shock to public relations spokeswoman. Alvarado clearly knew how to do her job.

"Well, we'll definitely reach out when we need your assistance," Murphy said, clarifying their conversation was over. Murphy and Harper ducked under the police tape and headed back toward their dark brown sedan. Murphy climbed in the driver's seat and turned on the air conditioner because she had practically sweated through her shirt. She was glad her black blazer hid her damp back.

"So, now what?" Harper asked.

"Now, we untangle this mess, but be ready for a shit show. Anytime we have Hollywood types involved, it's going to be a mess."

Murphy sighed as she turned the key in the ignition and headed back into town to the FBI Field Office.

Murphy pulled the car up to the curb and found a spot down from the main entrance to the NOLA FBI Field Office.

"Why don't you go tell Jackson what we know so far when we get inside," Murphy said.

"What are you going to do?" Harper questioned.

"I'll call the Office of Public Affairs and give them a heads-up. This will be a media circus as soon as they find out we're involved."

"Too late," Harper said, pointing to the camera and reporter staking out the front entrance of the building.

Murphy had barely thrown the car into park when the cameraman and reporter stalked toward their vehicle.

"Fuck," Harper said under his breath.

"Say nothing. I'll handle it," Murphy responded.

Harper opened the door and got out quickly. Murphy did the same.

"Stephen McNeil, RTN—" the reporter started as Harper trudged past him, heading into the building with his head down and not saying a word.

Hearing Murphy's door shut, the reporter spun his head toward Murphy. Murphy took a deep breath and put on her game face before stepping up to the curb.

"Stephen McNeil, RTN—"

"Yes, Mr. McNeil, I heard you the first time."

"What can you tell me about the grizzly assassinations of Cynthia Dunning and Daniel Hawthorne?"

"Absolutely nothing," Murphy said, shrugging. "You know I can't talk about an ongoing investigation."

"So, it's true they were assassinated?" McNeil asked.

"You know I won't answer," Murphy responded, easily batting away his question without breaking a sweat.

"What will you tell me?" McNeil countered.

"Nothing," Murphy said flatly. "If you want to speak to someone, call the Office of Public Affairs in Washington, DC, and they'll point you in the right direction."

"We already tried," McNeil said. "They told us to contact the local FBI Field Office because they knew nothing."

"Well, that must be the official statement from the FBI," Murphy said.

"So, you're saying you learned nothing while on Dunning's houseboat?"

"How did you know — ?"

"I have eyes and ears all over this town, Agent Murphy. The second the NOPD asked for help on this case, I knew about it."

Murphy took a deep breath before staring past McNeil and right into the camera. "The FBI does not comment about ongoing investigations. I have no statement to make. Any official statements from the FBI about this case or any case will come directly from the Office of Public Affairs." She then looked at McNeil, "There, you have your soundbite. Now, could you please get that thing out of my face? I need to go to work."

McNeil motioned for the cameraman to turn off the camera as he lowered the microphone himself. "So, off the record," McNeil started. "What happened?"

"Off the record?" Murphy asked.

McNeil's face lit up like a kid on Christmas about to open his first present, expecting some piece of juicy information.

"Off the record, the FBI does not comment on ongoing investigations."

"Oh, come on!" McNeil said exasperatedly. "You gotta give me something here."

"I don't *gotta* give you anything, Mr. McNeil," Murphy countered. "We're in the initial stages of this investigation. I don't have any information to give you."

"Well, if you hear anything — "

"If I hear anything? How's this? I'll let you know once I arrest someone."

"Remember," McNeil started. "I came to you first."

Murphy narrowed her eyes at the reporter and took a half step toward him, slightly invading his personal space. "What's that supposed to mean?"

Murphy watched as McNeil unconsciously took a step backward as he said, "I mean, I want to help. I meant nothing else by it at all. I promise," he rattled nervously.

"Well, Mr. McNeil, if you hear anything, please let me know. I'm sure you can figure out how to reach me," she said before stepping around him and the cameraman and heading into the building.

* * * *

*Dr. Hennigan*

Dr. Hennigan led the new recruits into a gray locker room. On one wall was a giant monitor, which was currently showing newscasts from around the globe. Wooden benches bolted to the ground were in the center. On the other three walls were a series of lockers.

"Find the locker with your pre-determined access code on it and stand in front of it," Dr. Hennigan said. She watched as a dozen women looked around the room for their lockers. When they were all facing them, Dr. Hennigan told them to open them, strip themselves and place the new clothes inside. "Don't worry. Any valuables will be returned at the end of your training."

Once all the women were dressed in their new Foundation-issued uniforms—a drab olive color that didn't make anyone look good—Dr. Hennigan instructed them to sit on the benches and stare at the monitor.

"Please keep at least five feet between you and the next person," Ms. Wilson said as the recruits sat.

As soon as everyone was seated, the screen in the front of the room came to life.

"Welcome to The Foundation. I'm Sara Hennigan, the current chairwoman. I wish I could be there with you in person to greet and welcome you on your journey, but my duties running The Foundation prevent me from that," the silver-haired woman said. "The Foundation was originally established by Deborah Sampson during the Revolutionary War in the United States. Sampson disguised herself as a man and fought in the war for almost three years before becoming ill in Philadelphia. The doctor who treated her discovered her biological sex and protected her until she was better."

A statue of a woman in military regalia filled the screen with the words 'Deborah Sampson' written under the image.

"Deborah was honorably discharged from the Army in 1783 and sent back to Massachusetts. She received a pension for her military efforts." There was a close-up of Sara Hennigan's face. "Deborah realized she could never publicly serve in the military again, so she devised a plan to continue her patriotic duty. Clandestinely, she recruited other like-minded women in Stoughton, Massachusetts, to create a spy ring that helped the thirteen colonies win their freedom from British tyranny. After the war, Deborah expanded her reach to all Massachusetts — then all thirteen colonies."

A map showed red dots and a timeline, illustrating how quickly The Foundation had spread throughout the colonies.

Sara Hennigan continued, "Although she died at the young age of sixty-six, her two daughters, Mary and Patience, continued her legacy and grew The Foundation into what it is today."

The Foundation's logo appeared with the organization's slogan, *Ad pugnam hodie melius cras*, "*Fighting today for a better tomorrow.*" The women in the locker room were focused on the video, so they didn't notice when Dr. Hennigan and Ms. Wilson slipped out of the room, locking the door behind them. The two slipped into the control room next door while the video still played.

"*Each of you was recruited because you contain specific knowledge, skills or connections that help strengthen the influence of The Foundation in American politics and global affairs. Over the years, The Foundation has had many highly visible members.*" A series of images of former senators, first ladies, actors and media personalities swam across the screen. "*But The Foundation is primarily built on the backs of women from all walks of life. Each of you was selectively recruited to join The Foundation to help us build a better tomorrow and continue the legacy of Deborah Sampson.*" The video ended with a shot of an American flag waving across the screen.

On the other side of the screen, Dr. Hennigan and Ms. Wilson watched as the women sat there, unsure of what to do next. Dr. Hennigan didn't leave them waiting very long. She flipped the switch next to a microphone and prepared to give the speech she'd given too many times to count.

"Welcome. You may have noticed there are currently a dozen of you in the room. We only have ten spots for recruits." Dr. Hennigan paused for effect and watched the looks of uncertainty cross the women's faces. "Your first task is to determine which two recruits don't measure up to the high standards of The Foundation. To help you figure this out, I will unleash a nerve toxin that will kill all of you in two minutes. If your decision hasn't been made, we deem none worthy of continuing."

The screen in the room started a countdown clock. The women looked at each other anxiously for the first few seconds, unsure if Dr. Hennigan was serious.

"My money is on the actor. You would think she'd be the first to go, but she's scrappy, which is why we recruited her," Ms. Wilson said.

"I think one of the marines will draw first blood," Dr. Hennigan responded.

Both of them were surprised when suddenly a homemaker leapt at the state senator from Nevada and started clawing at the woman's eyes. Then all hell broke loose.

Dr. Hennigan smiled.

Two of the former marines engaged each other in hand-to-hand combat. The ex-CIA operative went after the actor, who lived up to Ms. Wilson's expectations. Within forty-five seconds, the state senator and a homemaker lay motionless on the floor. As the monitor showed the second woman die, the door to the room flung open and a contingency of armed guards swarmed into the room, breaking up the other attacks and restoring order.

"Well done, ladies," Dr. Hennigan said, slowly clapping as she entered the room. "I knew you had it in you."

Behind Ms. Wilson, a blonde woman wearing combat fatigues entered the room and stood slightly with her arms behind her back in military parade rest.

"Recruits," Ms. Wilson said, "this is Instructor Emerson. She will be your guide through the intake process."

"I won't lie to you," Dr. Hennigan added. "Our average recruit class of twelve is cut down to six by the time the intake process is over. Do what Instructor Emerson tells you to do, and you will be one of the six left standing."

Dr. Hennigan spun and left the room without waiting to see the recruits' response.

After walking a few paces away from the open door, Dr. Hennigan asked, "Where are we with the other situation?" She didn't need to look. She knew Ms. Wilson was behind her.

"After you liquidated the primary target, we believe two secondary targets received the parcel."

"And?"

"We're waiting for the board to decide whether the next step is simple loss prevention or liquidation."

Dr. Hennigan stopped in the hall and turned to Ms. Wilson. "No one needs to involve the board. Liquidation is in order."

"I'll put out the kill order immediately."

# Chapter Six

*Blayne*

The students in the cavernous room pretended to be attentive, but Blayne could tell some were practically asleep. Those listening were curious about the content or were furious they were required to sit through a presentation about combating homonegativity and gender-based discrimination in their high school assembly.

Blayne clicked the remote control, and the PowerPoint presentation went to the next slide. Blayne watched as his co-presenter and close friend, Kira Strickland, read the slide.

"In 1977, Dr. Martin Rochlin created a list of questions for heterosexuals. The list obviously is a play on the many questions LGBTQIA2+—lesbian, gay, bisexual, transgendered, queer, intersexed, asexual, two-spirit and others—individuals are asked regularly." Kira read several items off the list. "When and how did you first decide you were a heterosexual?

Why do heterosexuals place so much emphasis on sex? Your heterosexuality doesn't offend me as long as you don't try to force it on me. Why do you people feel compelled to seduce others into your sexual orientation? Heterosexuals are noted for assigning themselves and each other to narrowly restricted, stereotyped sex roles. Why do you cling to such unhealthy role-playing?"

Blayne watched as a few students chuckled at the questions. A student raised his hand toward the back of the room, so Blayne called on him, "You, in the back of the room with your hand up." The kid had a cocky smirk Blayne knew all too well.

"Isn't this some kind of leftist propaganda? I mean, homosexuality isn't natural, so why are we being forced to listen to this crap?"

Blayne took a deep breath before starting. "Define 'natural'. If, by natural, do you mean *does homosexuality exist in nature?*' Then the answer to your question is a resounding yes. Scientists have documented homosexuality in all kinds of species, including reptiles, insects, birds, fish, etc. If you want to focus on mammals, homosexuality definitely exists in nature. Scientists have documented homosexuality in over two-hundred-twenty-five mammals, including bears, cats, cows, dogs, elephants, kangaroos, lions, monkeys and many, many others. Oh, and of course, humans."

"That's leftist propaganda," the student replied.

"If by leftist propaganda, you mean science, then sure," Blayne smirked. He watched the student grit his teeth, but the kid said nothing else.

"As I was saying," Kira started, "LGBTQIA2+ individuals are often asked some pretty intrusive and ludicrous questions about their sexuality or gender identity. Sometimes people don't realize how intrusive or embarrassing the questions are."

"For example," Blayne said. "Many LGBTQIA2+ individuals are asked about specific sex acts by complete strangers they would never ask a heterosexual person. These questions can be embarrassing. If you wouldn't want someone to ask you that question, then the best rule of thumb is to not ask it of someone else."

Blayne clicked to the next slide and listened as Kira continued her discussion. The students periodically asked questions, but mostly the presentation went pretty seamlessly.

When it ended, the school principal thanked them for coming. The students gave a polite round of applause right as the end-of-the-day school bell rang.

"I really want to thank you both for doing this," the principal said after the students had cleared the auditorium. "We've been having some incidences of bullying, so we thought this would be a good way to put a stop to it."

"What policies do you have in place to prevent bullying?" Kira asked. "As you know, David's Law has some pretty strict requirements for handling it."

"True," the principal said, his face dulling to a blank expression. "But as you know, David's Law doesn't protect any specific classes of students."

Blayne watched as Kira's eyes narrowed. By watching her facial expression, he could tell that Kira was trying to avoid exploding on the principal.

"As you know, schools that do not have adequate protection under David's Law could find themselves easy targets for lawsuits. As a lawyer, I've already mediated a handful of bullying cases in the Houston area. The last thing you want is to be on the receiving end of one of those. Not only could it be seriously detrimental for the school and the school district, but it could also prove very costly."

"How so?" the principal asked.

"Take the older case, *Mitchell v. Georgetown Independent School District.* Here, a gay student was spit on, knocked unconscious. A bully even threw his books in the trash. He was called derogatory names daily. The final straw was when bullies broke his fingers. Although the exact final settlement amount with the school district was undisclosed, legal circles say it was pretty large. And that was back in two-thousand-ten before David's Law went into effect in 2017. The penalties for these types of cases today would be much higher."

"Well," the principal said, "that's why trainings like this one are so important."

"True," Blayne noted. "But training only gets you part of the way there. The training won't get you very far if you don't have adequate policies and mechanisms to help bullied victims. Ultimately, all students, faculty and staff must be held accountable for bullying. As soon as you let one case slip through the cracks, you open the floodgates for more."

The principal shook his head before walking away. Blayne shot Kira a side-eye but said nothing. Blayne turned off his laptop and disconnected it from the school's audiovisual system.

"Well," Kira said, "that was fun." The sarcasm practically dripped from her mouth.

"It wasn't that bad," Blayne countered. "We could definitely have met up with a lot more resistance. All things considered, I thought it went well."

"Whatever."

"Thanks for doing this with me. I think it's always good for kids to hear a lawyer's take on some of these issues. The queer kids need to know there are resources for them, and the bullies need to know someone will hold them accountable — even if the school won't."

Blayne placed his laptop in his attaché case, and they left through a side door. The heat and humidity were still pretty bad. Blayne immediately loosened the tie around his neck.

The two walked along the sidewalk, saying nothing to each other. A car on the other side of the parking lot suddenly lowered its window, and the same jerk from earlier leaned out and yelled, "Fag!" before the car sped away. Blayne rolled his eyes.

"Want to tell the principal?" Kira asked.

"I'll shoot him an email when I get home. At least that way, it's documented."

"CYA behavior. Always a smart move."

"CYA?" Blayne questioned.

"Cover your ass."

Blayne pulled out his key fob and clicked the unlock button to open the doors on his Prius. He'd been able to buy a used one the previous summer for less than twenty-thousand dollars. The car was his pride and joy and he kept it in pristine condition. He heard the click as the car unlocked. He opened the back door and laid his attaché case on the floor behind the driver's seat.

"Blayne," a voice yelled, "do you have a minute?"

Blayne looked up to see a kid he knew all too well.

"Hey, Jamie. What's up?"

"Hi, Jamie," Kira added before giving the young guy a brief hug.

"Sorry about that jerk in the meeting," Jamie said, looking down at the ground.

"We've faced worse," Kira noted. She gently grabbed Jamie's chin and raised his eyes to hers. "What's wrong?"

Jamie had been a perpetual victim of bullying at Pennington High School. In fact, this bullying had led the school district to mandate the school-wide training that afternoon. Usually, Kira and Blayne didn't talk to high school students about queer issues and bullying. Still, when Blayne's professor, Dr. Madeline Reich, had asked if he would do this for her, he had to agree.

"I was thrown into my locker yesterday...again. I told the principal, but he said I was '*making stuff up again just to cause drama*,'" Jamie said in an imitation of the principal's gruff voice.

"Have you told your mom?" Blayne asked.

"What's she going to do? She knows what's going on and has done everything she can to stop it, but the kids keep getting away with it."

"How often is stuff like this happening?" Kira questioned.

"Well, if I'm not being called queer, fag, gay-boy, fairy, pillow-biter, fudge packer — well, you get the idea."

Kira's eyes narrowed. "And the principal knows this is happening?"

"Yes and no."

"Explain," Kira demanded.

"Well, I tell him it's happening, but he says if he doesn't see it himself, or if another teacher doesn't see it, there's nothing he can do."

"And of course," Blayne started, "these bullies know this, so they make sure none of this happens in front of an adult."

"Pretty much," Jamie said, looking down at the ground again, kicking at the pavement.

Blayne looked over and noticed Kira's mouth was set in a hard line. She was pissed. Blayne had been friends with Kira long enough to know exactly what was going through her mind.

He turned to her and asked, "Shall we?"

"We shall," was all she said.

"Hey, Jamie. Go on home. Tell your mom we talked, and I said 'hi.' We're going to go have a brief conversation with your principal," Kira said.

Jamie's eyes widened. "Do you have to?"

"Jamie," Kira started, "your principal is violating the law. I need to remind him of that. What's the point of being a lawyer if I can't protect people like you?"

Jamie didn't seem convinced, but he said nothing else as he turned around and skulked away. Kira and Blayne walked back into the high school and found the main office.

The principal's domain was an institutional gray color with a few school-spirit-type posters hanging on the wall. Blayne looked at one of them and saw a poster that read, '*Stay Cool. Stop Bullying.*' He almost barked out a laugh but caught it before he did. Blayne nudged Kira and jerked his head in the poster's direction.

"Yeah, like that's going to stop anything."

"Wow," Kira said, letting the word hang in the air. "Pathetic. What is this, the eighties?"

"Excuse me," a woman behind the reception desk said as she entered from a side office. "How can I help you?"

"Is Principal Reynolds in?" Blayne asked.

"Let me see if he's available. And you are?"

"Tell him it's Kira and Blayne," Kira said, pasting on a fake smile.

The receptionist went around the corner, and Kira could hear her all the way out in reception.

"Tell them I'm not here," Blayne heard the principal say.

Kira raised her voice and said, "Tell him we can hear him."

The principal said several choice words. A few seconds later, the receptionist came back around the corner. She was in a bit of a tizzy and unsure what to make of the principal's vulgar language.

"I'm so sorry you had to hear that. He normally doesn't talk like that," she said, shaking her head. "He'll see you now."

Blayne and Kira went through the side gate and behind the reception area to the hallway where the principal's office was. Without waiting, Kira opened the door and walked inside. She pulled out one of her business cards and handed it to the principal.

"I'm here to talk to you about my client, Jamie Reich."

"What has that boy done now?"

"Excuse me?" Kira asked.

"Well," the principal started, "he's always getting himself into trouble with the other boys. You know how it is. He provokes them by flaunting his 'gayness', then is surprised when they disagree with his lifestyle choices. Then he comes whining to me about it."

"Wow," Kira said, a look of utter amazement crossed her face. "There is so much to unpack in what just came out of your mouth."

Kira pulled out a legal pad and wrote what the principal had said. She repeated it to him, making sure she had nothing wrong. She then spent the next twenty minutes reexplaining David's Law and his ethical and legal obligations to his students under the law.

"You make it sound like I've done something wrong," the principal responded. "I'm doing what's best for *all* the students, not just Jamie."

"That may be your opinion," Kira said. "But Jamie is my client, so I'm only concerned about *his* safety and wellbeing."

"I almost feel like I should call my lawyer."

Kira took a deep breath before staring the principal down. The man was clearly not used to being talked to in this fashion. After an awkward pause, Kira said, "I will formally send you, the Superintendent and the district's legal representation a legal complaint tomorrow." The principal's mouth fell silently open as he puckered his brow.

"I think you need to leave my office, missy."

Kira tilted her head to the side as her expression hardened. "Did you just call me 'missy'?"

"Well, don't get your panties all up in a bunch. I meant nothing harmful by it."

If Kira's eyes could have shot lasers, the principal would be a smoldering pile of smoking ash. She took a short, calming breath before saying, "Principal Reynolds, if anything happens to my client—and I mean anything—the lawsuit I will bring against you and this school district will be so sweeping they'll bury you to get out from under it."

The principal stared at her. His demeanor quickly sobered as he realized this conversation was over.

Without saying a word, Kira stood and left the office. Blayne was shocked by what had happened. Blayne looked at the principal. Then his eyes shot toward the door where Kira was no longer standing, so Blayne scrambled out of the chair and was out of the office and down the hall. Kira had almost reached the school's front door when Blayne finally caught up to her.

When they were outside, Kira said nothing as they walked back to his car. He unlocked the car, and they piled inside before Kira finally exploded. "That fuckwit! That insolent, cockwomble, douchecanoe, wankpuffin."

"Did they teach you all those names in law school?" Blayne said, trying not to laugh.

Kira turned and looked at him, but as soon as she saw Blayne's smirk, the piss and vinegar went right out of her.

"How's meditation doing for your anger issues?" Blayne asked, raising his eyebrows and tilting his head.

"Fuck you," Kira said, as she chuckled and rolled her eyes.

"He really got under your skin."

"Well, it was bad enough he's not living up to the standard of care for his students under the law, but when he called me 'missy' and told me not to get 'my panties in a bunch', I wanted to reach across his desk and punch that smirk right off his face."

Blayne put the key in the ignition. "See? I call that progress. You didn't hit him."

Blayne threw the car into reverse, pulling out of the parking space. The parking lot was pretty empty as he righted the car and drove toward the exit. Blayne glanced out of the passenger-side window as they left and saw the principal walking to one of the few other cars left in the lot.

"Hey, look," he motioned with a jerk of his head. "It's the cockwomble."

* * * *

After he dropped Kira back at her place, Blayne picked up some Chinese takeout before heading to his apartment. When he got inside, he kicked off his shoes, laid out his food and turned on the TV to catch the news. He was only half-listening about some murder in New Orleans. He flipped the channel, looking for something mindless to watch. He finally settled on an old episode of *NCIS*.

Gibbs was doing something with Abby in the forensics lab. Blayne watched and spooned in a mouth full of noodles. He reached down, picked up his phone and scrolled through the messages. He had a few emails from students that he shot back quick answers without saying, "It's on the syllabus."

He was about to put the phone down when his dating app *EndZone* told him he had a message. He pulled it up and read.

*Hey B.*
*Hope all is good in your world. Thanks for the response last night. Yesterday was one of the crappiest days of my life. I need a friend right now. I can't talk about these things with my colleagues.*

Over the previous year, Blayne had learned that Roy's job enabled him to do quite a bit of traveling, but he was also tied down to his job and his coworkers. When Roy was venting about work, he frequently mentioned his coworkers were like family.

For Blayne, he had more of a split personality. He did his best not to have his two lives overlap often. There was his work and school — then his personal life. He felt life was more balanced and manageable when he could keep the different parts of his life clearly separated.

*Hey, Roy.*
*I'm here for you any time you need me.*
*B.*

Blayne almost hit send but amended the message.

*If you ever want to talk, let me know.*

He gave Roy his phone number. Blayne paused before hitting send. He knew giving a stranger his phone number over the Internet was asking for problems, but he'd been talking to Roy for almost a year, so giving Roy his phone number seemed like a natural progression in their friendship.

He set his cell back on his coffee table and went back to eating his dinner as he finished the rest of the episode of *NCIS*. As usual, Abby solved the case, and Gibbs made the arrest.

After dinner, Blayne packed away his leftovers in the fridge and pulled out a book he needed to read for one of his classes, which was all the rage in 2020. He read the back cover, which seemed reasonable. Still, he knew Pluckrose and Lindsay's *Cynical Theories* was controversial to progressive academics like himself. He laid back on his couch and opened to the prologue.

The buzzing sound on the coffee table drew his attention away from the book before he'd even gotten started. He picked up his cell and saw that the call was blocked. *Probably a telemarketer*, he thought as he put the cell back down. The buzzing stopped. Within seconds, the phone was vibrating again. He picked it up and again saw a blocked number. He ignored it again. On the third time, he picked it up and said, "What?"

"Hello?" a voice said hesitantly on the other side of the line. "Is this Blayne?"

"Yes, it is. Who's calling?"

The voice immediately turned lighter. "Hey, B. It's Roy."

It took Blayne a second for his brain to process what was going on. "Roy, as in *EndZone* Roy?"

"That's me," Roy said sheepishly.

"It's nice to finally meet you. Well, not actually meet you, but you know what I mean," Blayne stammered out.

There was a chuckle. "I get it. So how are you?"

"I'm doing okay. Lying on the couch. Was about to read a book for class."

"Oh, if this isn't a good time —"

"No, it's fine. I'd rather talk to you. I may have tossed the book across the room in a few minutes."

"Not a fan?"

"Not yet. Frankly, it's pissing me off. But anyway, how are you? Sounds like you've had a rough couple of days."

Blayne listened as Roy let out a quick breath before he dove into what happened to him. "Basically, I was in a work meeting when I found out a friend died."

"I'm so sorry to hear that. Was this a friend or a *friend*?" Blayne asked.

"He was a *friend*, as you put it."

"I didn't realize you had a boyfriend. Good for you."

"Nah, it wasn't like that. Sure, we were friends, but we fooled around occasionally. We're sort of in the same line of work, so it was convenient," Roy said, his voice trailing off.

Blayne wasn't sure what was going on in Roy's head, but he could tell there was a lot more to this story than Roy was willing to share.

"Yeah, I didn't take it well," Roy said, bringing Blayne back to the present.

"What happened?"

"I passed out."

"During the meeting?"

"Yep."

"Dude, that sucks."

"Especially since no one knew what had happened."

"So, your coworkers still don't know you're gay?"

"Nope. And before you start, I know I should tell them…someday."

Blayne and Roy had discussed Roy's issues with being gay and out many times since they started talking on *EndZone*.

"So, what did you tell them triggered it?"

"The doctor assumed I was dehydrated. The labs came back negative today, so there's nothing *wrong* with me. Everyone quickly assumed dehydration as a diagnosis, so we've all moved on."

Blayne and Roy talked for a few more minutes as Roy periodically dropped in a few more details here and there about the last couple of days. Roy had gotten up this morning and returned to work as if nothing had happened.

"I wish I could escape from my life," Roy admitted.

"We've all been there."

"Who knows? Maybe one day I'll come to visit you, Blayne, and we can really *meet* for the first time."

"You know what? I think I would like that. It'd be fun to hang out in person instead of on the app for a change."

"Really?"

"Yes, really."

"In my line of work," Roy started, "there aren't too many people who do things for others without wanting something in return."

"That sucks," Blayne said. "I can't imagine living like that from day to day. Sure, academia has its trials and tribulations, but mostly, people are supportive."

"That's cool."

The two spent the next hour talking about a wide range of topics, from growing up in the South to politics. Throughout the conversation, Blayne could sense Roy opening up more and more to him.

"So, earlier," Roy finally said, "you mentioned you'd like to see me face-to-face sometime. Are you up for that?"

"Sure. Let me know if you'll ever be in the area. I'd love to have you over. Hell, I have a spare room you can use. It's technically my office, but I have a spare bed in it."

"Sounds like you have a big place?"

"Not really. It's about nine hundred square feet, but it was designed well."

"I'm sure it feels like you."

"I've definitely left my mark on the place. It's not too cluttered but not too clean, either. Thankfully, I have a houseboy who comes by and cleans every other week."

"You have a houseboy?" Roy asked.

"I just call him that. He's a friend of a friend who was looking for work, and his rates were amazing. So I thought, what the hell? Besides, I hate housework."

"More of an outdoorsy, yard-work guy?"

"More of a none-of-the-above-type guy," Blayne replied.

Blayne listened as Roy chuckled on the other end of the phone. "You know what—and I know this is an absolutely crazy idea—and feel free to say no—can I come to visit?"

"Sure. When?"

"Tomorrow?"

"What?" Blayne replied without thinking.

"Too soon?"

"No, just taken aback. Are you going to be in the area?"

"I can be."

Blayne sat there for a second, not sure what to say. He'd opened the door for this, but was he ready to have company? He liked Roy, and they seemed to get along. So, having Roy visit for a couple of days wouldn't be too bad. Worse came to worst, he'd tell Roy to take a hike.

"You know what? This is also going to sound crazy, but why not?"

"My turn to ask," Roy said. "Really?"

"Of course. Yep, really."

"Awesome! I'll look at flights and let you know when I'll be there. I'll shoot you off a text and let you know my travel plans. I'll grab an Uber or something when I get there."

"Depending on when you get in, I'd be glad to come pick you up," Blayne added.

"I can't believe we're doing this," Roy said. Blayne heard Roy shuffling in the background. "Okay, so I'm pulling up flights from here to there."

"Where are you now?"

"New Orleans, so a hop, skip and a jump to Houston. It looks like I could be there about twelve-fifteen. Would that work for you?"

"Fits into my schedule," Blayne replied, shaking his head in disbelief that he was letting a virtual stranger come to stay with him, though Blayne didn't see Roy as a complete stranger. "How will I find you at the airport?"

"Oh, that's right," Roy said. "We haven't exchanged pictures."

"You always said you were photo shy."

"I am, but I'll shoot you off one right now."

Blayne pulled the phone away from his ear and read his text messages. An image of a blue-eyed, brown-haired guy was staring back at him with a smile that looked like it should be in a toothpaste commercial.

"Killer smile," Blayne said. "You're pretty cute. I was afraid you had a second head or something."

"Nope, no second head," Roy replied. "Like I said, I don't put my picture out there too often."

"Well, I need to get some work done around the house if I'm having company tomorrow," Blayne said, standing and doing a quick survey of the living room. *Definitely have a few piles I need to pick up.* "Thankfully, my houseboy is scheduled to clean tomorrow morning, so the place will be ready when you get here."

"Sounds like a plan. I'm going to book my flight and text you the information. I'm going to wait to make my return flight, just in case you want to kick me out sooner rather than later."

"Isn't that going to be crazy expensive?"

"It makes it a bit more expensive, but I'm not worried. I want you to know you don't have to keep me around if you want me gone. I know this is going to be awkward."

"Hey, if we get along half as well in real life as we do online, we'll have a blast."

The two said their goodbyes and goodnights. As soon as Blayne hung up the phone, he looked around the apartment again and immediately started decluttering. Thankfully, he had a ton of closet space, so he could shove everything in there and not open it until Roy was gone.

# Chapter Seven

*Ethan*

Ethan spent most of the night hatching his plan. He used a credit card no one knew about to purchase the ticket to Houston, but he still had to figure out how he would ditch ZERO. The band was flying out that morning to Seattle for the first leg of the new North American tour. They didn't have any dates for several days, so Ethan didn't think they would kill him when this was all said and done. At least, he hoped they wouldn't.

Ethan packed his overnight bag and threw in a few extra things he knew he would need that morning. At eight-thirty a.m., he opened the door to his suite and met up with the rest of the guys for breakfast. As usual, Orr was running late, so Ethan sat down in the suite's kitchen and grabbed a pastry room service had delivered.

"Morning, sleepyhead," Ric said as Ethan sat down.

"Anyone heard from planet Orr yet?" Ethan joked.

"I knocked on his door and made sure he was moving about twenty minutes ago," Zach told them. "Yeah, he totally slept through the alarm clock again."

"He could sleep through a hurricane," Ric said, biting into a piece of bacon.

"What time are the parents picking us up?" Ethan asked. The group often referred to their producer, Dan Rawlins, and their manager, Ron Hightower, as their parents.

"The 'rents should be by around nine-forty-five to pick us up and whisk us off to the airport," Rick said.

"Are we flying commercial or charter today?" Zach asked.

"I think they have us booked in first class on Peregrine Airlines. I checked it out last night. We're booked in sleeping pods, so at least we'll be able to lie back, watch movies or sleep some more," Rick told them.

The three ate the rest of their breakfasts, chatting about the day and the plans for when they hit the ground running in Seattle. Their choreographer, Sally Higgins, had flown up to the Emerald City, as some called it, the previous week to work with the backup dancers. ZERO had worked with one of her assistants, who had taken the redeye to Seattle the previous night. Ethan was amazed that Sally wouldn't force them into a late-night rehearsal when they landed. Still, there was some press junket Rawlins and Hightower had agreed to that afternoon.

After eating, Ethan put the plate in the kitchen sink. *House cleaning will deal with it after we're gone*, he thought to himself. He returned to his bedroom and gathered around the few last-minute items he still had out. He separated everything into two suitcases. One was his usual giant rolling suitcase, the other an overnight bag he wouldn't need to check. With everything ready to go, he wheeled the rolling bag into the common area and left it near the door. Ethan saw that both Ric and Zach had already beaten him. He heard a door opening from within the suite and glanced over his shoulder to see Orr coming out of his room, dressed in a pair of sweats and a hoodie. Orr may have been wearing sweats, but the outfit was probably crazy expensive, because they all wore designer clothing these days. The hoodie cost about nine hundred dollars, and the sweats were around thirteen hundred. Orr had topped the look with a ball cap and a pair of sunglasses. *Because, you know, who doesn't need to wear sunglasses in a hotel suite?*

"Morning, Orr," Zach yelled, a little too chipper with a goofy grin.

Orr tilted his head in Zach's direction and mumbled something Ethan thought were words but honestly wasn't entirely sure. Orr went over to the smattering of breakfast goods, selected a dry bagel and pocketed it before muttering, "Are we doing this?"

"Aye, aye, captain," Ric said, giving Orr a brief salute.

"Stop messing with Orr," Ethan said. "He clearly didn't get his beauty rest." Then Ethan swiveled his head to Orr and said in a high-pitched voice, "Does baby need his binky?"

"Fuck all of you. Just fuck all of you," Orr said before opening the door to the suite and rolling his bag into the hall.

Ethan, Rick and Zach scrambled to follow Orr with their rolling bags. There were only four suites on their floor, so there wasn't a long way for them to walk to the elevator. Orr had already pulled out his hotel key card and used it to call the elevator. This floor was only accessible by key card, making it almost impossible for random strangers or fans to access the set of suites.

Ethan looked up as there was a quiet ding and the steel doors slid open. Orr wheeled in first, followed by Ric, then Zach and Ethan were last. The four had to adjust a bit to get them and their luggage into the metal box before Ethan hit the lobby button.

"Anyone text the parents yet to let him know we're up and on our way down?" Ethan asked.

"I let Hightower know we would be down in ten about twenty minutes ago," Ric responded.

The four quietly rode the rest of the way to the ground level. When the elevator opened, they exited and went through a secondary security door before heading into the hotel's massive lobby. The marble tiling may have looked great, but it made everything echo loudly. Ethan could hear the rotation of his wheels on the flooring as he made his way to where Ron Hightower sat on an overstuffed couch reading *The Times-Picayune*.

Hightower looked up from the paper. *Probably heard our wheels rolling across the floor*, Ethan guessed.

"Morning, manager-daddy," Ric said. "Where's business-daddy?"

"Rawlins is out in the SUV waiting for you. He has some call to a booking agent in the UK. They're still trying to iron out your tour dates for that leg of your tour in the new year."

Hightower stood, folded this newspaper in half and slid the paper under his right arm. He pulled out his sunglasses and gave the group an 'after you' sweep with his left hand, and they headed to the side exit. Ethan could see two black SUVs sitting out front. There was a paid bodyguard standing on either side of the two SUVs. *They look like characters out of* Men in Black.

Mr. J., as the boys called him, was six-foot-five-inches and almost three-hundred pounds of solid muscle. Ethan was nearly amazed Mr. J. could find a suit to fit his giant frame. Mr. J.'s bald white head shone like a giant blazing beacon in the sunlight. Mr. S., on the other hand, was only about five-foot-eleven-inches, but Ethan knew the former Navy SEAL was not one to mess with. His black suit and even blacker skin created a visage of absolute badassery. Ethan couldn't see their eyes behind their dark sunglasses. Still, he knew their focus swiveled in their direction when the hotel's door opened and the five exited the building. Silently, the guards walked to the back, opened the hatchbacks and helped them with their luggage. Ethan and Zach chose the first vehicle with Hightower, and Ric and Orr chose the second.

Mr. J. helped Ethan and Ric with their luggage before closing the back door, then opened the side door to let them in. Ethan remembered how long it took him to get used to this kind of treatment by their security professionals when they started getting famous. After the release of their first album, Mr. J. and Mr. S. were hired full-time and were the group's constant shadows. If the group was out in public, they were always close behind.

"Good morning Ms. A.," Ethan said as he entered and found another one of their bodyguards already behind the wheel.

"Good morning, Ethan. Good morning, Zach," the guard said as she glanced at them through the rearview mirror. Ethan already knew from experience she would not turn her head to look at them. When she was behind the wheel, she was focused on potential threats or traffic.

"Morning, Ms. A.," Zach said as he settled beside Ethan.

Hightower was the last to enter, and Mr. J. shut the door as soon as Hightower was safely inside.

Mr. J. then opened the passenger side door, sat down, closed the door and buckled himself in.

"VIPs secured. Heading to MSY," Ms. A. said.

All four of their bodyguards were on the same closed-channel radio. Ethan saw Ms. A.'s head title slightly as she listened to a response in her earpiece. The SUV pulled into traffic and headed to Louis Armstrong New Orleans International Airport. The airport had been initially named Moisant International Airport, so it had the flight designation code MSY. The airport was officially renamed in 2001 to Louis Armstrong in recognition of the one-hundredth anniversary of the legendary trumpeter's birth.

Ethan closed his eyes and leaned against the window as they rolled through New Orleans. Before he knew it, he felt the vehicle slow down, and he opened his eyes to see them pulling up to a side entrance at the airport. A Peregrine representative was already standing outside waiting for them. As the SUV pulled to a stop, Mr. J. got out, retrieved the luggage from the back and put it on the sidewalk. After a couple of minutes, Mr. J. opened the door, and Hightower, Zach and Ethan exited to start the airline check-in process. A luggage handler with a large baggage cart appeared and put their checked items on the cart as the group was led into the building to a celebrity check-in area. The Peregrine representative talked with each person in the group, checking their IDs, tagging everything and issuing boarding passes.

\* \* \* \*

*Denzili*

The plane was on its initial descent into New Orleans. Denzili texted Richardson to let her know she would be on the ground in fifteen minutes. The handoff should be pretty straightforward. After texting Richardson, she'd sent an encrypted email to Dr. Hennigan, updating her on the mission's progress.

One of the nice perks of working for The Foundation was getting in and out of airports using corporate jets. Everyone on the plane worked for The Foundation, so there was no need for secrecy or to pretend that her phone would cause the aircraft to crash if she didn't stow it before landing.

"Please buckle in if you aren't already," the pilot's voice said over the intercom.

Denzili secured her seatbelt, raised the window shade and watched as the plane flew over swampland before heading into the airport. Denzili was supposed to be in New Orleans for less than an hour if everything went according to plan. She was supposed to land, meet up with Richardson, grab a coffee within the terminal, then she and Richardson would fly out. The plan was simple. Thankfully, a Foundation member who worked for the Transportation Security Administration had organized everything on the ground, making the entire series of events seamless.

Denzili felt the soft bump of the landing gear touch the tarmac as the plane's flaps stood in an upright position, slowing the aircraft as it landed.

"We'll be stopping in a couple of minutes," the pilot said over the intercom.

Denzili unbuckled her seatbelt and took her rolling bag out from the overhead compartment as the plane was taxiing to the part of the airport where private jets unloaded their passengers. When the aircraft came to a halt, Denzili walked to the front of the plane, opened the plane door and lowered the staircase. She walked down the stairs, stood on the tarmac for a second and stretched. She placed the small rolling bag down before lifting the handle and walking toward the terminal entrance. Right before she entered the terminal, she found an identical bag waiting next to the door. She swapped the bags and walked on inside.

* * * *

*Richardson*

Richardson watched as the Foundation plane landed and waited until Denzili entered the terminal before getting into the cart she'd borrowed to drive over the main terminal. She opened the side door to bag processing using the keycard she'd gotten from their inside source. She'd already been given a heads-up for the bag she was looking for. Another agent had already put Denzili's bag to the side so Richardson could locate it quickly.

Richardson meandered through the facility, using the map she had on her phone. Following the basic instructions, Richardson swapped Denzili's with an identical bag already in the system. The swap was necessary to ensure the baggage count didn't delay things. The switch took a matter of seconds. Richardson replaced the bag on the automatic conveyor belt and watched as it headed to its destination.

Thankfully, none of the other workers in baggage handling had even paid attention to her while she was making the switch, which meant one less body on her conscience.

She headed toward an exit she knew would take her into the terminal. Before heading into the airport, she slipped out of the coveralls and jacket she was wearing to blend in. She stowed the items in the empty carry-on bag now in her possession before opening the door.

* * * *

*Denzili*

Denzili sipped on a coffee at a small table right outside the Starbucks, which was the pre-determined rendezvous. Passengers strolled to and fro within the terminal. Richardson approached the table, sat down and said, "Package delivered."

Denzili didn't respond. She slid the coffee she'd already purchased for Richardson across the tabletop.

"Light cream, one sugar," Denzili said. "Just the way you like it."

"Thanks," Richardson responded. "Shall we head back to the plane?"

"Let's wait a few more minutes," Denzili responded. "I want to make sure no one is watching."

The two sat and pretended to converse, but they scanned what was happening around them to ensure they hadn't been followed. In their line of work, one could never be too careful.

Once Denzili was sure everything was safe, she said, "Shall we?"

The two stood and headed back to the private jet terminal, where their plane and flight crew waited.

* * * *

*Ethan*

Once the group was checked in, they were led to a private screening area where everyone was required to have their carry-on luggage screened by hand. They each walked through a metal detector before heading through a back tunnel to the Peregrine First-Class Lounge.

When the band had first experienced this type of royal VIP treatment, they had been awed by how smooth some airports were for celebrities. The guys in ZERO had quickly realized that not all airports were as celebrity friendly. Still, most tried to speed things up to avoid causing any kind of public scene within the airport that could be a security nightmare for all involved.

The group settled into a series of stuffed chairs. Ethan watched as Orr pulled out his bagel and started munching. Hightower and Rawlins both walked over to the coffee bar.

"I'll be right back," Ethan said. He stood up with his overnight bag slung over his shoulder and headed to the restroom. Thankfully, none of the other guys bothered to look up from their phones.

Ethan turned the corner and headed into the restroom area but continued past the restrooms to where he knew there were private showers and changing rooms. He found one empty and looked over his shoulder to ensure no one was watching before he slipped inside.

*Here we go.* Ethan unzipped his rolling suitcase, stripped and donned a fresh set of clothes. Next he pulled out a duffel bag, unfolded it and stuffed everything inside. His goal was to make himself look as different as humanly possible as he escaped the First-

Class Lounge. If everything went according to plan, he would slip out of the lounge with no one knowing.

The last piece of his disguise was a baseball cap with a fake black ponytail that ran out of the back. Ethan had picked up the hat several years earlier for a Halloween costume, but figured the accessory would be handy to help him slip out unnoticed.

He added a pair of oversized sunglasses that hid half of his face. He'd thought about adding some makeup and making himself look more female, but with his square jaw, Adam's apple and cleft chin, he knew that would not work very well. Instead, he'd gone for a more biker-esq look he knew he wasn't really pulling off.

With one last look in the mirror, he thought, *here goes nothing*. Ethan entered the hall right as Ms. Z, the other driver, walked in to use the restroom. The two passed each other in the hall, but Ethan kept his head down, tilted to the side, and kept walking.

*Keep moving. Don't look back. She didn't notice me.*

He moved through the lounge area, pausing for a second to look over where the band sat, and made a wide berth to avoid getting near the group. He walked through the front door of the lounge and entered the bustling airport. He found a display monitor and made sure his departure information hadn't changed. He had forty minutes before the plane left for Houston.

He'd flown in and out of Louis Armstrong so many times that he knew the layout like the back of his hand. Peregrine Airlines flew out of Terminal C and Roadrunner Airways Express flew out of B. Ethan knew he could easily walk from C to B and catch his flight with a few minutes to spare.

He strolled through the airport, doing his best to avoid looking at anyone. Even though he doubted anyone would recognize him in his getup, he didn't want to take any chances.

He arrived at his gate just as the announcer asked people to line up. Ethan had booked a business-class ticket, so he was one of the first to board the plane. He queued up with the other passengers waiting for the gate agent to start boarding.

"Good morning Roadrunner Airways Express Flight 1330. This is a non-stop flight from New Orleans to Houston Hobby, continuing to Denver, Colorado. We now welcome our Business Select passengers," a voice over the intercom chirped.

Ethan pulled out his phone, opened the airline's app and pulled up his ticket. The line started moving. The agent scanned Ethan's phone, the computer dinged and Ethan boarded with no problems.

He entered the jetway and walked down to the plane. The flight attendant greeted him with a "Good morning" as he stood in the front galley.

"Thanks," Ethan responded with a smile before walking down the narrow aisle and picking the window seat in the emergency exit row. He placed his duffel bag in the overhead compartment after pulling out a set of noise-canceling headphones. As soon as he could, he planned on blocking out the world. The last thing he wanted was a nosy seatmate who coveted a long conversation.

Thankfully, as the plane filled, another younger guy took the aisle seat. This guy looked about as interested in having a conversation as Ethan did.

The flight attendant came by and made sure everyone in the emergency exit rows was ready, willing and able to help in case of an emergency landing. Everyone orally agreed before the flight attendant left them.

Before long, the Boeing 737 pushed back from the gate, and the crew delivered the preflight safety briefing. Ethan pretended to listen but was still worried the plane would be turned around because someone figured out he'd escaped.

Ethan let out a breath as he felt the wheels leave the tarmac. He was amazed his plan had actually worked.

*Houston, here I come.*

# Chapter Eight

*Blayne*

"Have you completely lost your mind?"

Blayne looked at Kira. He knew this was how she would react when he told her he'd invited Roy to stay with him for a few days.

"How long have you known this guy? What do you know about him?" Kira continued to pepper Blayne with questions.

"Are you going to let me answer any of these?"

"How do you know he's not running from the mob? Or a serial killer?"

"Kira," Blayne started, letting out a breath and looking at the apartment ceiling, "I've known him for over a year. We met on a dating app, but we've just talked. And we weren't exactly sexting, either. We had normal, grownup talks."

Kira stared at Blayne from the other end of the couch, her eyes boring holes into Blayne when he finally got up the nerve to look at her. Blayne had almost opted not to tell Kira beforehand. When she'd called that morning asking for a ride to work since her car wouldn't start, he knew she would find out eventually, so he told her when she'd gotten over to his apartment, which was only two blocks from her house.

Kira sighed as her face relaxed. "You know, I'm worried about your safety, is all."

"I do," Blayne said. "I completely understand. And I would be lying if I said I wasn't a little anxious, but he sounded like a dog that had been kicked one too many times. I couldn't say no. And besides, I'm the one who invited him."

"One day, you said. You said you invited him to visit one day, not necessarily the next day."

"True," Blayne said, picking up one of the sofa pillows and hugging it to his chest. "I couldn't leave a friend in need. Even if it's a friend I only know virtually."

"When am I going to meet him?"

"Tonight?" Blayne asked. "After you get your car back, come on over. I'll have dinner waiting for you when you get here. If you are scared of him, I'll let you round up a lesbian mob and throw him out of my apartment."

"Lesbian mob?" Kira questioned, raising an eyebrow. "Since when do lesbians do anything as a mob?"

"Melissa Etheridge concerts?" Blayne said with a grin.

Kira picked up a pillow and threw it at Blayne's head. Blayne was about to throw the one he clutched to his chest when his phone vibrated on the coffee table. He put the pillow back in its place and grabbed the phone.

"Speaking of Roy, he just texted to let me know he's on the plane and can't wait to meet me at baggage claim."

"I still don't like this idea. If there is anything fishy about this guy, you leave him at the airport."

"Yes, *Mother*."

"You best be glad I'm not your mother. I'd spank some sense into you if I was."

"Okay, let's get you to work. I have a serial-killing mobster to pick up."

Kira narrowed her eyes at Blayne, setting her mouth in a thin line. Blayne stared right back, going wide eyed and shaking his head back and forth, trying to get Kira to laugh. After a couple of seconds, Kira rolled her eyes as the corner of her mouth lifted.

With the half-smile, Blayne knew he'd won the 'argument', so he stood up and headed toward the door.

"You coming?" he asked, grabbing his keys off the hook next to the front door.

Kira stood, grabbed her briefcase and followed Blayne out of the apartment. Blayne pulled out the key fob and opened the doors. Kira slipped into the passenger seat as Blayne buckled in and pushed the start button. The vehicle quietly roared to life.

Kira and Blayne talked about nothing specific as he drove her to her office. He pulled up right in front, and Kira unbuckled her seatbelt and got out of the car. Before shutting the door, she leaned back in and said, "If he's crazy, leave his ass at the airport." And without waiting for a response, she closed the door.

Blayne smiled, looked over his left shoulder and pulled out into traffic as he pointed his car toward Houston Hobby, since Roy was flying in on

Roadrunner. If he'd flown in on almost any other airline, he would have picked him up at the George H. Bush Intercontinental Airport, which was actually closer to Blayne's home. The trip would take about forty-five minutes at this time in the early afternoon, so he should make it there a little faster, as long as there weren't any major backups on the 610.

Blayne plugged in his iPhone, keeping one eye on the road and one eye on his phone as he scrolled through and found the audiobook he'd been listening to. With his audiobook playing, he sat back to enjoy the drive.

* * * *

*Zach*

Zach pulled out his phone and shot Ethan another text.

*Where R U?*

The band had been sitting in the Peregrine Airlines First-Class Lounge when Mr. J. had asked about Ethan's location. The band had looked at each other and realized they had no idea. At first, everyone figured Ethan was in the bathroom, so Zach had gone and checked it out, but when he hadn't found him anywhere in the lounge, Zach had broken the news to the group.

The bodyguards immediately started working with airline security to track Ethan down. They'd given everyone a general description of their bandmate and what he was wearing. The security people had even let

Ms. Z. scroll through the internal security feed to see if they could find out what had happened. Of course, everyone's biggest fear was that Ethan had been abducted.

When the airline came to escort the group to the plane, Rawlins had decided to re-book until they had Ethan safely back. Peregrine had been very accommodating and worked with Rawlins and Hightower to arrange tickets for a flight later that evening. With those logistics in order, Hightower had called Seattle to give Sally Higgins and the backup dancers a heads-up about Ethan's disappearance.

Zach watched the front door of the lounge as it opened. A uniformed NOPD officer walked in and purposefully made her way to the group. "Hello, I'm Officer Petty. I was alerted you have a missing person's problem."

"Yep," Zach responded. "Ethan Bond has been missing for almost sixty minutes now."

The officer wrote something in her small notebook, then asked, "Has he ever disappeared before?"

"No," Zach responded flatly. "And before you ask, he's not the type to up and run away without telling anyone."

"Okay," Officer Petty said, clearly trying to calm Zach down with her smooth tone. "I can only imagine how freaked out this has you, but I have to ask these questions. Anything you know could help us."

Zach understood what she was saying and felt the wind blow out of his sails as he took a calmer stance. "I know. He's my best friend, and I'm pretty fucking worried. Sorry about the language."

"So, what can you tell me?" Officer Petty asked.

Zach quickly described what had happened the entire morning.

"If anything, he seemed better this morning than yesterday."

"What happened yesterday?" the officer questioned.

"We were at a television shoot for RNN, and he'd passed out before going on camera. The doctors said he was fine, so we hadn't worried about it." Zach watched as the officer jotted in her notebook again. "You don't think these two are related?"

"Who knows?" Officer Petty said. "I'm gathering all the facts I can right now. The more information we have, the easier it will be to find him."

Right then, Ms. Z approached the group. Zach introduced Officer Petty to the entire group.

"Nice to meet you, Officer," Ms. Z said. "I was in Vice for the NOPD for about a decade before I became an independent contractor."

"Ahh, so you make the big bucks now," Officer Petty said.

"Anyway," Ms. Z continued, bypassing the officer's comment, "the security feed in here is pathetic – too many blind spots. There are cameras on all the doors, and no one forcibly removed Mr. Bond from the area. I'm going to go see if I can access the airport security feeds and do the same thing."

"Why don't I come with you?" Officer Petty said. "Maybe I can help grease the wheels around this place. I know pretty much everyone who works in security here."

"That would be appreciated," Ms. Z said, following Officer Petty out of the lounge.

Once Zach was alone with Ric and Orr, he whispered, "Do either of you know anything?"

"Nah, dude," Orr said.

"Me neither," Ric added. "You?"

"Nope. I texted him. Still haven't heard from him. I'm about to text his best friend, Stephanie, to see if she knows anything. I was putting it off, hoping we'd find Ethan hanging out signing autographs somewhere in the airport."

"This is so fu —"

Orr was cut off by a rolling, thunderous explosion. The sound was so loud that Zach's ears went numb as a viewing window facing the tarmac exploded inward, showering a section of the lounge with shards of glass. The sudden bloody carnage in front of him shocked him as he was tackled to the ground by Ms. A., who shielded his body from the flying debris.

Zach was suddenly jerked upward by a pair of firm hands. He was still trying to process what had just happened. Ms. A. ushered him toward a side door, heading him into the belly of the airport. He ran behind a man from Peregrine Airlines security through the maze of halls before finding himself in an inner room. Orr was already inside, and Ric came into the room seconds later, escorted by Mr. J., Hightower and Rawlins.

"What the hell was that?" Hightower said to no one when he finally caught his breath.

"Still finding out, sir," Mr. J. said, talking into a walkie-talkie he had on him.

Moments later, a Peregrine Airlines employee came into the room, escorting a politician Zach had seen a few times on the news. The asshat was one of those good-old-boys White Republican racists. The older man had cut marks on his face. Nothing fatal, but the man would need some stitching...and soon.

"Is everyone okay?" the Peregrine Airlines employee asked. "Anyone injured? Besides you, senator," she said to the politician.

Mr. J. looked everyone over and said, "Shook up, but no injuries here."

"J, it's Z. Come in?" Zach heard Mr. J.'s walkie-talkie squawk.

"Z, it's J. What the hell was that? Over."

"Hold, J." A pause over the walkie-talkie was brief before Z started talking again. "It looks like an airline exploded on takeoff. Still getting information from Federal Aviation Administration—FAA. It looks like it was Peregrine Flight 923 traveling from New Orleans to Seattle. Holy fuck!"

It took Zach a second to realize what the *"holy fuck"* was about. But from the grave look on Mr. J.'s face, he clued in immediately.

"That was the flight we were supposed to be on," Rawlins said.

Zach's face went slack as he slumped into the nearest chair in the room, unable to say anything. His mind raced a million miles an hour. *If Ethan hadn't disappeared, we'd all be dead right now.*

# Chapter Nine

*Ethan*

The flight to Houston was uneventful. Ethan spent most of it listening to music on his phone, staring out of the window at the Gulf of Mexico beneath them before they turned north into Texas.

As the plane approached Houston, the flight attendants came through the main cabin picking up trash and making sure everyone's tray tables were up, their seats straight and the luggage stowed. Ethan closed his eyes as they landed. He tried to predict when the plane would touch the ground based on how it felt. He'd been playing this little game in his head since he'd been a kid. He'd gotten pretty good at guessing when the first wheel would touch the tarmac, but sometimes he was a bit off. He loved feeling of the first little hop planes had when the back wheels touched the ground before the plane's nose settled on the runway and the plane reversed thrusters and slowed rapidly.

"We'll be arriving at the terminal in a few minutes. For those making connections here at Houston Hobby, please see the gate agent or the electronic boards once you enter the terminal. On behalf of your Dallas-Fort Worth-based flight crew, we welcome you to Houston. We know you have many options when flying. Thank you for flying Roadrunner Airways Express. And remember, keep your butts in your seats until the captain has turned off the seatbelt sign."

Ethan heard a slight chuckle from the woman behind him when the flight attendant said the last part. He took a deep breath and kept staring out of the plane. He turned off the airplane mode, waited for the phone to connect then scrolled through several texts and emails. Zach had texted him a few times asking where he was.

Ethan shot him back a quick response.

*Needed a breather. Don't worry. I'll be in Seattle in a few days. Sorry to worry you. I'll explain when I see you.*

The flight was right under an hour and a half, so he figured the band was getting ready to take off. *I'm sure they're all pretty pissed at me right now.* Ethan knew everyone depended on him, but he needed to get away from it all—even if it was only for a few days.

The plane pulled up to the gate and unloading began. The Houston terminal was bustling but not crazy, which was great, because it made blending in and moving fast to luggage claim easy. He stopped by the restroom and looked at himself in the mirror. *Blayne's going to think I'm some crazy-ass punk.* The baseball cap with the ponytail and the giant sunglasses covering half his face should be a dead giveaway to anyone paying attention that he was trying to disguise himself. Thankfully, most people never seemed to see what's going on right in front of their faces.

He followed the signs to baggage claim. On the way, he pulled out his cell phone and texted Blayne.

*On the ground, heading to baggage claim.*

*Great, already here. Wearing a light blue polo, khaki cargo shorts and sneakers. You?*

*Look for the person who looks like they're trying not to be noticed.*

*Huh?*

*Trust me. You'll get it when you see me.*

Ethan made his way through the airport maze, then down a final escalator into the baggage claim area. He followed the mass of people who had disembarked from his plane, assuming they all knew where they were going.

Within a few minutes, he stood next to the baggage carousel, looking for Blayne. Ethan spotted him almost immediately.

*Damn, he's hotter in person than in his EndZone profile pic.*

Ethan maneuvered through the crowd and made his way to Blayne.

Saying nothing, he stood beside Blayne and whispered, "Howdy, cowboy. Can you help a stranger out?"

Blayne's eyebrows rose as he yelped, "Dear God!" before quickly putting his hand over his mouth. "Fuck, I can't say that in Texas."

Ethan laughed. "Sorry... I couldn't resist the temptation... What?" Ethan asked as he examined the strange look crossing Blayne's face.

"What's with the getup?"

"Don't worry. I'm not in witness protection or wanted by the FBI. I didn't want anyone to see me when I left New Orleans. I knew some people in the airport, and I wanted to be anonymous today." Ethan had already come up with the lie when he realized he'd have to explain the odd getup.

"Okay, you can tell me all about it on the ride back to my place. What color is your bag?"

"I didn't bring one. Just the duffel," he said, lifting the bag for emphasis.

*Long Night* from his album, *Dog Days,* started playing over the intercom. He looked over and saw Blayne bopping his head to the song.

"You a fan?" Ethan asked, a bit nervously. The last thing he wanted was to hang out with a giant fan. That never ended well.

"Of whom?"

"ZERO? You were grooving to the music."

"Grooving? Who says that anymore?" Ethan chuckled before continuing. "I had no idea they recorded it. Tells you what I know."

"Okay."

"Sorry... Pop culture isn't something I'm up-to-date on. I remember hearing this song at the club a few years ago, back when I used to go clubbing."

"You're not a clubber?"

"Not anymore. Got too old for the scene. Besides, the local club has a bunch of undergraduates, and I don't want to socialize with people I teach."

"I can see how that could get awkward."

"Well, can I carry your bag for you, at least? My mother taught me to be a southern gentleman, after all," Blayne said with a big goofy smile.

"Nah, thanks, partn'ah," Ethan said in his worst attempt at a southern accent.

Blayne's eyebrows rose. "Please, never do that again."

"Promise. I won't use another bad accent."

"Okay, then. Follow me."

Ethan followed Blayne through the airport and across the street to the short-term parking garage. They took the elevator up to the third level and to an older model Prius. Blayne pulled out his keys and wirelessly opened the trunk.

"You can put your bag in there."

"Thanks! Let me get out of this getup first." Ethan took off the hat and sunglasses. He also stripped out of the sweatshirt he'd been wearing, which was becoming increasingly sticky in the hot, humid air of the Houston afternoon.

He heard a noise coming from Blayne, so he shot him a quick sideways glance and caught Blayne staring at him. *Great, he just recognized me. So much for anonymity.*

"So, this is me," Ethan said, closing the trunk. *If he wants to say anything about my celebrity, let him get it over with.*

"Okay, let's get on the road."

Blayne opened the driver's side door and sat inside. Ethan stood there for a second, a bit shocked because the scene was not playing out like he'd expected—which was good, but definitely surprising.

He walked up to the passenger side door, let himself into the car and buckled up. Blayne plugged his iPhone into the dashboard as he pushed the button to start the vehicle. A voice reading an audiobook filled the car. Blayne grabbed his iPhone, swiped and hit a couple of buttons.

"Sorry... I was listening to the latest Neil Gaiman book on the ride over."

"Who?"

"Neil Gaiman, an amazing fantasy writer. Hell, he's written stuff for DC Comics, too."

"Sorry... I admit I don't read nearly often enough."

Blayne sighed softly, and Ethan saw his face go blank. *He must think I'm some kind of backward swamp boy.* "And before you ask, I went to college. I graduated with a degree in accounting. Sadly, they didn't stress reading literature much. If you need me to balance an Excel spreadsheet, though, I'm golden." The corner of Blayne's mouth tilted up.

"Hope you don't mind listening to Broadway?" Blayne asked. "Honestly, besides audiobooks, it's the only thing I listen to."

"Cool. You know I'm game," Ethan replied. He knew a few people in the industry on Broadway. Heck, ZERO's choreographer had played a swing role for like six shows. One day during one of their rehearsal breaks, she'd explained to Ethan that a swing's job was to know fifteen different roles in a show's ensemble. She could be in one part for the matinee and a completely different one at night. Sally had told him some pretty funny stories about her first year as a swing. Once, she had found herself completely lost in the middle of a song because she'd forgotten what role she was playing that night. Thankfully, the dance captain saw the look of fear in her eyes, grabbed her and put her in the correct position during the middle of the number.

"Earth to Roy?"

"Huh?" Ethan asked, coming back to the moment. "Sorry… My mind wandered for a moment."

"Where did it go?" Blayne asked.

"A friend of mine was a swing on Broadway. She covered nine ensemble tracks in the show. If something happened to any cast member, she stepped right in as if nothing had transpired. Anyway, she told me some of the backstage antics." Ethan recounted the entire story as close to how Sally had told it to him as was humanly possible.

Ethan found it easy to talk to Blayne, even easier than when he had chatted with Blayne on the app. He looked at Blayne in the driver's seat and smiled at the man.

"What?" Blayne asked when he caught Ethan staring.

"Nothing," Ethan replied. "Glad to finally meet you after all this time. It feels like I've known you forever."

"Because we have known each other for a long time."

"You know what I *mean*. You're exactly like I expected you to be…all smart and handsome."

"And you, dear Roy, are nothing like I expected."

Ethan narrowed his eyes in confusion. "How so?"

"Well, look at you," Blayne said, gesturing at Ethan. "And?"

"You're going to make me say it, aren't you?" Blayne asked with a bit of a huff. "You're definitely a hell of a lot hotter than I expected. You're even hotter than the pic you sent me last night. I didn't think you'd have a third head or anything, but when you wouldn't trade pics for the longest time, I kind of had images of Quasimodo in my head."

"Like the cute Quasi from the Disney movie or the old black-and-white movie?"

"Well, you're definitely more Disney," Blayne said with a wink.

"Thanks, I think," Ethan laughed.

"Take it any way you want."

"Why don't you find us the show your friend was in?"

"You may not have it," Ethan said.

"I seriously doubt that," Blayne said with a grin.

Ethan looked through the iPhone, located a show, pushed play and the orchestration began.

"I loved this show on Broadway," Blayne said.

"You saw it?" Ethan asked with a bit more shock than he'd intended.

"Yes," Blayne said matter-of-factly. "This Texas boy tries to visit New York City at least a few times a year to catch up on his shows. Would love to live there, but the job of an academic doesn't lend itself well to picking where you want to live."

"What do you mean?"

"Academics have to specialize in specific areas. Then we must find jobs at colleges and universities looking for that specific skill set, teaching ability and background to fill a specific gap within a department. In my area, there may be three or four job openings across the country in a given year."

"Damn!"

"Damn, is right," Blayne replied. "Having taught public school for a couple of years out in West Texas while in graduate school will give me a huge leg up when I start looking for jobs after I finish my doctorate."

"Cool. How much longer do you have?"

"I should finish coursework in the spring. Then next year, I will focus on writing my dissertation."

"Your what?" Ethan asked.

"Big long book," Blayne responded. "You know, those things you don't read many of."

"Bitch," Ethan said in mock fury.

"Hardly the first time I've been called *that* in my life," Blayne shot back.

The two spent the rest of the ride to Blayne's apartment in easy conversation.

\* \* \* \*

*Dr. Hennigan*

Dr. Hennigan got off the phone before she rapped on her mother's office door.

"Enter," an authoritative voice said from within, followed by a beeping sound letting Dr. Hennigan know the door had been unlocked.

She opened it and walked inside. The vice-chair of The Foundation was on the phone with someone. Deborah Hennigan had a hawk-like nose and a gaze that could chill anyone to their core. Of course, Deborah was Dr. Hennigan's mother.

"Yes, Senator. I look forward to receiving your report," Deborah said before hanging up the phone.

Dr. Hennigan had been in this office countless times over the years, but it always reminded her of a queen sitting upon her throne. The north wall of the office was filled with a bank of television monitors that captured live feeds from television stations worldwide.

From her experience, Dr. Hennigan knew those channels could just as quickly capture feeds from the various internal cameras stationed throughout the facility.

"How are you doing this afternoon, Mother?" Dr. Hennigan asked.

"I'm fine, Philippa. What news have you for me?"

Dr. Hennigan noticed her mother hadn't asked about her. Dr. Hennigan learned long ago she had no mother when Deborah Hennigan sat in this room. Deborah could be the doting mother when they were at her estate outside Santa Fe, but in this compound, she was not her mother. Here, she was the vice-chair. And while Dr. Hennigan technically controlled the day-to-day operations of The Mesa Juamenes Complex, just called 'The Complex' by most who worked for The Foundation, Deborah Hennigan oversaw all operations worldwide while Dr. Hennigan's grandmother oversaw The Foundation overall. Three generations of women controlled the outcomes of elections, coups, the media and many other vital parts of society — all cloaked in The Foundation's mystery.

Many people had heard of The Foundation. Some had even learned to fear it. But only those few hand-picked women who survived their intense training could learn its secrets. Dr. Hennigan wasn't a fan of death, and she never took joy in watching others suffer and die, but she knew death was necessary for progress.

"We believe the target was not liquidated in the Peregrine explosion. We're not sure if other forces are at play or if it was absolute dumb luck at this point. We are still investigating."

"So, you're telling me The Foundation sanctioned the extra-liquidation of two-hundred-eighty-five people and managed to miss the one target?"

"Yes, Mother."

"That wasn't actually a question, dear."

The way her mother stressed the word "*dear*" was like a slap to the face. Although her mother would never come out and express her fury, let alone show it, using a familiar term while she was working was virtually unheard of.

*Well, two can play that game*, Dr. Hennigan thought to herself. "Vice-Chair," she started. The only reaction she got from her mother was the slight arch of a single thin eyebrow. "We are trying to find out what happened. Our agents on the ground were kept out of the loop about the target's non-appearance on the plane. The plan was already in motion, and a communication blackout had commenced. There was no way to stop once it was in motion."

"You followed procedures to the letter?"

Dr. Hennigan knew the question was less of a question and more of a statement. If her team hadn't followed procedures to the letter, her team would have been liquidated. And although she knew it would be hard for her mother and grandmother, Dr. Hennigan never took it for granted that she could find herself taken out.

"Of course. The plan proceeded flawlessly. There was an unknown element, and we're still trying to find out what happened."

"I will expect a full internal audit of this fiasco."

"Of course."

"I'm assigning Ms. Brighton to oversee the audit."

*Fuck!* "Understandable."

"I know you and she have…history, but I trust her discretion and thoroughness. I've already talked with the chairwoman and requested Ms. Brighton's presence at The Complex. She should be here late tonight."

"I will try to have as much information as is possible ready for her when she arrives."

"See that you do."

Deborah turned and looked at her computer monitor, a clear sign Dr. Hennigan was summarily dismissed. Without saying another word, she spun on her heels and walked toward the office's door. She heard the beeping sound as she approached, opened the door and let herself out.

With the door firmly shut behind her, she took a second to lean against it. "Well, it could have gone worse," she said to the empty hall. She took a couple of deep, comforting breaths, like she'd learned to do in the meditation class she'd taken in college. When she pulled herself together, she pointed her feet toward her lab.

She walked with a clear purpose, and everyone she met along the way gave her a wide berth. *Apparently, I'm radiating 'don't fuck with this bitch today'.* She rounded the corner into the hallway where her lab was located and quickly got inside. Her lab was one of the few places where she knew her mother didn't have cameras. They had long agreed that her lab was her refuge, and no one was to have any kind of surveillance there. She also had one of her underlings sweep the room daily for audio or video transmitters.

"How did it go?" Ms. Wilson asked as Dr. Hennigan strode into the room.

"Better than it could have. We're both still standing, so that's good."

"But?" Ms. Wilson asked with a questioning look on her face.

"Mother has asked Ms. Brighton to fly out to The Complex today to conduct the post-action audit."

"Indeed." Ms. Wilson responded as her expression hardened, and she put the palms of her hands on the table in front of her.

Ms. Wilson would look perfectly calm to an outsider — almost quizzical, if anything. Dr. Hennigan knew the look for what it was. Ms. Wilson was seething with rage.

"Don't worry," Dr. Hennigan started. "We did everything by the letter. We have nothing to worry about from an audit."

"Still…" Ms. Wilson let the word hang in the air.

"I know. We both have history with Ms. Brighton, but she is a consummate professional. She won't let our history interfere with a fair audit."

"And if she does?"

"If she does," Dr. Hennigan started, "we have ways of making people disappear. Don't we?"

"That we do," Ms. Wilson said as her eyes crinkled and the corners of her mouth tilted upward ever so slightly.

*From rage to joy in under a minute. I'll need to watch her to ensure she doesn't use this opportunity to take care of Ms. Brighton permanently.*

# Chapter Ten

*Agent Murphy*

Special Agent Sarah Murphy entered the Peregrine VIP holding area and took in the scene in front of her. She could tell some were in shock, and a couple had tight fuses that could explode easily and quickly if she didn't handle this delicately.

Murphy had joined the FBI after law school. She was a second-generation FBI agent, taking after her mother. Her father had been a professor at Tulane, which was one of the primary reasons she'd requested to be stationed at the field office in New Orleans. After her mother died from cancer, she wanted to be closer to her father. At thirty-five, she'd been on the job for almost ten years.

After the explosion, Murphy and her partner were dispatched to the airport to help coordinate efforts with Homeland Security, National Intelligence, the NOPD, the Bureau of Alcohol, Tobacco, Firearms and Explosives — ATF — the FAA and several other lettered agencies within the federal, state and local governments. Forensic specialists from the CIA, ATF, FAA and FBI were already en route to examine the debris field. Of course, half of the debris field was over swamplands, so the investigators had their work cut out for them.

"Who's Dan Rawlins?" Agent Murphy asked after taking in the room.

"I am," a man with silver hair and an expensive suit said. "And you are?"

"I'm Special Agent Sarah Murphy, FBI." She pulled out her badge and showed it to the gentleman.

After appearing to vet her credentials, *like this yahoo could tell a real FBI shield from a fake one*, she said, "I hear you missed your flight."

"What are you insinuating?" The man's eyes narrowed as a vein popped out on his neck.

"Nothing," she said, trying to defuse the situation. "Trying to figure out the facts on the ground."

Rawlins deflated a bit, but Murphy knew she would have to tread lightly with this guy, or he would request his lawyer, which would do nothing to expedite the investigation. She stared at Rawlins, waiting for him to continue.

"Yes," he started, "we missed our flight. We're rescheduled for a later one."

"What happened?" Rawlins looked nervous at the question, so she probed further. "From ticketing, I was told your entire party was here, so what caused you to miss the flight?" Of course, she already knew the answer from the Peregrine staff, but she wanted to see how this guy would respond.

"One of our party's members went missing," he said.

She thought he was doing an excellent job of selecting each word carefully, which wouldn't speed things along. "Okay, Mr. Rawlins, let me start by saying I already know most of the story from Peregrine Airlines. I need you to fill in the pieces of the story from your side. My goal here is not to cause a scandal. I'm here to investigate why a plane you were supposed to be on just exploded in the sky."

"Do you think it was terrorism? Were we the targets?" he asked.

"We are still waiting for our forensic experts from across the country to arrive in New Orleans. Until they survey the debris field and start piecing the plane back together, who knows what caused the accident? As for you being targeted, I have no reason to suspect this had anything to do with you. I still have to check every potential avenue. You weren't the only ones to miss the flight, which is normal. But, you were the largest group who missed it."

Rawlins motioned to the table where he'd been sitting with another gentleman. Murphy pulled out her notebook as they sat down.

"Agent Murphy, this is Ron Hightower, the band's manager," Rawlins said.

"Good to meet you, Agent Murphy," the man said as he extended his hand.

Murphy took his hand and shook it firmly. "So, tell me what happened."

Rawlins and Hightower spent the next few minutes filling in Agent Murphy about their entire morning leading up to Ethan's disappearance, then the explosion.

"So, you do not know where Ethan Bond is right now?"

"No," Hightower said. "We have no clue where he is. Our security team was working with airport security to find him when all hell broke loose."

Murphy jotted a few quick notes in her notebook before Rawlins asked, "Any chance he was on the plane?"

"There's always a chance, but Peregrine didn't have a record of him boarding," Murphy informed the gentlemen.

"Thank God," Hightower responded. "Sorry... I know that sounds horrible, considering how many people died. I don't know what we'd do if he'd been killed."

Murphy spent the next few minutes getting more details from the men before proceeding to interview the boys in the band, the bodyguards, then the senator. Everyone kept asking her questions she simply didn't have answers for yet. She understood everyone was a bit freaked out and wanted to know what was happening. Still, it was too early in the investigation to have any theories.

After wrapping up the interviews, she returned to the airport security suite, where she'd left her partner. She approached the door with a giant yellow sign that read 'Authorized Personnel Only' and knocked loudly. A guard opened the door, and she held up her shield. The man glanced down before standing back and letting her into the room.

"Find anything, Agent Harper?" she asked as she entered the room. The room was abuzz with people and energy. People were scouring every second of the video, trying to find clues.

"Come over here for a second," Harper said. Harper may have been eleven years older than Murphy, but he looked like a fit man in his late thirties. His well-fitted black suit highlighted his trim runner's physique. "I may have found something related to the boy band situation."

"Really?" Agent Murphy asked as she walked across the room. "Why were you looking for a missing person?"

"Wasn't intending to, but we caught something irregular and started tracking it." Agent Harper walked Murphy through a series of camera shots.

"What should I see here?"

"Watch the shoes," Harper said.

Murphy studied the video streams of the boy band arriving at the airport. She paid attention to the shoes of everyone as they went through security. "Okay, what am I looking at?"

"Look at Ethan Bond's shoes."

"Can you zoom in?"

"Sure," Harper said as he motioned for the tech person at the computer terminal to enlarge the video feed.

The image that filled the screen was a pair of generic-looking white sneakers. She spent a moment taking in the details.

"Okay, what's so special about 'em? They look like runners to me."

"Those are Alexander McQueen's."

"They're what?"

"Famous fashion designer. I went through a high-end sneaker phase. McQueen's are not cheap. They probably cost six-hundred-bucks."

"Okay, shoe boy, what does this have to do with anything?"

Harper cued up the second video of a young man or woman leaving the Peregrine Lounge. The person wore a baseball cap with a black ponytail and sunglasses covering half their face.

"Okay," she started, "who's this?"

"Look at the shoes."

She squinted at the screen. "Can you zoom in?" Saying nothing, the tech zoomed in. Sure enough, they were identical to Ethan Bond's. "What are the chances two people were wearing the same shoes?" she asked, looking up at Harper.

"Not very. The likelihood of someone else wearing those same shoes in our airport today is pretty much nil."

*Why would he need a disguise? What the hell is going on here?*

"Were you able to follow him through the airport?"

"Yep," Harper started. "We tracked him as he moved from Terminal B to C. He got on a flight bound for Houston. We have a message into Roadrunner Airways Express to see if he was flying under his actual name or an alias."

"And?"

"Haven't heard back yet. Things at all the airlines are chaotic right now. The FAA hasn't grounded planes yet, but all traffic in and out of New Orleans has been halted."

"Once we figure out where he's gone, we should probably send someone from the Houston Field Office to get his statement," she said, more to herself than anyone else.

"I guess this means we don't need to worry about the missing person situation anymore?" Harper asked.

"True, but Rawlins and the director go back apparently, so we don't want to end anything prematurely—if you get my drift."

Murphy watched as Harper shrugged while shaking his head. "Damn politics! Gonna be the death of me."

"You and me both, Harper. You and me both."

\* \* \* \*

"Agent Murphy," a voice yelled as she exited the airport and headed back to her car. The alphabet soup of specialists had arrived and was already taking control of the situation. Murphy and Harper were free to hand over the investigation. Harper had stayed behind because the agent who had flown in from DC was someone he'd gone through the FBI Training Academy with, so Harper had wanted to catch up quickly.

Murphy swung her head and saw Stephen McNeil and his RNN cameraman standing on the other side of the police tape. She thought about ignoring him and getting out of there, but she knew that wouldn't get her very far, so she tried not to scowl and threw on a fake smile.

"How can I help you, Mr. —?"

"McNeil. Stephen McNeil from RNN. We talked yesterday about the *NOLA Nights* murders."

"Ah yes," she responded, as if she'd completely forgotten about their run-in. "How can I help you, Mr. McNeil?"

Suddenly, the bright light of the television camera shone on her face as McNeil thrust a microphone into her face.

"What do you know about the bombing of Peregrine Flight 923?"

"Bombing?" she questioned. "Who said anything about a bombing? The forensic specialists who will put this case together have been on the ground for less than an hour. It will take a few days, if not weeks, before they'll have a definitive answer to what caused the explosion." She knew he was trying to fish for information, but Murphy had enough experience dodging reporters' questions over the years. "Wish I could provide more information, Mr. McNeil, but I have nothing else to say. Besides, you know I can't comment on an ongoing investigation."

McNeil made a cut motion across his throat. The cameraman turned off the light then relaxed the camera from his shoulder.

"Okay, off the record, what can you tell me?" McNeil asked.

"Again, right now, there's simply not much to tell. The news outlets probably have as much information as we do now."

"Come on. You have to know something about this. Any suspicions?"

"Of course, I have suspicions, but none of them are backed by evidence or facts, which is why I won't share them with you. Wish I could provide you with additional information, but I don't have any to give. As soon as we know more, I'm sure the various agency heads will have a press briefing." Murphy turned to leave, feeling pretty good about how she'd handled McNeil.

"Is Ethan Bond a suspect?"

She spun around quickly and tried to mask the look of surprise that washed over her face. "Excuse me?"

"I said, is Ethan Bond a suspect?"

Murphy watched as a few other reporters' ears suddenly perked up as they heard the possibility of a juicy story about to break. Murphy walked over to the police tape instead of saying anything, lifted it and gestured for McNeil to follow. His cameraman tried to follow, but she put the tape back down and said, "Sorry... This is only between us."

She motioned for McNeil to follow her. Once she was out of earshot of the rest of the press, she casually asked, "So, what do you know about the kidnapping?"

"Kidnapping? From what I hear, he purposefully ditched his security detail. He flew the coop, leaving the rest of ZERO in a bind. I also know ZERO was supposed to be on the flight to Seattle. So, you tell me, is this a coincidence?"

*Fuck! They already had a leak somewhere in the airport.* "Well, all avenues of investigation are ongoing. Ethan is no more a suspect than a dozen other people who missed the flight. Besides, there are countless possibilities. I can say, on the record, we are exploring any and all leads. Nothing is ruled out."

"You won't say he's a suspect, but you also won't say he's not a suspect."

"It's too early in the investigation to know if suspects are even needed. It's entirely possible there was simply some kind of mechanical failure. We have to wait and see what the forensic investigators piece together." She then narrowed her eyes at McNeil. "Please do not go spreading rumors. These investigations are hard enough without rumors flying around the Internet bogging down important investigatory resources."

"How's this?" McNeil started. "I'll give you some information on your other case if you promise to keep me in the loop on any actual developments."

"What other case?" Murphy asked.

"The *NOLA Nights* Murders," McNeil responded. "You know, the one we talked about previously."

"Sorry, of course," she started. "The explosion has my mind preoccupied."

"Understandable."

"So, what do you know about *NOLA Nights*?" Murphy asked. "And before you ask again, I can't guarantee anything. I can say that if there's a public break in the case, I'll be happy to talk to you."

"I'll take what I can get," McNeil said. "Let's say insider birdies have told me Cynthia Dunning and Daniel Hawthorne were not lovers. In fact, my team of researchers found an old picture of Daniel Hawthorne making out with a guy years ago. Although we can't confirm it, we have every reason to believe Daniel Hawthorne was gay."

"And what does this have to do with Ethan Bond?"

"Do I need to spell it out for you?" McNeil asked with a twinkle in his eye.

She thought about it for a moment. *Holy fuck! It could make sense.* "You think Bond and Hawthorne were more than just friends?"

"A definite possibility," McNeil started. "Again, I have no evidence of this. In fact, there's zero evidence Ethan Bond has ever dated anyone at any point in his life. Sure, he has taken a few starlets to various award ceremonies, but those are usually one-offs, and both he and the starlet always say they're just 'great friends'."

The wheels in Murphy's head spun when her thoughts were interrupted by Agent Harper as he approached. "Murphy? Need me to get this guy out of here for you?"

Murphy quickly snapped out of it and looked at Harper. "Nah, we're good. I explained to Mr. McNeil that the FBI will not comment on ongoing investigations." Murphy then looked directly at McNeil, narrowed her gaze and added, "Nor will we comment on rumors and innuendos."

\* \* \* \*

*Ethan*

Ethan let the warm water of Blayne's shower run over his body. After he had escaped from New Orleans and flown to Houston, he had wanted to wash the day off before settling in at Blayne's place.

Ethan had found conversing with Blayne effortless. He had never felt this at ease with his bandmates or even with Danny. With Danny, everything had always been to keep up the public image. Don't touch each other in public, secret rendezvous and clandestine kisses when no one could see them. Sure, it had been fun for a while, but it had gotten old quickly. Ethan had wanted more with Danny, but their 'relationship' had been doomed from the start because neither of them would let it interfere with their careers.

Thinking about Danny brought tears to his eyes that were quickly washed away by the falling water spilling out of the showerhead above him. For the first time in days, he let all his emotions ride over him as he sat down in the shower and cried. He cried for Danny, sure, but he also cried for himself—crying because he couldn't be the grieving boyfriend in public. *Hell, it's not like Danny and I were boyfriends. Not really.*

After finishing his cleanse, physically and spiritually, he turned off the water and toweled himself off. He ran the towel through his hair, leaving it a floppy mess on the top of his head. *I can't go out looking like this,* he thought. But then he remembered there were no lurking paparazzi ready to snap his picture if he didn't look cover-model ready. Ethan finished drying the rest of his body and hung up the towel Blayne had given him on the hook behind the door. He then brushed his teeth, just because.

He pulled on a pair of Armani boxer briefs and Under Armour shorts he liked to lounge around in. He applied deodorant and went to put on his T-shirt he'd grabbed out of his bag but couldn't find it in the bathroom. *Must have left it on top of my bag.* Ethan slipped out of the bathroom and walked down the hall. He passed Blayne's door as Blayne came out of the room and smacked right into him.

"Sorry," Ethan said immediately, noticing Blayne's hand resting on his chest. "I should have been watching where I was going."

"No. It's my fault. I didn't look both ways before leaving my room," Blayne joked as he removed his hand. "In reality, it's neither of our faults. Sometimes, people accidentally bump into each other in a hall."

"That they do."

Ethan noticed then Blayne was also wearing a pair of Under Armour shorts and a T-shirt that said Pennington University. "Hey, that's where you teach, isn't it?" Ethan asked, pointing at Blayne's shirt.

"Yep. And where I'm working on my doctorate."

"Cool, cool," Ethan responded, nodding his head. "Anyway, I need to grab my T-shirt. I left it in the bedroom."

"I'll get out of your way then," Blayne said, stepping back into the primary bedroom's door frame, moving his right arm in a sweeping motion.

"Thank you, kind sir," Ethan said as he passed.

Ethan opened the door at the end of the short hall and saw his T-shirt sitting on top of the bag. He'd gone with the one he'd gotten from a friend who had been in the *Spiderman, Turn Off the Dark* cast when it had been on Broadway. He thought Blayne would find it kitschy and fun. He picked up the shirt and slid it over his head before letting it fall around his waist. It was oversized on him. He found the material really soft, which was why he liked to lounge around in it.

He moved to pick up his phone and found it dead. *Dammit!* Ethan searched through his bag, looking for his charging cable. *Dammit again*, he thought as he couldn't find the blasted thing.

He grabbed the dead phone and walked out of the room and down the hall into Blayne's living room.

"Blayne, do you have a Samsung Galaxy charging cable by chance?" Ethan asked as he walked into the room.

"Sorry, I'm an iPhone guy."

"No worries. I'll pick one up when we're out and about."

"Actually, I think my friend Kira is a Galaxy person. I'll text her and see if she has an extra cable you can borrow or if she'll at least bring hers over so you can charge tonight."

"Thanks! I want to make sure I miss nothing important," Ethan said. "You know, just in case."

"Not a problem, Roy. I'm sure Kira would be happy to help."

Ethan watched as Blayne picked up his iPhone and started composing a message. Blayne looked so cute, all focused on his phone. His T-shirt rode up just enough for Ethan to see the lower part of Blayne's belly button. He noticed Blayne was pretty smooth but had a treasure trail leading into his shorts.

"What's wrong?" Blayne asked suddenly.

"Oh, sorry," Ethan said, diverting his eyes back to Blayne's face. "I was lost in my head," he lied.

"Kira said she has a spare in her office that she'll bring with her tonight. She said you could borrow it until you can pick one up yourself."

"She's a godsend," Ethan said.

"Wanna watch some TV?" Blayne asked.

"Nah," Ethan said. "I don't want to see what's happening in the world. Being with you here is like an oasis away from all my life."

"Ahh..." Blayne said, looking at him sympathetically. Blayne motioned to the couch. "So, tell me about what happened? If you don't mind."

"I can't give you all the details because it's only partially my story," Ethan started as he sat down.

"Okay, I sense this is going to be a long one," Blayne started. "Cocktail first?"

Ethan looked up and grinned at Blayne, whose genuine smile reached from his lips to the lines around his eyes.

"You know what? I don't drink much..."

"Me neither," Blayne admitted. "But sometimes, cocktails are a necessity." Blayne launched himself off the couch. Ethan caught himself watching Blayne's backside as he walked away. "Cran and vodka good?"

"Umm…vodka's always good in my book," Ethan replied. *Dude, stop staring at his ass. He's a friend. And you don't want to destroy that friendship. Besides, you don't even know if you're his type. Don't ruin a friendship on a fling that can't go anywhere.*

"Coming right up."

Ethan leaned back into the couch and thought about what he should tell Blayne about his life. He wanted to be honest, but he still wasn't ready for Blayne to know everything.

Blayne walked back into the living room with two martini glasses in hand. "I know, not exactly a martini, but I love how festive they look. Something makes me feel like an adult when I drink out of one of these glasses."

Ethan took his glass and sipped. His face puckered.

"More vodka than cranberry," Blayne said. "Sorry… Should have warned you. I can water it down if you want me to."

"Nah, this is fine. I hadn't steeled myself for it before I took a drink. I'm more used to drinks in clubs where everything is overpriced and watered down."

"Thankfully, most bars around here don't water alcohol down. I don't think 'the good-old-boys around these here parts' would allow them to get away with that shit," Blayne said in his best attempt at a thick Texas accent.

"Okay, no making fun of my fake Texas accent after that one." Ethan laughed.

"Yeah, but I'm from here. I'm allowed to make fun of Texas. You're a damn Yankee."

"Not really," Ethan started, taking another sip from his glass. He looked up and saw the questioning look on Blayne's face. "I already admitted, I have a lot I need to tell you. So, I guess I'll start there. I grew up in Louisiana and did my undergrad at Tulane."

"Nice school," Blayne interjected.

"Yeah, it was a great place," Ethan agreed. He placed his martini glass back on the stone coaster Blayne had set out for him on the coffee table. "I was majoring in business and intended to attend law school. But, as often happens, an opportunity opened for a close group of friends and me. After graduating, we jumped on it and ended up living in New York for a few years as we got the venture up and running." Ethan was still trying to figure out what to say without giving everything away.

"That must have been when we first met on *EndZone*?"

"Yep," Ethan said, nodding his head. "Once we were a bit more established, we ended up moving back to New Orleans, where we're now based full-time."

"That's cool. I love New Orleans. Admittedly, I've only been there in mid-November, not for Mardi Gras or Gay Mardi Gras. Thought about going to both, but I don't like crowds much. I found Bourbon Street overexciting on a random Wednesday. I can't imagine how crazy things are during Mardi Gras."

"I live in the Garden District, so I don't have to go very far. I can just open a window, step out onto a balcony and watch the craziness below me unfold. As for what happened that led to this little getaway weekend…I don't even know where to begin. Let's say that I had been kind of seeing a guy. Well, not actually. We're both a bit in the closet."

"Okay," Blayne said, staring Ethan in the eyes.

"So, two nights ago, he was murdered."

"What the fuck?" Blayne blurted as his whole facial expression turned into a mask of shock and incomprehension. "Do they know who did it?"

"I don't know. And besides, it's not like I can go into the police station and ask. No one knew we had a thing going. Everything about our relationship was hush-hush and behind closed doors. It didn't help he was on a soap either... Shit, I shouldn't have said that."

"Whoa, Whoa, Whoa. Back up. You were dating a guy who was on a soap opera?"

Ethan diverted his gaze and sheepishly said, "Yeah. On and off again for about three years." Ethan looked up and stared into Blayne's face before adding, "But we weren't dating. We were sort of friends with benefits. Neither of us was looking for a boyfriend, and a mutual friend introduced us. Actually, my best friend Stephanie introduced us."

"Your best friend hooked you up with a soap opera star?"

"It's not nearly as seedy as you make it sound," Ethan said, trying to add a bit of levity to the conversation. "I don't even know if she knew we were screwing on the side. Everyone thought he was madly in love with his costar, who knew he was gay. His costar was the only one who knew about me."

Blayne reached out and touched Ethan's knee. "How are you holding up?"

Ethan took in a deep breath and let it out slowly. "I'm holding up. I'm still a bit conflicted about what I think, anyway. I don't think I loved him. I never loved him. He was just fun. And I will miss what we had, but I feel horrible for saying I don't miss him."

"Explain," Blayne said, softly caressing his thumb across Ethan's calf muscle.

"This is going to sound horrible, but here goes." Ethan let out a sharp breath before going on. "As long as I had him, I didn't need to date. It's like he gave me enough of what I needed, so I didn't worry about myself, my own feelings or relationship needs. I got all the physical intimacy I needed and the rest of my needs from my family and friends. It's hard to mourn a person when you were both using each other."

"That's pretty deep," Blayne said.

"I've spent the last couple of days running all this over in my mind again and again. I know I'm sad about what I lost. I'm mad as hell someone killed him, but maybe this frees me to find something else, something more."

"Come here." Blayne opened his arms to Ethan. Ethan scooched across the couch and let Blayne wrap his arms around him in a gentle hug. "Now I completely understand why you needed to get away from life for a few days. Damn. I don't know what I would do if I were in your shoes."

Ethan pulled back a bit to look up at Blayne. "You wouldn't be in this position, because you wouldn't have been dating a hopelessly closeted soap opera star."

"True that," Blayne said, nodding his head. "But I've dated and slept with a ton of closet cases over the years. Okay, well, maybe not a ton, but I've had more than my fair share of them."

"Oh, and there's one more thing I need to tell you," Ethan started.

"Yes?" Blayne said, nervousness flashing across his face.

"My name's Ethan, not Roy."

\* \* \* \*

*Agent Murphy*

After she spent the afternoon at the airport helping coordinate the first responses to the Peregrine Airlines crash, Agent Murphy had wanted to go home and sleep. Sadly, leaving her office wasn't on her agenda any time soon. The sound of a new email hitting her inbox broke her concentration as she wrote her report from the afternoon. She grumbled a moment at the loss of her train of thought but opened it, anyway.

She read the subject line, *Dunning and Hawthorne Forensic Analysis Report*. She double-clicked the email and began skimming through the document, looking for the important parts. The female victim's neck had been snapped. *Expected that one.* No bullet had been recovered from the male victim. However, shards of ceramic in the wound were found during the autopsy. *Wow, didn't expect that.* On a hunch, Murphy pulled up the ViCAP—Violent Criminal Apprehension Program—database and looked for unsolved murders where a ceramic bullet had been suspected. She skimmed through the information. Several pretty high-profile assassinations had been, and a few lesser-known ones stood out as being eerily similar. *Clearly, we're dealing with a pro. How has no one put this together?*

She kept reading the report. Based on the evidence pulled from Daniel Hawthorne's cell phone, he had received a message from Cynthia Dunning earlier in the evening. The report read...

*Our specialists believe a message was received, but we could not find what the message contained. We checked his phone and the server backup after getting a court order. Both were wiped clean. Someone went to great lengths to delete any evidence of the content of the email. We know the email was automatically forwarded to two other cell phones. However, the email trail may be a red herring, not the message sent and received.*

*Unfortunately, both email addresses were associated with freemail.com accounts. We're still in the process of getting a court order to get access to those. However, previous experience with freemail.com has led us to believe those will be dead ends. Freemail.com prides itself on the anonymity of its users, so there's no way to trace the emails back to their originators. Again, let us reiterate, we are still not one hundred percent sure the email is even the right trail to follow. We need to get our hands on a phone with the message still intact.*

Murphy reread the paragraphs, trying to make heads or tails out of it. She moved on to the next segment of the report. She read through the trace evidence found at both Dunning's and Hawthorne's residences. There was little-to-no evidence at Dunning's place, which didn't surprise Murphy. The assassin was clearly a pro and knew how to clean up after themself. She then read the evidence from Hawthorne's house.

*The DNA within the condom did not match the victim. However, DNA outside did.*

She took a second to let that tidbit of information settle. *This definitely backs up what I learned from McNeil this afternoon. If I were a betting woman, the other sample is Ethan Bond's.*

She sent the forensics team a quick email asking them to get sample DNA from Ethan Bond for the missing person case. She wasn't sure how, but Ethan seemed to be the center of this shitstorm.

\* \* \* \*

*Blayne*

Blayne had put the spaghetti in the boiling water when there was a knock on his front door. He added a quick dash of salt and olive oil before heading to it.

"Good evening," Kira said, walking into the apartment with a bottle of shiraz.

"Good evening," Blayne said. "The spaghetti just went in the water, so we should be ready to eat in about fifteen minutes."

"Perfect. I'm starving. I missed lunch." Kira entered the living room, strolled right up to Ethan, extended her hand and said, "Kira Strickland."

Ethan stood up, grabbing Kira's hand, saying, "Ethan Bond. It's nice to meet you."

"Ethan? I thought your name was Roy."

"Long story," Blayne interjected. He watched as Kira raised an eyebrow. He could only imagine what was going through his friend's head. Thankfully, she didn't pursue the interrogation any further.

"So, I hear you need a charger." Kira put her purse on the table and pulled out a cable.

"Thanks. You're a godsend," Ethan said, putting the charging cable on the coffee table.

"Don't you want to charge your phone?" Kira asked.

"It can wait," Ethan replied.

"Kira, want to open the bottle of wine and pour us three glasses?" Blane asked, hoping to distract Kira before she went into full lawyer mode.

"Sounds good to me," she replied. "I'm guessing you have an opener somewhere in here."

"Of course, I do," Blayne started. "Let me find it." Blayne opened a drawer in the kitchen and rummaged through it before finding the wine opener. He then handed it to Kira. "Here ya go."

Kira cut the foil from the bottle and made quick work of the cork. She clearly had done this a few times.

"So, *Ethan*," Kira said, turning to look at him, "what brings you to Houston?"

"Short story or the long one?" Ethan said in response.

Thankfully, Blayne had prepared Ethan for Kira, so Ethan took everything in stride.

"Let's go with the short version…for now."

"Well, without giving too many specifics," Ethan started.

Kira's eyes narrowed at Ethan's statement. *Great… Suspicion is reading all over her face.* Thankfully, Blayne could tell Ethan was picking up on the change in Kira's facial expression.

"Part of the story is mine to tell, and parts aren't. For my part, I was seeing a guy casually who died. I needed to get away from things because it was overwhelming."

"Okay," Kira said. Blayne could sense the skepticism in her voice. "What aren't you telling me?"

"A lot, honestly. He was a celebrity and in the closet, so our 'relationship' was not exactly public. And before you ask, I'm pretty much a closet case myself—for professional reasons."

"What profession?" Kira asked.

"The entertainment business."

"That's how we met originally," Blayne jumped in, trying to take some of the heat off Ethan. "I was in New York seeing some shows, and he was there working on a project."

"And you two met on *EndZone*?" Kira asked.

"You told her that?" Ethan asked in disbelief.

"Trust me," Kira said. "There's very little Blayne doesn't tell me."

Blayne turned his attention to the spaghetti, continuing to stir the pasta to ensure it wasn't clumping together.

"So, yea," Ethan said. "We met on *EndZone*. We didn't hook up, if that's what you're thinking."

"I know," Kira responded. "Again, Blayne tells me everything."

"Good to know," Ethan said flatly. "So, we met, and we've been chatting ever since."

"Why did you lie about your name on *EndZone*?" Kira asked.

"Wow," Ethan said. "You really don't pull any punches, do you?"

"Nope. It's the lawyer in me. I learned a long time ago it's best to get to the point and not pussyfoot around things."

"Okay. Well, it's a dating app. Again, closeted for professional reasons. I've never used my actual name on those things. I also don't post face pics for the same reason."

"Why aren't you out? I don't get what would keep someone in the closet in this day and age."

"Well, if it was just me, I probably would be fully out, but it's not. I need to consider my coworkers."

Kira narrowed her gaze, but she said nothing. Blayne wished he could read minds to figure out what was going on in Kira's head.

"So, what are you two boys going to get up to while Ethan's here?"

"Honestly, I'm not sure," Blayne said. "I still have class this week, so we're going to play things by ear, I guess."

"As I said," Ethan started, "I needed to get away and let myself process everything that's been happening in my life, so I'm looking forward to hanging out with Blayne and getting to know him better."

The rest of dinner went by with no more third-degree interrogations from Kira. Blayne noticed that the longer Ethan and Kira were around each other, the more comfortable they seemed. He was glad he had someone like Kira in his corner, who was almost like a mother-hen, always there to protect and defend him.

After dinner, Ethan volunteered to help Kira clean up the kitchen. Blayne settled in on the couch and watched Ethan and Kira as they made quick work of the cleaning.

"Well, I best be getting home," Kira said once the dishes were in the dishwasher and the leftovers were safely put away. "Have an early morning tomorrow, working on a deposition for a civil rights case we're hoping to argue in front of the state supreme court."

"Pretty impressive," Ethan said.

"It'll be impressive if we can get the damn conservative court to see the importance of civil rights in this state," Kira said with a bit of venom. "Let's just say, Texas isn't exactly known for its progressive views on civil rights."

"Neither is Louisiana," Ethan responded.

"I thought you were from New York?" Kira asked.

"He's originally from New Orleans," Blayne interjected. "His business was started in New Orleans. Then they moved to New York to get things going. And now they're back in New Orleans since things are off and running."

"What he said," Ethan added.

Blayne watched Kira, trying to figure out what was running through her head. She'd slipped into lawyer mode again, so her face wasn't giving away any emotions.

She expelled a quick breath before saying, "Well, it was certainly nice to meet you, Ethan. I look forward to getting to know *all* about you while you're here."

"Likewise," Ethan responded.

Blayne opened the door for Kira and gave her a quick hug before she left the apartment. Once he closed the door, he let out a deep breath.

"Congratulations, you survived Kira interrogation 101."

"Do I get a medal or trophy?"

Blayne snorted. "No, but we don't end up with Kira deciding to sleep on the couch to make sure you don't kill me in my sleep, so that's something."

Ethan smiled at Blayne. Blayne noticed for the first time that Ethan's chin had dimples when he smiled. *He has chin dimples?*

"What?" Ethan asked suddenly. "Do I have something on my face?"

"Sorry… I just noticed your chin dimples when you smile."

"You're not the first person to comment about my chin dimples. I guess I'm genetically lucky is all."

"And I'm lucky you're staying in my apartment," Blayne said without thinking.

There was a brief silence before Ethan said, "And I'm glad you're letting me stay here. I can't explain how much this means to me. I know it had to be nerve-racking to let a stranger into your humble abode."

"You're not a stranger," Blayne said.

"You know what I mean. There aren't many guys out there who would be as welcoming as you have been."

"You are more than welcome. I'm glad you could visit, even if the circumstances behind your visit royally suck."

Ethan sat there for a moment. "Well, I know it's not too late, but I'm pretty tired. It's been a long day. I think I'm going to head off to bed."

"I understand. I'm going to watch the news before hitting the hay myself. I'll keep the sound low."

"Thanks," Ethan said.

Blayne thought he would lean in and hug him goodnight, but Ethan stood and headed off to the guest bedroom without making another sound.

\* \* \* \*

*Agent Murphy*

It was one a.m. when the email came in on Agent Murphy's account. She had submitted the paperwork for an expedited warrant for FreeMail right before five p.m., so she called a judge she knew at the federal courthouse in New Orleans.

"Why should I care about a gay tryst between a soap opera star and a member of a boy band?" Judge Katherine Vangelisti had asked.

Sarah had known she was walking some major lines on conjecture, but she went on a limb and took a wild chance. "Well, it's possible he's linked to the murder."

"*Possible* won't get you a warrant, Agent Murphy," Judge Vangelisti had warned. "Besides, do you even have evidence Ethan Bond and Daniel Hawthorne were having an affair?"

"DNA collected from Hawthorne's residence suggests the affair," Murphy had said, hoping the DNA didn't come back to bite her in the ass.

"Explain."

"A condom was retrieved from Hawthorne's residence, and it had DNA from both Hawthorne and Bond." She heard nothing, so she'd added. "One's DNA was on the outside, the other inside — if you get my drift."

"Okay, so you have evidence of the affair, but it's still pretty flimsy to get a warrant requiring FreeMail to fork over user information."

"I don't want all user information. I'm looking specifically for information on two email addresses in their system. That's it." *Did she even bother to read the warrant package I emailed*?

"I'm sorry, Agent. I don't think you have the evidence to secure this warrant. It's not like you're dealing with terrorism and need to cut through red tape quickly."

Murphy had thought for a second and decided she might as well try a Hail Mary. "Actually, there might be a connection to today's Peregrine Airlines explosion."

Murphy had woven a conspiracy involving the killings of Cynthia Dunning, Daniel Hawthorne and Ethan Bond. "It may be a coincidence, but Ethan's definitely connected to two murders. Then he magically misses being on an exploding plane because he disappeared at the airport." Murphy had avoided telling the judge she already knew Ethan had flown to Houston. If she got the warrant, it would make working with the Houston FBI easier, maybe.

"So, you think Ethan Bond, a known boy-band member, is a terrorist?"

"I would venture not, but there's definitely a link worth investigating. And who knows? We may find evidence in his email account. And since Ethan Bond has disappeared, we can't get his permission to enter the account."

"Hmm…" Judge Vangelisti had said over the phone.

"And if we use the 1986 Electronic Communications Privacy Act and the Patriot Act, we have legal grounds for requesting a warrant."

"How soon can you get this revised version of your request on my desk?"

"Twenty minutes?"

"Make it ten, and I'll sign it today. If it's more than that, it'll have to wait until the morning."

"I'll have it to you in nine," Murphy had promised.

True to her word, Murphy had the revised warrant request to Judge Vangelisti in nine minutes, and the judge signed it and had it emailed back in fifteen. As soon as she had the warrant, she'd called up FreeMail's counsel. After some legal maneuvering, FreeMail promised to send the information within twelve hours.

Murphy had gone home, eaten, watched some TV and sat waiting in her home for the email, which was where she now found herself at one a.m.

She read the email. The account was established from a public Internet Protocol — IP — address in New York about five years earlier. The company did not have a legal name associated with the account. And because the company didn't require identity verification to establish the account, there was no way to know who owned it. *Dammit!*

The lawyers surmised, since the warrant didn't ask about the contents of specific communications between individuals, they did not provide any specific correspondence information. All they offered was a litany of IP addresses used over the years to access the account.

Murphy ran through the six-page list of IP addresses. Either the person who used this account was purposefully bouncing email servers to make it hard to track, or this person accessed their email from around the world.

She forwarded the list to the FBI cyber forensic department and asked them to track the IP addresses. Hopefully, they could narrow down who the owner of the account was. She knew it was a long shot, but she had to try anything.

She wasn't ready to put out an official 'person of interest' notice on Ethan Bond yet. Technically, she wasn't in charge of the Peregrine Airlines explosion. Heck, it might not be terrorism at all. At this point, the FAA hadn't made an official determination for the crash, so Murphy was running only on the conspiracies she had running around in her head. She powered down her computer and headed to bed.

# Chapter Eleven

*Ethan*

Ethan was up at four-thirty a.m. the following day. He lay there in bed, trying to force his mind to shut down and go back to sleep, but he was awake, whether or not he liked it. He stared at the ceiling, willing himself back to sleep. He did the only thing he knew could exhaust him. He looked around and saw a box of tissues on the nightstand, grabbed a couple, and laid them next to him on the bed in the dark. He lifted his shirt and reached down into his shorts, pulling out his cock. The elastic waist of the shorts rested just below his balls. "Damn, I don't have any lube. I guess I'll do this the good, old-fashioned way." He spat into his hand.

He started stroking himself. Immediately, images of the last time he'd had sex with Danny filled his head. He remembered how they had fit perfectly together as Ethan had spooned into Danny from behind. Making love with Ethan as the big spoon and Danny as the little spoon had always been their favorite position. There was something intimate about the position — maximum body contact as Ethan's chest pressed into Danny's back. Ethan wrapped his arm around Danny's waist, pulling him close as he drove into him. Danny turned his head to kiss Ethan. *What the hell?* The face staring back at him was Blayne's. The face hungering for Ethan's lips was Blayne's. Ethan's cock exploded in his hands.

Ethan cleaned himself up and lay in the bed, still staring at the ceiling. Now, his head swam with what had just happened. Around five-thirty, he left the guest bedroom and headed for the bathroom in the hallway. He passed Blayne's room, pausing to hear the soft, rhythmic sound of Blayne's breath as he slept. *At least one of us is still asleep.*

He used the restroom, flushing the remnants of his mess. He looked at himself in the mirror and decided he might as well get a run in before Blayne was up and about. *I'll grab my cell and be on my way.* Ethan realized he had never charged his phone the night before. He walked into the living room and saw the charging cable right where he'd left it the previous night, when Kira had loaned it to him. He returned to the room to charge his phone when he realized he didn't have a USB wall charger to plug the darn thing into.

His watch had a GPS map tracking software built into it, so he at least wouldn't get himself lost. He put on a pair of shorts, a tank top, a baseball cap and sunglasses. The sunglasses were not the giant ones from the day before but a pair of more fashionable Oakley's. He slipped some cash into his pocket in case he picked something up while he was out.

He walked back through the living room, found a notepad on the bar separating the kitchen from the dining room slash living room area and wrote Blayne a quick note saying he'd headed out for a run and would be back soon.

Ethan slipped out of the apartment and left the front door unlocked so he could get back in. Thankfully, the sun was creeping over the horizon, so he wouldn't be running in the dark. He walked into the parking lot and stretched for a minute to get his body warm before taking off running. He turned on the GPS part of his watch before he took off east out of the apartment complex. He found a sidewalk in a residential area adjacent to his location and decided to stick to the smooth surface. He started slowly before building into a steady pace. He pounded the sidewalk, and his heart thumped smoothly.

After running for thirty minutes, he told his watch to plot the course back to the starting point. His watch vibrated whenever it wanted him to turn the corner, so he could glance down and see what direction he needed to head. Thankfully, the entire run was through residential streets, so he had no stoplights or traffic at this early hour.

When he was almost back to Blayne's, he noticed a small grocery store already open. He quickly noted the rest of the trip back to Blayne's apartment and turned off the GPS so he could slip inside the grocery store.

He had a sheen of sweat over his body, so he didn't want to spend too much time hanging out in public. A worker near the door who gave him a quick once-over greeted him. Ethan asked if they carried phone charger accessories. The young woman looked almost annoyed at having to do her job. Still, she pointed in a general direction and said, "Aisle seven," before she went back to watching the front door.

Ethan walked through the store and found aisle seven. He searched through the accessories and found a phone charging cord and a USB wall charger combination kit, so he grabbed the plastic vacuum-sealed package off the shelf. He turned around and headed toward the checkout counter. On his way, he passed the cosmetic line, and on the end of the row was a display for hair dyes.

*No? Should I? Couldn't hurt. It would definitely help me stay low.* He looked at the various kits and settled for one that had a guy on the box advertising natural blond hair. *I've always heard blonds have more fun.*

* * * *

*Blayne*

Blayne was an admitted non-morning person. He left his bedroom only because he smelled the enticing scent of freshly brewed coffee wafting through the house. *Ethan must be up already,* he thought to himself as he rolled over and looked at the clock on his nightstand. *Eight-thirty.* He slipped on a T-shirt before opening the door and heading into the bathroom. After relieving himself, he brushed his teeth. He noticed his fly was still open on his boxers, so he made sure the button was shut before leaving the bathroom and headed into the living room.

Blayne walked into the room and did a quick double-take because he wasn't ready for the blond guy sitting on his couch.

"Whoa," was all Blayne got out before Ethan looked up.

"Morning, sunshine." Ethan looked up from the book he was reading.

Blayne stared, not sure what to say. "Morning," Blayne mumbled. "Whatchya reading?"

"*Death Nail* by Robert Evans. It's on the *New York Times* bestseller list. Saw it at the store and picked it up on a lark."

"Cool," Blayne said. "I haven't read his work. I hear he's good. Unfortunately, I don't get much of a chance to read for pleasure these days. I have too much to read for my classes."

"Hope you don't mind. I picked up some coffee at the store and made a pot."

"You've been...busy."

"I was up at five-thirty, so I went for a run and found the grocery store a couple blocks from here."

Blayne stood there, staring at Ethan.

"Do I have something on my face?" Ethan asked.

"Oh, umm, sorry. I—"

"It's the hair?"

"Yeah," Blayne managed to get out.

"I felt like a change. I saw the display at the grocery store and thought, 'why not?' — so here I am."

"There you are." Blayne took a second to take it all in. Ethan had also shaved his stubble off. He barely looked like the guy he'd picked up at the airport the day before with the facial hair gone and the blond hair. "Looks good. Different...but good."

"Thanks."

Blayne walked into the kitchen. Ethan had already put out a mug on the countertop for him, so he poured himself a cup of coffee and added a dab of milk from the refrigerator. He noticed a few new items Ethan must have picked up when he was out and about.

"I didn't pick up anything for breakfast. I figured I'd take you out somewhere when you got up. Any ideas of a fun, trendy place to grab a bite?"

Blayne took a sip, noticing the bold flavor of the dark roast as it entered his mouth. *Not bad.* "Yeah, there's a coffee shop that serves breakfast not too far from here. Why don't I get ready, and we can head over there?"

"Sounds like a plan."

* * * *

The Dream Bean was a cozy little coffee house located a block from Pennington University. It was close enough for Blayne to walk there from his apartment, between classes or on his way home. Okay…so Blayne stopped in Dream Bean a lot. The café had enough room inside for a backroom where they roasted their beans, about eight tables with chairs inside and another ten on the raised porch in front of the store. The café had its own line of merchandise that lined one wall. There were beans in nightgowns, beans in bed, beans with nightcaps and beans drinking coffee. If you could put a bean in some kind of sleep, Dream Bean had already done it.

Blayne approached the main counter and recognized the employee immediately.

"Todd, I didn't know you worked here," Blayne said in as pleasant a voice as he could muster.

"Hey, Professor Dickenson. I started working here last week. What can I get ya?"

"I'm going to have the medium flat white with the egg white turkey wrap." Blayne turned to Ethan, who had sidled up next to him, "And you?"

"I'll have whatever he's having. I trust him."

"Sure thing." Blayne's student entered the information into the cash register and gave him the total. He pulled out his credit card.

"Blayne," Ethan started.

"My treat. I'll let you get dinner or something."

Ethan scrunched up his face, clearly not excited that Blayne was paying for breakfast. "Hey, you got coffee this morning. This one's on me."

Ethan nodded.

Blayne swiped his credit card and punched in his four-digit code. The beeping sound on the card reader let them all know it had gone through.

"Thanks, Professor! I'll have those right out to you," Todd said as he handed them a metal stand with the number ten atop.

"Want to sit outside?" Blayne asked. "It's not too hot yet, so it should be pretty nice."

"Sure," Ethan agreed. "Sounds like a plan."

The two walked out into the mid-morning sun. A few students had the same idea, so Blayne directed Ethan to a table in the corner, away from the students and the front door.

"So, who was that?" Ethan asked.

"The barista?" Blayne asked. Ethan nodded. "Todd Rice. He's in my English Composition class. He's a nice enough kid but a bit of a handful." He then told Ethan about the time Todd had sidled up next to him at the urinal and the most recent incident at the gym. "He doesn't know boundaries. And I don't know how to politely say, 'don't talk to me when you're naked or have your dick in your hand'."

"That would work."

"Yeah, if I wanted to get fired," Blayne said. "With this generation of kids, you gotta be careful with everything you say. You can't have anything seen as sexually suggestive or innuendo because you don't want to create a 'hostile' environment for your students."

"Really?"

"Yep. I agree with it somewhat, but I think we can sometimes go a bit overboard with everything."

"How so?"

"In today's litigious world, you've gotta be careful about every word coming out of your mouth. Heaven forbid you're not 'woke' enough for one student or are perceived as discriminatory toward one. I'm all about being polite and courteous and giving people the benefit of the doubt. These kids would rather sue or run to the Title IX coordinator if there is a perceived slight. We've lost all sense of discussion and debate in higher education. Instead, it's 'I'm more woke than you are, so you should be ashamed of yourself'."

"Yeah, the entertainment industry isn't anything like that. We've become more conscious about how we treat people after cases like those in the Me Too movement or even the Scott Rudin bullying allegations, but people's behavior has to be pretty abhorrent before anyone even bats an eyelash."

"Most industries aren't woke. I worry we're failing our students. How prepared will they be for the world if someone accidentally uses the wrong gender pronoun in a conversation? And trust me, these aren't exactly opinions I can go around sharing in my graduate classes because it's just as bad there. If your opinion doesn't align with the majority's, then you are evil and not to be tolerated."

"So, are you a Republican?"

"Oh, God, no. I'm not a sheep who buys into everything the radical left is selling. And that's the problem with today's students. Everything is so black and white, good or bad, right or wrong. They've lost all sense of gray. And heaven forbid you compromise or collaborate with 'the enemy' to get things done."

Blayne took a deep breath, looked at the sky, and let it out slowly. "Sorry. I get so worked up sometimes."

"It's cool. You're cute when you're all worked up. You turn this shade of pink."

"Thanks, I think," Blayne replied.

"Okay, guys," Todd said, approaching the table with a small tray. "Two medium flat whites and two egg white turkey wraps."

Todd set the cups and plates in front of them.

"Let me know if you need anything else," Todd said as he walked away.

"I think someone has a crush on his teacher?" Ethan joked.

"I hope not. I don't think I could handle that."

Ethan took a bite of the wrap. "This is fantastic."

"Glad you like it. It's my favorite thing on the menu. I've been known to grab one on the way home from class for dinner."

Blayne and Ethan enjoyed easy, casual conversation through the rest of breakfast. They were wrapping up when Blayne looked over and saw Kira walking up the steps.

"Kira!" Blayne yells. He watched as she spun her head in his direction.

"What are you two doing here?" she asked as she walked up to the table.

"Having some breakfast," Blayne said. "Shouldn't you be at work?"

"Coming back from a deposition. Thought I would stop in for a coffee pick-me-up."

"Want to sit down?" Ethan asked.

"Sure, but only for a minute."

Ethan stood and moved to a chair so Kira could sit directly next to Blayne.

"Thanks." Kira sat, took her sunglasses off, opened her purse, found the glasses' case and stowed them.

"You're more than welcome," Ethan responded.

"What was the deposition about?" Blayne asked.

"Simple civil rights case. A senior manager admitted in an email that he didn't hire a teller because she was too old. The moron wrote, *'we don't need any grannies in this place.'* It's a slam dunk age discrimination case. When the woman came to us and told us that she'd heard through the grapevine that she had been discriminated against, we told her the chances of winning were slim. But when we found the email during discovery, I almost jumped for joy. The manager did not know the bank had forwarded all his emails involving the position and the individual in question. He sat there slack-jawed when I pulled it out this morning. It was kind of fun to watch him squirm."

"Do you think this will go to trial?" Blayne asked.

"I doubt it. I could already tell the opposing counsel was trying to figure out how high the settlement will have to be to settle out of court. I'm sure I'll have an offer by the end of business today."

"Congratulations," Ethan said.

"Thank you. I can't stay long. I must get back to my office and let the partners know how it went this morning." She reached out and grabbed each of their free hands. "I hope you two have a great day." She gave them each a squeeze and stood.

When she was out of earshot, Blayne turned to Ethan and said, "Wow, she totally just touched you."

"Yeah, it was weird, wasn't it?"

"More than you know," Blayne said. "She's a total touch-me-not. Either she's drunk off her power after the deposition this morning, or she likes you."

"I'm going to hope it's the latter."

"I'm sure you're right. I mean, what's not to like?" Blayne said with a quick raise of his eyebrows.

Ethan took a sip of his flat white. "Do they have computers in there?"

"Yeah, they have a few public terminals."

"Cool, I'm going to run in and check my email. I totally forgot to charge my phone last night. It's back at your place now. I picked up a wall charger and a new cable when I was out this morning—which reminds me... I need to make sure Kira gets her cable back."

"I'll let her know she can come by and pick it up if I catch her on her way out."

Ethan walked back into The Dream Bean.

"Pick your chin up off the ground, lover boy," Kira said as she approached the table.

"What?" Blayne tried to stammer out.

"Please. You're talking to me. You have the hots for Ethan."

Blayne sat up a little taller as Kira sat down again. "I'm neither confirming nor denying I think Ethan's kinda hot. But it doesn't matter. I doubt he sees me the same way. Besides, his lover was murdered. Not exactly the best way to start a new relationship."

"Who needs a relationship? Just take him for a ride or two."

"Kira!"

She laughed as she rummaged in her purse, pulled out her sunglasses and put them back on. "Hey, you're both adults. So, if you want to have some adult fun, go for it. It's about time you did."

Without waiting for a response, Kira stood up with her coffee and walked away. Once she was out of sight, he remembered he'd forgotten to tell her about the charging cable.

# Chapter Twelve

*Dr. Hennigan*

Dr. Hennigan read the after-action report from Denzili and Richardson. From what she could tell, everything had gone entirely according to plan and protocol. The two had slipped in and slipped out, with no one being remotely aware. She also pulled out the initial analysis from the FAA. Her person inside the National Transportation Safety Board had already forwarded several doctored reports.

After reading, she shot her contact a quick email.

*Any way we can blame this on a rogue drone? It would help us kill a couple of problems. We're looking to introduce federal legislation to tighten restrictions on non-commercial drones. This would give our people some further evidence to point out to push our cause.*

She hit send and waited for a response.

She knew she wouldn't wait too long. No one took too long to return her emails. Taking your time or ignoring her was never good for anyone's health.

Ping!

She opened the email and read the cursory response.

*I'll get the drone theory circulated today. We can add drone parts to the mix in the swamp when we're out scavenging later. There's still so much we haven't found in the debris field. Also, don't worry. The black box won't be found.*

*Good, everything is in cleanup mode.* There was a light rap on her door. "Enter."

"Dr. Hennigan," Ms. Wilson started as she opened and closed the door. "The email address linked to Ethan Bond was just located at a coffee shop outside Houston. The IP address was public, so we doubt he'll be there by the time we have operatives in place, but we at least now have a general location in Houston to look."

"Thank you, Ms. Wilson. The more eyes we have out there, the faster he'll be to find."

"Actually, we pulled an image from social media. Someone uploaded it from their phone. We immediately scrubbed the picture from social media and deleted it from the person's phone."

"What was the image?"

Ms. Wilson lifted her tablet, punched a few things on the screen, and said, "It's in your inbox."

Dr. Hennigan opened the file and saw a picture of a woman with her hand on Ethan's. It wasn't a perfect shot of Ethan. Half his face was covered in a ball cap and sunglasses, but it was clearly him.

"We double-checked identity confirmation through facial recognition?" Dr. Hennigan asked.

"Of course, ma'am. I did that before I bothered you. From this image and the opening of the email at the same establishment, we know Ethan Bond was there less than thirty-five minutes ago."

"Indeed," Dr. Hennigan said, steepling her hands under her chin.

"Are Denzili and Richardson back yet?"

"I think they should land in the next thirty minutes. Why?"

"Once they've been debriefed, let's send them to Houston. They need to finish the acquisition and liquidation."

"Yes, ma'am." Ms. Wilson turned to leave.

"One more thing, Ms. Wilson…"

"Yes?" Ms. Wilson asked, turning around once more.

"Any word from Ms. Brighton and her audit team?"

"None yet. There was a problem with her plane in San Diego. I *can't imagine* what happened there," Ms. Wilson said, her eyes glittering with mischief.

"These things happen," Dr. Hennigan said, raising a single eyebrow and one corner of her mouth.

\* \* \* \*

*Agent Murphy*

Agent Murphy sat at her desk, tracking Ethan's and Blayne's movements through the Houston Airport on her computer monitor. She'd gotten the TSA to send over the video files that morning. She had to say it was a missing person case again because the National Transportation Safety Board said the explosion was looking more and more like an accident. The plane may have collided with a drone in the air.

Jason Wrench

"Where y'at?" Agent Harper asked, standing in Murphy's doorway without knocking.

She'd jumped a little in her seat at the sudden voice but did her best to mask her annoyance at being interrupted. "I'm frustrated at the moment, watching Ethan Bond and an unknown male at the Houston Airport and trying to see if I can get any information on the unknown male."

"Why?"

"Why?" Murphy said, spinning a little in her chair to face Harper. "Something doesn't sit right with this case. I mean, last night, I would have sworn that Ethan was connected to the murders on the houseboat, then slipped out of New Orleans right before the flight he was supposed to be on exploded, which connected the events somehow."

"How? The NTSB's all over the airwaves saying it's an accident."

"Since when did the NTSB do anything quickly? That doesn't strike you as odd?"

"Murphy, you're looking for a forest fire because you saw a little smoke in the air. Sometimes, coincidences happen in life. We don't have to like them. And they sure as hell screw with investigations, but that doesn't mean they don't happen."

"And sometimes coincidences are a clear sign something is going on. I don't know which it is here."

"You're like a dog with a new bone, aren't ya? If this is how you want to have a good time, do it. I'd rather head over to some hole in the wall, listen to jazz and get shit-faced. To each their own, I guess."

"Is there a reason you dropped by this morning?"

"Yeah, I wanted to give you a heads-up. I heard from Geraldine Jackson's assistant that she knew about the warrant from FreeMail last night. She got an earful this morning from Judge Vangelisti. The judge is pissed that you used terrorism as a ploy to get private email data since the NTSB has ruled the explosion an accident."

"Fuck!"

"Yeah, fuck is right. Thought I'd see if you wanted to get out of here for a bit to let Jackson cool off before she finds you."

Without saying another word, Murphy stood, grabbed her coat from the back of her chair and put it on. She then unlocked the top drawer of her desk to grab her shield and service revolver. She holstered the gun and pocketed the shield.

"Where are we going?" Murphy asked.

"Another Broken Egg?"

"You love that place."

"Got the best beignets in New Orleans," Harper said with a smile. "And the coffee ain't half bad, either."

She followed Harper out of the building and found their usual sedan parked out front. She threw Harper the keys. "You drive. I'm going to make a phone call on the way."

They got into the sedan, buckled up and Harper merged into the traffic. Murphy fished in her pocket and found the business card ZERO's manager had given her the day before. She dialed Ron Hightower's number.

"Hightower," a voice said in a clipped fashion.

"Mr. Hightower. Special Agent Sarah Murphy."

"Agent Murphy," Hightower responded, his voice changing in recognition. "How can I help you this morning?"

"Ethan," she said, letting the boy's name hang in the air for a second.

"Ethan, what? You find him?"

"We tracked him through airport security videos. He boarded a Roadrunner flight to Houston."

Murphy heard Hightower swear. "Sorry," he apologized. "Not sure how my people missed seeing him get on another plane."

"In their defense," Murphy said, "he'd disguised himself. It would have been easy to overlook. He'd wanted to slip away."

"What the hell is Ethan doing?" Hightower said into the phone.

"I was hoping you could tell me. Do you know if he has friends or relatives in the Houston area? We're trying to track down where he's staying."

"I don't know of anyone specifically. I'll ask the band and see if they have any ideas. Can I call you back at this number? I'm heading over to our rehearsal space now. I can get back to you in the hour?"

"Perfect. I'll be waiting." Agent Murphy pushed the end-call button.

\* \* \* \*

*Zach*

Zach lounged on the couch in the hotel suite listening to his iPhone. He glanced up when he saw the suite door open. Hightower and Rawlins walked into the room.

"Guys," Rawlins yelled, "can I get everyone in the living area, please?"

Zach pulled out his AirPods and sat up on the couch. Ric and Orr left their rooms where they'd been napping and sauntered into the living area. Ric had some pretty bad bed hair going on, and Orr was a rumpled mess. Of the three of them, Zach was the only one who looked even remotely awake.

"Okay. What do you know about Ethan's disappearance?" Rawlins asked.

The bandmates looked at each other before they mumbled some version of *nothing*.

"Let me rephrase," Rawlins started. "What do you know about anyone in Houston? Does Ethan have family or friends in the Houston?"

"None I know of," Zach said. He looked at the other guys, who shrugged. "What's this about?"

"I got off the phone with the FBI," Hightower said. "Ethan flew the coop and headed to Houston. Any idea why?"

"Not at all," Zach replied without hesitating. "Let me call Stephanie and see if she knows anything."

"Who?" Rawlins asked.

"Stephanie, Ethan's best friend," Zach said. "If anyone knows if Ethan has family or friends in Houston, it's going to be her."

"Do it."

Zach walked out of the living area and into his bedroom to get a bit of privacy before looking up Stephanie in his phone contacts. He hit the call button and listened to the ringing.

"Zach? Any news?"

"Not yet," Zach said. "We still don't know what's going on. We found out Ethan flew to Houston yesterday. Do you know if he knows anyone there?"

There was a lull on the other end of the line. "Honestly, I don't know," Stephanie admitted. "I think I know most of his family and friends, but we both know Ethan keeps some parts of his life private."

"Yeah, I know. He thinks no one knows, but he'd be surprised to find out how all of us pretend not to."

"I take it he still hasn't responded to your messages or texts?" Stephanie asked.

"Just a cryptic text about 'needing a breather'. Beyond that, nothing. You?"

"I didn't even get an obscure text. What is he doing? This is *so* not like him."

"I would say he's having a midlife crisis, but since when do twenty-five-year-olds have midlife crises?" Zach heard a quick laugh.

"Well, call me if you hear anything," Stephanie said. "I'll do the same."

"Thanks," Zach said as he hung up the phone. He drew a heavy breath and let it out before returning to the living area.

As soon as he opened the door, Rawlins asked, "Anything?"

"Nope, she's as clueless about all this as we are."

"So, where does this leave the rest of us?" Orr asked. "I don't want to be insensitive, but Ethan's timing here was pretty crappy."

"Orr!" Zach said.

"Sorry, dude," Orr said flatly. "He screwed us all with his little disappearing act."

Zach wanted to say something scathing in rebuke, but he knew Orr was right. Ethan had left them all hanging, which was totally not cool.

"Well, I'm glad you asked," Rawlins cut in. "I've asked Sally Higgins to fly back from Seattle. She's going to rehearse with the three of you on a new version of the show in case we can't find Ethan."

"What?" Zach blurted. "Shouldn't we at least wait a few days?"

"I know he's your best friend, Zach," Hightower interrupted, "but, we have obligations and millions of dollars on the line already. If we delay any longer, we'll all be out a ton of money. So as much as I wish we had time to wait for Ethan to come back to us, we have to move forward and prepare for a worst-case scenario."

Zach wanted to say something to counteract Hightower and Rawlins, but they were right. Ethan had royally screwed over everyone.

*What the hell is Ethan thinking?*

\* \* \* \*

*Dr. Hennigan*

Dr. Hennigan knocked on her mother's office door for the second time that day. She waited for the buzz before entering.

Her mom stood in front of a bank of display monitors, watching an operation going down in the Middle East in real time. The Foundation had an asset captured and tortured, so a small strike force was sent in on a retrieval mission. If rescuing was impossible, the asset would be liquidated.

Everyone, even the chairwoman and vice-chair, knew liquidation was a possibility. It was part of their line of work. The Foundation tried to stress that liquidation was always the last thing they wanted to do after investing so much time and energy into their training. Still, The Foundation was always greater than the individual members.

Dr. Hennigan stood beside her mother, knowing better than to interrupt her viewing of the mission in progress. The helmet cameras captured death-shot after death-shot as the team made their way through what looked like an abandoned warehouse.

The operation was borderline picture-perfect regarding its infiltration and sweep of the warehouse. The team finally came upon a clearly booby-trapped room. One specialist quickly worked the trap and hesitantly opened the door to ensure there wasn't a secondary one.

A gunman entered the hallway on one of the camera feeds, and one of their operatives put a bullet between his eyes before he raised his weapon. *Good shot!*

The strike force entered the room and found their asset. Unfortunately, she was already dead.

"Alpha to Mission Control," one agent said. "The target is down. How should we proceed?"

A voice chirped over the intercom, "Alpha, this is Mission Control. You are clear for disposition."

"Copy, Alpha out."

Dr. Hennigan watched as one operative set an explosive device under the seat where the asset had been bound.

"I trained that asset," Deborah said, a somber look on her face. "She was an excellent acquisition for almost two decades. I hate this is how her legacy ended. Fucking Aegis Concordat! How did they even know she was one of ours?"

The two watched as the strike force exited the building before it exploded behind them. A Blackhawk was waiting to exfiltrate the team back to a Foundation staging area. Once the helicopter left the ground, Deborah clicked on the monitors and turned to her daughter. "How can I help you?"

"I wanted to give you a quick status update on Target E. We've traced his email use to a coffee shop in

Houston. We also found a picture of him at the same location, so we're sending Denzili and Richardson to finish the job."

Deborah made her way back to her desk without saying a word. Once seated, she gestured for her daughter to sit in the chair in front of her desk.

"Your grandmother is not happy," Deborah said with no emotion. "She recommended I reassign this case—"

"Mother—"

"I told her," Deborah said, raising her voice to cut off her daughter's objection, "that I fully believe you and your team will finish the job. Of course, it would be helpful if Ms. Brighton was here completing her audit. Too bad she was delayed."

Dr. Hennigan thought about saying she had nothing to do with the delay, but she knew her mother wouldn't believe her, so she sat still and quiet.

"For their sake, I hope Denzili and Richardson get it right this time. Let's say your grandmother is looking for heads to roll after the explosion missed Target E."

"If there are any more problems, I'll take care of Denzili and Richardson myself."

"I'm going to hold you to that."

\* \* \* \*

*Agent Murphy*

Murphy and Harper finished breakfast when Murphy's phone vibrated in her pocket. She pulled it out and looked to see who was calling.

"Shit!"

"Who is it?" Harper asked.

"The boss," she said, immediately standing. "I'm going to take it outside."

She started maneuvering through the restaurant as she accepted the call. "Agent Murphy," she said as she was opening the door.

"Agent Murphy, it's Geraldine Jackson's office. Hold to speak to Special Agent in Charge Jackson," a voice said.

There was a momentary pause before an audio recording was picked up mid-message, extolling the virtues of the FBI. She walked toward the parking lot. The sun was already up and heating the muggy town. They'd been on a series of recording-breaking-temperature days with temps hitting the low nineties. Though October heat wasn't unheard of, Murphy was ready for things to cool off in New Orleans for many reasons. She found some shade on the side of the building and leaned against the wall.

"Agent Murphy. What in the hell is going on? I got read the riot act by a federal judge and the director this morning."

Murphy stood and collected her thoughts, not knowing quite where to start.

"Talk!" Agent Jackson's voice said, with no emotion over the phone.

"Yes, ma'am." Thankfully, Murphy knew lying to the boss was dangerous, so she laid out her entire reasoning and investigation. She could hear Jackson's pencil moving over a legal pad over the phone. Jackson was a furious notetaker, and Murphy had seen her fill an entire pad in one meeting.

When Murphy finished the case rundown, Jackson said, "Let me look at something really fast...." She then heard the clickity-clackity noise of Jackson's keyboard.

"Your assumption about the DNA was correct. I read the report. The trace evidence on the contraception found in Mr. Hawthorne's place was a match for Mr. Bond. However, since Bond is not a suspect in any crime, I better not see that information reported anywhere."

"It won't come from my end of the investigation, sir," Murphy responded. "I have no desire to out anyone. But I know Stephen McNeil from RNN has the story about Hawthorne and Bond's relationship. He's like a dog with a bone."

There was a huff. "I've dealt with Mr. McNeil before. He's itching to make a name for himself. He's one rung above working at *The National Enquirer*. Send him directly to the FBI National Press Office if he reaches out to you again. I don't even want so much as a 'no comment' coming out of your mouth on camera. Understood?"

"Yes, ma'am."

"You're lucky, Agent Murphy. The physical evidence and your logic support the claims you made in the warrant. I wouldn't plan on taking a warrant directly to Judge Vangelisti anytime soon, though. Someone leaned on her heavily. Not sure who it was, but she was not a happy camper this morning. I'll make sure you have coverage from the director. But in the future, anything like this is to be run by me first. Understood?"

"Yes, ma'am," Murphy said, wiping sweat from her brow. *Damn, it is getting hot out here.*

"Now, with all that said. I have other news for you."

"Yes?" Murphy asked hesitantly.

"The man Ethan Bond left the Houston Airport with is named Blayne Dickenson. The director had a few field agents looking into this missing person situation himself."

"What do we know about this man?"

"Not much. I'll email you the dossier I received."

"What should I do with this information, sir?"

"Nothing. Officially, this is neither a missing person nor a *terrorism* case. And since I have evidence Mr. Bond was busy during Cynthia Dunning and Daniel Hawthorne's murders, he is no longer a concern to you. Maybe it's time you refocus your energy on who killed Dunning and Hawthorne."

"What evidence, ma'am?"

"The director has seen Mr. Bond's schedule, along with a video of Ethan's whereabouts at the time of the murders."

Murphy wanted to let out a series of 'fucks' over the phone but held it in. Instead, she asked, "Why did we not have this information ourselves?"

"The footage was taken by one of Mr. Bond's press team and uploaded to the cloud around three a.m. this morning. Someone anonymously sent the director the link."

"That doesn't seem suspicious at all."

"My thoughts exactly, Agent Murphy. I won't lie to you. Something about all this doesn't sit well with me. I feel like our office is being manipulated. Unfortunately, this manipulation comes from the top, so there's not a damn thing you or I can do about it."

# Chapter Thirteen

*Ethan*

After breakfast, Ethan and Blayne headed back to the apartment. Blayne had to teach that afternoon, followed by a graduate seminar he was taking. Ethan was glad he got some alone time with Blayne that morning before Blayne had to head off for the day.

"Dude, I'll be fine. I have no problem lounging around your apartment for the day. Honestly, it's been ages since I've had nothing scheduled, so it will be nice to chill for once. Besides, I have the new book I bought this morning."

"Okay," Ethan responded. "If you need anything, call my cell."

"Speaking of cells, I should probably finally check mine. I'm almost worried to see what messages people have left since I up and disappeared."

Ethan noticed the strange look cross Blayne's face, but Blayne said nothing. Instead, Blayne went about putting together his attaché case for the day.

"God, I feel like we're Ozzie and Harriet. I'm leaving for work while you stay home eating bonbons on the couch."

"More like Lucy and Ricky," Ethan countered. "I promise not to blow anything up while you're gone." '

"Lucy, you've got some 'splaining to do!" Blayne replied in a dismal Ricky Ricardo impersonation. "Well, I'm out of here. I have enough time to get to class."

"Have fun, Teach," Ethan said. He walked Blayne to the front door of his apartment, which felt odd. *I'm acting like I own the place.* Ethan reached out and grabbed Blayne, pulling him in for a quick bear hug. "Thanks for everything. You have no idea how much this means to me."

Blayne gave him a quick peck on the cheek before pulling away. "It's not a problem at all. I enjoy having you around. But I hope you take the time to deal with whatever's going on with you. In the immortal words of Lucille Ball, *'It's a helluva start, being able to recognize what makes you happy.'* Or maybe you need, *'Not everything that is faced can be changed, but nothing can be changed until it is faced.'* Lucy's great for a lot of wisdom."

Ethan pulled away a bit and looked Blayne in the face. "You sure know your *I Love Lucy.*"

"If you get bored, I have the full series on Blu-ray under the TV," he responded with a quick flash of his eyebrows and a mischievous grin. Blayne turned the door handle behind him and left the apartment.

Blayne was right, though. But then, so was Lucy. Ethan had a lot of shit he hadn't been dealing with. How did Blayne put it? *"You can't change everything, but you can't change anything until you face it?"* Guess *it's time for me to face the music.*

Ethan walked through the apartment to the guest bedroom and found his cell phone. The green light on top showed that it was fully charged. He unplugged the device and powered it on.

As soon as it powered on, he saw the stream of texts immediately start blowing up his phone. He puffed his cheeks and let out a slow breath before diving into them. He felt his eyes widen more and more with each new text he read. The more he read, the more panicked he became. *What the fuck? What the actual fuck?* The first texts were Rawlins and Zach sounding worried, which turned into Rawlins sounding pissed about Ethan's disappearing act. Those turned to fear as his brain registered what had happened after he'd left New Orleans.

*Wait! Back up! The plane exploded?* Ethan inhaled and exhaled in short waves as his pulse raced. His head started to fog as his mind raced. Ethan had experienced enough stage fright in his early days, so he knew to bend over and put his head between his knees as he tried to return his breath back to normal. Once he was no longer light-headed, he read the text from Zach saying they were safe and hadn't been on the plane.

Ethan opened the RNN app and looked at the top headlines on his phone. He quickly found the report about the explosion at the airport the afternoon before. *Whoa! That was the plane ZERO was supposed to fly to Seattle?* He read the information in the texts and the news report. However, it took his brain a second to process the incoming information.

He kept reading through the stream of texts. The ones from Hightower and Rawlins had once again become pissy, but that was to be expected. The last one from Zach said Sally Higgins was flying back to New Orleans to re-choreograph the show with the three remaining members.

*Rawlins isn't saying he's pissed, but he's pissed. At this rate, they're going to find someone whose name starts with "e" to replace you. I think they should find another "o" guy so we can rebrand as ZORO. I hope you're well.*
*Peace,*
*Zach*

He needed to talk to someone but wasn't ready to talk to anyone in ZERO. He scrolled through the names in his phone and called the one who was probably the most important name in his Rolodex...Stephanie. He hit call.

"Where the fuck are you?" Stephanie said, answering the phone. "What the fuck are you doing? Everyone is worried about you." She rapidly peppered him with more questions, not even giving him the chance to answer any of them. Ethan knew this was her way of showing concern, so he let her go on until she took a breath, and he could naturally jump in.

"I'm fine. I'm in Houston. I'm at the house of a guy I know. I forgot my charger, picked one up this morning and finally got my cell working again." He paused, waiting for Stephanie to say something.

"Thank God!" she finally said. "I barely slept last night. I was worried sick. If you ever disappear like this again, Ethan Bond, I will hunt your ass down and make sure it stays lost forever."

"I'm sorry. I really am. I needed space."

"I get it...more than you realize," Stephanie said, her voice softening. "I spoke to Danny's mom today. She's still in shock."

"I can only imagine," Ethan started. "No, I can't even imagine. I'm a fucked-up mess, and I lost a *friend.* She lost her son."

"She's holding it together somehow. She asked about you."

"She did?"

"Yep. Even though Danny never *came out* to her, mothers know." Ethan could hear the hesitation in her voice before she added, "I think Danny may have seen your relationship as more than he let on. Now, I'm admittedly speaking out of my ass here. Still, his mother knew about you and that you were a special person in his life, which leads me to believe she was aware you were together."

"Whoa," Ethan said. "I kind of wish Danny had said something to me. I purposefully never allowed myself to develop feelings for him — well, at least not romantic feelings. He was also so crystal clear with his intentions. I always thought we were on the same page."

"Danny was a complicated man. That's for sure. I think he loved you the best he could."

"Sadly, I guess we'll never know," Ethan said, his voice trailing. He wiped a tear away from his eye as he closed his eyes and attempted to hold back the rest of the flood works building inside him. "So, switching gears. Have you talked to Zach?"

"Yes," Stephanie said. "They're all worried about you. They know you're in Houston."

"Really? How?"

"The FBI tracked you down."

"Holy fuck!"

"Yeah. Your producer or manager — you know, one of them — pulled some strings to get them to look into your disappearance. You need to call him."

"I will. I promise. I need to work out a few things in my head before I do."

"Can I at least tell him we've talked?"

"Sure. I wouldn't ask you to hide that from him." He pondered what he should say next. He knew Zach and the guys had a right to know he was safe, but he still wanted a few days to figure everything out for himself before he headed back. "I guess I should at least respond to his texts."

"That would be a start," Stephanie encouraged. "Well, I have a meeting in ten minutes and need to prepare for it. I'll call you when I get home. Cool?"

"Of course, it is."

They said their goodbyes and hung up. He pondered for a moment what he wanted to say in his text to Zach. He finally started typing.

*I'm safe. Something happened in my personal life, and I needed a few days to get over it. I don't want to get into it in a text, but let's just say I needed some serious alone time and didn't know what else to do. I should be back in New Orleans by the end of the week. I promise to explain to everyone when I get back.*

*E.*

\* \* \* \*

*Blayne*

After his seminar in Educational Theories, Blayne swung by Flip'N Pizza to pick up an order he'd called in when he was leaving campus. Flip'N or F'N Pizza, as most people called the place, was a local establishment created by a second-generation Italian family. By sight, if not by name, Blayne ate there enough that he knew everyone. Rosolino, the matriarch, sat behind the cash register. Blayne guessed she was in her late seventies or early eighties, but she still had the energy of a woman half her age.

"Mr. Dickenson, good to see you this evening. Your order's almost ready. I noticed you ordered more food than usual. Have a date tonight?" Rosolino asked with a playful smile and a wink.

"Nope. But I have a houseguest in from New Orleans who's staying with me."

"New Orleans, did you say? Awful business there with what happened yesterday."

"What happened?" Blayne asked, with a puzzled look swimming across his face.

"The Peregrine Airlines explosion?"

"I guess I've been a bit too preoccupied to have even seen the news. I know nothing about it."

"Well, the news is reporting some serious equipment failure after the plane collided with one of those stupid drones during takeoff." Blayne watched as the old woman beckoned him to lean in closer before she whispered, "Between you and me, I think the CIA assassinated someone. I mean...how did they determine the cause of an explosion this quickly when most of it is still somewhere in the swamp?"

"*Porca vaca*, Mother," a voice yelled from the kitchen. "We can still hear you back here."

The youngest member of the Randasso family, Mansueto, came out of the back. The man was in his early- to mid-twenties. He was about six feet tall, had olive-brown skin, dark black hair and brown eyes one could get lost in for days. The five o'clock shadow he was sporting added another layer of sex appeal to the guy. Blayne had had a crush on Manny when he'd opened the door to his apartment and found Manny standing on his doorstep with the square box in hand. In that moment, Blayne had hoped his pizza delivery boy porn fantasy was about to happen. Sadly, it hadn't.

"Don't listen to this old woman," Manny said with a smile. "She's a member of the tinfoil hat club. Never met a conspiracy theory she didn't like."

"Listen here, *il nipotino*. I trust those people on Reddit more than I trust the lame-stream news media."

"Whatever," Manny said with an over-exaggerated roll of his eyes. "You know I love you, you crazy old woman." Manny turned around and headed back into the kitchen. Before returning to the room, he spun around and whispered, "Tinfoil Hat Club!"

Blayne stifled the laugh trying to escape him. Rosolino entered Blayne's bill into the cash register, saying, "It'll be thirty-four dollars and ninety-nine cents."

Blayne reached into his back pocket and pulled out his billfold. He flipped it open and handed her a credit card. She took the card and swiped it as they waited for the transaction to go through. The little machine started spitting out a receipt. Rosolino gave Blayne the receipt and a pen. He added ten dollars and one cent to the bill to make it an even forty-five.

"Here you go, Mr. Blayne," Manny said, handing him a couple of boxes and a single bag. "I put plates, napkins and plastic wear in the bag. I slipped in a couple of cannoli for you and your beau, on the house.

I figured you deserved restitution after listening to a *persona pazza*…crazy person."

Blayne thanked them and headed back into the early evening heat. *Wait, a second? Did he say the cannoli for me and my beau?* He smiled and shook his head. When he got to the apartment, he one-armed the pizza boxes, fished out his keys and unlocked the door.

"Honey, I'm home," he yelled in his best Ricky Ricardo impersonation as he pulled the door closed with his foot. "Hope you're hungry. I swung by and picked up pizza on the way back from class."

Blayne put the boxes on the counter. Ethan wasn't in the living room. *Probably in the bedroom.* Blayne walked through the apartment and knocked lightly on the closed door. He waited to hear if there was movement inside. After not hearing anything, he turned the nob and walked in.

Ethan was lying on the bed, face down, his head turned away from the doorway. Blayne couldn't help himself. He took a moment to examine Ethan's chiseled, god-like back. Ethan's shorts rode down low enough on his hips that Blayne could see the start of a farmer's tan. And when Blayne's gaze traveled south to Ethan's perfectly sculpted ass, he swore Michelangelo's David's ass had nothing on Ethan's amazing-looking bubble butt. Blayne felt himself stirring in his own pants. *Down boy!* Blayne willed his member back to a swinging state before walking into the room.

He crossed the room, gently put one of his hands on Ethan's shoulder and jostled him a bit. Ethan yelped and jerked away from him, rolling over quickly, looking like a cat who had been startled.

"Oh shit!" Ethan let out.

"Sorry," Blayne said, his eyes going wide. "I tried knocking and calling your name. Didn't mean to freak you out."

Blayne could see Ethan's heart rate was already going back to normal as Ethan's chest's fast rise and fall slowed.

"Sorry," Ethan said. "I guess I was sleeping."

Blayne glanced down and noticed the remnants of what looked like had been a pretty hot dream from the way the thick outline in Ethan's shorts was trying to escape and point in his direction. Blayne felt himself getting hard again, so he spun around and said, "I'll get everything in the kitchen laid out. Come, eat when you're put together."

He closed the door behind him and walked down the hallway. *Too bad sausage isn't on the menu tonight.* He flicked himself in the crotch, muttering, "Down boy. Heel." He shook his head from side to side as he tried to get the images of Ethan's fucking hot body out of his mind.

He grabbed the bag with the plates and cannoli, put the dishes on the table and slipped the cannoli in the fridge to keep them cool. He then put the pizza and breadsticks on the table. He heard Ethan come in behind him.

"Smells amazing," Ethan said.

Blayne hoped Ethan would come in behind him, slip his arms around him and pull him in for a long embrace, but Ethan pulled out a chair and sat down. Blayne stopped himself from sighing before asking, "What can I get you to drink?"

"Water's good for me."

"Two waters coming up." Blayne grabbed two bottles of water out of the fridge. He knew plastic wasn't the best for the environment, but sometimes convenience trumped social conscience.

"Here ya go," Blayne said, tossing a bottle to Ethan. Ethan reached out and snagged the flying bottle with ease. "Good catch."

"I guess all those years playing wide receiver paid off."

"You played football?"

"Through high school and some of college."

"Well, that explains your kickass build," Blayne said before he realized what he'd said.

"Yeah, between football, dancing and running, I rarely see the inside of a gym. If I'm frank, I've never been a fan of gyms," Ethan replied.

"Dancing?"

"You think I have a kickass physique?"

Ethan motioned as if to say 'you first'. "As if you don't know your body is fucking amazing. You could be on the cover of *Men's Fitness*."

"Why, thank you, kind sir. I'm genetically gifted. And while I haven't seen much of you yet, you're easy on the eyes yourself there, professor. As for dancing, I have a background in dance. I did some musical theater, so there's that, too."

"Wow, star jock and dancing queen. Who'd have guessed?"

"Who are you calling a queen?" Ethan joked as he flexed one of his biceps in his direction.

"Eat your pizza," Blayne said.

"I see what you're doing. You're just trying to fatten me up," Ethan joked.

"Yep. Now eat." Blayne reached for a plate, a couple of breadsticks and the marinara dipping sauce. "I got you your own dipping sauce. Us Texans have a thing against double-dipping anything. It started with chips and salsa but works equally well with any foods you can dip."

"What if you're eating with your boyfriend?" Ethan asked.

"I can kiss you, rim you and swallow your cum, but don't you *dare* double dip a chip in my salsa. That's nasty," Blayne said with a huge grin.

"You Texans are weird," Ethan said, his face contorting into an exaggerated look.

"Sure thing, swamp boy — eat your pizza."

Ethan laughed and grabbed a plate, a couple of breadsticks and a couple of slices. "My dietitian, if I had one, would not find this meal healthy at all. It's carbs, carbs and more carbs."

"There's cheese and meat. That's protein," Blayne added.

"Hmm...*protein*," Ethan said seductively before taking a bite of his pizza.

"Kinky. Should I leave you two alone?"

Ethan was still chewing, so he let out a guttural moan that sounded like half orgasm and half choking goose. Blayne busted out laughing. He was glad he had nothing in his mouth, or he'd have spit across the room. When he finally got it under control, he looked at Ethan and asked, "What the hell was that? An impression of two prairie dogs fucking a moose?"

Ethan scrunched up his face and looked at Blayne, and said, "Two prairie dogs fucking a moose?"

"It was the first thing that popped into my head. I originally thought about saying 'a goose having an orgasm,' but thought I'd rein myself in a bit," he said sheepishly.

"Well, you definitely have a colorful imagination."

The buzzing sound on the table distracted Blayne for a second. He flipped it over and saw 'Reich' on the screen. "Give me a second. I need to take this. She never calls me at home." Blayne hit the call button and raised it to his ear, "Dr. Reich?"

"Blayne, I wanted to let you and Kira know, but I don't have her cell number." The woman on the other end sounded strange. Blayne knew Dr. Reich to be a confident and brilliant person, so this disoriented woman sounded off.

"Dr. Reich, what's wrong?" Blayne asked, lowering his voice to calm her.

"It's Jamie," she spat out quickly between what sounded like tears. "He's been attacked. They took him into surgery."

Blayne felt the blood drain from his face. He looked across the table at Ethan, whose face turned solemn. "Pennington?" Blayne asked.

"Yes, the university hospital."

"Are you in the ED?"

"Yes," still sounding confused.

"I'm on my way. And I'll call Kira and let her know."

Blayne hung up the phone. "There's an emergency. I've got to go."

"Give me a minute to throw on something more appropriate," Ethan said.

"You don't need to—"

"Shut it," Ethan said with a remarkable amount of compassion as he reached across the table, grabbed Blayne's hand and stared into his eyes. "I'm coming."

\* \* \* \*

## Blayne

Blayne and Ethan walked through the sliding doors into the Pennington University Hospital Emergency Department—ED. The institutional white walls and fluorescent lighting gave it a dreary look in the best of times. There were some random paintings of West Texas landscapes on the walls. Someone must have felt the extra pop of color made it look homier, but the artworks added to the desolate look of the ED.

Blayne had been in the ED twice—once after he had tried to slice off his thumb when cutting red peppers and another time when a friend had broken a leg during a pickup game of soccer during the summer. Blayne steered Ethan toward the waiting area, which he knew was right off the main entrance and down a short hallway.

Blayne walked into the waiting area. Dr. Reich stood and immediately threw her arms around Blayne. He could tell she'd been crying. Her face was puffy. Her mascara had been washed away, leaving black streaks running down her cheeks.

When they finally separated, he turned to Ethan and introduced her to Dr. Reich. "Ethan Bond, this is Dr. Madeline Reich. Dr. Reich, Ethan Bond."

Ethan extended his hand and shook the woman's hand, grasping it on both sides. "It's nice to meet you, Ethan." She gave him a once-over. "Have we met?"

"I doubt it," Blayne jumped in. "He's visiting from New Orleans. He flew in yesterday to hang out in Houston for a few days."

"Well, it's nice to meet you, Ethan," she started, before choking back a sob, "even if it is under these circumstances."

Blayne helped her back over to a chair. Thankfully, the waiting room was quiet, so Blayne sat down next to her and held her hand while Ethan took a seat across them.

"How is he? What happened?"

Blayne gestured with his head to Ethan toward a box of tissues on a table toward the front of the room. Without saying a word, Ethan stood and got the box before handing it to Blayne. Blayne mouthed, 'Thank you'.

Blayne watched as Dr. Reich took a deep breath while staring at the ground. She slowly exhaled before she told Ethan what she'd learned from the police. "Jamie was coming home from school. Someone jumped him, and he was beaten badly. The police think it was just with their hands, but they couldn't rule out that he'd been attacked with something else. They found his phone on him, which is how they called me. Thank God I made him put me in his phone as ICE."

"ICE?" Blayne asked.

"In case of emergency," Dr. Reich said. "I don't know where I read to do that, but thank God I did."

"What have the doctors told you?"

"Dr. Giest-Mueler was on call tonight. I met with him right before they wheeled Jamie into surgery."

"Dear God," Blayne said, his eyes wide in shock. "What did they do to him?"

"He has at least one broken bone and some nasty lacerations across his face and upper torso. There's also fear he might have been—" She choked back another sob, then took a deep breath before continuing. "He might have been sexually violated."

Ethan gasped. His eyes widened as the color drained from his face.

Without going into too much detail, Dr. Reich told them the police were afraid whoever attacked Jamie had used some kind of object to victimize the young man. The surgery they were performing right now was threefold. A plastic surgeon was working on Jamie's face. An orthopedic surgeon was waiting to fix his arm. And Dr. Giest-Mueler was making sure there was not any permanent damage to Jamie's rectum or colon.

Blayne pulled Dr. Reich into a hug. "I am so sorry." He felt the hot tears streaming down the side of his face. Ethan leaned over, grabbed a tissue and handed it to him.

"Madeline," a voice came from the doorway. Blayne looked up to see the fluorescent light above Kira's head like a strange oblong-shaped halo, "what happened?" Kira asked as she walked into the waiting room and came and sat next to Ethan. Kira grasped one of Madeline's hands as Blayne caught her up so Dr. Reich wouldn't have to go through it all again.

When she finished, a couple of detectives entered the room. "Dr. Reich?" one of them asked.

"Yes?" she said, pulling back from Blayne and Kira.

"I'm Detective Wilson, and this is Detective Spector. We're with the Pennington Police Department. Can we talk to you for a few minutes?"

"Dr. Reich," Blayne said. "Do you need anything? Coffee? Something to eat?"

"Coffee would be great," she said, almost absently.

Blayne nodded toward the door, and Ethan followed him into the hall. Kira was right on their heels.

"I'm going to stay with Madeline," Kira said. "I think she needs Jamie's lawyer right now." Blayne noticed Kira's jaw set, and her face hardened, masking her emotions. She spun around, walked back into the waiting room.

"That poor woman," Ethan said, "What kind of monster would do this?"

"Sadly, there are many of them in this world. In fact, I think I may know who did this." Blayne filled Ethan in about the harassment Jamie faced at school.

"So, that's why Kira has turned into lawyer-zilla?"

"You saw it too?" Blayne asked.

"Yeah, it was like a switch turned on, and all her pleasantness disappeared. I'd hate to be on the other end of her in a case."

*Ethan*

Ethan followed Blayne as he walked through the maze of corridors making up the hospital interior. *Thank God he knows where he's going. They'd have to send out a search party to find me.* After a few more twists, turns and an elevator ride, they were in the hospital cafeteria. The line was short, so they moved through it quickly. They picked up four large coffees, a small milk and some packets of sugar, in case someone wanted to doctor their brew. Blayne also grabbed a tuna sandwich from the display. He made some comment about not letting Madeline off the hook when it came to eating.

"She's going to need her strength for this," Blayne said.

Ethan watched the look of dismay and despair cross Blayne's face. Blayne's body had lost the vigor and energy Ethan was already becoming used to seeing in the man beside him. Ethan threw his arm around Blayne's waist without even thinking as they walked back to the ED waiting room. He felt Blayne lean into him as they walked. Blayne didn't need Ethan to help him walk, but Ethan didn't mind being there to support his friend.

They walked into the room. Kira looked up from where she was sitting, holding Madeline, who was once again crying.

"Here's your coffee," Blayne started. "I wasn't sure what you'd want in it, so I got milk and some sugar packets, just in case. And I know you said you weren't hungry, but I got you a tuna sandwich. You'll need to eat at some point, so at least you'll have something." Blayne placed the milk carton on the chair next to Madeline and emptied his pockets of the packets. Madeline glanced up at Blayne, giving him a weak smile.

"Madeline," a male's voice came from the doorway. "Oh, hey, Ethan, Kira and someone I don't know," the middle-aged man said as he walked into the waiting room.

"Hey, Arnold," Ethan said to the surgeon. "How's he doing?"

Dr. Giest-Mueler looked to Madeline for permission to say anything. She nodded, so he went on. "Things are about as good as we could have hoped for. The plastic surgeon is still working on a couple of facial lacerations, but he thinks there will be minimal scarring."

"Maybe not externally," Kira said under her breath.

Dr. Giest-Mueler clearly heard Kira, but he continued without responding, "Jamie's arm was set. The orthopedic surgeon had to insert two pins and a plate. He will be in a cast for about four to six weeks, depending on how things heal." The surgeon took a breath. The look that washed over the surgeon's face told Ethan everything he needed to know. The surgeon was trying to figure out the most delicate way to put the next part. "Despite the bleeding, there was only minor damage internally," Giest-Mueler said, drawing out the last word. "There was some ripping, and I cauterized those wounds to stop the bleeding. Neither the rectum nor colon were perforated, which is a minor miracle."

"When can I see him?" Madeline asked, her quiet voice barely audible.

"The guy from plastics said he should be finished in about fifteen minutes, so we should have Jamie in the intensive care unit in about thirty minutes at the latest. I'll take you back there now, Madeline, if you want."

Saying nothing, she stood up, grabbed her coffee and the sandwich and followed the surgeon out of the room.

As soon as they were gone, Blayne sank into one chair. Ethan sat down next to him. "You, okay?"

"Definitely been better. I feel so powerless right now."

"Not me," Kira said. "I'm fucking pissed. I'm ready to rain down a fucking shitstorm on that asshat principal of his."

"Whoa, back up," Blayne said. "What happened while we were gone?"

"Let me show you." She pulled out her cell phone and pulled up the video the detective had forwarded to her since she was Jamie's lawyer. She hit play and handed her phone to Blayne, who watched in horror.

"They recorded it?" Blayne asked in horror as the images of Jamie's assault played out.

"And posted it to social media," Kira said, barely opening her clenched jaw. "That's how the cops found the perpetrators. The smug, entitled little pricks streamed it while they were doing it."

"Have they been arrested?"

"Yes. The police have the three fuckweasels who did this to Jamie in custody. Big surprise. The one who sat there with the camera egging the other two on was the asshat kid from the assembly the other day."

Blayne's jaw dipped open as he rocked his head from side to side. "We knew the kid was a dick. I can't believe he'd do this. But I can't believe anyone with any kind of conscience could do this to another human being. What kind of fucking monster do you have to be?"

"What happens now?" Ethan asked.

"Now, I sue the shit out of everyone who let this happen—the school district, the school, the principal and the kids' parents. Trust me… When I'm done with these monsters, Jamie won't need to work a day in his life."

Kira's purse suddenly buzzed, so she reached in and grabbed her phone. "Look at that," she said sarcastically, "It's the school district's attorney. I'll be right back." Ethan heard her answer the phone as she left the waiting room.

"Damn, she's fucking scary," Ethan said. "If I ever need a talented attorney, I'm hiring her."

"She's pretty damn good at what she does. From what one of her partners told me once at a Christmas party, most of the lawyers in the region would rather settle than face her in court. The few times she has taken something to trial, the initial settlement offers were chump change compared to what the juries awarded her clients."

"Remind me not to get on her bad side," Ethan said.

"Don't hurt the people she loves, and you'll be fine."

"Well, I have no intention of hurting anyone," Ethan said, "let alone anyone she loves," he added.

Ethan watched as Blayne's face softened for the first time since they'd gotten to the hospital. Ethan had been acutely aware of the tension running through Blayne's body, which was one reason he'd held Blayne on the way back to the waiting room. *He looks so vulnerable right now. I want to wrap my arms around him and tell him it's going to be okay. But I also know it won't be. I feel so fucking useless.*

The two sat in their chairs, their thighs touching. Ethan tried not to notice the contact, but it was hard to ignore. Blayne seemed to effortlessly let his body move toward Ethan without a care in the world. Ethan was always so worried about public displays of affection and what they could do to his career. In this moment, he enjoyed sitting in the waiting room with Ethan. Life seemed so simple here. His phone buzzed in his pocket.

Blayne looked at him. "Do you need to get that?"

"Nope. There is no one I need to talk to right now and no other place I'd rather be." They sat in silence for a couple of minutes. Ethan finally blurted out, "Blayne, there's something I gotta tell you—"

"Guys, Jamie is back in the intensive care unit. He's awake," Kira said, poking her head in. "I ran into Arnold in the hall and told him I'd tell you." Kira didn't wait to see if Ethan and Blayne followed.

As they scurried after her, Blayne said, "You were about to say something before we got cut off."

"It can wait," Ethan said as they followed Kira out of the door, hurrying to catch up. Blayne was right behind him.

Ethan and Blayne saw Kira halfway down the hall and jogged after as she led them through the hospital maze. Clearly, Kira knew where she was going. When they got to the ICU, a nurse stopped them.

"Can I help you?"

"We're here to see Jamie Reich," Kira said.

"I'm sorry, but visiting hours are over. You'll need to come back in the morning."

"Nurse Emerson," Dr. Giest-Mueler said, poking his head around the corner, "it's okay. They're the kid's family. He just woke up. They promise they won't stay long."

Blayne, Ethan and Kira all nodded in agreement. The nurse soured her face, but she let them by without saying another word.

Kira knocked on the door before going into the room. "Come in," Madeline said from inside. Kira slowly opened the door, stepped inside. Then Blayne and Ethan followed.

Jamie was a little groggy, but he gave a kind of half-smile as he saw Kira and Blayne. Then his entire expression changed as he practically squealed, "Ethan Bond!"

# Chapter Fourteen

*Blayne*

Blayne looked from Ethan to Jamie and back to Ethan with a look of absolute confusion. Ethan smiled, walked in and said, "Hey, kid, it's nice to meet you. I'm Ethan."

A look of surprise and joy flooded Jamie's face and dumbfounded everyone else in the room.

"Who are you?" Kira exclaimed once she'd gotten past the shock. Blayne watched as Kira looked Ethan up and down, as if seeing him for the first time.

"I'm Ethan Bond—"

"He's Ethan Bond," Jamie said with a look of awe. Ethan nodded to Jamie, who continued. "He's only like one of the most famous people in the world. Where have you three been? What's with the blond hair?"

Ethan shrugged and put on one of his dazzling smiles. "That's me. As for the blond hair, I was trying not to be recognized."

"Good luck with that," Jamie said, trying to fully sit up.

Blayne saw the wince flash across Jamie's face. Knowing Jamie was still in pain caused a pang of anger in Blane's heart.

"Still confused," Kira said, tilting her head at Blayne, looking for some explanation. Blayne shot her back a look of absolute befuddlement.

"He's the E in ZERO. God, you guys are old," Jamie said, before returning his attention to Ethan. "Why are you here?"

"I'm staying with Blayne for a few days."

"You're friends with Blayne?" Jamie questioned in absolute wonderment.

"We've known each other for a long time." Ethan then looked at Kira, who was narrowing her gaze on Ethan. "I told Blayne I was in the entertainment business. I never told him exactly what I did in the business."

"We're so going to have this conversation later," Kira said flatly.

"Are you and Blayne dating?" Jamie asked excitedly.

Blayne caught the look of panic that flashed over Ethan's face. "We're just friends, Jamie," Blayne cut in. "As Ethan said, *'We've known each other for a long time.'*"

"I knew I recognized your name," Madeline said, entering the conversation. "How I missed it is beyond me. Jamie dragged me to one of your concerts at the Toyota Center last year."

"I wish I could say I remembered even being here in Houston, but that tour was such a blur. We did something like sixty cities in ninety days before crossing the pond and doing another thirty around Europe."

Ethan bounced from the shy boy next door to the confident, internationally recognized performing artist he was. *And he's staying at my apartment. And I've probably seen more of him than any of his fans will ever see.* His Peeping Tom experience from earlier that afternoon flooded into his memory, bringing a grin to Blayne's face.

"Do you mind?" Ethan gestured, pointing to the corner of Jamie's bed. Jamie nodded. Blayne could tell the teen was still star-struck and surprised one of his musical idols was in his hospital room about to sit on his bed. "How are you doing? Need anything?" Ethan's tone was smooth. Blayne wondered how many of these types of hospital visits Ethan made over the years.

"Kinda crappy," Jamie admitted. "Feel like I was run over by a Mack truck. Honestly, I'm wondering what meds the doctors gave me, because this is one fucking awesome dream."

"Language," Madeline chided her son.

"Yes, Mom," Jamie said, winking at Ethan conspiratorially. Ethan winked right back.

"Well, we wanted to check up on you," Ethan said. "I'm sure we'll see you again soon once you're feeling up to it. Okay?"

"Promise?" Jamie asked.

"I promise. And who knows? Maybe before you're out of here, I'll figure out a way to get Ric, Zach and Orr here, too. The four of us can sign your cast."

A look of absolute excitement rushed over Jamie's face, beyond anything Blayne had ever seen on the boy. Somehow, in one sentence, Ethan had done more to raise Jamie's spirits than anyone else in Houston could have.

"Good night, everyone," Ethan said. He shook Madeline's hand, who Blayne thought looked a bit tongue-tied. Ethan looked at Jamie and said, "I would give you a hug, but I don't want to hurt you any more than you already are."

"I'm fine—"

"No, you're not," Ethan said gently. "And that's okay. I'll owe you a hug once you're back on your feet. Okay?"

Jamie nodded. Blayne said his round of goodbyes, then grasped Jamie's hand when he was sure he wouldn't hurt the poor kid.

Kira followed them out into the hall before they headed home. "I'll call you tomorrow," she said, looking at Blayne. Kira brought Blayne in for a hug, then extended her hand to Ethan. Ethan shook Kira's hand, and she pulled him closer to her. She pointed to her eyes, then pointed at Ethan, letting him know she was watching him. She then smiled and brought him in for a quick embrace.

* * * *

The ride back to Blayne's was somber. Once back in the apartment, he pulled the cannoli from the refrigerator, and he and Ethan sat out on the couch. Ethan had gone back to his room and come back out in a pair of soccer shorts and casual tank top to lounge in. Blayne's jaw dropped as Ethan yawned and stretched his arms overhead. First there was the incredibly ripped stomach and treasure trail. Then Ethan twisted his torso from side to side and Blayne caught sight of Ethan's side nipple.

Blayne refocused his attention on the countertop and looked down at the cannoli. *I'd like to see his cannoli.* He shook his head and pulled himself together. He finished plating the cannoli and headed back into the living room. Ethan had sat on the couch.

"Here you go," Blayne said, handing the plate and fork to Ethan. Ethan reached out and accepted the plate and their hands grazed each other in the pass off.

"Thanks," Ethan said, looking up at Blayne.

"I'll be right back," Blayne said, worried that his resprung erection would slap Ethan in the face if he didn't cool it…and fast.

"You, okay?" Ethan said after Blayne made a hasty retreat toward his bedroom.

"Yeah, just need to change. Be right back."

Once inside, Blayne leaned against the closed bedroom door and took several calming, centering breaths. "What the fuck was that?" Blayne asked, looking down at his dick, which was clearly bulging. "Dear God, I hope he didn't notice." Blayne walked over to his dresser and fished out a simple pair of shorts and a T-shirt. Once dressed, Blayne waited until he'd completely deflated before heading back to the living room.

"So," Blayne started as he left his room, "right before we went in to see Jamie, you said you needed to tell me something. Let me guess what that was." Blayne looked at him with a knowing smile.

"Guilty as charged. I was on the verge of telling you about my career before we were interrupted. I figured you had enough other things on your plate. You didn't need to deal with my bombshell."

Blayne came over to the couch, sat down and grabbed his own cannoli from the coffee table. He snagged a throw pillow and put it on his lap as an improvised table, and to hide himself in case his dick got a mind of its own again. He crunched through the pastry crust and savored the first bite. He was enjoying the sweet flavor of the shell and filling when a memory popped into his head.

"Dear God."

"What?" Ethan looked up in concern.

"In the airport…when we first met, one of your songs was playing. You even told me ZERO was the band."

The smile lines around Ethan's face crinkled as he remembered. "Yep, I was in the weird getup. At least you can now understand why I was trying to go incognito through the airport. If I don't, I'll get swarmed."

"And that's why you dyed your hair."

"That's also why I wear a ball cap and shades when we leave the house. Hundreds of thousands of kids like Jamie would spot me from a mile away. I'm less worried about them than I am of the middle-aged women. Some of them can be downright scary fans."

"I'll take your word for it," Blayne said, narrowing his eyes in confusion. "Since we're in the middle of a truth fest, I should at least say I had sex with Dr. Arnold Giest-Mueler and his partner Harry, who's a professor on campus."

"Really? You had a threesome with a surgeon and a professor? That's kind of hot."

"It was fun, but it was awkward more than anything. It was a onetime fling. We're still friends, and I swear they're always subtly trying to get me to join them again. I'm not into that. I don't mind threesomes. Who doesn't?"

"Never had one," Ethan said, a flush of awkwardness crept across his face. "I haven't had many experiences at all, to be perfectly honest."

"Oh, sorry to hear that," Blayne said before joking, "Well, now I sound like a slut."

"I don't think you're slutty at all. You've just lived a very different life than the one I have."

"So, between you, me and the wall," Blayne said hesitantly, "who was the guy you were seeing? You said he was a soap star, but that's all."

"His name is Daniel Hawthorne."

"The *NOLA Nights* guy?"

Ethan cocked his head, a pretense of a pout on his face, "Sure, you know who the soap star is and don't have a clue about the multi-platinum-selling musician."

Blayne scrunched his face and shrugged. "I went through a phase when I was in college. My best friend at the time and I got together every day for lunch on campus. *NOLA Nights* was always playing, so we got caught up on the plotlines, whether we wanted to or not."

"You are a man of mystery, Blayne Dickenson."

"Pot, meet kettle," Blayne said with an impish grin. "Tell me about him."

"What would you like to know?"

"What was he like? How did you two meet? What was your *relationship* like?"

Blayne listened as Ethan told him the story about how Stephanie had introduced the two men. Blayne had some pieces based on their earlier conversations, but now having names and contexts associated with the story made it easier to understand. He disagreed with Ethan's and Daniel Hawthorne's insistence on staying in the closet to protect their professional lives. Still, he admitted to himself that he struggled to imagine what it would be like to be in their circumstances.

In academia, being out and proud was pretty protected by most administrations across the country. Sure, there was the random crazy-conservative student who would freak out if he mentioned a past boyfriend as an example. Still, most took it in stride and didn't even think twice about Blayne's sexuality. Hell, he'd run into a few students over the years on *EndZone*, which was always awkward. He'd even used the app once to message a student, to let him know he was behind in the class and on the verge of failing. Thankfully, Blayne kept his online profile pretty squeaky clean for that very reason. Now, he had a couple of dirtier profiles with a few pictures he wouldn't want to get out, but those profiles were kept on websites and apps where his face was not shown at all. He knew some of his straight colleagues wouldn't get this part of gay culture, so he understood the necessity of keeping aspects of his life private.

"I'm going to the bathroom," Ethan said. "Be right back."

They had finished their cannoli, so Blayne took their plastic to-go boxes and spoons to the kitchen. He then grabbed a couple of water bottles from the fridge and put them on coasters on the coffee table.

Blayne closed his eyes and laid back on the couch for a minute. He didn't hear Ethan come back into the room.

"Lift your legs," Ethan said. "Wow, that sounded dirtier than I intended."

"You're assuming I don't like it dirty." Blayne gasped and threw a hand over his mouth. "I'm sorry. I just blurted that out. Sometimes, my mouth seems to have a mind of its own." The heat rose in his cheeks. Blayne looked at Ethan's big grin and the playful look on his face. "I can just sit up."

"No need. Lift your legs so I can get under them. Use me as a leg rest. You've had a bit of a day."

Blayne lifted his legs, keeping the pillow firmly in place on his lap. Ethan sat on the couch, and Blayne lowered his legs onto Ethan's lap. Ethan draped his arms on top of his legs and stared down at Blayne from across the couch. The warmth of Ethan's forearms against Blayne's bare legs caused him to strain against the throw pillow.

"TV?" Blayne asked.

"Sounds good."

Blayne picked up the remote control and turned on the TV, which was set to RNN. Blayne was about to change the channel when Ethan's face flashed across the screen.

Tika Downs was sitting behind the desk as she started reading the teleprompter. "*In an RNN exclusive, Stephen McNeil has tracked down the story of the mysterious cancellation of the Seattle performances of the boy band ZERO.*"

*Ethan*

Stephen McNeil's face filled the screen in a standard medium close-up shot.

"Thank you, Tika. Fans in Seattle were dismayed to find their tickets were being refunded today for a scheduled upcoming tour launch for the boy band ZERO's North American tour."

RNN used B-roll from ZERO's last tours interspersed with interviews from fans who were devastated. One young girl was on the screen in tears.

"Geez," Blayne said. "You would have thought you killed her pet with those waterworks."

"Fan reactions are always interesting. Most are perfectly normal, loving people. But there are definitely some obsessive ones who take us *way* too seriously."

The package ended, and Stephen McNeil reappeared. "In an RNN exclusive, we can now confirm the reason the North American tour was postponed is because Ethan Bond has disappeared." Ethan's face once again filled the screen. "Fans will wonder why. I'll have more information after this break."

"Gre-eat," Ethan said, drawing out the word. "This should be interesting." He glanced down at Blayne and added, "I hope I haven't brought a shitstorm to your door."

"If you did, we'll deal with it."

The two remained silent through the rest of the commercials before Stephen McNeil filled the screen once more. "Before the break, we told viewers that Ethan Bond of the boy band ZERO has gone missing. Although some fans may wonder why he did this, I must mention Ethan's disappearance probably saved ZERO's lives."

A new segment ran that tied Ethan's disappearance to the explosion of Peregrine Airlines Flight 923. The video showed Ethan sneaking out of the First-Class Lounge and making it onto a Roadrunner flight.

"Well, fuck," Ethan said. Absently, he grabbed one of Blayne's feet and started rubbing on it. This was a position Danny and he had taken up many times. Danny always loved Ethan's foot massages. "You don't mind, do you?" Ethan asked, glancing from the TV to Blayne. "My hands just like to be doing something. I mean...I like to rub things. Oh wow, that sounded worse." Ethan felt the heat rise in his cheeks and didn't dare look at Blayne in the face. Ethan felt himself stir.

"It's cool. It feels amazing. You're great at that." Ethan finally looked down at Blayne, who added, "You can rub *me* any day."

Both busted out laughing. *Is he flirting with me? God, I hate flirting. I never know if a guy is flirting with me. I'm like a fucking teenager.* He rested Blayne's foot down and picked up the other one.

Blayne moaned slightly as Stephen McNeil's face flashed back on the screen. "As you can see, if Ethan Bond hadn't ditched the band to fly to Houston this week, the entire band would have been on Peregrine Airlines Flight 923, and we'd be telling our viewers a very different story. Many of you may wonder why Ethan escaped to Houston. RNN has an exclusive photo of Ethan Bond and a mystery person looking very couply in Houston."

Ethan worried for a second, fearing there would be an image of him and Blayne together. The image that McNeil displayed was one of Kira touching Ethan's hand earlier that day at The Dream Bean.

Blayne busted out laughing. "Oh, my God," he squeaked out between breaths.

Ethan looked at Blayne, not seeing nearly the same humor in the situation as Blayne did. "It's not funny."

"Really?" Blayne countered. "They accused you of having an illicit affair with the biggest lesbian in Houston. That's fucking funny."

Ethan thought about it for a second and realized Blayne had a point. "On the positive, it will be fun to watch RNN try to explain how they got this story so wrong."

Ethan's phone vibrated on the coffee table. He picked it up to see a stream of texts coming in.

*Dude, you have a new girlfriend? You could have told us,* a text from Orr read.

*It's about time you got some,* Ric's text read.

*Who the hell is that woman?* Stephanie's text read.

*What the fuck?* was all the text from Zach said.

*We need to talk,* read the text from Rawlins.

*Ethan, what is going on?* asked Hightower.

Ethan looked at the stream of texts as a few more came in. He turned off the notifications and set the phone back on the table. "I can't deal with this mess right now."

Blayne's phone started vibrating, so he grabbed it off the table. Kira's face showed as the caller, so he hit the accept button.

"Hey, Kira—"

"What the hell is going on?" she groused. "I got a text from my mother asking me if I was turning straight. I've had an unbroken stream of texts from people wondering how I know Ethan Bond, international man of mystery."

"I'm putting you on speaker." Blayne hit the button. "I take it you haven't seen RNN?"

"Nope, been having an emergency call with some of the partners about our Jamie strategy."

Blayne quickly filled Kira in on the RNN package and her starring role. Blayne did his best to suppress his laughter a few times while telling the story. Blayne's entire body shook with silent laughter as he got out the last parts.

"I'm so sorry for this," Ethan said. "I'll have my publicist release a statement in the morning."

"Your publicist?" Kira said, letting out an exasperated laugh.

"Welcome to my world," Ethan said. "Once we're done, I'll shoot her off a text and deny everything. I'll say you're a friend and not a romantic partner."

"Kira, would you mind if Ethan waits a day or so?"

"Why?" Kira asked. Ethan could practically hear the skepticism dripping from her voice over the phone.

"Let's see if this thing blows over," Blayne said.

"It won't," Ethan said. "In my experience, these stories snowball if you don't get out ahead of them. I wouldn't be surprised if the paparazzi case Dream Bean by morning." Ethan heard an exasperated sigh from Kira. "I should also warn you, Kira. You may experience paparazzi following you or showing up at your workplace tomorrow."

"What?" Kira said. Ethan could hear the sense of alarm in her voice.

"My recommendation would be, use it to your advantage," Ethan started. "Think about it. You're going to have a ton of reporters pointing cameras in your direction. Use it. Talk about Jamie and the case every chance you get. It's a great way to get public opinion on your side."

"Wow," Blayne said, "I wouldn't have thought about doing that in a million years."

"Welcome to my world," Ethan said. "You don't have any kind of longevity in show business if you don't learn to be media savvy. I'll be the first to admit my life is different and sucks at times, but it gives me a platform. And now, Kira will have this platform, at least for a few days."

"Interesting," Kira said. "I'm going to talk to the partners about this strategy before I jump into this."

The three chatted for a few more minutes and devised a game plan for the next couple of days. After they hung up, Ethan quickly emailed his publicist asking her to stall all interview requests. He promised to call her in a few days to schedule a more formal announcement. He then spent almost an hour responding to the litany of texts he received while talking to Kira.

He glanced over at Blayne and saw his eyes were closed. *He is pretty damn cute. But, after all this, I seriously doubt he'd ever consider me anything but a friend. Oh well. Such is life.*

He put his phone down on the table, doing his best not to disturb Blayne. He sat there for a few minutes, watching as Blayne's chest went up and down with his breaths. Blayne's shirt had ridden up slightly, showing the treasure trail. Ethan felt himself stirring down south, so he lifted Blayne's legs gently.

"Oh, sorry," Blayne said, waking up. "I must have dozed off."

"Only for a few minutes."

"I guess, I should head to bed, but I don't feel like moving."

Without thinking, Ethan bent over Blayne and hefted the other man into his arms.

"Whoa," Blayne said in shock. "Damn, you're strong."

"Put your arms around my neck," Ethan replied. "I don't want to drop you."

Thankfully, Blayne did as he'd been told and rested his head against Ethan's chest. Ethan lifted Blayne a little higher than necessary to keep his dick from poking the other man in the back. He walked around the coffee table and across the room. He shifted Blayne's weight when he got to Blayne's bedroom door, so he could turn the doorknob. Ethan turned sideways and carried Blayne into the primary bedroom, crossed to the queen-sized bed and laid Blayne down.

"That was fun," Blayne said. "We should do it again some time." He barely got the words out of his mouth before he yawned loudly.

"Maybe we will," Ethan said. "Good night."

Ethan turned to leave the room. Blayne reached out and grabbed his hand. "I don't... I don't want to be alone."

Ethan took a deep breath before turning around. A pleading look on Blayne's face melted Ethan's heart. "In all honesty, I don't want to be alone, either."

Blayne moved to the other side of the bed as he got under the covers. Ethan lowered himself behind Blayne. "I'll sleep on top of the covers. I tend to run hot, anyway."

He laid down on his side, stared at the back of Blayne's head and ran his gaze down his body to Blayne's runner's ass. *What I wouldn't give —*

Blayne had scooched closer to Ethan's body, so Ethan settled in behind him and snaked his arm across the man's chest. Blayne let out a contented sigh. Ethan rocked his hips back to keep his erection from impaling Blayne accidentally and laid there stiffly for what seemed like an hour.

Ethan knew the moment Blayne had drifted asleep. Only then did he relax behind Blayne as he allowed himself to close his eyes and let the darkness of the night wrap its embrace around them.

* * * *

*Dr. Hennigan*

Dr. Hennigan was ushered into the dining room by an attendant and told that her dinner host was running behind and would be with her in a moment. She'd been in the room once before, but she'd been a young girl at the time, and the room had been renovated since then.

She took a minute to take in the decor while she was waiting. The wallpaper was vertical stripes of light and dark green. Two giant windows stood on the far wall from the door, framed by opulent red and gold drapes. She looked out of the window and couldn't see much past the security lights sweeping across the front lawn.

She turned and noticed someone had lit a fire in the fireplace. Above the glowing flames was a mirror running all the way to the top of the twenty-foot ceiling. *Where does one even find a mirror that large? Clearly, it's custom-made.* In Washington, DC, the October weather was already chilling, so the fire made for a pleasant addition. Opposite the fireplace was an armoire filled with various knickknacks the First Lady had brought back with her from multiple trips abroad.

"Dr. Hennigan, it's so good to see you again," Cleo Barnes said as she entered the room, walked over to her dinner guest and grasped Dr. Hennigan's hand.

"Cleo, dear. Call me Phillipa. We've known each other forever," Dr. Hennigan responded with a fake smile.

"Please, sit," Cleo said, gesturing to one seat at the table. "Cocktail?"

"Vodka, please."

Cleo smiled and went to the small bar area in the front corner of the room. She pulled out two cocktail glasses from the bar. "Ice?"

"No thanks."

Dr. Hennigan watched from her seat as Cleo pulled out a bottle of vodka she hadn't seen before. "What brand is that?"

"It's called CLIX and is produced by Buffalo Trace Distillery. They only make two thousand bottles of this ever. They distill it almost one-hundred-sixty different times before it's bottled. As a native Kentucky girl, they sent me a couple of bottles from their distillery for the inauguration. We keep one bottle in the residence kitchen and the other here."

Cleo walked back over and handed the glass to Dr. Hennigan. "Let's toast to another four years," Dr. Hennigan said as she raised her glass and clinked it with Cleo's. "I've been looking at the internal polling data, and your husband's a shoo-in for another four years."

"Well, he's been good for the economy and good on social justice. It's almost amazing, because members of both sides of the aisle have come out to support him. That never happens anymore."

"Very true. But then, having a unified force behind a specific presidential candidate has never been in The Foundation's best interest."

"I know. The Foundation worked for years to get me here. So many things fell into place to get me to this point."

"Well, you were one of our top picks," Dr. Hennigan noted. A measured look of surprise crossed Cleo's face. "You didn't think we'd put all our eggs in one basket, did you?"

Cleo's face returned to the masked, tight-lipped smile she was known for on the campaign trail. Cleo was a former lawyer who worked in the Department of Justice. The Foundation had recruited her in law school. They had gotten her a clerkship with one of the Supreme Court justices, then she took the job at the Department of Justice.

Dr. Hennigan's mother had recognized the potential in a low-level military officer named Jeffry Barnes. After a few moves, The Foundation had arranged an 'accidental' encounter between Cleo and Jeffry at a cocktail party in the district. The two were engaged in six months and married in eleven. From there, The Foundation pulled strings behind the scenes to get Jeffrey elected to the Maryland State Legislature, then Governor. When he ran for President five years earlier, he was the longshot on the ticket. Of course, the longshot won easily as people were manipulated or paid off behind the scenes to show their full support of Governor Barnes.

The staff opened the door and wheeled in dinner. "What are we eating tonight?" Dr. Hennigan asked.

"Honey-roasted duck, grilled asparagus with light butter and crispy roasted rosemary sweet potatoes, ma'am," the server said as she put the plate in front of her and removed the metal lid.

"It smells divine," Cleo replied. "Give my compliments to the chef. She outdid herself tonight."

Dr. Hennigan stabbed one of the asparagus and put it into her mouth. The tiny tree had the combination of crispy and chewy you get when correctly prepared. And just like the server said, she noticed the hints of the butter without it being drowned by the yellow stuff.

When the door shut, Cleo let her facade drop. "We're clear to talk in here. This room is swept daily."

"Good to know. Where are you with our priority situation?" Dr. Hennigan asked.

"I've reached out through back channels to someone I know at the Department of Homeland Security — DHS. Ethan Bond is staying with some guy he met online, a Blayne Dickenson."

"We knew he was in Houston but hadn't located him yet. What do you know about their relationship?"

"We intercepted their messages on a gay dating app. Until Ethan left New Orleans, the men had never met. Heck, they'd never even talked on the phone until earlier this week."

"What do you know about this Mr. Dickenson?"

"DHS doesn't have much on him. We know he's a graduate student at Pennington University. I can tell you his grades going back to elementary school, but nothing in his background should worry The Foundation."

"Your assessment?"

"Mr. Dickenson is a bystander, and liquidating him could probably cause more problems. As for Mr. Bond, we have no way of knowing what he does or doesn't know," Cleo said as she cut a sliver of duck and placed it in her mouth.

Dr. Hennigan thought for a moment. "What do we know about the file?"

"We know little. Here's what we've found out. When Mr. Hawthorne's phone received the message, it immediately sent two emails. One email is a complete dead-end, and the other was sent to Ethan Bond. When the email was sent to Ethan Bond's cell, two separate actions simultaneously occurred. One made it look like an email was sent then deleted, which is a complete red herring. The email is piggybacked by a data burst. Honestly, if you didn't know what you were looking for, you'd waste years trying to go after the emails and learn nothing. We know the data burst buries itself in the receiver's cell phone and can only be located and decrypted by someone with the passkey. We think the file is being automatically transmitted to the person listed as ICE."

"So, the file is sent automatically. That's how it went from Cynthia to Daniel to Ethan?"

"That's our analysis, ma'am, yes."

"And when Ethan accessed his cell today, who did it get forwarded to?"

Cleo reached down and picked up her own secure device and looked for the file in question. "A Ms. Stephanie Anne Mitchell. When we hacked into Bond's phone, we saw the file was transmitted to her today."

"And the ICE thing?" Hennigan questioned.

"That's how we finally saw how it was being transmitted. Mr. Bond has Ms. Mitchell listed as his ICE and vice versa. The file started bouncing back between both phones."

"Would the owners of the phones know this was happening?"

"The National Security Agency analysis says there's no reason to think the recipients would know."

"Could the NSA figure out what was in the file?"

"They can watch what's happening, but unless we get our hands on a device being used, we have no way of locking the file down. And even then, if we don't have the key, there's no way to crack the encryption code."

"Interesting," Hennigan said, steepling her fingers under her chin. She took a bite of her duck and chewed, coming up with her own assessment of the situation. "What would you recommend?"

"Best-case scenario, asset retrieval with no liquidation. However, if it's not doable, then liquidation followed by asset retrieval or destroying all the assets in play. Whatever this file is, it's much too dangerous to have floating around," the First Lady said.

"Indeed."

"If I may be so bold as to ask," Cleo started. "When did The Foundation first realize Cynthia Dunning was working as a double agent for Tiandihui out of Hong Kong?"

"We'd heard chatter that the Tiandihui had been reconstituted and were looking to make inroads into the US. We didn't know it had happened until an unauthorized data retrieval was linked back to Dunning. She was liquidated as soon as we traced the data to her, but the file was already forwarded. We've been trying to put the cat back in the bag, so to speak, ever since."

"What did she retrieve?"

"That's the terrifying part. We don't know. Whoever helped her with the hack was good...very good. Our techs have been working around the clock to figure out how the hack happened and to secure The Foundation network all week. Your intel from the DHS mirrors what we've discovered."

"Any chance we're exposed?"

"Cleo," Hennigan said with zero emotion, "there's a chance every facet of The Foundation has been exposed, which is why we're taking this leak seriously."

"So seriously, you blew up an entire jumbo jet of innocent people to get one target?" Cleo asked with an arched eyebrow.

"Watch yourself, Mrs. Barnes," Hennigan replied.

Dr. Hennigan's phone started vibrating. She picked it up, still staring at Cleo Barnes as she said, "Hennigan."

"We have one team heading to New Orleans to handle Target S and the other on the ground in Houston going after Target E," Ms. Wilson said over the phone. "Orders?"

"Liquidation and asset retrieval."

# Chapter Fifteen

*Ethan*

Around six a.m., Ethan's eyes popped open. He was still cradled against Blayne's back. He had to pee. Ethan unwrapped himself from Blayne's body and smoothly exited the bed. The bedroom was dark, but a sliver of light shone under the door. *We left the hallway light on.* Ethan quietly padded over to the door and slipped out, using his body to block as much of the light as possible. He then closed the door behind him.

After relieving himself, he opted to go for a run to clear his head. He wanted to jump back into bed with Blayne but went back to the guest bedroom and slipped into his running gear. *There had been a spark last night. If yesterday hadn't been so insane...* He let the thought fall from his mind. He wasn't even sure if Blayne saw him that way. Sure, they'd flirted a bit, but Ethan questioned if that meant Blayne was into him or just being a good host.

Ethan headed out of the apartment and stretched for a minute in the parking lot before taking off on the same path he'd run the previous morning. He quickly found his running groove as he quickened his pace. Ethan's mind was a jumble of thoughts, from revealing who he was to Blayne the night before, to Jamie's attack, to issues with ZERO, to how amazing Blayne's body had felt next to his. With each additional problem entering his head, he tried to run faster, hoping he could outrun all the difficulties in his life and have no blood running anywhere but his arms and legs.

Halfway through his run, he deviated from the previous morning to run by Dream Bean, pick up breakfast and a couple of coffees for himself and Blayne. He paused on a corner, waiting for a traffic light to change colors. He spoke into his watch, "Dream Bean," and waited for the GPS to plot him an alternative course.

"*Proceed to highlighted route,*" his watch said in his ear buds.

Ethan took off in the new direction and found himself a block away from the coffee house in a few minutes. He rounded the corner and stopped dead in his tracks. In front of the building was a gaggle of paparazzi. *Fuck! The vultures have arrived.*

Over the years, Ethan had gotten good at spotting paparazzi from a mile away. The celebrity photographers were part of being in the public eye, but to say they were intrusive was an understatement. Half the reason Danny and he had always been so careful with their relationship was because the paparazzi were always around the corner. Ethan knew it made him sound paranoid, but he also knew they really were out to find him. If they could find him in a compromising position, the photographers would have snapped a shot and sold it to the highest bidder.

A photographer glanced in his direction. Since the photograph he'd seen online the previous night showed him in his hat, he took it off to show his newly blond hairdo. He rolled up the cap and put it in his waistband under his tank top. The photographer lowered his camera when he saw Ethan's blond hair. *Thank God, that guy didn't look through his telephoto lens.* Ethan crossed the corner, going the opposite direction from the coffee shop, which forced him to take a much longer way back to Blayne's house.

By the time he got back to Blayne's, it was almost seven-fifteen. He walked into the house and found Blayne sitting on the couch, drinking coffee.

"Good morning," Blayne said as Ethan walked in. "How was your run? I didn't even feel you leave the bed this morning. I must have really passed out last night."

"Well, yesterday was a rough day…for both of us. As for the run, it was great. The paparazzi, on the other hand, are out and about."

"They are?" Blayne asked, putting the newspaper down. "What's that like?"

"Yea, I saw a group scoping out Dream Bean—"

"I know you mentioned it last night, but I thought you were blowing it out of proportion. I should text Kira to let her know your warning last night was right. If they found The Dream Bean, they may be staking out her house."

"As for what it's like," Ethan said, "I've been dealing with them or avoiding them for so long, it's part of my life. I almost forget that normal people don't have to worry about photographers jockeying to get a photograph of their worst possible moments."

"I can't imagine what it's like to be that *public*."

"Most paparazzi are pretty considerate and treat us like humans. Heck, celebrities are often pretty friendly with the paparazzi because we get they have a job to do. It's those that cross the line and become stalkers who cause problems."

"Hey, I made coffee," Blayne said. "Want me to get you a cup?" Blayne asked as he got up off the couch.

"Don't get up. I can get mine," Ethan said. "Remember... I made it yesterday, so I know where you keep everything."

\* \* \* \*

*Blayne*

Blayne had already set out a mug on the counter, so Ethan grabbed the pot off the coffeemaker and poured himself a cup. He then watched Ethan grab the milk he'd purchased the day before and pour a small amount into his mug.

"So, how will you get the paparazzi off your ass?" Blayne asked.

"You really don't. Once they know where you are, there's not too much you can do to get rid of them. Think about them like cockroaches. Once you see one, you know there's another twenty lurking around somewhere nearby."

Ethan walked back into the living room and sat down next to Blayne. Instinctively, Blayne draped his arm around Ethan.

"Eww... I'm hot, sweaty and gross."

"And I don't care," Blayne said. "Cheers?" He held up his mug to clink it with Ethan, who shook his head, smiled and clinked his mug. "Did they see you?"

"One looked in my direction, so I pulled off my hat and tucked it into my shorts. Apparently, the blond hair was just enough to keep him from looking closer. Not sure how long it will last, though."

"Why would the hat give you away?" Blayne asked.

"Probably because I've worn it and been photographed in it a lot. Speaking of which..." Ethan leaned forward, reached around and grabbed the cap from under his shirt before setting it on the coffee table. When he leaned back, he leaned a little more into Blayne.

Blayne sat there for a moment, trying to come up with some kind of plan. "Anything else you're known for wearing? Is there a uniquely Ethan look?"

"Hmm," Ethan said. Blayne watched Ethan's eyes look skyward in a look of concentration. "Probably my shoes."

"Your shoes?"

"Yeah, they're designer, and there aren't too many pairs around, so they're part of my signature look, I guess."

Blayne thought for a second, saying "hmm" to himself, trying to develop a plan.

"What are you thinking?" Ethan asked.

"I'm not sure yet. What if we could distract them into thinking you weren't really you?"

"If only I had a clone."

"You don't need a clone, just someone who looks close enough to confuse them." Blayne took a sip of coffee and thought about it for a moment. An idea sprang into his head. "What size shoe do you wear?"

"Ten and a half or eleven, depending on the brand. Why?"

"So do I. What if I played you for the morning?"

"We don't look alike," Ethan said.

"True, but we had similar hair before you dyed it. We're basically the same build," Blayne said before adding, "with our clothes on. I mean, you're all dancer, hot muscles, and I'm all lithe, thin runner."

"Do you realize how cute you are when you get all flustered?" Ethan asked.

"I... Well, I'm not..." Blayne sat there, unsure what to say.

"I think I see where you're going with this idea of yours," Ethan said. "It could work. I doubt it, though. Paparazzi aren't stupid. You're a good three inches taller than me."

"True, but if I was with Kira, would they tell the difference from afar?"

"Depends on how well they saw the grainy photograph from the cell phone, I guess."

"If you dressed me up in your best Ethan Bond look, could it be enough of a similarity to make them think twice?"

Ethan eyed him up and down. "I don't think it will work, but it's worth a shot."

"Let me call Kira and get her in on the plan. Might as well give it the good old college try."

"Hold up," Ethan said. "I hate putting the brakes on your enthusiasm, but you realize if the paparazzi see through this, you're setting yourself up for being followed."

"What if we had them follow me on purpose?" Blayne asked. A mischievous smile broke across his face. "What if we sent the paparazzi around in circles on *our* terms?"

Blayne spent the next ten minutes laying out a plan that could bore the paparazzi to death, causing them to leave Pennington and keep Ethan safe. The excitement in Ethan's eyes became obvious. It was time to play the parent trap.

"I need to go get showered," Ethan said, standing up. "This plan is so ridiculous, it's brilliant."

"Sometimes crazy works because no one's expecting it," Blayne said, standing up. "I should get ready, too."

Blayne stood almost toe-to-toe with Ethan when Ethan said, "Your plan might work."

* * * *

*Dr. Hennigan*

Dr. Hennigan exited the Osprey after returning from Washington, DC. She slept a bit on the plane, but hardly enough to feel rested. Even with the sleeping cabin in the private jet, Dr. Hennigan never quite slept when she was flying. Thankfully, the onboard shower had allowed her to put herself together before boarding the Osprey and heading out to The Complex. She had many moving parts on the board that day, so she needed to ensure she was ready for anything.

Ms. Wilson greeted her at the door with her tablet in hand. "We have operatives on the ground in New Orleans to complete the Target S project."

"Who do we have on it?"

"Agents Fox and Kramer," Ms. Wilson said as she checked the information on her tablet. "They were trained in the last batch, so this is their first major assignment."

"Are these placed agents or full-time?"

"Both of them are full-time. Agent Fox is ex-CIA, and Agent Kramer is ex-NYPD."

Dr. Hennigan nodded as she and Ms. Wilson meandered through the facility, heading toward Dr.

Hennigan's office. Ms. Wilson entered the smaller office next door. Dr. Hennigan went over to her computer and pulled up her internal email. Most of the information she received that morning was after-action reports from various operations currently underway. She scrolled through the list to see if anything needed her immediate attention. She responded to a recruitment question. An operative in London had been working on a new member of the House of Lords. So far, the deep dive research showed nothing troubling, so Dr. Hennigan gave the operative permission to broach the idea with the potential recruit.

Over the years, The Foundation had created a seamless script, making recruitment straightforward and relatively risk free.

There was a sudden knock on her door. "Come in."

"Dr. Hennigan," Ms. Wilson started as she entered the office, "I have Agents Fox and Kramer for you."

Dr. Hennigan nodded, and Ms. Wilson used her tablet to connect to a wall monitor. Immediately, two women showed up on the screen.

"Status report?" Dr. Hennigan demanded.

"The incendiary device has been placed in Target S's house."

"How will it be triggered?"

"We have it linked to the target's cell. As soon as the device recognizes the target's phone is within range, Target S, along with the device, will be liquidated."

Dr. Hennigan thought for a moment, trying to see if there were any holes in the plan. Seeing none, she said, "Travel separately to Safe House Zeta Epsilon Alpha and await further instructions."

Dr. Hennigan nodded in Ms. Wilson's direction as the call disconnected. "Send the coordinates to the safe house, just in case they are unfamiliar with this one."

"On it, ma'am."

Ms. Wilson's fingers flew over her tablet as she sent instructions to the agents in-field.

"Done, ma'am."

"Thank you. If there's nothing else, you're dismissed."

"Yes, ma'am."

Ms. Wilson turned and left her office. Dr. Hennigan walked back to her desk and sat behind her computer to fill out the report for her mother and grandmother.

# Chapter Sixteen

*Blayne*

Blayne looked at himself in the mirror. With the baseball cap and Oakley sunglasses, he could pull off Ethan Bond as long as people didn't get too close. Where Ethan had a cleft chin, Blayne's was smooth. Where Ethan had rippling muscles that could be seen if he flexed his arms, Blayne had a lither build. Ethan styled Blayne's hair to give it an even more Ethan Bond look. Blayne planned on wearing the baseball cap but figured he'd need to take it off at some point to sell the ruse.

"So? Do I look like you?" Blayne asked.

"You could be my doppelgänger," Ethan said, shooting Blayne a smile through the mirror. "This crazy plan might work."

Blayne pulled out his phone and texted Kira to see where she was. She shot him back a text saying she was ten minutes out.

"I forgot you have an iPhone," Ethan said with a concerned look.

"What's the problem?"

"I have a Samsung Galaxy."

"Still not seeing the problem."

Ethan gave him a questioning look.

"What?" Blayne asked.

"I forget how little you know about pop culture," Ethan said with a smile and a half chuckle. "I've been their spokesperson for about a year now. It would violate my contract to be seen with an iPhone in my hands."

"Oh," Blayne said, "I see how that could be a problem."

"I guess we'll have to trade phones," Ethan said. "It will give me some time to scroll through all your nudes."

"Sorry to disappoint you, but you won't find any on mine," Blayne said as his eyebrows rose a bit. "Gonna see a lot of dick pics on there?" he asked suggestively.

"Nope. Everything is password protected or completely boring in case my phone gets lost or stolen. The last thing I want is someone hacking into my phone and finding things out about me I don't want them to discover."

"What about *EndZone*?" Blayne asked. "If someone hacked your cell, how would you explain that?"

"It doesn't say *EndZone*. I put some skills I learned through an online course to change the app logo," Ethan said. "Trust me. I'm careful *and* paranoid."

Blayne couldn't come up with a reason for needing his cell phone, but they agreed to forward any emergency texts throughout the day. Blayne and Ethan swapped phones, and Ethan gave Blayne a quick tutorial on using his device.

There was a knock at Blayne's door, so he walked through the apartment, checked the peephole and opened the door.

"Whoa," Kira said. She took Blayne in as he stood framed in the doorway. "This is pretty damn eerie."

"Were you followed?" Ethan asked, standing out of the way of the front door.

"At least two photographers followed me. I had to slow down several times to ensure they could tail me."

"Shall we give them a big show?" Blayne asked.

"I would prefer a friendly handshake," Kira said, her annoyance shining through. "But, let's put on the show. If you grab my ass, though, I'll deck you."

Blayne laughed audibly and hoped it would make for a magnificent picture before he embraced Kira in a bear hug. He then ushered Kira into the apartment and shut the door.

"So, what's the plan?" Kira asked.

"We'll wait a few minutes, then head over to Dream Bean," Blayne said.

"We think the more ridiculously public you two can be, the better," Ethan said.

"Let's get this over," Kira said. "My car or yours?"

"Ethan and I talked about it," Blayne said. "We both think it makes more sense for you to drive since Ethan wouldn't have a car here."

"Fine," Kira said.

"Call me if you need anything," Ethan said.

Blayne opened the door, and Kira left the apartment. Blayne made a big show of locking the front door of the apartment. He grasped Kira's hand as she practically dragged him to her car.

Within minutes, Kira pulled into a parking space about a block from the coffee shop. There were cars everywhere. *Hopefully, Dream Bean is getting some good publicity and business out of this*, Blayne thought.

"Shall we hold hands?" Blayne asked.

"Only if you want me to squeeze your hand so hard one of your bones will break," Kira said with a sickly sweet smile.

"Okay, so no hand holding."

"Smart idea."

Blayne and Kira walked the block and pretended they didn't see any of the paparazzi along the way who were taking a ton of photos. Someone had asked the paparazzi to move off the property, so Blayne and Kira could make it into the café unaccosted.

"Stage one is complete," Blayne muttered as they entered the café.

"Thank God."

The two walked up to the barista. Once again, Blayne found himself face-to-face with his student.

Blayne watched as Todd did a double-take as Blayne removed the baseball cap and moved the Oakleys to the top of his head.

"Morning, Todd. I'm going to have a large flat white." Blayne motioned to Kira, saying, "And whatever she's having."

"Large bold coffee, cream, no sugar."

"Why don't you wait at the end of the bar? I'll have those right up," Todd said.

Blayne watched the facial expression on Todd's face. Blayne guessed Todd had seen the news and was now thoroughly confused about what was happening. *Good, if I can confuse a student, maybe we can do the same to the paparazzi.*

Blayne kept a smile plastered on his face the entire time. He kept his back to the bar and watched the patrons inside, pretending not to notice Blayne and Kira's presence in the coffee shop. He even caught a couple of patrons discreetly taking his and Kira's pictures. *Good… Instagram that shit!*

"Mr. Dickenson, your order is ready," Todd said.

"Thanks, Todd." Blayne turned around and grabbed the coffee. He handed the large regular coffee to Kira. "Shall we sit outside?"

Kira said nothing as she walked toward the front door. Blayne moved the Oakleys down on his face as he headed out. He wanted his face partially covered as he exited. As soon as he was back in the sunlight, he placed the baseball cap back on and followed Kira to a table near the front of the patio.

"So, now what?" Kira asked once they'd both settled in at the table.

"We smile and have a conversation. Pretend like nothing strange is going on. Remember… Our goal is to look like we do not know what's going on."

Blayne watched Kira take a deep breath through her nose and let it out slowly. "Did you talk to your partners about Jamie today?"

"I had a conversation this morning with one of the senior partners. He's on board with taking Jamie's case pro bono. I already called Dr. Reich and set up an appointment for coffee this afternoon."

"Where are you two meeting?"

"Fuck! Dammit, I didn't even think about that," Kira said, a look of disgust washing over her face. "We're meeting here."

"Well, use it to your advantage," Blayne suggested.

"What do you mean?"

"Like we talked about last night, you'll have a ton of reporters who want to point cameras in your face. You might as well use the publicity. Get public opinion on your side."

"I'll think about it. I still need to run this past the senior partners before I do something like that."

"How did you explain the whole Ethan thing to them?"

She let out a sigh. "I told them the truth. I told them you were friends, and the picture was taken completely out of context. They weren't concerned. If anything, they thought it was pretty damn funny, since they all know I'm not into guys."

Blayne and Kira sat for another thirty minutes before deciding to leave. While waiting, Blayne purposefully removed the baseball cap and sunglasses. He hoped the paparazzi would get a perfect shot of his face.

\* \* \* \*

*Agent Murphy*

Agent Murphy got up early in the morning and went to the gym before heading into the office. Thankfully, after her conversation with her boss the previous morning, not much else had come through her email. At least no one was calling for her head again.

She pulled into the nondescript three-story white-paneled and red-brick building. After parking her car, she headed into the lobby, flashed her badge at security and walked up the stairs to the third floor where her office was located. The building was still quiet, so she didn't run into anyone, which was great in her mind. She had a bunch of paperwork to finish after their interviews with the cast and crew at *NOLA Nights* the previous afternoon.

She set her coffee down on the table and booted up her computer. She then entered her sixteen-digit password and the keycode on the dual-authentication device she kept on her keychain. She scrolled through the email to see any additional information from NOPD on the forensic analysis. Since the New Orleans FBI Field Office was small, they worked closely with the NOPD on most cases. Of course, the FBI didn't run around sticking their noses into local law enforcement cases unless they were invited in or some national security issue trumped local jurisdiction.

She deleted a handful of emails that were not pertinent. She was amazed at the amount of spam she received in her FBI email inbox. *You would think we would have better spam filters by now,* she thought as she continued deleting. She almost deleted one by accident but stopped herself when she saw the address was from a colleague who worked with the National Cyber Investigative Joint Task Force — NCIJTF.

Murphy opened the message.

*Agent Murphy,*
*Your case has come across my desk. There are some peculiarities we need to discuss. When you get this email, please contact me using the NOLA sensitive compartmented information facility – SCIF. I'll be in my office by eight a.m.*
*Agent Annie Little*

Murphy responded, letting Agent Little know she was in the office herself and would be in the SCIF in ten minutes. *Very strange. So, cloak and dagger.*

Murphy descended the stairs and crossed into the annex part of the building where the SCIF had been built. Along the way, she said hello to a couple of agents and other personnel she knew. She used her ID badge and submitted to an iris scan to gain access. She entered the room, logged in then set up the connection with Washington, DC.

A minute later, a woman in her late thirties appeared on the screen, sporting a shoulder-length bob cut. "Agent Little, good to see you. It's been a while," Murphy said as the woman's audio turned on.

"Yes, it has, Agent Murphy. I believe it was at a cybercrime training seminar I gave at Quantico two years ago."

"You're probably right," Murphy said, nodding in agreement. "So, what's this all about?"

Agent Little scrunched her brow, looking at the screen. "I don't know quite how to explain what I've found. Let's say an anomaly in your case got flagged when someone at NOPD tried to access Cynthia Dunning and Daniel Hawthorne's phone records."

Little explained that this only came to anyone's attention because an irregularity was noticed. "We have tower information showing a quick data burst from their phones. But the data burst was not recorded on the cellular hard drives."

"Data burst? I thought we were tracking down email addresses?"

"Let me guess," Agent Little said. "You reached out to FreeMail.com and received a litany of IP addresses?"

"Yes," Murphy said quizzically.

"I've run into that problem with them before. It doesn't matter. The email addresses are dead ends. From what we can tell, a data burst piggybacks on one of the emails as it heads to the intended target's cell. The emails are immediately deleted from the target's phone, so the recipient never knows it happened. Even the data burst isn't noticed by the target. We've seen the trick before, but the addition of decoy emails was a new one."

"How has this happened?"

"Only a handful of times I'm aware of, which is why it's troublesome. The other times we've seen this irregularity, it was detected after someone was assassinated."

"Which is exactly what it looks like we have here," Murphy said, finishing Little's idea.

"Exactly," Little said. "However, the other assassinations were always high-value targets. I'm not sure how two soap opera stars qualify as high value," she said with no sense of irony in her voice.

"Hmm…" Murphy started. "You think the people behind these assassinations here in NOLA are linked to previous ones?"

Little nodded. Murphy took a minute to make sense of this extra information. "Let me run a theory I had by you," Murphy said. She then floated her idea about Ethan Bond's connection to the Dunning and Hawthorne murders and the Peregrine Airlines Flight 923 explosion. "Now, I say this," Murphy hedged, "knowing full well the NTSB ruled this an accident."

Murphy watched as Little rolled her eyes. "Since when does the NTSB do anything quickly?" Little asked, her voice dripping with contempt. "That investigation was a coverup before any investigators hit the ground in New Orleans."

"This case is leading to more dead ends than answers," Murphy noted. "I feel like one of those conspiracy nuts who think the US is run by lizard people."

"But sometimes conspiracies are real and not imagined. To pull off a complete sham investigation of a bombing of an airline flight on US soil, some pretty powerful people had to be involved in the coverup," Little said. "As for Mr. Ethan Bond, he leads me to another peculiarity in your case."

"How so?"

"The same data burst sent from Dunning to Hawthorne was sent from Hawthorne to Ethan Bond. More recently, the data was sent from Bond's phone to Stephanie Anne Mitchell, who lives in New Orleans."

"Have you tried capturing the data?"

"We've tried. The encryption used is unlike anything we've ever seen," Little admitted. A look of intense concentration washed over the woman's face before she spoke again. "Honestly, it's lightning years beyond what should exist. It functions like a text message but worms its way into the phone's internal hard drive. As far as we can tell, it doesn't do anything after that beyond send it to the next person then wait on the hard drive. I'm betting the recipients don't even know they've received anything."

"So, you're telling me we have some strange Internet worm embedding itself into people's cell phones, and we don't know what this worm does?"

"We're not sure what the data is. We're not even sure why it's jumping or why the cell companies have no data transfer record. It's like a worm that fills in the dirt behind it as soon as it's passed through. Or, maybe the worm burrows into a new hole, clones itself, then digs a new hole. We don't know—and that's what worries me. We've not seen anything like this — and I mean anything."

"Okay. What do you need me to do?"

"I need you and your partner to secure Stephanie Anne Mitchell and get her cell phone. I hope to have a Foreign Intelligence Surveillance Act — FISA — warrant for Mitchell's phone as soon as I can get the warrant. My team is currently figuring out which judge to approach."

Something about the way Little said this last sentence sent shivers up and down Murphy's spine. "Back up. What do you mean by figuring out who to approach?"

"I'll deny what I'm about to say, but I want to be upfront with you," Little said, narrowing her gaze on Murphy through the screen. "This type of technology could be created domestically or by a foreign adversary. We don't know who to trust. I can say my boss sanctioned our meeting, but not even your boss or your boss's boss knows we're talking."

"And you'd deny this conversation occurred if asked," Murphy finished. Murphy didn't need Little to say 'yes', because the look on the woman's face said everything she needed to know. "Fuck me!"

"If this goes as high as we're afraid it does, fuck all of us."

"As soon as you have the FISA warrant, my partner and I will discreetly serve it without letting Special Agent in Charge Geraldine Jackson know."

"When you have secured Ms. Mitchell, we'll simultaneously read in the director on our end, but not before."

Murphy and Little spent the next few minutes discussing logistics before Murphy ended the call. She logged out of the computer and exited the SCIF to find Agent Jackson standing outside. A quick look of shock crossed Jackson's face but was quickly masked.

"Agent Murphy," Jackson said, more as a question than a statement. "I'm surprised to see you here."

"I was asked to read someone in on the Dunning and Hawthorne murders from the DOJ. The Attorney General doesn't like the idea of two celebrities being murdered. It makes law enforcement look weak," Murphy lied.

Jackson's face softened. "I wish those bureaucrats at the DOJ would stay out of our investigations until we are finished."

"My thoughts exactly."

"Anything I need to be aware of?" Jackson questioned.

"Not at the moment. Still waiting on some of the forensic evidence to come in from NOPD. We should have it today or tomorrow, according to their lab."

"I expect to see a report later this morning."

"I was about to work on it when I got this email," Murphy acknowledged. "I'm heading back to my office to finish it. You should have it in your inbox within the hour."

\* \* \* \*

*Blayne*

Blayne spent the rest of the afternoon followed by the paparazzi. Some, he guessed, thought he'd lead them to Ethan, but most were still following him because they thought he was Ethan. He caught them out of the corner of his eye a few times, even after he went to campus. He texted back and forth with Ethan several times, still clumsy using Ethan's phone. Blayne'd had an iPhone for so long. The switch to the Galaxy was more awkward than he would have imagined.

He walked into class later that afternoon and noticed a young woman do a double-take. Blayne was still wearing the hat and Oakley's as he unpacked his attaché case, pulled out his laptop and plugged it into the computer terminal in the room's front.

"Mr. Dickenson, what's with the fresh look?" the young woman asked.

"Got up a bit later than usual," he responded, taking off the hat and sunglasses.

"Were you at Dream Bean yesterday?" the woman asked.

"Yep, I was there with my best friend. Why?"

"Have you seen the picture?" she asked.

"What picture?" Blayne lied.

She got out of her desk and brought up the image of Ethan and Kira. "Where did you get this? That's me and my best friend, Kira."

"You don't know, do you?" the young woman asked.

"I do not know what you're talking about," Blayne lied. *Thank God for those drama classes in high school.*

"Someone posted the picture of you saying you were Ethan Bond."

"Who?"

"Ethan Bond? Member of the group ZERO?"

Blayne wrinkled his brow and tried to deliver his best look of confusion.

"Oh, my God, this is hysterical," the woman said. "Can you please put the hat and shades back on for just a minute?"

"Why?" Blayne asked, drawing the word out.

"People think there's a celebrity hiding here in Pennington, but it's just you. I want to post your picture on Twitter, telling the world who you are."

"I'm not sure I like this idea," Blayne said. *She's going to make this easier than me walking around all day.*

"Trust me, Mr. Dickenson. It's in your best interest to do this."

"Okay," he said, giving her his best awe-shucks look.

She snapped his photo a couple of times with the chalkboard behind him. She had him take off the hat and sunglasses and snapped a couple of more pictures. She then uploaded them to Instagram.

"This is going to double the amount of my Instagram followers," Blayne heard her say as she returned to her desk.

Blayne turned his back to the class and glanced down at his watch. *And I still have five minutes to spare.* Blayne pulled out Ethan's phone and sent him a text, letting him know what the student had done.

Ethan texted back.

*She already has one hundred likes and a few dozen forwards. In the next hour, this will explode all over social media.*

*Why don't you post something from my social media accounts in an hour confirming it's me? You think this will stop the paparazzi from following me all day?*

*Wait! You have multiple social media accounts? Pulling up the app now. Awe, you were a cutie in high school.*

Blayne rolled his eyes and was glad his back was to the class because he felt the heat increasing in his cheeks. He typed a quick *Thanks* before pocketing the phone and turning to the class.

"Okay, so today is going to be a writing workshop day. I hope everyone has their outlines ready to go. If you forgot to print off three copies of your outline for your groups, there's a computer lab down the hall. Go do it now. If you don't have your outlines finished, there's the door," Blayne said. "Go to the library and get it done now. If you're not ready to work, you're wasting yours and your group's time."

Blayne watched as one student left with his book bag and a couple of others walked down the hall to the computer lab.

"Okay, break into your groups."

\* \* \* \*

After class, Blayne pulled out Ethan's phone and told him he was heading back to Dream Bean to meet up with Kira and Dr. Reich to discuss Jamie's situation.

*Tell them I said hello and wish I could be there. By the way, congratulations. You're trending on Instagram and Twitter.*
*#SexyProf #NotEthanBond #CanIGetExtraCredit?*

Blayne groaned as he read the text. *I don't know how he lives like this.* Thankfully, Blayne saw no more paparazzi on campus, so the Instagram posts were working.

He made his way off campus and enjoyed the stroll in the afternoon heat. He unbuttoned the cuffs on his long shirt and rolled up the sleeves while walking. When he rounded the corner to The Dream Bean, no paparazzi were hanging out this time. He walked up the stairs and went inside. Neither Dr. Reich nor Kira had arrived, so he ordered a mint-infused iced tea and went to sit outside under one of the umbrella-shaded tables. The outdoors would give the trio more privacy than sitting in the closely packed interior.

He kept the Oakleys on and hung the baseball cap off one of his knees. He thought about putting the hat on the table but found it disgusting. Of course, Blayne had been wearing Ethan's sweaty hat all day without complaining. Every time he put it on or took it off, Blayne smelled Ethan's scent, which Blayne had grown to enjoy. As much as he loved having Ethan's hat near, he didn't think Kira and Dr. Reich would react similarly to the sweaty ball cap.

Kira arrived a few minutes later and put her bag in the chair beside him. "Whatever you did, the leeches stopped following me about an hour ago," Kira said. Blayne explained how the student had posted about him on Instagram and how he was now blowing up on social media.

"Is it a good or a bad thing?" Kira asked.

"I'm not sure, either," Blayne admitted, opening his eyes wide and shrugging. "I've been assured by Ethan it's a good thing."

Dr. Reich arrived as they were talking. Blayne noticed the dark bags under her eyes. He doubted the poor woman had rested.

"How's Jamie?" Blayne asked.

"He's doing much better than I am," Dr. Reich admitted.

"Madeline, I'm going to get something. Can I get you anything?" Kira asked.

"A large coffee with cream. You can bring me a couple of packets of brown sugar if they have them."

"Sure thing," Kira said. Blane watched as Kira put her hand on Dr. Reich's shoulder and squeezed it before she headed into Dream Bean.

"So, what's with the getup?" Dr. Reich asked.

Blayne barked a laugh and told her the cloak and dagger story of his day.

\* \* \* \*

*Agent Murphy*

Murphy spent the rest of the morning completing reports and filling out paperwork. By one p.m., she finally got the FISA warrant from Annie Little with the NCIJTF. With the warrant in hand, she also officially received permission to read in her boss and her partner. Her conversation with Jackson and Harper had been a bit tense, because Jackson felt she was being kept out of the loop on cases involving her own agents. Thankfully, Jackson didn't blame Murphy for the bureaucracy and secrecy of Washington, DC.

Harper took everything in stride. By two p.m., the group loaded into one of the pool sedans and took off into the city's heart to pick up Stephanie Anne Mitchell and her cell phone. The agents swung by the high school where she taught, only to find that Mitchell had left early for some kind of medical appointment, so they headed over to her residence instead.

Murphy pulled the car down the block from Mitchell's house in the first available street-side parking space she could find.

"How are we playing this?" Harper asked.

"Nothing in this woman's background suggests she's anything but on the up-and-up. We assume the intel from NCIJTF is correct, and she doesn't even know there's a file on her cell phone," Murphy explained. "She's a victim, and our job today is to get her to a safehouse until DC can figure out what's going on."

The two exited the car and walked down the sidewalk. Murphy noticed an older man who sat on the stoop of one house across the street smoking something that didn't look like a cigarette. *I'm sure he has a prescription.* She caught him eyeing them as they walked past, but he didn't try to hide his pot-smoking. *Ahh, this city!*

The buildings in this part of town were all two-story Creole-style townhomes. Even though the Mardi Gras parades didn't purposefully come through this neighborhood, the traditional second-story porch with the iron railing ran along both sides of the street. As they approached Mitchell's address, she noticed the townhome had potted plants fastened to the railing. She glanced up at the balcony and saw a chaise lounge chair and a large fern potted in an oversized terracotta pot. *Homey.*

She climbed the three steps and knocked on the front door as she pulled out her FBI shield to have at the ready. Harper stayed below and off center of the front door, in case things went sideways. Murphy heard some movement inside before the door opened partly. A chain lock prevented the door from fully opening.

"Can I help you?" a young woman said as she peered out of the door.

Murphy opened her shield and held it up to the door. "Stephanie Anne Mitchell?"

"Yes, that's me."

"Can I ask you to please step outside?"

A look of concern flashed across Mitchell's face. Ms. Mitchell closed the door briefly, and Murphy heard the metal chain being unlatched. When the door opened again, Murphy noticed a purse on a small table inside the front door.

"Grab your purse," Murphy said.

Mitchell's eyes grew as her eyebrows shot up with concern, but she did as Murphy instructed.

"I know this is scary," Murphy started. "But let's walk down the street and chat in our car. Don't worry. You're not in trouble."

The woman hesitated a second but followed Murphy down the stairs as Harper followed them from behind.

"Okay, you're freaking me out here," Mitchell said.

"Let's wait until we're in our car. It's down the street." She nodded toward the older man, still eyeing them from across the street. "I want to have this conversation…privately."

The three walked in silence. When they returned to the car, Murphy gestured for Mitchell to sit in the front while Harper sat in the car's back. Murphy started the engine to get the air conditioning running again.

"Does this have something to do with Ethan Bond?" Mitchell asked when the doors were closed.

"Yes, and no." Murphy told Mitchell about the data burst and its potential implications for national security without giving away too many details.

"You realize how crazy you sound right now, right?" Mitchell said when Murphy finished laying out the parts she could.

"Trust me, I do. And for your records," Murphy said, "here's a copy of the FISA warrant issued by a federal judge this morning." She pulled the printed copy from her coat pocket and handed it to Mitchell. Murphy watched as Mitchell glanced through the document quickly.

"Wait a second," Mitchell said. "This authorizes you to take me into protective custody?"

"Yes, ma'am," Harper said from the backseat. "There are parts of the FISA warrant sealed for national security."

"National security?" Mitchell gasped. "What the hell is going on? I thought this was about Ethan secretly dating some guy in Houston."

Murphy made a quick mental note to follow up on that last tidbit of information once they had Mitchell safe and secure. Murphy reached into the middle console separating the driver and passenger seats and pulled out a small bag.

"This is a Faraday cage. The bag will block signals to and from your cell until we can have someone see what's going on," Murphy said, opening the bag. "Please retrieve your phone and place it inside."

"I can't," Mitchell said. "My cell's in my house still. The blasted thing didn't charge fully last night, so it died earlier today. I plugged it into the charger beside my bed when I got home."

"Not a problem," Murphy said. "We can either go with you back to your house or have Agent Harper go get it for you. I'll let you make a choice."

Murphy watched Mitchell's face as she decided and started rummaging through her purse. She pulled out a set of keys and handed them to Harper. "The key with the purple band around the top is the one to the front door. You'll see the staircase off to the left when you get inside. Go up the stairs and find it right at the top."

Harper nodded in understanding and exited the car. Murphy watched as Harper made his way down the street.

"Do you think I'm in danger?" Mitchell asked.

"Honestly, I don't know what to think. The evidence that something strange is going on here is pretty convincing," Murphy said as she turned her head to look at Mitchell while keeping one eye on Harper as he made his way down the sidewalk. "If I hadn't seen the look of concern this morning when I talked to the cybercrime people in DC, I wouldn't believe any of this, either."

The vehicle rocked violently as a shockwave hit them, followed by the whumping sound of an explosion. Harper was thrown off his feet as a raging fire wall rose skyward from where Mitchell's house used to be. Car alarms along the street immediately started whining.

With her ears still ringing, Murphy looked at Mitchell and yelled, "Don't leave!" Murphy threw open the car door and ran toward her partner.

When Murphy got to Harper, he was already pushing himself into a sitting position. "You okay?" she yelled.

"What happened?"

She pulled out her phone and dialed nine-one-one as she helped Harper to his feet. She glanced across the street and noticed the old man still sitting on his stoop, smoking his weed as if this were the most normal thing in the world.

# Chapter Seventeen

*Ethan*

Ethan was bored out of his mind. He'd lounged on the couch for most of the afternoon. He'd even busted out Blayne's *I Love Lucy* collection and watched a few famous episodes after googling a list of ones he should see. He didn't want to tell Blayne, but his knowledge of *I Love Lucy* was limited. He remembered watching a few episodes with his great-grandmother when he was a kid, but it was so long ago he probably didn't even know which ones he'd seen.

When he wasn't watching TV, he was plowing through his novel or taking a nap. Thankfully, they had plenty of leftover pizza, so he would not starve anytime soon. *What army did Blayne think he was feeding?* He'd gotten up, gone to the bathroom and come back into the living room when he heard Blayne's iPhone buzz on the table. *He's got a text.* He plopped back down on the couch and picked up the phone.

*E it's B. Love the cloak and dagger. I just had a text from someone named Zach. It looks like it's important. All it said was 'nine-one-one! Zach – call now.'*

Ethan shot back a quick thanks before asking, *This is horrible, but can you send me his number? I know nothing by memory anymore.*

There was a momentary pause as Ethan waited for the next text. He imagined Blayne trying to figure out where the Galaxy address book was located, then trying to find Zach's contact information. The phone buzzed, so he picked it up and got the info from Blayne.

*Thanks for the fast response. Hope all is well in paparazzi-confusion land.*

*All is good. Having coffee with Kira and Dr. Reich. Should be home in an hour.*

*I'll be here. Not going anywhere.*

He then hit the phone number Blayne had texted him and waited as the call went through. *Come on, Zach. Pick up!* He figured Zach wouldn't because he didn't recognize the number. When the call went to voice mail, Ethan texted Zach.

*Dude, pick up the phone. I'm borrowing someone else's cell. Long story.*

He hit send. Almost immediately, the iPhone vibrated in his hand. He looked down at the screen to make sure it wasn't someone else before hitting the answer button.

"What's the emergency?" Ethan asked.

"It's Stephanie," Zach said. "Something's happened."

Ethan felt himself bolt upright on the couch. "What do you mean, something happened?"

"There was an explosion," Zach said.

Ethan's brain immediately started swimming. He barely heard anything as the blood ran to his ears after the word 'explosion'. His heart started thudding in his chest as his mouth ran dry. Breathing was hard and becoming more difficult with each passing second.

"Ethan!"

"Give me a second," Ethan screeched out between shallow, almost nonexistent breaths.

"Dude, breathe!" Zach yelled. "You're having a panic attack. I remember what they sound like from our early years on stage together."

Ethan heard the words, but their meaning wasn't clear. His vision blurred like he was looking through a fish lens.

"Ethan!" Zach yelled again. "Breathe, damn you. Do what the doctor taught you."

Ethan closed his eyes and tried to focus on his breathing as he bent over the waist and put his head between his knees. He heard a voice. It sounded like it was a million miles away, and Ethan couldn't make out any of the individual words. Ethan forced himself to inhale then exhale deeply. As his breathing and pulse normalized, Zach's voice sounded like it was getting closer, even though Ethan knew it was all in his mind.

"Whoa," Ethan said between breaths.

"How you doing, buddy?" Zach asked.

"I haven't had one of those in years, and now I've had them two days in a row." Keeping his eyes shut, Ethan slowly returned to a normal sitting position. "Okay, tell me what you know about Stephanie."

"I don't know much. The FBI only let her make one call, so she called me because she had my number on a slip of paper in her purse."

"Whoa, FBI?"

"Oh yeah, totally missing some pieces here. Let me backtrack."

Ethan listened as Zach told him about the explosion at Stephanie's house. Thankfully, Stephanie hadn't been in the house because she was talking to the FBI. Even though Zach did his best to tell the story, pieces of what was going on were still absent.

"If you talk to Stephanie again, give her this number. I'm going to get on the first flight back to New Orleans. I'll call you as soon as I have plans," Ethan said. Zach promised he would as they hung up. *I need to talk to Blayne.*

* * * *

*Dr. Hennigan*

Dr. Hennigan sat in her office, reading an email she'd received from an agent on the ground in New Orleans. Ms. Wilson sat on the other side of her desk, waiting for Hennigan's reaction.

"How the hell do you miss killing someone when you use a bomb?" Hennigan seethed.

"In Agents Fox and Kramer's defense," Ms. Wilson said cautiously, "their plan was flawless. The asset was destroyed as soon as the target's cell phone was within range of the incendiary device. Unfortunately, the target was not with the asset at the time of the explosion."

"What aren't you telling me?" Dr. Hennigan asked without emotion as she narrowed her gaze on Ms. Wilson.

"That look doesn't intimidate me, Phillipa," Ms. Wilson said.

Using her first name was like a slap across the face. She knew she'd overstepped a line with Ms. Wilson. "I'm sorry, Ms. Wilson," Dr. Hennigan said as she rubbed the bridge of her nose. "This entire operation keeps going to shit."

"Well, Dr. Hennigan," the switch to her honorific was immediately noticed, "the FBI arrived immediately before the incendiary went off."

"Then the bomb didn't work."

"One would think, but the explosion perfectly coincided with the cell signal. We think her phone must have been dead when she entered the house. She probably plugged it in, and once it rebooted and got the cell signal, it triggered the incendiary."

"This is speculative?"

"Of course it is," Ms. Wilson said. "But speculation doesn't mean it doesn't fit the facts on the ground."

"Any word from Denzili and Richardson?"

"They are on the ground and making their move on the target. Target E should be liquidated within moments."

"Do we have a live feed?"

"Let me see if I can pull it up," Ms. Wilson said as she started typing and swiping on her tablet. Within a few moments, the large screen in Dr. Hennigan's office showed two live feeds, one from each agent.

Superimposed over the feed was a green dot where Target E was located.

"What's the green dot?"

"That's the cell phone we've been tracking."

"Do the agents on the ground have access to this information?"

"Yes, they do, sir."

Dr. Hennigan stared at the monitor. The image was grainy, but then these feeds were always that way. She could see the agents were on a higher perch, probably eight to nine hundred yards from the target. The target was with the same woman from the photo and wearing the same baseball cap and sunglasses. An umbrella was partially in the way, but she knew Denzili could make the shot. Dr. Hennigan had seen her make much more complicated ones in the past during a blizzard, so this should be like shooting fish in a barrel.

* * * *

*Blayne*

Blayne looked over his shoulder and watched Kira emerge from Dream Bean with Dr. Reich's and her coffees in hand. Dr. Reich was barely keeping it together, so Blayne reached out and grabbed her hand, reassuringly squeezing it as Kira settled and pulled out a yellow legal pad and a pen.

"Have you spoken to anyone from the school district yet?" Kira asked.

"No, I haven't," Dr. Reich started. "Should I?"

"No," Kira said as her pen moved across the pad's surface. "Please don't talk to anyone calling from the school district. When they reach out to you, direct them to me. From a legal perspective, you shouldn't get in the middle of any discussions. The school fucked up. They're going to try to cover their asses. And their lawyers will probably attempt to get you to agree to something. We don't want that."

"Okay," Dr. Reich said, sipping her coffee. "What else?"

"Well, I spoke to the district attorney this morning. They are debating whether to file charges against the criminals as adults. At first, the DA had considered trying them as juveniles, then she saw the video for herself. As you know, it's damning."

Blayne watched as Dr. Reich shuddered. "I wish I'd never seen the video. I can't get those images out of my head," Reich said as tears formed in her eyes.

Kira reached into her bag, pulled out a travel-size pack of tissues and handed them to Dr. Reich.

"Thanks," Dr. Reich said. "I couldn't sleep last night. Every time I closed my eyes, those images flooded my mind. I don't understand how people can be so fucking cruel."

"I also talked to a former friend who works for the Department of Justice. Given the history and background of this case, the DOJ could indict the teens on federal charges to ensure this trial is heard in a federal court."

"Why?"

"To be perfectly honest, hate crime cases have not fared well in Texas courts. Since its first passing in 1993, Texas' hate crime law has rarely been used. There's still a huge political bias against these laws because of right-wing talking points 'about punishing bad behavior' and not 'people's politically incorrect opinions and beliefs'." Kira accompanied her emphasized speech with air quotes to stress how she felt about these ideas.

"Where does this leave us?" Dr. Reich asked.

"There are two separate cases here. One is the legal case where the criminals who attacked and sexually assaulted your son will face criminal prosecution. The case will be handled by either a state or federal prosecutor. I'm trying to get it kicked up to the federal level because Texas has a horrible history with these cases. And finding juries who will convict teenagers is harder at the state level. Too many Texan good-old-boys and good-old-gals see bullying as a normal, natural part of childhood, so they're less likely to hold these vile creatures culpable for their actions—especially when they're white, suburban kids. Also, kicking it up to the feds would put it squarely within the federal court jurisdiction in Houston, which has a more sympathetic jury pool."

"What's the second case?" Blayne asked.

"It's a civil case under David's Law, where we show the school district was negligent in handling Jamie's repeated harassment. We can show the district knew of the threats against Jamie, and they did not follow through with Texas law to adequately contact his parents, nor did they stop the harassment from happening. And since Jamie's lawyer," she pointed her index finger at herself, "warned them two days before the attack, they can't claim ignorance."

"You think they'd try?" Dr. Reich asked.

"Of course, they'd try. In these cases, school districts' first line of defense is always to claim they did not know what was happening. Or if they knew, they did not know how bad it was."

There was a sudden buzzing sound, and all three looked to see whose phone was making the noise.

"It's mine," Blayne said, recognizing his number on the screen. He immediately hit the button. Well, he tried to hit the button. He cursed under his breath as he tried to tap and swipe at the screen. *Whose bright idea was it to tap and swipe to get the fucking thing to answer?*

"Hey, Ethan," Blayne said, "what's up?" Blayne heard a sound, but it wasn't clear. "You're breaking up. Let me see if I can find a better place to talk." He stood, forgetting he'd placed Ethan's hat on his knee. He bent quickly to pick it up.

*Fuck!* he thought to himself, as what felt like a bee stung him in his shoulder. An intense burning sensation followed. He looked to see where the bee was. Instead, he saw a red spot on his shoulder that seemed to get larger. *Did I bump into paint?*

The sound of the bullet now lodged in his shoulder finally hit his ears as he felt himself half-spinning, crumpling to the ground. He saw the blue sky next to a brightly colored umbrella. He heard a noise, twisted his head to the right and saw Kira knock over her chair. The sound of a woman screaming behind him caught his attention. Kira's face was animated, and it looked like she was yelling something, but Blayne couldn't tell what she was saying. He sensed motion around him. His head spun, his eyelids went limp and the world around him went dark.

# Chapter Eighteen

*Agent Murphy*

Murphy stared at the drab walls of the safe house. Special Agent in Charge Geraldine Jackson stood in the living room, pacing back and forth. Her anger, mixed with anxiety, was wearing on Murphy's last nerve, but Murphy kept her wits about her...so far. Murphy listened again as Stephanie Mitchell explained that she did not know what was happening. She detailed her relationship with Cynthia Dunning, Daniel Hawthorne and Ethan Bond for what seemed like the gazillionth time.

Murphy's cell phone vibrated, and he looked down to see Agent Harper calling. She stood up and tiptoed into the kitchen. "Murphy."

"Hey, Murph, you okay?"

"Shouldn't I be asking you that? You're the one who got knocked unconscious out there."

"The docs said I'm fine. Just had my bell rung pretty good. It's gonna leave a nasty bump on my head."

"Always knew you had a thick skull."

"Hardy-har-har," Harper said, the hint of an upbeat in his voice.

"As for here, Jackson is in the other room grilling Ms. Mitchell. Mitchell's already talked to ATF, and I even had Little from the NCIJTF talk with her for a few minutes — on an unsecured line at that."

"Did you let her reach out to anyone?" Harper asked.

"Yeah. I was curious to see who Mitchell would call," Murphy admitted.

"And?"

"She called Zach Reeves."

"Who the hell is that?"

"One of Ethan Bond's bandmates. I didn't know who he was, either. Thank God for Google."

There was a pause. She could hear the muffled sounds of Harper arguing with a doctor or nurse about being discharged. The doctor wanted to keep him overnight for observation, but Harper was being his typical stubborn self. She walked over to the fridge and grabbed herself a bottle of water. The fridge had a few staple items, but not much else was in the safe house. And with the layer of dust on most things, the place hadn't been used in a long time. She twisted the cap off the bottle and took a swig.

"Still with me, Murph?"

"I'm here. Guess you're not taking doctor's orders?"

"Me? Nah. They wanted to keep me. When I played football, I had worse things happen. I'll be fine. I promised I wouldn't go to sleep for at least eight hours and to come back if I had any symptoms."

"Better safe than sorry," Murphy said. She knew better than to tell Harper to follow the doctor's orders and stay in the hospital, so she didn't even bother.

"Holy shit!" Harper said suddenly in her ear.

"What's wrong?"

"You near a television?"

"Can be."

"Turn on RNN."

Murphy hustled into the living room, where Jackson still grilled Ms. Mitchell. She pulled up the remote control.

"What do you think you're doing?" Jackson growled as she shot daggers at Murphy.

"Sorry, ma'am. Something's happening."

She waited for RNN to appear on the screen. Stephen McNeil stood on the corner of a street. A coffee shop was in the background, surrounded by police cars and blue and red flashing lights.

"The country mourns the death of musician Ethan Bond at this hour."

A sharp gasp escaped Murphy's mouth. She heard a garbled moan escape Mitchell's lips as well.

"From what we can tell, Ethan Bond has been assassinated." McNeil spun a tale of how he was shot from a high-powered rifle. The camera swiveled to show a taller building on the opposite side of the street from where the coffee shop was located. "Although it hasn't been confirmed, we believe the assassin shot Bond from somewhere in this building. We'll have more on this developing story right after the break." The RNN logo flooded the screen, which was followed by an advertisement for some kind of erection pill. Murphy absently hit mute.

Murphy stood in stunned silence for a second. She heard the muffled cries coming from Mitchell's direction as she heard Jackson let out a few curse words. Murphy's phone vibrated in her hand. She hadn't even realized she'd hung up on Harper. She looked down to see who the incoming call was from.

"Agent Little, what the hell is happening here?" Murphy said. Jackson shot her a questioning look, so she whispered, "It's the cybercrime agent," before telling Little, "I'm putting you on speaker." Murphy hit the speaker button on the phone.

"Sorry, Agent Murphy, I'm just getting information. Somehow this happened, and it didn't get filtered into the computer system properly, which is why we just heard about it. From what I can tell, Ms. Mitchell's house exploding and someone taking a hit out on Mr. Bond happened within minutes of each other."

"So, you're telling us that there is no way these are coincidences?" Jackson said.

"Who's that?" Little asked.

"Supervisory Special Agent in Charge Jackson. She came by to talk to Ms. Mitchell," Murphy said. "I should also mention Ms. Mitchell is in the room with us now."

There was an interruption on the other end of the line. "Sorry... Some additional information is coming in now from Houston. Give me a minute."

Murphy hit the mute button. "What the fuck is going on here? What is so important about this data burst?"

"That's an excellent question," Jackson said. "Whoever these people are, they're equipped and trained, which is pretty fucking scary."

"I'll say." Murphy turned to Mitchell. "I can't believe you had to hear like this." Murphy watched as the young woman sat on the couch, tears streaming down her face. She looked to be in complete and utter shock. Murphy spotted a box of Kleenex on the other side of the room, so she walked over and grabbed the box and handed it to Stephanie. "I am so sorry for your loss," Murphy said.

Mitchell looked up from where she was sitting. "Tell me you'll nail these fucking bastards."

Murphy wanted to reassure her, but she knew better than to over-promise things to victims. "We'll do everything in our power to make sure these people are brought to justice." Although the words weren't a commitment, they seemed to mollify Mitchell.

"Agents Jackson and Murphy," Little said, coming back on the phone, "I'm going to have to call you back. Things are getting more complicated on the ground with every passing second. The Houston Field Office has dispatched Agent Raymond Anderson to the scene. I'm liaising with him from Washington. I'll call you back as soon as I have more information."

There was a click on the other end of the line as they were disconnected.

"What now?" Mitchell asked in a small, quiet voice.

"Sadly," Murphy started, "we wait." An exasperated groan escaped Mitchell's mouth, which Murphy agreed with all too well. "Trust me... We hate the waiting game as much as anyone. As agents, we'd much rather be doing than sitting."

There was a sudden knock on the door of the safe house. Murphy shot Jackson a quick glance.

"You expecting anyone?" Jackson asked.

"No. You?"

"Nope." Jackson turned to Mitchell. "Please quietly go into the back bedroom." A look of fear flashed over Mitchell's face. "It's a precaution."

Mitchell stood and walked to the back of the safe house. Both Murphy and Jackson unholstered their weapons as they approached the front door.

"Murphy," a voice yelled, "it's just me. I come bearing pizza."

Recognizing Harper's voice, both Murphy and Jackson holstered their weapons. Jackson went to the back of the house to tell Mitchell it was okay as Murphy opened the front door.

"Ya know," Murphy said as she bit her lower lip, "you could have been shot. Why didn't you call to let me know you were on your way?"

"Figured I'd surprise you."

She let her partner into the house. Jackson came back into the living room from the back. "She's passed out asleep," Jackson said.

"Wow, that was fast," Murphy replied.

"Probably the afternoon's stress finally getting the best of her."

"Pizza?" Harper said, with a goofy grin on his face.

* * * *

*Ethan*

Ethan was a wreck. Between Stephanie's house blowing up and Blayne getting shot in the shoulder, he blamed himself for everything that was happening. He was sitting with Kira in the same waiting room they'd been in when they'd waited for Jamie to get out of surgery. Now, they were waiting for Blayne to get out. Thankfully, the shot wasn't fatal, but the surgeon didn't know what damage the bullet had done to Blayne's scapula.

The emergency department was busier this evening than it had been earlier in the week. *Earlier in the week? That was just yesterday.* Ethan first learned a shooting had happened when an alert flashed across Blayne's iPhone on the Associated Press's app saying, *Ethan Bond Assassinated in Texas.* Ethan had freaked out and immediately started calling his phone. Then he had tried calling Kira repeatedly to find out what was happening. He had finally called an Uber and headed to the hospital to find out what was going on himself.

When Ethan arrived, paparazzi were already pooling around the main entrance, so he'd walked around the building until he discovered a side door that let him in. He had spent fifteen minutes walking through fluorescent-lit corridors, lost. He found an orderly who had taken pity on him and helped him locate the emergency department waiting room.

He had found Kira up and pacing, trying to keep it together. When Ethan came into the room, she glared at him as she hissed, "You!" She had walked right up to him and slapped him across the face before pulling him into a giant bear hug as the tears started flowing. Ethan wasn't sure which shocked him more, the slap or the hug.

Now, he sat in the waiting room, holding Kira's hand. He heard a buzzing sound from Kira's bag. She picked it up and pulled out her phone.

"Oops, I believe this one's yours," Kira said, handing Ethan his Galaxy. "I picked it up before the police got there."

Ethan looked at the phone like Kira was handing him a scorpion. There was a small crack on the screen and a streak of blood on the side of the case. The device continued to buzz as he reached out his hand and took it. He looked down at the screen and saw a slew of messages. He wasn't sure where to start first. He texted his parents to let them know the media news reports were wrong. He then sent a group text to the ZERO family, saying he was fine. Last, he texted Zach directly.

*Got my phone back. My friend Blayne was shot. He was pretending to be me.*

Ethan hesitated before he added, *I think the bullet was meant for me.* He hit send.

"Kira," a male's voice came from the door.

Ethan kept his eyes on his phone, waiting for the series of texts he knew would come his way. He saw the hem of the man's white coat, blue scrub pants and clogs.

"Arnold," Kira said, looking up from her seat standing, "how is he?"

"He's fine. Thankfully, the bullet went through the outer part of the arm, missing his subclavian artery."

"Arnold," Kira snapped, "speak to me like I'm a human."

"Sorry," the surgeon replied. "If Blayne had been shot on the inside of his arm, it would have pierced a major artery. He would have bled out before he got here, if not on the operating table before we could have figured out what was going on. Thankfully, this is not what happened. Instead, it was right under the shoulder on the outside. The bullet grazed his humerus but missed the major nerves, which was my biggest concern when I took him into surgery. The bullet didn't hit the bone directly, which would have caused both bullet and bone to fracture, causing considerably more damage. All in all, this is a stroke of one-in-a-million luck. He's going to hurt like hell, and rehab will take some time, but he shouldn't lose any sensations. He's a very, very lucky man."

Ethan let out his breath. He hadn't even realized he'd stopped breathing while the surgeon had been talking.

"When can we see him?" Kira asked.

"We?"

Ethan felt Kira put a hand on his shoulder. "Dr. Arnold Giest-Mueler, let me introduce you to Blayne's friend, Ethan Bond."

Ethan tilted his head up to look at the older man.

"Holy shit, it is you. Jamie said you'd been in his hospital room last night. I figured it was the drugs talking."

Ethan shook his head, offered a weak smile and extended his hand. "Thank you for taking care of Blayne." A tear welled in the corner of his eye, and he reached up and brushed it away with the back of his hand.

"So," Kira said, trying to get back to business, "when can we see him?"

"He should be in his room in about thirty minutes. You can go there now. I put him in the same room as Jamie. I figured it would make everyone's life easier if Blayne and Jamie could be together."

"Does Jamie know what happened to Blayne?" Ethan asked.

"I honestly don't know," the surgeon said. "Dr. Reich probably said something to him. I saw her in there, but we didn't talk."

"Thanks," Ethan said. "Let's go wait for Blayne." From the corner of his eye, he saw a young woman with her cell phone held up in his direction.

*I don't even care.*

* * * *

*Blayne*

Blayne's eyes fluttered open before closing again. His brain was still coming out of the anesthesia fog. He listened to the steady beeping coming from somewhere to his left. He moved his head from side to side. His eyes felt heavy. He mentally took stock of his various body parts. His feet were covered. He could feel the weight of a blanket on top of him. *Where am I?* He felt a weight on his hand, a throbbing sensation in one of his arms. He tried to speak, but his mouth was as dry as the West Texas tundra in August.

"Water," he finally grumbled as he forced his eyes open halfway to take in his environment.

"Hey, sleepyhead," a voice said to his left. The voice belonged to someone who was holding his hand.

Blayne twisted his head to look, but could only see a blurry figure. "Where... Where am I?"

"You're in the hospital," a different voice said from his right.

A straw was placed between Blayne's lips, so he sucked the room-temperature liquid into his mouth. Almost immediately, his mouth started to function normally as it was coated in juice, and his salivary glands also produced their own moisture.

"Slow down. The nurse said you'd be thirsty, but he also said to make sure you took sips and not gulps."

Blayne forced himself to slow his sucking on the straw. When he was done, he coughed and drifted back to sleep.

The next time Blayne woke, he opened his eyes, and the room was dim and quiet. He shook his head from side to side, trying to shake the sleep out.

"Hey there," a voice to his right said. "Welcome back to the land of the living."

Blayne opened his eyes fully and found Ethan looking at him. "What happened?" Blayne choked out.

"You were shot," Ethan said, his forehead scrunching.

"I was *shot*?" Blayne asked. He'd heard what Ethan said, but the words weren't computing in his head.

"Yeah, you took a bullet to your upper arm," Ethan replied. "Don't worry. The surgeon expects you to make a full recovery."

Blayne took a second to let Ethan's words wash over him. He stared at Ethan's face and registered the look of concern and fear that was abundantly clear, even in Blayne's dazed state. Blayne also looked down to find Ethan holding his hand. Ethan's thumb was moving across the back of Blayne's hand in a soothing motion.

"What happened?" Blayne asked.

"I'll tell you everything. But first, do you need anything?" Ethan asked.

"Water?" Blayne asked after a beat.

Ethan got up, grabbed a bottle of water with a straw and held it up to Blayne's lips. "No. Go slowly. The nurse warned that patients often try to drink too fast when waking up, so take it easy."

"Yes, Mother," Blayne said with a weak grin before he sipped.

When Blayne was done drinking, Ethan put the bottle on the table and told Blayne everything that had happened. When Ethan got to the part where he thought the assassination attempt was meant for him,

Ethan choked back tears. Without needing to be told, Blayne could tell Ethan was blaming himself.

"Dude," Blayne said, interrupting Ethan, "you're not to blame for this. You had no way of knowing what was going to happen. Remember... This plan was pretty much my idea."

"I know," Ethan said, letting out a quick breath. "I can't help but blame myself. I wish I knew what was going on. None of this makes sense."

Blayne looked at Ethan as tears started welling in his eyes. Blayne gave Ethan's hand a reassuring squeeze. "It's not your fault, Ethan."

"Still, you could have died," Ethan said, his voice barely escaping his throat. "I...I don't think I've ever been so scared in my life than when I saw the Associated Press message saying I'd been assassinated.... Well, *you* were assassinated." Ethan raised Blayne's hand to his lips and gently pressed them against the back of his hand, just above where the IV needle was placed.

Blayne shifted his body to stare at Ethan, but he winced as a sharp wave of pain shot from his left arm. Without skipping a beat, Ethan put a cylindrical device in his hand with a button on top.

"It's a patient-controlled analgesia pump for pain management," Ethan said. "Any time you hurt, push the little button, and you'll get a dose of medication through your IV."

Blayne pushed the pump, and within seconds he felt a soothing sensation wash over his body. "Whoa," Blayne said. "That stuff's fast."

"He's finally awake," Kira said, entering the room. She pulled back the curtain separating his bed from the other one in the room. He glanced to his right and saw Kira, Dr. Reich and Jamie sitting on the other side.

"Wow," Blayne said. "I didn't know anyone else was in the room."

"We didn't want to interrupt," Dr. Reich said. "We knew you two needed some privacy."

Blayne looked at Jamie, who had a goofy grin on his face. Blayne tilted his head slightly, and Jamie mouthed, "He loves you."

# Chapter Nineteen

*Dr. Hennigan*

Dr. Hennigan listened to the soft clicking sound of her heels as she walked through The Complex's halls. She'd received a phone call moments earlier from her mother, requesting her immediate presence. Dr. Hennigan had terminated highly skilled operatives who had caused her fewer problems than Ethan Bond and his friends. As she approached the door, she steeled herself for a conversation she knew wouldn't be pleasant.

She knocked on the door and waited to be buzzed in. She walked into her mother's office and almost stopped in her tracks. Not only was her mother there, but her grandmother was there as well...and Ms. Brighton. *Well, fuck!*

"Thank you for joining us so quickly," Deborah said. "Please sit." She motioned to an available seat. In this corner of her mother's office, a couch, a coffee table and two chairs formed a cozy square. Her mother and grandmother were in the chairs, and Ms. Brighton sat on the other end of the couch.

"Let's start by saying this is not a formal inquest," Sara Hennigan said. Dr. Hennigan looked at her grandmother's face for any trace of emotion, but her grandmother's demeanor was utterly affectless. Sara could just as easily be talking to a wall as her own granddaughter. "Ms. Brighton, if you would."

Ms. Brighton sat a tablet PC in her lap. "From my initial analysis of this operation, everything has been completed per The Foundation protocols." Dr. Hennigan wanted to let out a sigh of relief, but she did her best to mirror her grandmother's countenance. "However, we have clearly run into a series of problems outside the parameters of expected success rates given the *nature* of the targets in question."

"Yes?" Dr. Hennigan asked.

"Honestly, I'm not sure what to make of this situation," Ms. Brighton admitted, turning to look at Dr. Hennigan directly. "I fully expected to see a glaring flaw in your initial assessment and plan, but I haven't. Now, this doesn't mean the audit has concluded. Still, my initial assessment is that what has happened could not have been anticipated."

"Thank you, Ms. Brighton," Sara said. "You may leave us now."

Ms. Brighton got up and left the room. As soon as the door was closed, Dr. Hennigan watched as both her mother and grandmother's postures relaxed.

"Phillipa," Sara said, "what the hell is going on here?"

"Grandma," Dr. Hennigan started, "every move we make has been counteracted by things we could not predict. If I believed in luck or the fates, I'd say they were conspiring against us."

Sara Hennigan steepled her hands under her chin as she pondered the situation. "Walk me through everything. I've read the reports, but I want to know what's not in them. Off the record, of course."

Dr. Hennigan told her mother and grandmother about the entirety of the operation from the initial realization that Cynthia Dunning had stolen classified files to Denzili and Richardson's failed attempt at assassinating Ethan Bond.

"Like Ms. Brighton said," Deborah started after Dr. Hennigan finished, "you have run a textbook operation. From what I can tell, this has been one giant clusterfuck from the beginning."

"Deborah, language," Sara chastised.

"Sorry, Mother," Deborah apologized.

"Language aside," Sara said, "the sentiment is accurate."

"Trust me," Dr. Hennigan said. "I've repeatedly debated every move my team has made, and I would have made the same calls each time."

"So, where does this leave us?" Sara asked.

"Depends on what our priorities are at this point?" Dr. Hennigan asked. Her mother and grandmother pondered the question.

"Liquidation of the target seems too risky and too public," Deborah said. "Do you agree, Mother?" Sara nodded.

"As such," Sara started, "our primary concern must be asset retrieval. We need Ethan Bond's cell phone. If we can't retrieve the asset, it must be destroyed."

"I agree," Dr. Hennigan said. "I'll fly to Houston immediately and oversee this op myself."

\* \* \* \*

*Ethan*

Ethan shifted uncomfortably in the chair beside Blayne's bed. He insisted on staying by Blayne's bedside all night, even after the night charge nurse tried to have him leave since it was *"after visiting hours."* Ethan had politely looked at the woman and said, "No." The nurse had threatened to call security on him. Still, Kira had come into the room like a white knight and informed the nurse she was Blayne's lawyer and that Ethan had every right to stay in the room as she rattled off some legal precedent that included the words "national security risk." He had sort of figured Kira was bullshitting, but the nurse had thrown up her hands and left.

Around six a.m., Kira left to go home and prepare for the day. Before she went home to shower and change, she'd gotten Ethan a cup of coffee, which was already getting cold on the bedside table. Ethan looked at his watch. *Damn, it's already seven-thirty.* Ethan stretched in the chair. Sitting up straight, he rolled one shoulder forward, then the other. He arched his back and let his neck fall backward before twisting it from side to side in its own set of stretches.

"Good morning, sunshine," Blayne said as Ethan stretched.

"Hey, you." Ethan smiled at Blayne. "How are you feeling?"

"Like I was shot," Blayne said, giving Ethan a weak grin. "But other than that, I'm hunky-dory. You?"

Ethan rolled his eyes and joggled his head back, "What am I going to do with you?" Blayne shot him a goofy smile but said nothing. "As mother used to say, *'you don't want to be the boy whose face froze like that,'"* making his own goofy grin right back at Blayne. "I'm a little stiff, but sleeping in a chair can do that to you."

"You could have hopped into bed with me. There's plenty of room up here for you," Blayne joked as he gestured to the narrow hospital bed.

"*Oi*, old people! There's a minor in here!" Jamie said from the other side of the curtain.

"*Oi*, young'n. No autographs for you!" Ethan joked back. He stood up, walked around the bed and drew the curtain back so Jamie could see into their side of the hospital room. "And how are you doing this morning?" Ethan asked.

"Better than he looks," Jamie quipped, hooking a thumb in Blayne's direction.

"Ouch!" Blayne said, narrowing his eyes in fake anger. "Is that how your mother taught you to respect your elders?"

"Breakfast," an orderly said, entering the room with a cart. The orderly put a breakfast tray in front of Jamie and Blayne.

"What did the hospital gods bring us this morning?" Jamie asked, smirking. Jamie dramatically lifted the foil cover as Ethan looked down. There was some kind of omelet with cheese on top, a couple of wedges of fried hash browns, a blueberry muffin and a small cup of fruit. There was also a carafe of coffee, a carton of milk and a small glass of orange juice.

Before handing Ethan a tray, the orderly looked around as if engaging in some kind of dastardly conspiracy. "Don't tell anyone," the orderly said with a wink before backing his cart out of the room.

Ethan returned to his chair and sat down with his tray on his lap. The three dug into their breakfasts. Ethan couldn't remember the last time he'd eaten. Still, the hospital meal was not half bad, even if it looked grossly institutional.

The three chit-chatted for a few minutes as they ate their respective breakfasts. "Jamie," Blayne asked, "when is your mom coming back?"

"She had a class this morning, so she left around six a.m. after bringing a coffee to Ethan."

"You were awake?" Ethan asked.

"Yep, kept my eyes closed so you two could think you were talking in private."

"Sneaky little one, aren't you?" Ethan said with a half-grin. Jamie stared back at Ethan with a smile and forked another bite of egg into his mouth.

"The innocent ones are always the most trouble," Blayne said.

When they finished their breakfasts, Ethan helped stack their trash on one tray to make it easier for the orderly when he came back by the room. Almost like clockwork, there was a knock on the door.

"I was getting everything tidied up for you," Ethan said, turning his head as the door opened.

A man in a dark blue suit with a sky-blue tie stood there. "Ethan Bond?"

It took Ethan a second for his brain to shift gears. "Yes, yes... I'm Ethan Bond?"

"I'm Special Agent Raymond Anderson with The Houston FBI Field Office," the man said as he pulled out a badge and flipped it open to show Ethan.

Ethan read the badge as he said, "FBI? How...how can I help you?"

"I'm going to need you to come with me, sir." The FBI agent made it very clear it was not a request.

"Let me grab my phone," Ethan said.

"You're not going anywhere without me," Blayne protested as he swung his legs off the side of the hospital bed.

"It's okay," Ethan said, picking up his phone from the nightstand. "I've been expecting this."

"What?" Blayne said, a bit incredulously.

"Let's see." Ethan leveled his gaze at Blayne. "My lover was assassinated. A plane I was supposed to be on blew up. My best friend's house exploded last night. And someone tried to kill me but took a shot at you instead."

"Well, when you put it like that," Blayne said, a little of the bravado leaving him. "Will I ever see you again?"

Ethan leaned forward and kissed Blayne on the forehead. "You can't get rid of me that easily." He then turned toward the FBI agent and asked, "Is anyone staying here to watch out for him?"

"Yes, sir," Agent Anderson acknowledged as he opened the door and two more agents entered the hospital room. The room was getting a bit too cramped with all six people standing in there.

"Excuse me," another voice said, entering the room. "What the hell is going on here? Visiting hours aren't for another hour."

Ethan turned from Blayne to see Arnold Giest-Mueler pushing both agents out of the way to get into the room. His surgical getup was gone, and he was now wearing a pair of khakis, a buttoned-down blue shirt with a yellow tie under his white lab coat with the Pennington University seal and his name embroidered on it.

"And you are?" Agent Anderson asked as he blocked the surgeon's entry into the room.

"I'm their surgeon," Giest-Mueler said, his expression hardening. "And you are?"

The FBI agent pulled out his badge and explained who he was. "And these other two agents are Special Agents Marianna and Brooks. One will stay inside this room, and the other will check the IDs of anyone entering until I can safely transfer Mr. Dickenson to the FBI building downtown."

"No," Giest-Mueler responded. "Your agents can stay outside this room, but for patient confidentiality, you have no reason to be here unless both patients allow it. And one of them is a minor, and his legal guardian is not here to agree."

"I'm sorry, doctor, but I must insist," Agent Anderson started.

"You can insist all you want," Giest-Mueler said. "Unless one of these men is under arrest, you must follow hospital privacy policies. If you have a problem, I'll gladly give you the hospital lawyers' number."

"I don't have time for this," Agent Anderson said, adrenaline dilating the blood vessels in his face.

Ethan could tell Agent Anderson was on the verge of exploding at the surgeon, so he said, "Are you ready to go, Agent Anderson?"

"Yes," the agent said. He turned around and left the room in a huff.

"Ethan?" Blayne said.

"It's okay," Ethan reassured Blayne. "I'm going to be okay. Call Zach and let him know what's going on. His number is now in your phone." Ethan nodded toward Blayne's phone, which was plugged into a USB port next to the hospital bed. Ethan had a million things he wanted to say to Blayne. He blinked back a tear and said, "Talk to you soon," without turning around as he left.

# Chapter Twenty

*Zach*

"And five, six, seven, eight," Sally Higgins yelled as ZERO broke into their first number in the dance studio. Their backup dancers had made the trip from Seattle to New Orleans the evening before so the group could start putting everything together. For the time being, the group blocked everything, assuming Ethan would be there for the tour's first leg.

Zach was a natural dancer. He swung and moved his hips with the best of them. It helped that he'd been in gymnastics, ballet and football growing up. He'd fought the dance stuff early on because he didn't want to do that *'girly shit'*, as he used to call it. Then he had learned several NFL Hall-of-Famers studied ballet. Zach had figured if greats like Lynn Swann and Herschel Walker could plié at the dance bar, so could he. Of course, that was back when Zach had idolized Walker before Walker had become a crazed conservative and run for office in Georgia.

The music started. Zach stood on the counterweight platform below his star trap. The beginning orchestration was a remix of ZERO's hit songs. They'd been working with the star traps before everything had been sent up to Seattle, so it was the first time in a while he stood below the wooden octagon above him. The counterweight would get triggered and propel Zach through the wooden octagon. The triangular pieces were each hinged to open as he went through them skyward, then close as he landed back on them. Since Zach came first in ZERO, he was the first of the four guys to get shot up onto the stage. At the mention of his name, the stagehand next to him triggered the counterweight. Zach flew through the trap about one foot above the stage before landing in his posed position. Once all three of the guys landed on stage, the song began in earnest. A giant double staircase appeared behind them, and their backup dancers danced down the stairs, wearing little-to-no clothing.

Each of the guys had their own solo in the first song, which was why they chose it to start this show. Well, that and because it was a high-energy pop number they knew would get the crowd in a tizzy.

Orr executed a series of flips. Then Ric dove into the dancers' hands, who flipped him over and landed Ric on his feet right when his solo began.

Zach made his way upstage, where a stagehand latched him into a harness and double-checked the locking mechanisms. Zach gave the stagehand a thumbs up to let him know he was secure before the stunt. If Zach didn't feel secure, he'd give a thumbs down. If that happened, the harness would be removed, and Zach would run to the front before his solo started. Zach felt his body slingshot forward through the air over the heads of the rest of the group and dancers to land right at the edge of the stage. Well, from the audience's perspective, it looked like the edge of the stage, but Zach had a good three or four feet of buffer. He began his solo the second his feet landed, and four gyrating backup dancers flinging themselves around his body while seamlessly unhooking him from the harness. The choreography was sexy and functional.

The rest of the song was high energy, with several dance solos and stunts. Zach was always amazed at how much Higgins had crammed into three minutes and twenty-two seconds. Zach positioned himself and did a two-step run before executing an aerial cartwheel with no hands. He landed and immediately went to his knees and slid to the front of the stage, where ZERO and the backup dancers converged.

The song ended, and all of them breathed heavily and held the position until they heard Sally's voice over the system, "Take five and reset at the top." Everyone moved back to their starting points.

"Really? We're doing it again," Rick said through clenched teeth. "How many times are we going to run this one today?"

"Until Sally is happy, I guess," Orr replied.

Zach's assistant met him as he exited backstage and down the stairs leading to the basement where ZERO's first positions were.

"Zach, you received a call from Blayne Dickenson," Zach's assistant said. "He said it was urgent and to have you call him back." The assistant handed Zach his phone, and Zach immediately hit the callback button.

"Zach?" a voice on the other end said.

"Yes, Blayne? As in Ethan's Blayne?"

"Well, I don't know if he's mine, but yea, that's me."

"Give me a second," Zach said as he muted the phone. "I'm going to take this outside. Come get me when they're ready for me," Zach told his assistant before turning around on the stairs to head up and out through the side door. When he was finally alone outside, he unmuted Blayne, "Sorry that took so long. We're in rehearsals, and I needed to get somewhere private."

"I understand," Blayne said before correcting himself, "Yeah, I have no clue what your life is like."

"You're lucky," Zach said with a quick chuckle. "How are you? Ethan said you were shot?"

"I'm okay. A little out of it because of the narcotics they've been giving me after surgery. The surgeon doesn't think there's any permanent damage."

"Glad to hear. I could tell Ethan was pretty freaked last night."

"What about Stephanie? Have you talked to her today?"

"She's here with me at the rehearsal space. I convinced the FBI that being with our security team and us was just as secure as their safe house was."

"Glad she's safe, too."

"So, where's Ethan? Why are you calling?" Zach asked, now that they'd gotten the niceties out of the way.

"He was escorted out of the hospital by an FBI agent. The FBI left a couple of agents to watch my hospital room. The last thing Ethan said was to call you."

"What the fuck is going on?" Zach asked.

"I wish I knew," Blayne admitted.

"What did Ethan tell you?" Zach heard Blayne let out a quick breath through the phone.

"He doesn't know why any of this is happening. And I don't know what you do or don't know. And I don't want to break Ethan's confidence, but he told me to call you."

"What aren't you telling me, Blayne?"

Zach could tell Blayne was battling divulging Ethan's secrets. Still, the voice on the other end of the phone laid out a conspiracy involving the soap stars, the plane, the bomb and Blayne's bullet hole.

"What the hell did he get himself into?" Zach asked aloud when Blayne stopped talking.

"I honestly don't think Ethan has any clue. He only took off and came to Houston because he needed someplace to grieve after Daniel Hawthorne's death."

"Dammit!"

"What?" Blayne questioned.

"I should have told him I knew about Hawthorne. Hell, all the guys have known Ethan is gay for years. Ethan always thought he was so secretive. His relationship with Hawthorne was known by everyone on our team. We said nothing because he said nothing."

"Not surprised. Often closeted gay guys think they're so hidden and have no idea the world is waiting for them to come out."

"So, what now?"

"I honestly don't know," Blayne admitted. "I'm unsure if I'm still in shock over getting shot or if all this is way out of my knowledge set. But, I don't have the foggiest idea what to do."

"I'm going to talk to our producer and manager. If anyone knows what to do, it's those two."

"Let me know if you need anything from my end," Blayne said.

"Just heal," Zach said. "I know it's what Ethan would want for you right now. Let us figure this mess out. You should stay out of it."

"No offense but fuck that shit. I'll have my lawyer work things from this end. You work things from yours."

"But it's not what—" Zach started before hearing the clicking sound of a call disconnected. "He hung up on me."

\* \* \* \*

*Blayne*

Kira was a whirlwind when she got to the hospital. She demanded to see her clients from the FBI agents, who tried to stop her from entering the room by telling her that only family was being admitted. After a few choice words Blayne could hear from inside the hospital room, the agents smartened up and opened the door.

"What's going on?" Kira asked as soon as the door was closed. "I got your nine-one-one text."

Blayne spent the next few minutes filling Kira in on everything that had transpired that morning. "So, they came in here, took Ethan and left us with the goon squad out front."

"Blayne," Dr. Reich chided from the other side of the room, "they're not goons. They're just doing their job, and right now, their job is to protect you."

Blayne was about to say something, but he shut his mouth before uttering something he'd regret. He took a calming breath and let it out in one huff. "Dr. Reich, I know you're right, but…" he said as his voice trailed off.

Kira lowered herself into the seat Ethan had slept in all night long. "I get that you're scared. And I love giving law enforcement a hard time as a lawyer," she admitted. Blayne noticed the sheer amount of pain her face exhibited as she acknowledged it. "But they are here to protect you. Someone shot you less than twenty-four hours ago."

"They didn't try to kill me. They tried to assassinate Ethan."

"We think," Kira said as she interrupted him. "We don't know that for sure. What if you were the target for some unknown reason? What if we got you out of here, and the person tries again and succeeds this time?"

Blayne knew she was right, so he kept his mouth shut. He wasn't happy about it, but he knew what she was saying was true.

"If that's true, why don't we all go to the FBI building?" Blayne asked. "Wouldn't it be safer for all if we were there instead of a public hospital with only two armed guards?"

"Blayne—"

"Don't 'Blayne' me. Is this really the most secure place for me if I'm in danger?"

"Probably not," Kira said with reluctance.

"See?" Blayne said, nodding his head in vindication.

There was a sudden series of three knocks on the door then Arnold Giest-Mueler walked into the room.

"How are my patients doing?" the surgeon asked as he took in the facial expressions around the room. "I'm clearly interrupting something. I can come back?"

"You're just the man I needed to speak with," Kira said.

# Chapter Twenty-One

*Agent Murphy*

Murphy and Harper were leaving the FBI Field Office in New Orleans when a white van pulled up in front of the station, and the side of the door quickly slid open. For a brief second, Murphy almost went for her gun, thinking Harper or she was about to be kidnapped. She let her arm drop back to her side. *Worse... It's a reporter with a camera. I would much rather be kidnapped.*

Murphy slipped on her fakest smile and asked, "How can I help you, Mr. McNeil?"

"Where are you going?" McNeil asked, shoving a microphone in her face.

"None of your business," Murphy said as she rested her hand on her hip, a few inches away from her holster.

"Any chance it's because Ethan Bond was taken into custody this morning?" Murphy stared back at McNeil without blinking, her jaw set in a tight line. "Come on, Agent Murphy? The public has a right to know."

"Let me reiterate what I told you the other day. The FBI does not comment on ongoing investigations —"

"Comment on ongoing investigations," McNeil said, his words overlapping with Murphy's.

"See? You remember," Murphy said with a giant, still-fake smile. "Now, if you'll excuse me," she said as she stepped around McNeil and started walking toward a car waiting for them.

"I know this is all tied up with the Peregrine Airlines 923 explosion," McNeil blurted out.

Murphy spun on her heel without thinking and was about to say something when she noticed the camera was still pointed at her.

"Off," she said as she stared into the lens directly.

Murphy watched as the cameraman looked to McNeil for confirmation. McNeil nodded, and the red light on the front blinked out as the man lowered the camera. McNeil handed the cameraman his microphone saying, "You can wait for us in the van. If I need you, I'll let you know."

Murphy waited for the van's door to slide shut.

"What are you doing, Murphy?" Harper asked, whispering in her ear. He'd positioned his back to McNeil so McNeil couldn't try reading Harper's lips.

"Fishing," Murphy said as a predatory grin crept over her face. "So, Mr. McNeil, what do you think you know?"

"Well, let's see... We have two murders, a plane explosion, a bombing and an assassination attempt, and Ethan Bond is in the middle of it all. He's either the mastermind or the target. And since he wasn't walked out of the Pennington University Hospital this morning in cuffs, I'm guessing it means he's the target. My question is 'why?'"

"That's some interesting conspiracy theorizing you have there, Mr. McNeil. Are you sure you're not a member of the tinfoil hat society? Why not blame aliens or space lasers? Heck, maybe it's the child-eating lizard alien cabal running our government doing all this? You're as crazy as those Q-Anon whack jobs."

"You may joke, Agent Murphy, but the facts are the facts."

"And please tell me, what facts do you have to support any of this?"

McNeil stammered something about how the timeline worked, but Murphy looked at McNeil like he was a member of a tinfoil hat club.

"I'm not some conspiracy theorist," McNeil finally blurted out.

"Have you listened to yourself?"

"I'll let the American public judge what I have to say."

"You do that," Murphy said, shaking her head at him as she plastered on a look of concern. "I'll be sorry to see you leave RNN in shame. All things considered, you're not a bad guy."

Murphy spun on her heels and walked away without waiting for a response. Harper didn't skip a beat and fell in beside her.

Once they were in the sedan, they told the driver to take them to the Naval Air Station. They were catching a plane to Ellington Field in Houston. From there, they were boarding a chopper that would whisk them away to the Federal Building in Downtown Houston.

"You totally believe this theory, don't you?" Harper asked.

"Like he said, the pieces add up. Well, maybe they don't add up to anything, but they are definitely pieces of the same puzzle. The problem is, I can't figure out what that image is."

"I admit, when you first drew a line between the murders of Dunning and Hawthorne to Ethan Bond because of the plane explosion, I thought you'd lost your marbles." Murphy shot Harper a deadly look, but Harper threw up his arms in mock surrender. He quickly amended, "But after yesterday's explosion and the attempt on Bond's life, I think you're onto something here. Like you said, I don't have a fucking clue what, but it's something."

\* \* \* \*

*Ethan*

Ethan was bored out of his mind sitting in the silent car without even the radio playing. The FBI agent who grabbed him was silent the entire ride from Pennington to the Houston FBI headquarters. As the agent got off Highway 209, Ethan saw a green monstrosity ahead.

The building was an eight-floor rectangle with green glass plates, making it sparkle in the sun. Even the sign out in front of the building had the same green glass Ethan noted as the agent pulled into the parking lot. The ungodly complex stood out like a sore thumb against the rest of the community.

"I've gotta ask," Ethan said, breaking the silence. "Why is it green?

"Welcome to the Emerald City—or the Green Monster," Agent Anderson said. "I'll be the first to admit the building is ugly, but the blasted thing is safe. I hear it can withstand a nuclear blast."

"Really?"

"Yep, we hope no one tries to blow us up anytime soon, though. They built it after McVey blew up the Federal Building in Oklahoma City. Someone decided the FBI wasn't going to go through that again."

"So, you're taking me into a mini-fortress?"

"Pretty much, Mr. Bond. No worries about anyone trying to get you in here. The place is secure."

"Good to know," Ethan said, staring at the structure.

"It's also supposedly good for the planet, not that I honestly give a rat's ass. But some people do," Agent Anderson said.

Agent Anderson parked the car, and Ethan followed him into the building. They paused briefly to let two joggers pass by on a jogging path circling the building.

"It's basically a mini-city," Agent Anderson said as he opened the door for Ethan.

Ethan walked into the atrium area and saw a few agents here and there talking. Anderson filled out some paperwork for Ethan and gave Ethan a visitor's badge. *Visitor, ehh?* Ethan said nothing and followed Agent Anderson like a lost puppy. They went into an elevator and exited on the fifth floor. Ethan was led into a conference room.

"Stay in here," Agent Anderson said. "There're bottles of water in the mini-fridge and a small restroom in the back of the room," Anderson added, pointing to a door in the back. "I'll be back soon."

With that, Agent Anderson left Ethan in the conference room. Ethan heard the telltale clicking sound as Agent Anderson locked Ethan inside.

Ethan wasn't in the mood to be stared at, so he walked over to the glass wall and closed the blinds. Someone could still see he was in there, but at least Ethan didn't feel like he was a goldfish being watched anymore.

He walked around the room then pulled out his phone to text Blayne and Zach, but there 'was no cell service or Wi-Fi access. Well, there was certainly Wi-Fi in the building, but Ethan didn't have the password to log on, so he was left with nothing to do. He found a handful of pamphlets on a small table. Most of the materials were recruiting materials for the FBI. Ethan lost interest quickly.

Ethan sat for a spell, flipping aimlessly through his phone. He opened his Kindle app and found a half-read book he'd started a couple of years before. With nothing else on his agenda, he started reading.

After what felt like at least a day-and-a-half to Ethan, but he realized it was probably only an hour or two, Agent Anderson showed up at the door with a couple of paper sacks. Anderson let himself in and locked the door behind him.

"Hope you don't mind burgers?" Anderson said as he put a paper bag down in front of Ethan.

Anderson spotted the phone in front of Ethan and said, "Hate to do this to you, kid, but I'm going to have to confiscate your phone."

"Why? I'm not connected to cell service or Wi-Fi. At least let me read my book on here if you're going to keep me locked up in here too much longer."

The agent tossed around the idea before giving Ethan a noncommittal "Keep it...for now."

"What do you know about what's going on?" Agent Anderson asked.

"I know my ex and his best friend were murdered. I fled New Orleans to grieve because I couldn't talk to anyone I knew. The plane I was supposed to take to Seattle exploded. Then the paparazzi figured out where I was. My best friend's house then exploded. Last, Blayne, the guy in the hospital, led the paparazzi around yesterday looking like me and got shot because of it."

"Okay," Agent Anderson said, taking a big bite out of his hamburger. While chewing, Anderson asked, "Why are you so special?"

"Special? Besides being an incredibly talented, famous and rich musician, I'm not special." The agent's face contorted. *Clearly, not the answer he was going for.* "You want to ask me something, Agent? Just ask."

"Why is someone so determined to kill you that they'd murder hundreds of innocent people?" Agent Anderson asked as he popped a fry into his mouth.

Ethan took a long breath, staring the agent in the eyes as he rocked his head from side to side. "That's the million-dollar question."

"So, what's the answer?"

"I wish I knew." He added a shrug for emphasis.

"Not good enough," Agent Anderson said, his voice getting louder than the pleasant conversation they were having.

"What do you want me to say? I wish I knew. I don't." Ethan let the words fly out of his mouth rapidly. "I'm a boring popstar."

"You're a boring *gay* popstar."

"Are you fucking kidding me? Do you think this has anything to do with my sexual orientation?"

"You tell me. You're the one who was fucking...or was it getting fucked by two guys? One's dead in a morgue in New Orleans, and one is laid up in a hospital here in Houston. So, you tell me."

Ethan looked at the agent. His pulse rose, and he felt the tenseness in his jaw as he bit out the words, "I have never had sex with Blayne Dickenson. He's only involved in this because I dragged him into my world."

"Really? So, he's not one of your little butt buddies?"

"Butt buddy? Who says that? You know what? This conversation is over. I'm not saying another word to you until my attorney is present."

Ethan stood up and left the conference table, placing his back to Agent Anderson, looking out of the window. Ethan watched as Agent Anderson grabbed his fast-food back and left the room. The agent mumbled loud enough for Ethan to hear, "Fucking fagots."

Ethan whirled on the man and yelled, "What did you say?"

"Keep your voice down," the agent said.

"Why? So, you can use more homophobic slurs? I think not!" Ethan wasn't sure if anyone paid attention to his outburst, but he wasn't about to back down now.

**\* \* \* \***

*Agent Murphy*

Murphy and Harper exited the helicopter and looked up at the green glass building. *God, that thing is ugly.* A middle-aged man with a short-cropped haircut met them outside the helicopter pad.

"Agents Harper and Murphy," the man said, "I'm Agent Raymond Anderson. How was the trip?"

"Uneventful," Murphy replied, yelling over the roar of the helicopter blades. "What have you learned?"

"Not much. The suspect isn't very forthcoming."

Murphy narrowed her eyes at the man. "There's no reason to believe Mr. Bond is anything other than a victim in this case."

"Really?" Agent Anderson questioned. "He sure acts like he has something to hide."

The three agents walked into the building, and Murphy, for one, was glad to have her hearing back to normal. She was never a massive fan of helicopter rides. She didn't get motion sickness, but the blasted machines were always deafening, even with a headset or earplugs.

Agent Anderson led Murphy and Harper through the building to an elevator bank. On the ride up, the three kept silent. The small group approached the door to the conference room, and Agent Anderson pulled out his keys to unlock the door.

"You locked him in?" Murphy said incredulously.

"He should be glad we have him in a fancy conference room and not one of our interrogation rooms," Agent Anderson said before opening the door. "The little prick is not exactly the most cooperative person in the world."

Murphy glared at the Houston agent. Something about the man rubbed her the wrong way. She couldn't quite grasp what it was, but he didn't seem to be the right person for this job.

"Mr. Bond," Agent Anderson said as he entered the room, "I have some more agents for you to talk to."

"What, more agents to toss around homophobic slurs?" Ethan spat.

Murphy's eyes went round before she narrowed her gaze on Agent Anderson's back. "Thank you, Agent Anderson. That will be all," Murphy said flatly.

"If it's all the same, I'll stick around and see what he has to say for himself."

"Actually, no, you won't," Murphy said. "You were asked to put Ethan Bond into protective custody, not treat him like a criminal. Besides, this isn't your investigation." Murphy hoped talking down to Agent Anderson would put her in Ethan's good graces. She could only imagine what transpired before Harper and she arrived in Houston, but Agent Anderson clearly didn't follow FBI protocols.

"But—"

"You heard the agent," Harper said. "We thank you for your cooperation, but we'll handle it from here."

Agent Anderson pushed his way past Harper and Murphy in a huff and slammed the door behind him. The glass reverberated, and Murphy was a bit surprised the glass hadn't cracked.

She sat at the table across from Ethan, and Harper leaned against the door. "First, let me apologize for anything that happened before our arrival," she said with as much remorse as she could muster. "I don't know what Agent Anderson said or did, but it clearly wasn't what he was told to do."

Ethan stared at her with no emotion on his face. Murphy could read people's facial expressions, but Ethan's mask was pretty good.

"I'm going to lay out what we know," Murphy said. "When I'm done, I will ask you to fill in as many blanks as possible." Murphy pulled out her cell phone and looked through the notes she'd prepared before diving into everything she knew. While analyzing the situation, Ethan occasionally piped in with more information Murphy didn't already have. As time passed, Murphy noticed Ethan becoming more relaxed and open, which was precisely what she had hoped for.

* * * *

*Blayne*

Blayne looked up at the ugly green building as Kira pulled into the FBI parking lot. At first, Blayne thought they had made a wrong turn when he saw the green glass structure, but the sign out front said they were in the right place.

Kira parked the car in a visitor parking space and walked inside the building, with Blayne following her. Convincing Dr. Giest-Mueler to discharge Blayne hadn't been easy. Blayne promised not to drive and return if he showed any signs of problems. Kira swore up and down that she'd hold Blayne to that promise. With much reluctance, Giest-Mueler finally discharged Blayne, and noted in Blayne's chart he was being discharged against medical advice.

To get around the FBI agents stationed outside Blayne and Jamie's room, Kira convinced Madeline to distract them as she slipped Blayne out. Madeline wasn't too keen on tricking FBI agents, but Jamie had pled with her to help them. In the end, everything went as smoothly as possible. Blayne and Kira had slipped out of the hospital. Kira had plugged in the GPS coordinates for the FBI building in Houston, and they'd taken off.

Kira walked up to a reception desk in the atrium of the FBI building. A young man looked up from the desk as she approached and said, "Can I help you?"

"Yes, I'm here to see my client, Ethan Bond."

"Excuse me?" the receptionist asked.

"Ethan Bond was brought into this facility by Agent Raymond Anderson earlier today. I'm here to make sure my client has proper representation. I'm his lawyer."

The receptionist picked up the phone and dialed what Kira assumed was Agent Anderson's number.

"Agent Anderson, I have a lawyer here who represents..." He turned to Kira and asked, "Who do you represent again?"

"Ethan Bond."

"The lawyer represents Ethan Bond."

Kira wasn't sure what Agent Anderson had said, but from the look on the receptionist's face, whatever it was, it hadn't been kind.

"He'll be right down. You can sit over there." The young man gestured toward a small waiting area in the atrium's center.

Blayne and Kira walked to the waiting area, and Blayne sat down. Kira stood and started pacing.

"Calm down," Blayne said. "You're going to wear a hole in the marble flooring."

Kira let out an exasperated sigh and took a seat opposite Blayne. "How are you doing?" Kira asked.

"If you mean, 'are you in pain?' I'm doing okay. I still have enough happy drugs running through my system."

Kira nodded. There was a chime on an elevator bank, and Blayne watched as Kira's head swiveled toward the elevators.

"That's him," Blayne said quietly as Agent Anderson exited the elevator.

Kira stood and met Agent Anderson halfway between the reception area and the elevators. Blayne turned his head to watch the fireworks, just in case they happened.

"Agent Raymond Anderson," the man said, extending his hand. "And you are?"

Blayne watched as Kira gripped the man's hand and said, "Kira Strickland. I'm Ethan Bond's attorney. My understanding is you brought him here earlier today."

"That's correct," Anderson said.

"Great, take me to him," Kira demanded.

"I'm sorry, but he's currently being interviewed —"

"Without his attorney present?"

Blayne watched as Agent Anderson tried to come up with something to say, but Anderson finally shook his head and said, "Follow me."

Blayne stood up and followed Kira and Agent Anderson into the elevator bank. The agent hit the fifth-floor button, and the elevator climbed.

"How's the shoulder, Mr. Dickenson?" Anderson asked.

"Feels like I've been shot," Blayne said dryly.

"Been there," Anderson said. "I've taken three rounds throughout my career. Well, two of them were back when I was in the military. Only one of them since I've been in the FBI. What's the prognosis?"

"I'll live," Blayne said blandly, not in the mood for chitchat. "My surgeon said the bullet went through the outside of my right arm, so I was pretty lucky nothing major was nicked."

"People underestimate how bad getting shot in the arm can actually be. So many TV shows have someone taking a bullet to the shoulder. Trust me, that's not a simple wound, it can be deadly. All in all, count yourself lucky, Mr. Dickenson."

The elevator stopped, and the doors slid open. Agent Anderson started walking down a corridor. He paused outside a glass door. The blinds were closed, preventing anyone from looking into the room. Anderson rapped on the door twice then entered.

"Excuse me," a female agent said as Anderson opened the door.

Blayne saw Ethan sitting at the table and didn't hesitate as he barged into the room, dashing in his direction.

"Dear God," Blayne said, entering the room. "I've been worried sick."

"What the hell?" a male agent inside the room barked. "Who are you?"

Blayne ignored the FBI agents and made a beeline for Ethan, who was already getting out of his chair. As soon as Blayne was within arm's reach, Ethan enveloped him in a hug before grabbing the sides of Blayne's face and kissing him deeply.

# Chapter Twenty-Two

*Agent Murphy*

Murphy watched in stunned silence as two strangers barged into the room. Her jaw dropped as Ethan enveloped the young man in a sling and kissed him. *That must be Blayne Dickenson.* She noticed Blayne wince as he was hugged by Ethan. She waited for Blayne and Ethan to finish their kiss before trying to take the room back over.

"Okay," Murphy said loudly. "I think it's time for some formal introductions. I'm Agent Sarah Murphy, and this is my partner, Agent Benjamin Harper. You apparently already met Agent Raymond Anderson. I'm guessing," she started turning to Blayne, "you're Blayne. So, who are you?" she asked, turning to Kira.

"I'm Kira Strickland, attorney at law. I'm here representing my client, Ethan Bond."

"Ethan," Murphy started, "is she your lawyer?"

Ethan hesitated for a second before saying, "Yes. Yes, she is."

"Okay, so now that introductions are over, let's all sit down and have a pleasant conversation."

Agent Anderson closed the door and joined the group. "Agent Anderson, thanks for bringing Mr. Dickenson and Ms. Strickland up, but your presence isn't necessary."

Anderson's neck muscles twitched in anger. Thankfully, the agent kept it together and left the room. The only sign that he was pissed off was the slamming of the door behind him as he left.

"God, I hate that guy," Ethan said when Anderson left the room.

Murphy ignored Ethan and opted to get right to the point. "What do you know about the current situation, Ms. Strickland?" Murphy listened as Kira explained what she'd been able to piece together with Blayne's help. Murphy filled in a few details that weren't classified along the way.

"You really think someone is trying to assassinate my client?"

"I'm not one who normally believes in conspiracy theories," Murphy acknowledged. "But something is definitely going on here. To be completely honest, this puzzle has so many missing pieces."

The lawyer let out a long breath. "And you think this all has to do with something on my client's cell phone?"

"That's the working theory," Murphy responded. "I have a FISA warrant for your cell phone, Mr. Bond, but I would much rather ask for your cooperation. We want to clone your phone and send it to the NCIJTF for analysis—with your permission, of course."

Ethan turned to his lawyer for advice. She nodded, so Ethan pulled out his cell and slid it across the table. Murphy slid the phone to her partner, who pulled a box out of his pocket and plugged Ethan's phone into it.

"What now?" Kira asked.

"I think we need to do the same thing we did with Mr. Bond's friend Stephanie in New Orleans. We need to get him to a safe house. I think it's not a bad idea for all three of you to be put into protective custody at this point." The lawyer started to protest, but Murphy kept going. "I know it's inconvenient, but your picture is associated with Mr. Bond. For your safety, I think having you in a safe house until we know what's going on is the best move."

"What the fuck?" Harper blurted.

"What's wrong?" Murphy asked.

"Something happened to the cell phone. I think I tripped something with the clone. Fuck, fuck, *fuck*," Harper said as he unplugged the phone from the cloning device. Everyone watched as Harper punched at Ethan's phone.

"What happened?" Murphy asked.

"It's gone. It's wiped clean."

\* \* \* \*

*Dr. Hennigan*

Dr. Hennigan buckled her seatbelt. From her seat, she could stare out of the cockpit window and watch as the ground quickly approached the aircraft. She was always amazed at how much the airplane bumped to and fro when it descended into an airport. The plane ride may feel smooth, but the slightest pockets of turbulence could cause the plane to jostle left, right, up and down. In fact, when one looked out of the cockpit window, a landing was anything but a smooth process.

She closed her eyes, leaned back and waited for the wheels to hit the tarmac. She steadied herself for what lay ahead. Her mission from her mother and grandmother had been clear. Retrieve the phone or ensure it was destroyed. Ideally, she could walk up and threaten Ethan Bond with his life if he didn't hand the phone over, then take the blasted thing and walk away. She sighed internally, knowing things rarely turned out as easily as she wanted them to.

The wheels hit the tarmac, and she felt the force of the backward thrusters push her back into her seat as the plane slowed down. Dr. Hennigan opened her eyes and watched as the aircraft rolled past what counted as the airport's terminal. The words 'West Houston Airport' were emblazoned on the brown boxy building. A ground crew member ushered the jet to its parking point. Five black SUVs were parked, waiting for her to exit the plane. She changed into her tactical gear while in flight, so she was ready to move as soon as the aircraft stopped.

"Ms. Wilson?" Dr. Hennigan asked, tapping a communication device on her shoulder. "Can you hear me? I'm on the ground in Houston."

"Loud and clear, ma'am. I commandeered a satellite and can see your jet and the SUVs from my vantage point."

"How do things look at the Emerald City?"

"Dorothy is still in the Emerald City. Scarecrow and Tin Man showed up there, too."

"Thanks!" Before she'd left The Complex, she and Ms. Wilson had decided to use Wizard of Oz as the callsigns for this operation because of the FBI Complex's nickname. Ethan's callsign was Dorothy. And Kira Strickland was the Scarecrow because she was a lawyer. Blayne Dickenson was the Tin Man because he represented Dorothy's heart. Of course, Dr. Hennigan fashioned herself as the wizard because she was pulling all the strings behind the scenes, and no one knew it.

The pilot exited the cockpit and lowered the stairs for Dr. Hennigan so she could exit the plane. Denzili, Richardson, Fox, and Kramer were standing in a line of military parade rest as Dr. Hennigan left the plane. She looked at the operatives through her sunglasses and said, "Report."

Richardson spoke. "We have five SUVs. Each SUV has an additional three operatives — one driver and two strike force members. This gives us twenty personnel, including yourself, for this assignment."

"And the vehicles?" Dr. Hennigan asked.

"They exceed NATO's Standardization Agreement for kinetic energy, blast and artillery threats. We brought the BMW X Five series models. They're fast. All drivers have trained on right-hand driving consoles, so the European design isn't a problem."

"Good, good," Dr. Hennigan said. "Ms. Wilson, anything else?"

"Nothing from my end. The estimated time from your location to the Emerald City is approximately thirty minutes."

"Let's roll," Dr. Hennigan said. The operatives split up and headed to different vehicles. Dr. Hennigan took the one in the middle. She walked to the US driver's side of the BMW, opened the door and entered. She nodded at the operatives already in the SUV. Everyone had their balaclavas pulled down except for the driver, who wore the same pair of sunglasses she did. Dr. Hennigan looked through her sunglasses and was given an immediate readout on each person in the vehicle on the LCD screens in front of her eyes. She was still trying to get used to augmented reality, but she found the instant feedback and information very useful.

The first SUV left the airport, and the others followed, keeping two lengths behind each other. The caravan of five black SUVs was a well-oiled machine. All she could do at this point was sit back and wait until they invaded Emerald City.

* * * *

*Zach*

Zach had spent the rest of the morning rallying the troops and getting them in on his plan to storm the FBI in Houston and get Ethan back. He'd gotten Rawlins and Hightower to agree to the five-hour ride from New Orleans to Houston to save Ethan. Sally Higgins had not been thrilled about canceling yet another rehearsal. Still, Zach had convinced Rawlins that the publicity they could garner for the upcoming tour, if they played their cards right, made the day trip worthwhile. By eleven a.m., Zach, Orr, Ric, Rawlins, Hightower and Higgins, along with their bodyguards, had loaded into their SUVs for the five-hour trip. Zach had convinced everyone to let Stephanie come along for her safety. Rawlins had not liked the idea, but Zach finally got him to cave in.

Zach looked at his watch as they pulled into the Houston metro area. They made excellent time. *As long as we don't get stuck in traffic, we should be there by four.* Zach looked out of the window, watching the skyline pass. He was holding Stephanie's hand.

"How are you holding up?" he asked.

"I could be better. To say the last few days have been a crazy whirlwind is a colossal understatement," Stephanie said. "I wish I could make sense of this. I'll be curious to see if Ethan knows what's happening."

"When I talked to him, he seemed pretty clueless."

The two sat silently until the SUV turned off the highway onto a frontage road. Zach could see a strange-looking green building in front of them. *What the hell is that?* He was even more dumbfounded when the SUVs turned into the parking lot. *This is an FBI building?*

As Ms. A. parked the SUV, Zach posted a message to the local fans across his social media feeds. He figured he could garner attention by letting their fans know where they were. He had told no one about this little part of his plan.

He opened the door and exited the SUV, not waiting for Ms. A. to do it for him. After stretching for a second, he offered his hand to Stephanie and helped her exit the vehicle.

"Okay, troops," Rawlins said, "follow my lead."

The entire group walked to the front of the FBI building and entered. Rawlins immediately approached the reception desk.

"Can I help you?" the receptionist asked, a blank look on his face.

"Yes. My name is Dan Rawlins, and I'm here to see my client, Mr. Ethan Bond. It's my understanding you are detaining him here."

"And you are?"

"His lawyer."

"Let me get someone who can help you."

The receptionist made a phone call and talked to someone in hushed tones. "You can wait over there," the young man said, pointing to the lobby's sitting area. "An agent will be with you shortly."

Zach walked Stephanie to the waiting area, but neither felt like sitting down after the ride from New Orleans. Zach noticed Rawlins hadn't moved from where he stood, leaning against the receptionist's desk staring at the elevator bank. There was a dinging sound from the elevators. Zach glanced over and watched as a middle-aged guy in a dark navy suit exited.

"Who's Dan Rawlins?" the guy in the suit asked.

"I am," Rawlins said as he moved to greet the agent as he extended his hand. "And you are?"

"I'm Agent Raymond Anderson. How can I help you?"

"I demand to see my client, Ethan Bond," Rawlins replied.

"Interesting. He's already got a lawyer with him," Anderson said as he crinkled his forehead.

"I've been Ethan's lawyer for many years now. So, if you don't mind, I'd like to see my client now."

"I don't mind, but the agents questioning him might care," Anderson said. "I'll have to get their permission."

The agent walked to the reception desk and asked for the phone. The agent made a phone call, and there was a bit of back and forth before the agent turned back to Rawlins and said, "Sorry, no can do. They don't want to be disturbed. And since your *client* already has representation with him, I'm not inclined to take you upstairs until I get the go-ahead from the agents in charge."

A teenage girl entered the FBI building and let out a squeal before running over to Ric. "Oh my God, oh my God, oh my God, you're like my totally favorite member. Can I get a selfie?" the girl asked, but whipped out her cell phone and took the picture before Ric even smiled.

"What the hell is this?" Agent Anderson asked as the door opened, and a couple more groupies entered the building and let out delighted squeals.

"I guess we're trending on social media," Zach said quietly to Stephanie.

"You didn't?" Stephanie asked.

"I may have posted that we were here right before we left the SUV," Zach said with a wink. "I figured we could use the publicity in case the FBI tried anything fishy."

"Call security," Agent Anderson barked at the receptionist. "Did you do this?" Anderson asked, pointing a finger at Rawlins.

"I can assure you," Rawlins said in his best lawyerly voice, "I do not know what is going on."

Within seconds, a team of security personnel tried to escort the increasing number of fans from the building. In a look of exasperation, Agent Anderson yelled, "Lock the front doors. No one is coming in or out."

Zach shot Stephanie a sly grin. Stephanie shook her head and rolled her eyes. "Pray this doesn't come back to bite you in the ass," she said.

Zach looked through the glass door and noticed the first television crew in front of the FBI building. "Well, all eyes are officially on this place. Let's save Ethan."

\* \* \* \*

*Agent Murphy*

Murphy and Harper sat on one side of the table, looking at Ethan, Blayne and Kira, who sat on the other. The group had spent the last hour putting together the best timeline of events Ethan could muster. Periodically, Murphy or Harper would ask a question to clarify the information Ethan had provided. Thankfully, the lawyer hadn't jumped in to stop her client from saying anything. Murphy had a yellow legal pad in front of her and was jotting down notes, her pencil scratching the paper's surface furiously as Ethan provided details.

"So, let me get this right," Murphy asked. "You two," she said, pointing to Ethan and Blayne, "had never met before Ethan flew to Houston?"

"We'd been talking for over a year," Blayne said.

"On a gay dating app?" Harper questioned, stressing the last three words as he drew them out.

"Yes," Ethan said, squeezing Blayne's hand.

"And you two aren't dating?" Murphy asked.

"Nope," Ethan said. "Look... I know how this looks," he said, raising Blayne's hand off the table. "We haven't even discussed anything ourselves. We hinted at things and flirted a lot, but it's been a crazy few days."

"I'll say," Kira muttered under her breath.

"Okay. So, why was Blayne pretending to be Ethan yesterday?"

Murphy jotted Blayne's plan for getting rid of the paparazzi in her notebook. Blayne and Ethan detailed everything from the initial idea to Blayne wearing Ethan's clothes and using his cell phone to make sure everything looked good to the paparazzi.

"So, you were having coffee when you were shot?"

"Yes," Blayne said. "Same place where the photo had been taken the day before."

"And you were having coffee because you met with one of Kira's clients?"

"Yes. Dr. Reich, Kira's client's mother, is my graduate adviser. I've known Dr. Reich and Jamie for a few years. They're like family. When Jamie was bullied at school, Kira took him on as a client."

"Then, when Jamie was viciously attacked," Kira added, "I filed a handful of lawsuits on his behalf."

"First, I'm sorry to hear the kid was attacked. Second, I know someone who works in the civil rights department at the Department of Justice, so I'd be happy to put you two in touch if the Texas courts don't take your case seriously," Murphy offered.

"I'll definitely keep that in mind," Kira responded. Kira pulled out a small metal case containing her business cards. She slid one across the table to Murphy, who pocketed the business card in her jacket.

"I don't have any cards on me at the moment," Murphy said. "Let's ensure you get my information before we leave today."

There was a knock on the door. Murphy pushed away from the table, headed over to the door and opened it.

"Yes?"

"I'm sorry, Agent," a young man in a pinstripe suit said. Then he whispered, "Agent Anderson wanted me to let you know a mob is growing outside."

"A mob?" She turned to the room and said, "I'll be back. There's a situation unfolding I need to be briefed on." She noticed Harper shoot her inquisitive look as she closed the door behind her. "Okay, explain," Murphy said to the junior agent.

"It's probably easier to show you," the young man said. He gestured for her to follow him into another conference room. She walked over to the window overlooking the parking lot. She saw over one hundred people carrying signs reading *Free Ethan!* and *Ethan, We Love You!* Off in the corner, she saw three news vans already setting up for satellite telecasts.

"What about the back side of the building? Is there a way to get out of here with a few cars?" Murphy questioned.

"There's a side entrance covered by some trees. So far, all the protestors are in front of the building, but I don't know how long we'll keep them out there. I heard the contingent in the lobby brought the mob."

"What contingent in the lobby?" Murphy asked.

"The rest of ZERO is downstairs, along with their management and security. It's a bit of a mess down there, ma'am."

*This might work in our favor*, Murphy thought. "How quickly can you get a team of SUVs lined up?"

"Ten minutes. As long as the Special Agent in Charge approves."

"Do it. Get me that motorcade."

Murphy walked back across the hall and slipped into the conference room. Kira took one look at her and demanded, "What's going on?"

"Ms. Strickland, we need to move you, your client and his whatever-the-hell-Blayne-is, to a secure location. Right now, this location is no longer secure. Someone posted Ethan's location on social media, and there's now a group of screaming fans outside."

"So, there's a mob of teenage girls, and you think my client is not safe because of this?"

"I'm less concerned about the teenage girls than the threat posed if whoever is after Ethan attacks this place with everyone in it."

"I was told this place is a virtual fortress," Ethan said.

"Maybe so," Murphy noted. "But I don't want to take that chance with all the innocent civilians gathered. Whoever these assassins are, we know they have no qualms about killing hundreds of civilians to get to you."

# Chapter Twenty-Three

*Ethan*

Ethan held Blayne's hand as they rode the elevator to a subbasement with Kira and the special agents. On the lobby floor, the doors opened. Across from the doors, Ethan saw Zach and Stephanie pacing.

"Guys?" Ethan yelled. As he did, Agent Murphy hit the close button on the elevator door repeatedly. Ethan looked back at Zach and Stephanie, but he wasn't sure if either of them heard him over the loud chanting he could hear coming from outside. The door slid shut again, and the elevator went down one more level.

"That's all for you?" Blayne asked.

"Trust me, that's mild. You should hear what it sounds like when we're in one of our arena stops. Our earpieces are half sound suppression and half monitor. Without them, we can't hear ourselves think, let alone any of the music we're supposed to be singing to."

The elevator made a quiet dinging sound as the doors opened. A young male agent was standing there as they got off the elevator.

"Agent Murphy," the young male agent said. "If you'll follow me, I'll show you the way to the side entrance." The agent put a walkie-talkie to his mouth and pressed the button. "Everything still clear for the motorcade?"

"All clear on our end. The sounds from the front are getting loud, so we should get this show on the road," a female voice responded.

The group proceeded through several underground service tunnels. It ultimately came to a side door marked *Emergency Exit Online, Alarm Will Sound*.

"Don't worry. We've already disabled the alarm," the young male agent said.

Agent Murphy pushed through the door first. There was a short stairwell ascending in front of them. The younger agent then held the door open for everyone else. As Ethan got to the top of the stairs and looked at the motorcade waiting for them, he glanced back to see Agent Harper was the last person to exit the building.

The motorcade was comprised of three black SUVs. Agents in stereotypical black suits and sunglasses stood outside each vehicle and opened the doors.

"The three of you will be in the middle vehicle with me," Murphy said. "Harper, take the rear. Agent?" Murphy said, looking at the younger agent.

"Agent Michael Fritz, ma'am."

"Agent Fritz, ride in the front car and coordinate plans with the other vehicles. I take it you have a safe house you're taking us to?"

"Yes, ma'am. The Special Agent in Charge approved access to one we've never used. Once we've driven for approximately ten minutes, the vehicles will separate and go in different directions, just in case of a tail."

"Okay," Ethan heard Murphy say as he entered the SUV and sat beside Blayne. Kira had already flung herself into the rear seat, sitting in the middle.

"Don't want company?" Blayne asked.

"Nope. I want to see what's happening in front of us," Kira said.

She leaned in toward Ethan. "Did you pick up your cell?"

Ethan turned his head to ensure none of the agents were paying attention. "Yeah, I grabbed it when we were being ushered out of there. I figured it's already wiped clean, so I might as well trade it in for a new one."

"We'll talk later," Kira said, sitting back as Agent Murphy climbed into the SUV. Another agent ensured all the doors were shut before heading to the driver's side and entering the idling vehicle.

"Buckle up," Agent Murphy yelled from the front.

Ethan made sure his seatbelt was securely tightened before grasping Blayne's hand.

* * * *

*Dr. Hennigan*

Dr. Hennigan looked down at her watch and realized their convoy should be at the FBI facility within a few minutes. She mentally prepared herself to breach the building. According to the schematics they'd pulled up, their best entry point was a side door leading down to the subbasement. The subbasement meant they'd have a lot of ground to cover before they found

Dorothy, but that couldn't be helped. A frontal approach was pointless because the front doors were thick, bulletproof suckers. The only genuinely vulnerable entry point was the side door. The door was supposed to be bombproof, but the morons who built the building hadn't used reinforced hinges. Her team should be able to take out the hinges using a simple, targeted blast.

"Dr. Hennigan, please respond."

Hennigan reached up and pushed the send button on her communication device. "Yes, Ms. Wilson."

"There's a situation on the ground at the Emerald City."

"What kind of situation?"

"It looks like a gathering of Munchkins have come to the Emerald City to free Dorothy."

"Plainly, please," Dr. Hennigan said, trying not to sound too irritated.

"There is a protest of Ethan Bond fans at the Emerald City."

"Fuck!" Hennigan cursed. She pulled out a small tablet from a pocket and connected it to the SUV's Wi-Fi. "I've connected to the Wi-Fi. Please send information to my tablet."

Within seconds, Dr. Hennigan received the live feed of the protest outside the Houston FBI field office. *What the hell is going on?* From the overhead images, all she could see was a mass of people swarming the front.

"Can you get a better view of our infiltration point?" A few seconds went by as the camera they had in the sky sent to the side of the building and zoomed closer to the location. "Can you get a clearer image?" Dr. Hennigan asked. All she could see was a bunch of trees.

"Sorry... Those trees prevent us from seeing anything else there."

*Fuck!* She was about to switch over the tablet when the first black SUV left. "Ms. Wilson, are you seeing this convoy leaving?"

"Yes, I am."

"Did our inside source say anything about other dignitaries in the building?"

"No. Our inside source said the building was quiet until the last twenty minutes. I'm texting her now."

"Does she know who is in the convoy?" There was a pause as Dr. Hennigan assumed Ms. Wilson texted with the agent on the ground.

"Sorry," Ms. Wilson said. "Our agent was tasked with helping security in the atrium area. She was unaware of anyone leaving the grounds."

Dr. Hennigan thought for a second about how best to proceed. She ran through a range of different scenarios and settled on one that seemed to be the best. "Ms. Wilson, where can we set up an ambush?"

There was a delay as Ms. Wilson did something on her end. Almost immediately, the image of a frontage road appeared on her tablet with a red X. "This position seems defensible and would enable you to box them in."

Dr. Hennigan looked at the image and decided it made the most sense. "Send the details to the other vehicles."

She glanced into the back window to watch as two SUVs took an immediate exit ramp. The three front vehicles made their way around before stopping in the middle of the street. Two of the cars blocked the road under an underpass. The FBI convoy would have little-to-no time to maneuver before they saw them.

Jason Wrench

When Dr. Hennigan's team came to a stop, she radioed for everyone to get out and prepare for an ambush. She lowered her balaclava as she exited the SUV, Dr. Hennigan yelled at one of her operatives, "Pull out the M203s. I want the first vehicle immobilized the second it's around the bend, then immediately converge on the others."

Each vehicle had an M203 rocket grenade launcher retrofitted to work with Raytheon's new seventeen-inch rocket dubbed The MiniGriffin. The MiniGriffin carried an eight-pound warhead, unlike the thirteen-pound warheads of the much larger and less portable Griffin missile systems.

An agent Dr. Hennigan didn't know suddenly asked, "Rules of engagement, sir?"

"Necessary force to retrieve the asset. Once we have the asset, everyone will disburse and return to The Complex."

"Understood, sir," the agent said.

Dr. Hennigan heard her relay the orders to everyone on their commlinks. "Dr. Hennigan?"

"Yes, Richardson?"

"We are coming up upon our turnoff in forty-five seconds. Once we do, the FBI caravan will be cornered. We expect they'll notice immediately."

"Fine. How close are they to us?"

"Seconds, probably."

"I don't like probably, Agent."

"Twenty seconds, ma'am. Confident, ma'am."

"Okay. We're using the MiniGriffins to immobilize the front vehicle. Do the same with the back. Expect resistance. Minimize casualties. Our focus is on retrieving the asset."

"Understood, ma'am. Exiting in nine, eight, seven, six, five, four, three, two, one."

# Chapter Twenty-Four

*Ethan*

Ethan knew something was wrong when he heard Agent Harper's voice over the car's intercom.

"We have a tail," the agent said.

Ethan felt the shockwave as the first SUV in their convoy lifted off the ground and hurdled through the air toward the side of the road. He leaned to the right to see around the driver. Three black SUVs blocked the road. *Is that a missile launcher?*

The driver of their SUV took evasive action, breaking the vehicle and flipping it into a U-turn. The small rocket flew toward them. His body whipped against the seatbelt as the SUV tumbled. Various items in the vehicle flew around the cabin like miniature projectiles hunting for a target. He couldn't hear himself or anyone screaming in the car over the sound of the vehicle crunching and scraping against the pavement. The SUV finally came to a stop on its side. Ethan's body hung, suspended by his seatbelt.

He looked to his right and saw Blayne leaning against the door, which was now on the ground. Blayne looked dazed. The vehicle's rolling must have reopened Blayne's wound because blood seeped through Blayne's shirt. Ethan took inventory of himself and tried to figure out if he was okay. He blinked twice and moved every part of his body. He felt numb, but he wasn't sure if it was the vehicle rolling or the shock.

"Are you okay?" Kira yelled from behind them.

"I've been better," Blayne yelled back to her. "You?"

"Thank God for seatbelts."

Blayne rotated his body so his knees were firmly on the door before he unbuckled himself and rolled onto the door. *Blayne is moving faster than me*. Ethan grabbed the driver's seat so he wouldn't fall and land on Blayne when he unbuckled himself. Ethan pushed the button a few times. But it wouldn't budge.

"I'm stuck," he shouted.

The pinging sound of gunshots started reverberating off the SUV.

"Don't worry," Agent Murphy said, poking her head between the front seats. "The shots are outside."

"Yeah, but for how long?" Kira asked, finally making it down from her seat.

"Come on, Mr. Bond. Hurry up," Agent Murphy said. "We need to move. We're sitting ducks out here."

"I'm stuck," he cried out. "I can't get it to unbuckle."

"Just a second." Agent Murphy ducked back around her chair, out of sight. She returned with a metal gadget that looked like a 'T'. "It's a safety hammer," Murphy yelled over the gunfight happening outside. "Use the razor to saw through your seat belt."

Ethan reached out and grabbed the device from Agent Murphy and sawed through the polyester blend. He felt the snap as he finished cutting through it and braced himself for the quick fall to the ground. Ethan heard the thud of his feet hitting the door. Agent Murphy reached over, grabbed the safety hammer from Ethan's hand and started using it on the front glass.

"Will the safety hammer break through?" Ethan yelled, but the words were barely audible between the ringing in his ears and the muffled sounds of gunfire going on outside.

"It's specifically designed for these vehicles. It sure as hell better work," Murphy yelled back. "Check on him," she added, pointing in the driver's direction.

Ethan looked up to see the SUV driver hanging partially from his seat. Without thinking, he reached up and touched the driver's neck. He didn't feel a pulse. He lifted himself back up to see if he could get a better position to test for a pulse. The head lifelessly drooped to the side when he put his fingers on the driver's neck. The side of the man's head was banged up pretty bad. Part of his skull was exposed. *Is that…? Fuck it is!* Brain matter hung out. Ethan closed his eyes and tried not to hurl as he lowered himself back down.

"I don't think he made it," Ethan finally squeaked out as he opened his eyes and tried to shake the image of what he'd just seen from his conscious.

Ethan turned to Blayne and saw the look of concern in his eyes. Blayne reached out and squeezed Ethan's hand. "Remember… None of this is your fault."

Ethan returned Blayne's squeeze and gave him a single nod.

"Okay, before I blow this window," Agent Murphy yelled, getting their attention again. "I'm going to go out first. Right now, we're sitting here blind. We have no idea what's going on." As if to reaffirm her point, bullets ricocheted off the vehicle's undercarriage. "Do any of you know how to shoot a gun?"

"I do," Kira said.

"Great," Murphy said as she unholstered the deceased agent's gun. She handed Kira the weapon and showed her where the safety was. "Once I check things out, I'll return and get you. If anyone else shows their face, shoot it."

Kira nodded once. Murphy picked up the safety hammer and hit the center of the front windshield. She had to hit it three times, but it cracked like a spiderweb on the third strike. Agent Murphy positioned herself against the passenger side seat to give her leverage to kick the windshield out. She peeled back the half at street level before crawling through the hole.

Ethan, Blayne and Kira sat huddled, trying to be as quiet as possible. Ethan was the first to see Agent Murphy shimmy herself back into the SUV.

"Dear God, it looks like Fallujah out there," Murphy muttered. "Both sides have taken some pretty heavy damages. There's a small building about fifty feet off the side of the road. I'm going to lay down fire, and I want you to run like your lives depend on it to the backside of the shed…because they do."

They all nodded, then Agent Murphy helped them one by one to crawl out of the front window of the SUV. Ethan felt the gravel under his palms as he slid himself out of the window before he turned and helped drag Blayne out by pulling on Blayne's good arm. Kira was inside, giving Blayne a push. Once Blayne was out and crouched behind the SUV, Kira shimmied her way out and waited for further instructions from Agent Murphy.

Ethan watched as Agent Murphy snuck her head around the corner of the SUV. She made eye contact with someone and shot some hand signals Ethan couldn't understand. Once she was finished, Murphy joined the group.

"Thank God, Agent Harper is out there. He's taking fire, but his vehicle is in better shape than ours. Not great, but their SUV just fishtailed from the looks of it, though there's a nasty dent on one side. We're going to lay down fire in that direction. When we do, you three are going to run like hell. Understand?"

Ethan, Blayne and Kira all shook their heads. Agent Murphy gave all three of them one final once-over before she said, "Good luck," then slid back to the SUV's edge.

Murphy raised herself into a shooter's stance and pulled the trigger. That was their cue.

Like runners who had been waiting for the starting pistol at the beginning of a track meet, the three stood and took off running. Kira was first followed by Blayne, with Ethan picking up the rear. Blayne stumbled in front of him, so Ethan reached out to steady Blayne. Blayne over-corrected and fell back into Ethan, causing him to take a nosedive into the ground.

Blayne turned in horror as Ethan looked at him and yelled, "Run!" Ethan lifted himself when dirt nearby hit him in the face. It took his brain a moment to realize the shooting dirt was from a bullet lodged into the ground next to him.

"I wouldn't move if I were you," a woman behind him said.

He flipped over and looked up to see a woman wearing a black ski mask about fifty yards away walking in his direction, her gun leveled at him. Ethan instinctively crab-walked backward.

The woman shot at Ethan again. This one landed inches from his hand. "That's your last warning, Mr. Bond."

"How... How do you know who I am?

"You've been a pain in my ass for a few days, Mr. Bond."

"Why are you after me? Why did you kill Danny? Why did you kill all those people on the plane? Why did you try to kill Blayne?" Ethan yelled in rapid succession, hoping his barrage of questions would let Kira and Blayne get away.

"I'm sure you have lots of questions, Mr. Bond. But I'm not here to give you answers. If I did, I would have to ensure you didn't leave here alive."

"What do you want?" Ethan yelled.

"Your phone," the woman said, now within ten feet of Ethan. She lowered her gun to his chest. "Now, please."

Ethan reached into his pocket to pull out his cell, but it wasn't there. Ethan panicked, realizing his only bargaining chip was probably in the SUV somewhere. He started stammering.

"*Now*, Mr. Bond."

Ethan's eyes went wild as he tried to figure out what to do, and he saw his phone twenty feet away lying in the road. "It's over there," he yelled as he pointed wildly in its direction.

"I'm not going to fall for that, Mr. Bond."

"No, really," he pleaded. He reached into his pockets and turned them inside out to show he had nothing but his wallet.

She kept her gun on him, but quickly glanced in the direction Ethan indicated. "Ms. Wilson, confirm?" Then, "It's been nice meeting you, Mr. Bond." The woman turned and walked away. In a single scoop, she picked up his phone and disappeared.

Ethan didn't wait for an invitation. He picked himself off the ground and ran behind the shed where Blayne and Kira waited. Kira stood with the gun leveled at him as he rounded the corner.

"It's me."

"What happened?" she asked, letting him by but keeping her gun-holding stance.

"She wanted my phone," Ethan said. He was still trying to make sense of what had happened to them. "One second she was there, then she was gone."

"Wait...! What do you hear?" Blayne asked.

"Nothing," Ethan replied, his eyebrows knitting in confusion.

"Exactly. I don't hear anything, either."

"I'm not about to stick my head out there and find out what's going on," Kira said, pointing the gun at the corner of the building.

"Me neither," Ethan agreed.

"Makes three," Blayne chimed in.

The three stood in silence for a couple of minutes. They finally heard crunching gravel under someone's feet.

"Everyone okay back here?" Agent Murphy asked before coming into view. "You can lower your weapon now, Ms. Strickland. The bad guys left." Agent Murphy put her hand on top of the gun and helped Kira lower the weapon before gently prying it out of Kira's hand.

# Chapter Twenty-Five

*Blayne*

Blayne, Ethan and Kira were led back to where the remaining FBI agents who weren't killed were tending to their wounded in a makeshift triage area between their original SUV and the one behind them in the convoy. As Blayne took in their SUV sitting on its side, the entire scene looked like something out of a war movie. A couple of bodies were covered in aluminum foil blankets he associated with being stranded in the snow, which didn't happen very often in Texas. That's not to say parts of Texas didn't get blanketed with snow. Still, you were more likely to die of heatstroke than from hypothermia. He was glad whatever happened was clearly over. In the distance, Blayne heard sirens heading their way.

"Do any of you three have first aid experience?" Agent Murphy asked.

"I do," Kira said, raising her hand like she was in a classroom. "I volunteered as a firefighter when I was younger."

"You did?" Blayne asked.

"I'm a woman of many talents," Kira said with a playful wink. Kira may have been trying to make light of the situation, but Blayne saw right through her steeled resolve. She was shaken. Blayne thought helping would give her a sense of purpose in all this chaos.

"Great," Murphy said. "Agent Harper," she yelled. "I have a pair of hands for you — ex-firefighter." Blayne watched as Kira approached Agent Harper, who gave her a small medic kit and a pair of rubber gloves.

"So, what the hell just happened?" Blayne asked, looking at Agent Murphy, who stood in the middle of the wreckage and carnage, taking it all in.

"I wish I had answers for you, Mr. Dickenson."

"How's everyone on your team?" Ethan asked the agent.

"We have two dead and another three wounded. Trust me. This could have been much worse with the amount of firepower that group had. Hell, I think it should have been much worse."

Blayne found it hard to imagine what he saw around him being any worse than it was. "How could this have been worse?"

"Well, we were outnumbered and outgunned. I don't know who those guys were, but they were fast and skilled. They came here for one objective and killing us was not it."

"Okay?" Blayne started. "I don't get your logic. Admittedly, I'm just a graduate student in education with zero military knowledge, so walk me through this one."

Agent Murphy stopped looking around and turned to speak to Blayne and Ethan directly. "The two agents who died were killed in the initial attack. From what I can tell, whatever ballistics they used, those rockets could have taken out the vehicles and not just incapacitated them. After that, the only shots made to our men were superficial. Whoever they were, they knew what they wanted. And as soon as they got it, they left."

"I think we know what they wanted," Ethan admitted.

Agent Murphy stared Ethan down as he told them about their escape, his tumble to the ground and the woman with the gun.

"So, this was all about your phone?" Agent Murphy said as she let out a low whistle. "Too bad there's nothing on it now. Whatever they wanted, we accidentally deleted it when we tried to clone it earlier."

"Do you think they're going to come back?" Blayne said, his voice shaking a bit more than he intended. He looked down and saw his trembling hand caused Ethan to shake a little, too. Blayne took a calming breath and tried to center himself like they'd taught him in the one yoga class he'd taken as an undergraduate. *Fuck Namaste! She didn't prepare me for this.*

"If it was the phone they were after, well whatever was on it, they have it now. I wish we knew who *they* were. The woman you talked to, did she have any kind of discernible accent?"

"You mean, did she sound *foreign*?" Blayne asked, disdain entering his voice at the seemingly uncouth question.

"Any kind of accent," Murphy corrected. "Foreign or domestic. Anything that could help us identify her."

"American, I guess," Ethan said. "Blayne?"

"I heard nothing unusual, either. Her voice was cool and collected. She could have just as easily been scolding her kids at a playdate as she was pointing a gun at us."

"Can we go home now?" Ethan asked.

"Not yet," Agent Murphy said. "We need to go back over to the Emerald City." Then, realizing what she said, she corrected herself. "The Houston FBI Field Office. to get official statements from you. We should have you finished by sometime this evening."

Over the next ten minutes, a range of Houston Police, ATF and FBI descended on their little stranded group. Several ambulances arrived to whisk the injured FBI agents to area hospitals. An emergency medical technician tended to Blayne's arm. Thankfully, he'd only popped one of his stitches, which the EMT quickly replaced.

When the other groups arrived, a dark sedan took Blayne, Ethan and Kira back to the Emerald City, which Blayne found aptly named.

Blayne found himself singing *If I Only Had a Brain* as they entered the subbasement, they'd left less than an hour before. It may have been an hour, but it seemed like a lifetime ago.

"How appropriate," Kira remarked, quirking her head in Blayne's direction. "If you're the Scarecrow, does that make me the Lion?"

"Nah," Blayne said. "You showed a hell of a lot of courage out there."

"What does that make me?" Ethan asked.

"Dorothy!" Blayne and Kira said simultaneously before they both broke out into laughter that reverberated off the walls of the underground corridors.

"Why are we laughing?" Kira said, trying to catch her breath.

"Don't worry," Agent Harper said, patting Kira.

"Yep," Blayne said, finally catching his breath. "It's a coping mechanism. Many academic studies discuss how humor helps people cope with a wide range of tragedies."

"Whatever, egghead." Kira grinned at Blayne before busting into another fit of hysterics.

"It's your body's way of relieving some of the tension you've been holding. As I always say, 'sometimes the only sense you can make out of life is a sense of humor,'" Blayne said as he released Ethan's hand long enough to throw his good arm around Kira. "And let's face it. None of the past three days makes any sense."

The agents took them to the elevator bank and hit the fifth floor. When they exited the elevator, they were led to the conference room where they'd been earlier. Only this time, there were a few more people in it.

Ethan was immediately enveloped by a group of people. Without being told, Blayne quickly realized this must be his ZERO family. Blayne and Kira held back as Ethan was reunited. After a second, a guy with black hair and piercing blue eyes came up to Blayne and said, "You must be Blayne. I'm Zach. It's nice to meet you," the man said as he made to shake Blayne's hand. When Blayne extended it, the guy brought him in for a one-handed half hug. Blayne winced at the sudden jostling of his arm.

"Dude," Zach said. "Sorry about that. How's the arm doing?"

"Definitely had better days. Popped a stitch when we rolled the SUV."

"What the fuck?" Zach asked, his eyes widening.

Blayne looked quizzically at Zach before asking, "What did they tell you?"

"Not much, apparently," Zach said, his face sobering.

"Long story short," Blayne started, "international assassins shot missiles and guns at us, all because they wanted Ethan's cell phone."

"Say that again," Zach said.

A loud whistle broke through the conversations in the room. "I hate to break up this joyous reunion," Agent Murphy yelled. Once the room quieted, she leveled her voice to normal and continued, "But unless your names are Blayne, Ethan, Kira or one of their lawyers, I'm going to ask you to leave the room. There's a conference room across the hall. My partner, Agent Harper, will take you over there and answer any of your questions. Assuming, of course, we can answer those questions."

There were some protests, but the ZERO family left. Two older men tried to stay in the conference room, but Ethan shooed them away.

Once the room was empty, Murphy said, "Take a seat. Let's make this quick, shall we?" as she pulled out a digital recorder and hit record. Over the next hour, Blayne, Ethan and Kira told Agent Murphy everything they remembered about the attack on the convoy.

"Anything else you can think of?" Murphy asked. The three looked at each other and shook their heads. "I'm sure you'll be interviewed by several agencies over the next few days. Between you, me and the glass walls, this was a bit of a clusterfuck."

"Tell me about it," Ethan said before adding, "Sorry... I know this isn't your fault."

"Nor is it yours, Mr. Bond," Agent Murphy added. "I can tell you're going to blame yourself for everything, but you're not to blame."

"Then who is?" Ethan countered.

"I wish we knew," Agent Murphy admitted soberly. "From the moment I stepped foot on the houseboat in New Orleans to investigate the Dunning and Hawthorne murders, none of this has made any sense. And without the data, I don't know if we'll ever know for certain. I can tell you people at the highest level of our government will try to figure out what happened here."

Blayne looked at Agent Murphy and said, "So, what now?"

"Now, we get you out of here so you can have your reunion with Ethan's band, get some food in you and, if possible, get some sleep. I will put you in contact with an FBI Victim Specialist who can help you get any kind of mental health counseling and other assistance from the federal and state governments."

"Is that necessary?" Kira asked.

"You may not think it is now," Agent Murphy said slowly, "but victims of terrorism and violent crimes often need support over time. I'd rather you have a support system in place and not need it than not have the system in place and need it."

"I'll take your word for it," Kira said, clearly not convinced.

"I also want to ensure I can get hold of you over the next few days. I'm assuming I can get you at your regular numbers," Agent Murphy said, gesturing to Blayne and Kira.

"Yeah, I'm supposed to teach tomorrow. Well, maybe not tomorrow. I may take the day off and sleep for twenty-four hours," Blayne said.

"I still have cases to work on, so I'm not going anywhere," Kira said.

"And you, Mr. Bond?"

Blayne turned to see Ethan hesitate for a moment. "I haven't even thought about it yet." Ethan turned and looked at Blayne, "Can I stay with you for a few more days? I want to make sure you're okay while you're healing."

Blayne squeezed Ethan's hand. "Of course, you can stay with me. *Mi casa es su casa.*"

After Blayne, Ethan and Kira's interview with Agent Murphy, ZERO was let back into the room. Ethan informed the group of his plans to hang out at Blayne's for several more days because of his injury. The entire time Ethan laid down the law, Ethan kept his arm around Blayne. Blayne wasn't sure who was supporting whom right then.

Once the FBI released them, the group headed to the nearest restaurant, a dingy diner down the street. Thankfully, the lookie-loos and fans had dispersed earlier in the evening. There had been a few stragglers who politely asked for autographs and selfies with the band. The group smiled and spent a few moments with their fans. Even Ethan agreed to a couple of selfies, but he never let go of Blayne.

After dinner, Kira took Blayne and Ethan back to Blayne's apartment and promised to check in with them both in the morning.

After shutting and locking the door, Blayne sighed. "What a day."

"That's the understatement of the century," Ethan said as he wrapped his arms around Blayne and drew him close to him. "I don't know about you, but I'm exhausted."

"I need to pop a couple of pain pills, and I'll be out like a light."

Ethan leaned forward and gently pressed his lips to Blayne's. "Your room or mine?" Ethan whispered into Blayne's ear.

"You know my bed is bigger," Blayne said as Ethan dragged him through the apartment.

# Epilogue

*Dr. Hennigan*

Dr. Hennigan was not a fan of crowds, so she was glad she wasn't down in the throngs of the Toyota Center waiting for the concert to begin. She could see nearly everyone she wanted to see using her high-powered scope from her perch in a skybox. She swiveled the scope to find the locations she'd marked earlier. Finding seating arrangements hadn't been hard for a techie at The Foundation. *These ticketing companies need to up their security game.*

She pointed her scope toward the stage, then off to the left, where section one-hundred-seventeen was located. She found Blayne Dickenson and Kira Strickland sitting alongside a woman and her teenage son. Even though Dr. Hennigan didn't plan to contact anyone associated with Ethan Bond, keeping track of any potential problems was still good. Over the past month, Dr. Hennigan had received regular reports about Blayne's recovery, along with Kira's efforts to sue the school district on behalf of her teenage client. When the situation on the ground seemed to go sideways in Ms. Strickland's case, Dr. Hennigan made a few quick phone calls to the United States Attorney General and had the case taken out of Texas' jurisdiction. The local district attorney hadn't known what hit her.

The kids involved with the assault were informed they would face federal hate crimes convictions, and all took plea deals within a couple of days. Dr. Hennigan was glad she could at least prevent the young man from going to court and facing his assailants.

As for Mr. Dickenson, Dr. Hennigan felt somewhat responsible for his injury. When they audited the shooting at The Foundation, a slip in their protocol system was noted and corrected for future actions. There should have been a way for agents on the ground to be alerted to changes in social media. Suppose Denzili and Richardson had had access to social media feeds. In that case, there's no way Mr. Dickenson would have been shot because the agents would have known he was not Ethan Bond. *Oh, well. We keep learning and moving forward.* The Foundation had set up a special scholarship for Mr. Dickenson. He would be informed about it later in the semester. His last part of graduate school would be covered.

She was glad to see Blayne and Ethan's relationship deepening after it was made public, along with a highly sanitized version of their exploits with the FBI. Dr. Hennigan surmised that Blayne had been thrust into the spotlight, which was clearly not something he was comfortable with. It may be hard for outsiders to understand, but the decision to liquidate Ethan Bond had never been personal. She found out she liked the young man. But liking someone would never stop her from doing her job. As for Mr. Dickenson, she'd also see that he landed a teaching position at a school in New Orleans, if he and Ethan decided to stay together.

Though the FBI couldn't prove Peregrine Airlines Flight 923 was anything other than an accident, many conspiracy theories and rumors floated around on the Internet. Admittedly, The Foundation created half of them. An internal investigation at the FBI was technically open and ongoing, but Dr. Hennigan knew it would go nowhere.

As for The Foundation, the blame for the attack on the FBI was put squarely on a domestic terrorist group out of Montana. The Foundation had been looking to dismantle the group, so planting evidence at the ambush scene had been part of her mission. Dr. Hennigan knew Agent Murphy wasn't convinced, but she had enough on her plate to prevent her from being a nuisance. Still, The Foundation placed Agent Murphy on a watch list. She'd either be recruited or liquidated if she ever got too close.

Dr. Hennigan focused the scope on the seat next to Kira and noticed a dressed-down Agent Sarah Murphy. Murphy had transferred from the New Orleans Field Office to Houston last month. Dr. Hennigan wasn't involved in the transfer, but she'd made sure things went smoothly, especially when one of the Agents at the Houston Field Office started making some noise because Agent Murphy was transferred in as his immediate supervisor. Oh well, Dr. Hennigan hoped Agent Raymond Anderson enjoyed living in Anchorage. *Not that there's anything wrong with living in Anchorage.*

The lights in the arena suddenly dimmed as a voice boomed over the speaker system, welcoming them to the Toyota Center and the Launch of ZERO's North American Tour. "The use of photography, videography and cell phones to capture any part of this event is strictly prohibited by law. Violators will be removed from the concert and could be banned from the venue permanently. Get on your feet, put your hands together and let's hear some noise for Zach, Ethan, Ric and Orr…ZERO, live in concert!"

Dr. Hennigan turned on the night scope, so she could see in the dark. A loud, blaring orchestration started. Even though Dr. Hennigan wasn't familiar with the music, the fans clearly were. There was a loud, drawn-out note. Then Zach, Ethan, Ric and Orr were shot up on stage from underneath as the first musical number started. The frenzied motion on stage split people's attention until one band member sang a solo. She could hear the music, but the words were muffled from her perch. She wasn't sure if that resulted from being so far away from the stage or if that's what pop music sounded like these days.

After listening to three songs, Dr. Hennigan saw her real reason for being there. In another skybox, she saw the lights pop on. A group of five security guards and two dignitaries entered the room. The Foundation had been alerted that the heads of the National Democratic Party of Germany and the Constitutional Liberation Army, a domestic terrorism organization, would use the cover of the concert to meet.

"Denzili, Richardson, on my mark," Dr. Hennigan said into her communication device. "You are cleared to liquidate."

Want to see more from this author?
Here's a taster for you to enjoy!

# Love and Liquidation:
# A Choreographed Coup
## Jason Wrench

### *Excerpt*

*Blayne*

Blayne gave himself one last look in the mirror. *I look like an idiot*, he thought. His boyfriend, Ethan Bond — one of the five members of the pop group ZERO — had assured him that the outfit was perfect for a concert. It was a white T-shirt under a black T-shirt, black skinny jeans rolled up at the ankles and white tennis shoes without socks. To complete the look, he also had a black lambskin leather jacket, accented with navy-blue satin lining. "I look like I should be a model." In Blayne's mind, that idea was not exactly reassuring. He applied some pomade to his hands and worked it through his short, blond hair until it was tamed to his liking.

There was a buzz from his left. He glanced at a text message on his iPhone screen.

*Driver will be there in five minutes.*

"The driver will be here in five minutes," he announced to the small group of friends in his apartment living room. He grabbed his favorite cologne, gave a quick spritz and walked through the fragrant mist before pocketing his wallet, keys and cell phone. Coat in hand, he left his bedroom.

"It's about time," Kira remarked as he emerged. "I thought I'd have to rescue you." She paused for a second and let out a low whistle. "Look at you, all grown up." She pantomimed wiping a tear from her eye.

"That's it, I'm changing," Blayne declared.

"Why?" Kira asked.

Blayne gestured to his outfit. "It's not me."

"Wow, Mr. Dickenson, you look almost hot," Jamie Reich teased from the couch. The sixteen-year-old had short, green spiky hair and wore a cast on his arm, a remnant from an attack a month earlier. The bullies had turned into violent sexual predators and were now behind bars. And while Blayne didn't wish harm on anyone, he hoped the trio would experience a fraction of the fear and torment they'd put Jamie through.

"And, Blayne," Dr. Madeline Reich, Jamie's mother, said, "you look devilishly handsome. I'm sure you'll stand out tonight."

"Thanks," Blayne replied, letting the corner of his lip creep up as he averted his gaze. Blayne was in love. It had only been a little over a month since he had finally met his now-boyfriend, Ethan, but they had been pretty much inseparable ever since someone tried to blow up Ethan, shot Blayne then tried to kill them both, along with Kira, all for a fucking cell phone. And no one seemed to know what had been so fucking important on Ethan's phone that it cost hundreds of lives.

*Honk, honk.* The sound was right outside his front door. "I guess that's our cue." He took a deep breath through his nose and let it out as the rest gathered themselves, stood and headed toward the door. Kira opened it, and Jamie and Madeline followed as Blayne took up the rear. The last thing he did was enter his security code into the keypad next to the door, a recent addition to his apartment. The security panel was a 'gift' from Ethan's manager and a complete security upgrade after 'the incident', as the band had called everything that had happened.

"Door is armed," a robotic voice chirped as Blayne shut it behind him. He walked out into the parking lot and found Zahava Peretz standing next to the open door of the black SUV.

"Ethan told me he had arranged transportation. He hadn't told me it would be you, Zahava." The woman wore a black suit, white shirt and a black tie. He couldn't see her eyes behind the dark sunglasses.

"I was available. They don't need all four of us for a simple security detail at the venue."

Ms. Z. was one of four bodyguards hired by Ethan's band for their protection. While the other three bodyguards always seemed more stand-offish, Zahava had been friendly to Blayne from the start. Blayne knew little about her. She was in her late twenties or early thirties and had worked for the Israeli Institute for Intelligence and Special Operations before an injury had forced her into early retirement. Somehow, Ron Hightower, the band's manager, was given her information, and Zahava had been flown to the States and never left. She was technically a dual citizen, born on the East Coast before her parents moved to Israel.

Blayne heard the door shut behind him as he sat down and reached for the seatbelt. A moment later, the driver's side door opened, and Ms. Z. climbed in. Without checking on her charges in the back, her eyes were already scanning the road.

"ETA is approximately thirty-five minutes," she said, but Blayne didn't think she was talking to them. The SUV headed out of the apartment parking lot and headed to the Toyota Center for the ZERO concert.

He listened to idle chitchat around him, leaned his head back and closed his eyes. Immediately, Ethan's face, with his boyish features, brown hair and blue eyes, filled his mind, the image of Ethan smiling. Of course, Blayne immediately remembered all the other things Ethan's lips had done to him the previous night. Ethan may not have been the most experienced lover Blayne ever had, but Ethan made up for his lack of experience with a willingness to satisfy Blayne that was unparalleled. Ethan wanted to try everything with him. Since Ethan had come home with Blayne after the attack, he'd been like a kid in a sexual candy store. Millions of fans worldwide may have wanted Ethan, but only Blayne got to be with him — got to touch Ethan, got to taste Ethan, got to feel what it was like to be inside Ethan. Blayne's crotch stiffened against the skinny jeans as he remembered the night before. Ethan's nipples, like Blayne's own, were hardwired directly to his cock. Play with those while stroking or blowing him, and the ultimate climax would blow them away.

Blayne felt the SUV exit the interstate. He looked out of the front window and saw the Toyota Center looming ahead in the late afternoon sun. The SUV drove past the outer parking lots that would soon be filled with cars, trucks and SUVs, all there to see his boyfriend perform. They could watch him, but only Blayne got to have him.

The SUV drove around the outer perimeter of the Toyota Center before heading south on Jackson, then west on Bell. The SUV pulled into the Tundra Parking

Garage next to the arena. It slowly crept up to the third story before stopping near the sky bridge that would take them to the Center.

Ms. Z. parked the SUV in the middle of the garage and turned to them. "Make sure you keep this around your neck." Ms. Z. handed Blayne a stack of security badges and lanyards. "These are your all-access passes to the facility." Blayne wore a lanyard around his neck and handed the others theirs. "I'm going to let you out here. You're going to cross the sky bridge. When they scan you in on the other side, see Meghan, the Event Services Coordinator for the Center. She'll take you to the green room, where you can wait for the band until they're ready." Ms. Z. turned to Blayne. "Don't be surprised if Ethan's PA comes to drag you back to his dressing room. He's been worried all afternoon that something would go wrong with getting you here on time."

With that, Ms. Z. exited the vehicle and came around to open the door for Blayne, Kira, Jamie and Madeline. Blayne finally shrugged into the leather coat. He glimpsed himself in the glass bridge while the group started crossing as Ms. Z. drove away. Ahead, they could see ticket people already poised with their scanners. There was no one else on the bridge but them at this early hour, but a few people who worked there were milling around ahead.

"It's a shame Alan couldn't join us this evening," Blayne told Madeline. Madeline had been quietly dating the Pennington University Vice Provost for a while.

"Surprisingly, pop concerts just aren't his thing. He'd much rather hang back and chill at a wine bar or take in some jazz at a back-alley bar in New Orleans," Madeline said.

Her collar had flopped up when she'd put the concert lanyard around her neck. Jamie noticed and immediately reached over to fix it.

"Please have your passes ready," a ticket taker said as they approached the arena side of the bridge.

"We're supposed to be meeting Meghan," Blayne said.

"Ah yes," the woman said as she scanned their badges. "The guests. We were told you'd be here shortly. Let me call Meghan." The woman pulled a walkie-talkie from her belt and said, "Meghan, it's Sharice at the Tundra Entrance with the VIPs. Again, the VIPs have arrived."

A squawking sound came over the radio that Blayne couldn't make out, but Sharice said, "Ms. Flores said she'd be here momentarily. You can go stand over there." She motioned to a side lobby next to the glass that overhung Bell Street. Blayne looked down at traffic passing underneath.

"Good afternoon. You must be the friends of ZERO," a voice cut through the silence.

Blayne turned to look at the businesswoman walking toward the group. She wore a gray pantsuit. Her shoulder-length black hair had light brown highlights that popped in the foyer lighting.

"Blayne Dickenson." He extended his hand to greet the woman, who freely took it and shook it. "And with me are Kira Strickland and Madeline and Jamie Reich."

"Meghan Flores," the woman said, turning and shaking everyone's hand. "Welcome to the Toyota Center. Please ask me or anyone on my staff if you need anything while visiting us. If they can't help you, they'll find me. Are we all here?"

Kira answered. "Another one of our party will show up later—"

"Yes, Special Agent Sarah Murphy," Meghan cut in. "I'll ensure she is ushered into the greenroom as soon as she arrives." Then, without skipping a beat, she spun on her heels, all six inches. "Follow me." Meghan Flores started walking through the arena without waiting to see if anyone would follow.

She walked the group around for almost thirty minutes as a tour guide. "We broke ground in 2001 and opened in 2003."

"Have you been here this whole time?" Madeline asked.

"No. I joined the team in 2015. Before moving back to Houston, I worked at the Toyota Arena in Ontario, California, in guest relations and event management."

"How many seats does this place have?" Jamie asked. The group stood in one of the many social clubs with amazing views of the arena inside.

"The arena sits eighteen-thousand, three-hundred guests on game days, and we can seat about nineteen-thousand guests for concerts."

"There are going to be nineteen-thousand people here tonight?" Jamie asked, the shock in his voice clear.

Blayne walked over to the railing and stared into the arena.

"No," Megan answered. "Tonight's concert only uses about two-hundred and seventy of the full three-hundred-and-sixty degrees. The band's layout doesn't enable concertgoers to sit behind the stage. I think we're expecting some fourteen-thousand visitors tonight."

Blayne looked down across the arena at the stage on the other end. Behind it was a giant wall of monitors. Images flashed across the giant screens. The crew scurried back and forth on the floor like ants. He marveled at how so many people seemed to know exactly what they were doing and how their small part fit into the larger picture of a multi-million-dollar concert.

"Mr. Dickenson?"

The sound of his name snapped him out of his wonderment.

"Yes?" The words were out of his mouth more by instinct than anything else.

"It's time to head down to the green room," Meghan said.

Blayne smiled and started following the group. Meghan led them out of the club area to an escalator down to the stadium floor. She passed a few checkpoints, and everyone was summarily let through as they followed their guide, who continued to rattle off facts about the facility.

They walked through an entryway and right onto the floor of the Toyota Center. Blayne paused just for a moment to take in the arena's size. He'd been inside a large arena before but never a professional one.

"And it only cost us about two-hundred-and-thirty-five million dollars," Kira mumbled from his left. "Imagine what the city could have done with those funds."

"You're right, Ms. Strickland. The citizens of Houston made a substantial investment in the Toyota Center when they voted to increase the sales tax by zero-point-one percent. But it was an investment. For example, we held a UFC event several years ago estimated to have had an economic impact of twenty-five million dollars. Half of that was in direct spending by the organization and our out-of-town visitors. That one event garnered almost a half-million in direct tax revenue for the city. People only often hear about the initial investments in these facilities. Still, they rarely hear the full story about how these facilities pay for themselves over time."

"Mm-hmm," Kira responded, clearly not wholly buying the argument.

Meghan had clearly dealt with skeptics before, because she smiled and led the group through the arena floor to a side tunnel area to the left of the stage. For the first time, Blayne saw heavy amounts of security. Blayne recognized Mr. J. talking with security personnel Blayne didn't recognize. At six-five, with three-hundred pounds of solid muscle and a bald head that glinted in the stadium lights, Mr. J. stood out like a giant security beacon. Of course, Mr. J. wore his sunglasses. Blayne had seen none of the ZERO security team without sunglasses…ever.

The group was led through a metal detector, and their bags were checked by security personnel. In a few minutes, they entered the part of the arena that was more business than entertainment. The gray concrete walls had a few decorative items adorning them, reminding you that the arena was the home of the Houston Rockets. Still, it was mostly plain gray industrial walling.

"Here you go," Meghan said, opening the door to a room. "The band will be with you when they finish getting ready. You probably have" — she glanced down at her watch — "at least thirty minutes. So please, enjoy the buffet." She gestured to the tables of steel chafers. Caterers immediately began unrolling the tops of the dishes and the smell of food entered the room. "And if you need to use the facilities" — she gestured toward a hallway at the other end of the room — "they're right down there."

With that, she spun on her heels and left the group, who were now outnumbered by attendants and caterers to serve them.

"So, this is how the other half lives," Madeline commented. "I hate to admit this, but getting used to this kind of treatment wouldn't take me long."

# About the Author

Jason Wrench is a professor in the Department of Communication at SUNY New Paltz and has authored/edited 15+ books and over 35 academic research articles. He is also an avid reader and regularly reviews books for publishers in a wide number of genres. This book marks his first full-length work of fiction.

Jason loves to hear from readers. You can find his contact information, website details and author profile page at https://www.firstforromance.com/

PUBLISHING

Sign up for our newsletter and find out about all our romance book releases, eBook sales and promotions, sneak peeks and FREE romance books!